A NICK KISMET ADVENTURE

FORTUNE FAVORS

SEAN ELLIS

Fortune Favors (A Nick Kismet Adventure)

Copyright © 2013 by Sean Ellis

All rights reserved. No part of this book may be reproduced or transmitted in any form or by any means without written permission of the author.

This is a work of fiction. Names, characters, places, and incidents either are the product of the author's imagination or are used fictitiously. Any resemblance to actual events or locales or persons, living or dead, is entirely coincidental.

ISBN-10: 1940095263

ISBN-13: 978-1-940095-26-4

Cover Art by J. Kent Holloway

Gryphonwood Press
PO Box 28910
Santa Fe, NM 87592

www.gryphonwoodpress.com

Printed in the United States of America

PRAISE FOR SEAN ELLIS

"FORTUNE FAVORS has everything you want in an adventure story: pirates, treasure, assassins, legend, mystery, romance, two-fisted action, and immortality. Nick Kismet is an Indiana Jones for the 21st century, and Sean Ellis is the new Master of Adventure." ~ **Kane Gilmour**, bestselling author of RAGNAROK and THE CRYPT OF DRACULA.

"Sean Ellis is a thriller reader's dream come true."~ **Jeremy Robinson**, bestselling author of RAGNAROK and ISLAND 731.

"Another action-packed quest for the source of one of the world's most enduring legends. Ellis blends myth, legend, Biblical tradition, and history in the best Nick Kismet adventure yet!" ~ **David Wood**, author of BUCCANEER and ATLANTIS.

"Sean Ellis is an author to watch closely. *Into the Black* is one of the top ten thrillers of the year! An adventure story that will stay with you long after the read is finished. You can count this reader as a huge fan of Nick Kismet!" ~ **David L. Golemon**, NY Times bestselling author of the EVENT GROUP series and THE SUPERNATURALS.

"Sean Ellis has mixed a perfect cocktail of adventure and intrigue and this one is definitely shaken and not stirred." ~ **Graham Brown**, bestselling author of the thrillers BLACK RAIN and BLACK SUN.

BOOKS BY SEAN ELLIS

NICK KISMET ADVENTURES
The Shroud of Heaven
Into the Black
The Devil You Know (novella)

MIRA RAIDEN ADVENTURES
Ascendant
Descendant

DODGE DALTON
The Adventures of Dodge Dalton in the Shadow of Falcon's Wings
The Adventures of Dodge Dalton at the Outpost of Fate
The Adventures of Dodge Dalton on the High Road to Oblivion

JACK SIGLER THRILLERS (With Jeremy Robinson)
Callsign: King
Callsign: King--Underworld
Callsign: King--Blackout
Prime

SECRET AGENT X ADVENTURES
Secret Agent X: The Masterpiece of Vengeance
Secret Agent X: The Scar
Secret Agent X: The Sea Wraiths

OTHER SEAN ELLIS THRILLERS
Magic Mirror
Oracle (with David Wood)
Hell Ship (with David Wood)
Flood Rising (with Jeremy Robinson)
WarGod: An Ogmios Team Novel (with Steven Savile)

PROLOGUE
PAYABLE IN BLOOD
January, 1991

FOR A MOMENT, SILENCE REIGNED supreme in the desert; an otherworldly stillness that seemed an oddly appropriate punctuation mark for the violence that had occurred only a few seconds before. Sergeant Alexander Higgins, of the 6th Queen Elisabeth's Own Gurkha Rifles, listened intently, waiting for the one, insignificant sound that would herald the end of that quasi-peaceful instant of time.

The world did not disappoint.

He spied a hubcap turned on end and spinning wildly like some toy from his childhood, and almost smiled at the reminiscence. The hubcap was one of only a few pieces of recognizable debris left over from the explosion that had ripped a car apart right in front of him, and taken the life of his comrade-in-arms Corporal Sanjay Singh.

Singh's body lay between Higgins and the American army lieutenant Nick Kismet. Kismet was the nominal leader of the team—what was left of it—that made a covert insertion into southern Iraq. The mission called for them to rendezvous with a high ranking government official who had expressed a desire to flee what many believed was the sinking ship of Saddam Hussein's regime.

Higgins hadn't understood why they had been saddled with an American officer, or why CENTCOM had utilized his regiment for the assignment; Gurkhas were tough soldiers to be sure, but clandestine operations were not their forte. Nevertheless, orders were orders. They had crossed the desert sands in a CH47 Chinook helicopter, an aerial platform that looked to

Higgins like a school bus with rotors at either end, and made a flawless entry, arriving practically on top of their target without raising a single alarm.

Then things had gone south.

The American officer had left with the defector, offering no explanation for his decision. The two men climbed into a battered Mercedes sedan, leaving Higgins and his platoon to trail along behind them on foot. Along with three of his men, the Gurkha sergeant had set a murderous pace, hiking through the sand alongside the paved roadway that connected the river city of Nasiryah to the Bedouin communities of the desert. Higgins had begun to wonder about the wisdom of trying to follow Kismet; what if the defector was taking the lieutenant all the way into the city?

Nevertheless, after an hour of hustling across the austere landscape, they had spied the car, sitting abandoned on the roadside. Footprints led away, down into a narrow ravine, to the partially buried remains of some ancient Sumerian structure. Weapons at the ready, Higgins and his men had followed the trail expecting almost anything but what they discovered in those ruins.

Lieutenant Kismet held audience with the dead.

The defector and a dozen or so others—young men, women and children—had been lined up against the wall and massacred. A scattering of brass cartridges, shell casings for the 5.56-millimeter NATO rounds, lay on the floor a short distance away. Kismet was ministering to some of the mortally wounded victims, offering final comfort rather than assistance—all were beyond saving. Higgins had no idea what had happened, but one thing was glaringly obvious: the shots that had murdered the defector and his family had come from Kismet's weapon. The American's CAR15, a smaller version of the M16s Higgins and most of his men carried, stank of recent discharge.

Kismet had denied shooting them, but his protestation of innocence was wasted on Higgins. Civilians or not, the Iraqis were, after all, the enemy. Kismet's superiors would no doubt demand a more scrupulous accounting, but that was their business, and no concern of the Gurkhas.

They had returned to the car, anticipating a short ride back to their rendezvous site and an end to the mission. However, as Corporal Singh had reached for the door handle Kismet had shouted for him to stop. Too late, the Sikh had worked the lever and triggered the bomb. The blast ripped the car apart, smashing Singh into an almost unrecognizable pulp.

Kismet had known.

Even now, as he stared at the American officer, Higgins wondered what kind of trap he and his men had been sent into.

The burning car sent a towering column of smoke and fire into the sky, a beacon that was almost certainly visible in the nearby city where members of the Nebuchadnezzar Division of the Republican Guard had reportedly been stationed in anticipation of war; a war that had begun that very night in the skies over Baghdad. Those paramilitary soldiers would surely come out in force to investigate the explosion, and would find the shattered remnants of the Gurkha squad hastening across the sands.

And yet, there was something about the American that Higgins found strangely inspiring. He had seen young officers freeze up at the first sight of blood, the first taste of combat. Kismet was different. He could almost see the American reaching down into his deepest reserves of courage, tapping into an inner fire. It might not be enough to get them through the dark night ahead, but Higgins respected what he saw; he would willingly follow such a man into Hell itself.

Still, there remained the matter of the defector's death, the massacre of his family, and the nagging question of who had set the explosive device in the car.

He would follow this young lieutenant, he decided. But if they survived the night, he would have some tough questions of his own for the American with the strange name.

Private Mutabe, injured in the blast, was walking unassisted, but he would be useless if they were engaged by the enemy. The blood flowing from the long shrapnel wound in his left arm had been stanched, and although he still had the use of his right arm, the morphine injection administered by Sergeant Armitraj to dull the pain would also deaden his reflexes in the heat of battle. Armitraj had already freed Mutabe of the Minimi machine gun he carried, shouldering the burden of the weapon and its heavy ammunition bandoliers.

Higgins and Kismet shared the effort of bearing the slain Corporal Singh on a hastily assembled litter. The American seemed to understand the psychological importance of not leaving fallen comrades behind. At the same time, both men knew in the event of an encounter with the enemy, they might have to cut and run.

They stayed near the road as long as they dared. Though they were fully exposed to the eyes of anyone who might pass by, they knew that once they retreated to the desert dunes, their progress would slow to a snail's pace. For fifteen minutes they hastened along the roadside, until Higgins keen ears picked out the sound of a vehicle. Before he could voice a warning, they all heard it, and turned immediately into the open desert, seeking cover.

Higgins peered through his night vision goggles to get a better look at the approaching automobiles. He had no trouble locating them; the headlamps of two Land Cruisers burned brightly in the green monochrome display. He marked their location relative to the column of smoke that continued to hover above the bombed-out Mercedes. The Land Cruisers were on the move, following the distinctive trail of footprints left by the Gurkhas.

"Shit," he muttered. "That tears it."

"We'll dig in here," declared Kismet, not questioning Higgins' assessment. "If we can overwhelm them with an ambush, it might buy us a few minutes."

Higgins hefted his rifle and loaded a grenade into the M203 launcher affixed to the lower receiver. Armitraj laid out the Minimi on a dune crest, and then likewise readied a grenade. Kismet was left with only his CAR15, a weapon for close engagement if the grenades failed to remove the threat.

The two Gurkha grenadiers aimed at a spot roughly two hundred meters out, prepared to send the bullet-shaped grenades in a parabolic arc toward their destination. All that remained was to wait until the targets entered the kill zone. As it turned out, they didn't have to wait very long.

FORTUNE FAVORS

Higgins' grenade released with a popping sound followed an instant later by Armitraj's. Both men hastily ejected the spent shell casings, reloading in the seconds it took for their ordnance to sail into the sky and drop back onto the road. The task was completed before the first 40-millimeter high explosive projectile detonated.

Higgins' grenade hit directly in front of the lead vehicle, blasting its windshield inward. The driver instinctively swerved, careening toward the edge of the road even as the left front tire blew out. The Land Cruiser abruptly pitched over on its side, sliding gracelessly into the sand, as the other grenade found its mark.

The second Land Cruiser erupted in a pillar of fiery metal.

Armitraj laid his rifle aside, dove for the machine gun, and lit up the first vehicle. Higgins and Kismet also opened fire without hesitation on the wrecked vehicle, even as the dazed occupants tried to get free. Rounds from the Minimi cut through the Land Cruiser like a chain saw, killing anyone remaining inside. A lone figure—a soldier wearing the black beret and triangular insignia of the Republican Guard—struggled through the exposed driver's side door only to fall in the crossfire of 5.56-millimeter ammunition.

The ambush had been so quick, so decisive, that Higgins found himself doubting the certainty of their victory. He kept waiting for the real battle to begin, but the desert was plunged once more into silence.

"Sergeant!"

Higgins looked up at the American. Kismet was standing near Singh's litter, motioning for the Gurkhas to resume their flight. Higgins nodded, hastening over to join the lieutenant, passing by the glassy-eyed Mutabe. The engagement truly was over, but how long until the next? He doubted their luck would hold now that the element of surprise was gone.

There were two more Gurkhas waiting for them near the original drop zone with all the supplies they had brought in anticipation of a forty-eight hour long deployment. Those men also guarded the radio equipment. With any luck, they had heard the sound of gunfire and already called for a quick evac. Whether or not the small group now fleeing across the desert could reach the rally point, much less even find it, remained to be seen.

Even before they started walking, a noise reached their ears: a convoy of vehicles was racing toward them. Higgins looked to Kismet. "We won't get far."

"And we won't last long in a firefight. Maybe the sand will slow them down, too."

They ran. Armitraj took a position behind the wounded Mutabe, pushing the drugged soldier along at a halting pace. If Higgins and Kismet had not been burdened by the task of bearing Corporal Singh's remains, they would have easily outdistanced the first pair, but as it was, no one made rapid progress. Their pursuers quickly closed the gap.

After what seemed like only a few minutes of running, Higgins began to see strange patterns on the dunes; shifting figures of shadow that made the sand seem almost alive. He knew immediately what it was: the headlights of the approaching enemy convoy.

Armitraj turned and dropped to one knee, firing another grenade. Then, spread-eagled on the sand, he extended the bipod legs of the machine gun and gripped the trigger before the explosive round finished its journey, detonating harmlessly forty meters from the foremost troop carrier.

Kismet, at the front of the litter, stopped abruptly.

"Sir, we should keep moving. Armitraj will buy us some time."

"So they can hunt us down one at a time?" He lowered his end of the makeshift stretcher to the sand. "I don't think so. We'll make our stand here."

Neither man noticed Mutabe, still meandering forward in the grip of a narcotic fugue, but it would have changed nothing; Kismet and the Gurkhas knew that their lives were now measured in minutes, perhaps only seconds.

Sergeant Armitraj opened fire with the machine gun, sweeping across the approaching headlights. It was impossible to judge the strength of the advancing force, but there were two armored troop carriers, side by side, leading the charge. Higgins suspected they were only the tip of the spear.

The machine gun rounds seemed to have no effect, prompting the two Gurkhas to fire another volley of grenades. Armitraj selected a white phosphorus round, and both men fired together, point blank at the vehicles. This time there was no delay.

Higgins' round detonated on the hood of the APC on the left, decapitating the vehicle and lighting up the night. The WP grenade from Armitraj's launcher hit directly behind the other vehicle, and erupted in a blaze of solar intensity. The surviving personnel carrier continued to advance, now only fifty meters away, but the wreckage caused by the grenades hampered the rest of the column, forcing the other vehicles to swing wide out into the desert. Higgins now caught a glimpse of the size of the attack force: there were seven vehicles altogether. Two of that number were out of commission thanks to the grenades. Higgins had killed one of the armored personnel carriers, but there remained three more, at least a full platoon sized element. The white phosphorus grenade had showered an old military Jeep with flaming metal, forcing the surviving officers to abandon it to the flames, but there were two additional Land Cruisers, each stuffed full of combatants in black berets, charging nimbly around the wreckage toward their flanks.

Higgins quickly loaded another grenade, but the leading vehicle was already too close. Kismet meanwhile, opened fire with his CAR15, showering the driver of the APC with armor piercing rounds. The hardened tungsten and steel bullets ripped through the armor, and began ricocheting crazily inside the metal interior. The vehicle swerved and stalled.

Armitraj once more unleashed a stream of lead from the machine gun. Every tenth round was a tracer, zipping through the night like a red laser beam to mark the path of destruction as he homed in on one of the flanking APC's. A second line of tracer fire appeared from the opposite direction however, as the gunner in turret of the armored vehicle targeted his DShK 12.7-millimeter machine gun on the Gurkha sergeant's location. Armitraj knew what was coming but his only reaction as the incoming tracers walked across the sand toward him, was to close his eyes.

A bullet struck the Minimi gun, shattering its mechanism and exploding the unfired rounds in the feed tray. An instant later, Sergeant Taranjeet Armitraj erupted in a spray of red, his body shredded by an unrelenting torrent of enemy fire and fragments of his own weapon.

Higgins knew without looking that Armitraj had fallen; he had marked the cessation of heavy automatic fire from his fellow soldier's location. He did not mourn for his brother, not even to the extent he had felt grief at the earlier loss of Corporal Singh. The immediacy of the current battle, and the certainty that at any moment, he too would feel the icy hand of death on his shoulder, made such grief irrelevant. He emptied his magazine at a Land Cruiser, shattering its windshield, and then rapidly loaded another HE grenade into the launcher.

Not far away, Kismet was reloading his weapon, burning through magazines rapidly, but making every shot count. The enemy convoy had ceased advancing, their vehicles now a liability. The troops inside hastened from the impossible-to-miss targets, spreading out and seeking cover. More than a dozen had fallen, picked off by Kismet as they filed through the narrow doorways of the APCs; God alone knew how many more would never leave those vehicles, yet their numbers seemed undiminished.

Higgins dropped a grenade close enough to blast the nearest Land Cruiser over on its side. The fuel tank ignited in a secondary explosion that jetted sideways away from the exposed undercarriage. The shock wave momentarily stunned the Gurkha. His vision doubled, leading him to wonder if he had taken some shrapnel to the skull, but he ignored the side-effect of the concussion and slammed another magazine into his rifle. It was his last.

Kismet was attempting to fix enemy positions by the angle of incoming fire and rising from cover only long enough to snap off one round at a time before ducking down again. Higgins switched the selector on his own weapon to single shot as well, but knew it would merely delay the inevitable—that moment when he squeezed the trigger and nothing happened. He raised the M16 above a dune crest, firing at what he thought might be a sniper position, then ducked down again.

It would be over soon, he realized, and for some reason decided that he didn't want to die alone. He had always known death in combat was a possibility—for a Gurkha it was almost inevitable—but he had never imagined that he would be the last man standing. Kismet was only twenty meters away, but reaching his position would mean running a gauntlet of enemy fire.

Kismet wasn't a Gurkha. He was by his own admission barely a soldier; he was a reserve officer, engaging in military drills in order to pay for a college education, with no combat experience. Higgins would have willingly died for any man in his regiment, even the much-loathed officers, but for this American?

You're going to die anyway, mate.

He almost laughed aloud at the admonishment of his inner voice. "So I am."

He triggered a three-round burst over the dune crest, then launched into motion. He had gone three steps when a 7.62-millimeter slug from an enemy AK-47 ripped across the back of his right thigh. He winced at the unexpected burning sensation, but his leg did not fail and he did not stop running. After a dozen more strides, with blood streaming down his leg and into his boot, he made a desperate dive for Kismet's position.

"I'm out," shouted Kismet.

Higgins indicated his own weapon. "My last."

Kismet nodded gravely and laid his carbine aside. Then he did something that left Higgins stunned. He drew his blade, the *kukri* Higgins had given him earlier.

The large knife was the signature weapon of all Gurkha fighters, and this one had belonged to the fallen Corporal Singh. Higgins had offered it as a token of his respect for Kismet, in that now barely remembered moment when he had glimpsed a bit of steel in the young officer, but had never expected to see it used by the American.

You're one of us now, he had said. And at the time he had meant it, even though so much about what had happened that night remained beyond his comprehension.

How did I forget that? he wondered.

The lull in firing from their position gave a clear signal to the enemy. Higgins could hear the orders, barked in Arabic, for the soldiers to advance cautiously on their position. *Not much longer now.*

He had no idea how many rounds remained in the magazine of his M16—he figured he could probably count them on one hand. He set his gun beside Kismet's and drew his own *kukri*.

The first man to crest the dune led with his rifle, flagging his approach with the barrel of his AK-47. Kismet heaved the boomerang shaped blade against the gun, smashing it aside in a spray of sparks then reversed the edge, hacking across the soldier's torso. Higgins sprang at the next man, pivoting on his good leg and putting his full weight behind the cut.

A headless enemy soldier fell back into the arms of his comrades.

As if linked by a common mind, Higgins and Kismet dove into the heart of the approach. The stunned Iraqi riflemen had no idea how to repulse the crazed attack; they could not shoot for fear of hitting each other. They parried the assault with their rifles, swinging the wooden stocks like cudgels when they saw an opportunity, but several of their number prudently fell back.

As retreating soldiers formed a ring around the knife-wielding pair, Kismet and Higgins repositioned, back to back, to meet whatever attack was to follow. Both men were bruised from numerous blunt traumas and Higgins' right trouser leg was soaked in his own blood, yet the fire in their eyes was undimmed.

There was fire in the eyes of their enemy as well. The soldiers of the Republican Guard orbited their position warily, their visages twisted with a mixture of rage and trepidation. Some of them drew bayonets which they affixed to their AK-47s while others drew long fixed-blade combat knives.

One strident but nevertheless commanding voice was audible above the rest. Higgins didn't know enough Arabic to translate, but he had been a soldier long enough to know when an order to attack was given. The ranks began moving in, more cautiously this time, determined not to be taken off guard.

Higgins gripped the haft of his *kukri* fiercely and waved it back and forth in front of the advance. He assumed Kismet was doing the same. The American officer's back was pressed reassuringly against his own. At least he wouldn't die alone. "A pleasure serving with you, sir."

"The pleasure was all yours."

Kismet's voice sounded strange when he said it, and it took Higgins a moment to realize that the American was laughing; a harsh, sarcastic chuckle, but a chuckle nonetheless.

My God, thought Higgins. *He's actually laughing in the face of death.*

"Hey, Sergeant?"

"Yes, sir?" Higgins was in awe, wondering what the American would say or do next, but Kismet's voice was now only solemn.

"See you in the next life."

PART ONE
STRANGE BEDFELLOWS

FORTUNE FAVORS

1

The present

IN THE DEEPENING TWILIGHT, the becalmed surface of the South China Sea resembled an expanse of black velvet, stretching in every direction almost as far as the eye could see. The only landmass visible to the occupants of the Bell JetRanger 203 helicopter, beating the air high above the inky waters, was the eastern tip of the Malaysian island of Borneo, rising out of the sea to the south.

Nick Kismet gazed through the Lexan viewport, watching as even that last remaining link to terra firma dissolved in the distance, and then swung his gaze forward. He shifted uncomfortably in the cramped rear seat. The headset he wore over his close-cropped dark hair allowed him to converse both with the other passengers and the flight crew, but its primary function was to muffle the noise of the rotor blades as they hacked through the air, giving lift and speed to the craft. He knew from experience that the sound was almost deafening; even muted by the foam earpieces, it was still loud enough to destroy the illusion of floating peacefully above the darkened sea.

His fellow traveling companions were strangers, though he knew two of them by reputation. One of the female passengers had made a furtive effort at introductions, but no one else had manifested a desire to converse once the helicopter was airborne. The crossing would be brief and there would be plenty of time to socialize once they reached the ship.

The vessel to which they were bound was a mid-sized cruise ship, based out of Hong Kong. It was presently flying the flag of the Sultanate of Muara, from where it had just commenced a historic voyage that would, if all went according to plan, last nearly two years and take the ship to every corner of the globe. By arrangement with the shipping line, the craft had been renamed *The Star of Muara* and would be operating both as a fully-staffed maritime luxury resort and a museum of priceless antiquities for the next twenty-two months.

Unlike his fellow passengers, Kismet was neither enjoying the thrill of a helicopter ride, nor particularly looking forward to a week of being pampered aboard the cruise ship. With respect to the former, he'd had more than had his fill of helicopters during his brief time in the US military; even a sleek JetRanger held no more excitement than a drive to the corner store. As far as his stay aboard *The Star of Muara* was concerned—well, that would be work.

At the time of his death a few years earlier, the man who had ruled as Sultan of Muara for nearly thirty years had achieved an undreamed of level of wealth. Although ranked only as the forty-seventh wealthiest man in the world, his riches were unique in several respects. He was not an entertainer or athletic god, nor was he a politically elected figure; his affluence did not depend upon his popularity among a fickle public. Neither was he a hedge fund manager, or the chairman of a board of executives, entrusted with the responsibility of making money for others, and therefore beholden to his shareholders. The Sultanate of Muara, a sovereign nation nearly three hundred years old and occupying a few thousand square miles of the island of Borneo, guarded one of the largest petroleum reserves of any nation outside of OPEC. As the supreme ruler of its simple monarchy, the Sultan had been its sole protector and beneficiary.

Despite his wealth, the late Sultan had been a man of moderate habits. Although he had certainly made his share of impulse purchases and lavish gifts for his wife and son, he had been a careful manager of the royal treasury. Under his guidance, Muara's oil industry, and subsequently its economy, had thrived. So, in turn, had the royal family.

For all his frugality, the Sultan had succumbed to a single expensive vice: he was a collector. For nearly twenty years, he had set his heart upon accumulating art treasures and priceless historical relics, slowly building what was rumored to be the most impressive collection of antiquities anywhere. It was a difficult claim to verify since the international trade in such properties was highly restricted and most of the pieces in his private storehouse had been traded illegally many times over the centuries. During the Sultan's lifetime, only a few discreet visitors had the privilege of viewing the treasures of Muara. Because the relics were illicitly obtained, they were not reckoned as part of the Sultan's net worth, and inasmuch as many of the pieces were unarguably priceless, the Sultan of Muara would rightly have earned a place much higher on the list of the world's wealthiest men; perhaps at its very top.

And then he had died.

The heir to the wealth of Muara, the royal prince, had often demonstrated that he lacked his father's fiscal discretion but the state-run oil industry was virtually self-perpetuating, so there seemed to be no reason for alarm. The former Sultan had hired the best business managers and paid them well, and they in turn had created a sustainable pipeline of wealth for the small country. The new Sultan, now approaching his thirtieth year of life, needed only to sit back with his American movie star wife, and enjoy the good life for the rest of his years.

Somehow, the young Sultan had done the impossible: he had squandered his father's legacy. Five years after the death of the old Sultan, the royal house of Muara was bankrupt.

The oil had continued to flow unchecked from the earth's veins, but the wealth of Muara had hemorrhaged even faster, financing the Sultan's outrageous parties, expensive hobbies and extravagant gifts to friends and mistresses. It was rumored that guests to the royal residence could have their choice of carnal pleasures, including cocaine and heroin of such purity that doses were regulated and administered by a registered nurse.

FORTUNE FAVORS

The approaching storm had not gone unnoticed; several members of the household staff had openly warned the heir that the wealth of his father was not an unlimited resource. Rather than heeding the message, the Sultan had followed the time-honored tradition of killing the messenger. The staff was relieved of their duties and replaced; the business and financial advisors were dismissed and their jobs given to several of the new Sultan's friends. Silencing the voices of dissent however could not change the inevitable outcome, and a mere sixty months after his ascension to the throne of Muara, the checks began bouncing.

His newfound friends may not have offered the Sultan worthwhile advice, but they certainly had the wherewithal to get out before the collapse of the kingdom. Stunned at the disappearance of both his riches and his associates, the Sultan had at last turned to the advisors trusted by his father, begging for their help in saving the kingdom. Because they were men of conscience, and recognized that there was more at stake than merely the Sultan's standard of living, the advisors resumed their duties, laboring feverishly to salvage the wreck of Muara.

It was determined that the oil revenues would be sufficient to bring the Sultanate back into solvency in less than a decade, but that did not take into account the day to day operations of the kingdom. Nor did it address a growing threat from Muara's neighbor, and chief debtor, Malaysia. The government in Kuala Lumpur was already making overtures to bring the sovereign nation permanently into its fold. If Muara did not allow annexation and could not pay its debts, the Malaysian government would place a lien against any profits from the sale of petroleum in order to pay the interest on the Sultan's loans, keeping the country indefinitely in the red. What was needed, the financial ministers decided, was a rapid infusion of cash.

The old Sultan's collection of antiquities had not completely survived the appetites of his heir and the latter's friends. Several baubles of precious metals and jewels had been gifted to young ladies in exchange for a few hours of entertainment, and several other smaller curiosities of indeterminate value had likewise disappeared. Nevertheless, the bulk of the collection remained intact, an assemblage of artifacts each deservingly appraised as priceless. Yet the Sultan could not sell a single piece.

Although his father had been discreet in acquiring the antiquities, the existence of his private museum was nonetheless well known by those who enforced the laws governing the international art trade. As long as the treasures remained on the soil of a sovereign nation, no one could touch them. But a potential buyer had to face the very real possibility that law enforcement agents from any of a number of national and international bodies would be waiting to seize the relics should they leave the country, and perhaps arrest the purchaser as well.

At last, one of the Sultan's advisors had hit upon a solution that satisfied not only the letter of the law, but also guaranteed the future of Muara. The treasures of the kingdom would be put on display, touring the world on a floating museum, during which time every nation with a reasonable claim to individual artifacts would be able to make their case for rightful ownership. At the end of a two-year circumnavigation, the collection would be broken and distributed accordingly. Not only would Muara receive a modest finder's fee, but a percentage of profits from the tour and merchandising would also pour into the emptied treasury. It was a gamble to be sure, but for the young Sultan facing the dissolution of his kingdom, it was the only option.

The oversight of the world tour and the legal proceedings that would determine ownership of the relics fell to the only body capable of maintaining a semblance of objectivity: the United Nations Educational, Scientific, and Cultural, Organization's Global Heritage Commission. Each member nation sent their representatives to begin the tedious process, commencing immediately after the gala opening of the exhibit which was housed aboard *The Star of Muara*. As the Global Heritage Commission liaison to the United States of America, Nick Kismet was the lucky winner of an all-expenses paid cruise in the South China Sea.

The ship was easily distinguishable in the descending darkness. Its decks were strung with lights, causing it to resemble nothing less than an enormous funeral pyre in the middle of the ocean. Kismet cringed as that image sprang unbidden into his imagination; he tried to think of the lights in a more festive setting and failing that, he simply looked away, which was harder than it seemed. The eye was naturally drawn to the overwhelming light source as a moth to a flame. He turned his head away, deliberately gazing out into the darkest part of the sea.

Kismet's interest in the relics of ancient history was relatively new. Although he had studied world history extensively during his college education, his personal agenda had very little to do with solving the mysteries of another age. Kismet was interested in solving more contemporary enigma.

Many years earlier, a much younger Kismet had gone into the desert and everything about his life had changed. A junior officer with Army Intelligence, on the eve of Desert Storm, he had been sent on a mission which he believed to be simply the rescue of a defector who wanted to escape from Iraq. Instead, he had witnessed the curtain being thrown back on a conspiracy that seemed inextricably linked with the legendary treasures of the ancient world, and more importantly with his own life. After escaping the desert crucible, he had finished his education in international law and taken a job with UNESCO's Global Heritage Commission, from which vantage point, he had been able to maintain a vigil on the world of antiquities, watching and waiting for the conspiracy to reveal itself once more. Although he had found nothing conclusive, it had certainly proven to be an interesting career choice.

The dark water offered little insight into these ruminations, but was a welcome change from the gaudy shipboard lights. Kismet's dread of the days that lay ahead was returning. He didn't have the patience for a life of leisure; the thought of sipping cocktails poolside filled him with dread...

His brow creased as he caught a glimpse of something moving in the distance. He squinted, trying to bring the object into focus, but the ambient light in the interior of the helicopter confounded the attempt. All he could make out was a series of white streaks on the surface of the distant sea; half a dozen parallel white lines clawing across the velvet darkness. He blinked away the mild headache of eyestrain, and returned his gaze to the front of the aircraft. They were nearly there.

Up close, the lights of *The Star of Muara* seemed more benign. As the JetRanger flared above the helipad just aft of the towering smokestack, a score of party-goers on a nearby deck welcomed its arrival with pointing fingers and curious stares, doubtless wondering what celebrity was about to grace their presence, but Kismet also saw two other men dressed in dark suits, who did not gawk drunkenly at the approaching aircraft. Instead, their eyes roved methodically back and forth, constantly scanning the decks and passengers, with no trace of awe. Kismet figured them for security guards.

The pilot rattled off instructions for safe egress as the rotor blades began to slow; the operators of the air charter service weren't about to take any chances with their high-profile guests. Kismet sat patiently and waited his turn. From his brightly lit vantage, the sea was all but invisible. There was no sign of the white lines he had glimpsed from the air.

Including the crew, there were over five hundred people aboard *The Star of Muara*. A handful, like Kismet, were there for official purposes, but most were celebrity guests, taking advantage of the high-profile exhibit to keep their faces fresh in the minds of the adoring public. In turn, their presence elevated the notoriety of the traveling exhibit, drawing the interest of people who otherwise would not think of setting foot in a museum. It was a symbiotic relationship, based ultimately on the fickle values of the masses. It also greatly increased the threat level.

Immediately after leaving the aircraft, Kismet separated himself from the throng and made his way along the deck toward the stern of the pleasure craft. The superstructure of the cruise ship rode high above the sea, and its hull that was practically a sheer vertical wall all the way down to the waterline. Kismet estimated a four-story plunge awaited anyone unlucky enough to fall from her lowest open deck; boarding the craft from a smaller vessel would be virtually impossible. Nevertheless, Kismet found his unease growing. He was certain that the parallel lines he had witnessed from the air were caused by high-speed watercraft closing in on the cruise liner; boats that were running without any lights.

He scoured the dark horizon for any sign of the approaching armada, but could distinguish nothing. He cupped his hand over one ear, listening for the whine of what he knew must be powerful outboard motors, but heard only sounds of merriment.

FORTUNE FAVORS

"Jumping at shadows," he murmured, turning away from the railing. Even so, he decided a visit to the ship's bridge was in order. He had only taken a few steps toward his goal when the noise of the party was suddenly punctuated by the distinctive crack of gunfire.

The sound was muted by the layers of steel comprising the deck plates and bulkheads of the cruise liner. It might have been easy to mistake the noise for fireworks but for the sudden shrieks of terrified passengers. But the noise was repeated a moment later, and Kismet knew his first guess was correct.

He ducked instinctively, trying to present as small a target as possible, even while scanning the deck for some sign of a hostile presence. Seeing no one, friend or foe, he crept silently ahead.

When traveling, Kismet always brought his personal sidearm, a Glock 17 semi-automatic pistol, and the *kukri* knife he had carried since that fateful night in the desert when the Gurkha blade had been his weapon of last resort. This venture was no exception to that basic rule of preparedness, but he had made the error of assuming nothing dire would occur in the minutes following his arrival aboard the ocean liner. His weapons were safely tucked inside a suitcase, which was probably en route from the helicopter to his cabin. His sole remaining means of defense—or attack—was his Benchmade 53 Marlowe Bali-Song knife. The Bali-Song butterfly knife design was different than an ordinary pocket knife where the blade folded into the side of hand grip. The Bali-Song handle was split lengthwise, and the blade rotated on two pivot points out of the grooved channels on either side. In skilled hands, it could be deployed almost as quickly as a switchblade. Kismet could hold his own with the Bali-Song, but he was also a believer in the axiom of not bringing a knife to a gunfight. Nevertheless, he held the unopened folding knife in his right fist, and continued forward stealthily.

He felt a faint tremor pass through the deck, and recognized that the ship was no longer surging ahead at a steady twenty-five knots. In fact, just over the barely audible thrum of the engines, Kismet could hear the rushing sound of water being agitated at the stern—someone had reversed the engines, slowing *The Star of Muara*'s forward progress.

It seemed inconceivable that in just the short time since Kismet's arrival, the small flotilla of watercraft he had witnessed closing in on the cruise ship had managed to come alongside, putting a crew of raiders aboard to overrun the decks and seize either the bridge or the engine room. In fact, he realized, it was impossible. Those boats could not have been fast enough to execute such a takeover, leaving only one unarguable conclusion: the impending assault on *The Star of Muara* was being aided by someone already on board.

Kismet heard a loud clanking noise behind his position, and turned to find what looked like a small ship's anchor hooked over the deck railing and trailing a thick rope down into the sea. The noise was repeated as several more grappling hooks arced over the rail, falling into place along the metal barrier.

He crept forward and peeked over the edge at the boarding party. Two shapes were visible in the water directly below—fast-hulled jet boats, commonly known as cigarettes—matching the speed of the larger vessel as its mass carried it forward despite the reversal of her screws. In addition to the pilot helming each cigarette boat, there were ten armed men, five per boat, now attempting to make the four story ascent to the deck. Despite the awkwardness of the rope scaling ladders attached to the grappling hooks, the intruders were making nimble progress. Kismet was going to have company in a matter of seconds.

He resisted an impulse to cut nearest line. Doing so would only have served to attract the attention of the men below, and Kismet doubted even the razor sharp edge of the Bali-Song could slice through all the thick ropes in time. Instead, he melted back into the darkness, waiting for a better opportunity.

The armed boarding party swarmed over the railing, expecting no opposition and meeting none. They carried AK-47s or possibly a regionally produced variant; the sturdy assault rifle was easily obtainable from a number of different sources. The men, a scattering of Chinese among a majority of Indonesians, wore ragged jeans, cast-off military fatigues and t-shirts with English and Chinese language advertising logos. Despite their unprofessional appearance, Kismet recognized that they were trained combatants, not formally trained perhaps, but men who had honed their survival skills in an arena far more exacting than any military school. They fanned out as if they had intimate knowledge of the cruise vessel and her decks. Kismet didn't doubt that such was the case; the seizure of *The Star of Muara* had not been merely a spur of the moment attack on a target of opportunity.

He figured there were probably more groups like this boarding the vessel elsewhere. Additionally, there was an unknown number of pirates who had patiently waited, perhaps performing duties as members of the ship's crew, until the signal to strike was given. Though it was impossible to verify, Kismet estimated a force of at least fifty men were now swarming over *The Star of Muara*. There seemed to be little he could hope to accomplish against such overwhelming odds, but he couldn't bear to simply hide out in the shadows.

He moved toward the rail again and peered over the side at the boats below. The two jet boats were already pulling away, leaving the scaling ropes to dangle purposelessly against the side of the ship. Another vessel however, hove into view, slowly navigating toward the ocean liner. This craft appeared to be a Chinese junk, drawing motive power from a large diesel engine, rather than the sails which hung limply from the mast. Even with the modern power source, the craft would never have been able to match the cruise ship's speed. Here at least was an answer to the question of why the pirates' first objective had been to reverse the cruise ship's engines. The mystery of why were the attackers utilizing such a slow boat when they had so much speed at their command, both from the cigarettes and the cruise ship itself, continued to gnaw at him.

They're not staying, he realized. *This is a simple heist; take what they can grab and run like hell.* And if the pirates intended to use the junk to haul away their booty, they evidently had no intention of keeping the massive cruise ship as a prize.

Kismet didn't stop to think about what he was doing; under the circumstances it seemed like the right thing to do. Clipping his butterfly knife to his belt, he drew one of the grapnels from off the rail and carefully coiled the scaling rope over his shoulder.

The junk drew nearer to *The Star of Muara*, close enough for Kismet to see the figures moving about her deck. A moment later, its hull scraped against the larger craft as it pulled in parallel beside her. Kismet leaned out a little further, risking discovery, in order to observe the crew of the junk in action. The Indonesian men were using long strips of adhesive tape to affix something to the hull of the cruise ship.

Shaped charges, Kismet thought. *Probably detcord*. Once ignited, the substance could burn through steel in a heartbeat, even underwater. But the pirates were not placing their charges below the water line. Instead, they had marked off a section as big as a garage door that was roughly level with the deck of their own craft. Despite the immediate risk of discovery, Kismet was fascinated by what he was witnessing.

One of the pirates shouted something in Chinese, and the rest of the group sought cover. Without waiting for an all clear, the leader of the group activated the fuse. There was a resounding boom from near the water line as the ship's hull became instantaneously hot enough for the metal to actually begin burning. The pirates were ready for this however. Two men stepped forward with pressurized carbon dioxide fire extinguishers to rapidly cool the molten steel, after which a third used a pry bar to pop the excised portion of the hull loose, allowing it to slip into the depths.

A few minutes later, the process was repeated on the cruise vessel's secondary hull, breaching her completely and leaving a gaping wound in *The Star of Muara*. The gap was significant enough that even a modest rogue wave might inundate the ship, sending her to the bottom. The pirates evidently cared little for the ultimate fate of the captured ship or her passengers. The hole served only one purpose: it was a doorway through which they might bring whatever treasures they could seize. A dozen more armed men crossed over from the junk, entering the bowels of the ship and leaving their own vessel evidently unmanned.

Kismet saw his opportunity. He quickly repositioned one of the grappling hooks so that the rope trailed down above the junk's stern, then unhesitatingly climbed over the rail and rappelled down. Only as he slid down the thick line did it occur to him how ridiculous he must appear in his tux and shiny black shoes; he had dressed for the wrong party.

Although he was abandoning the cruise ship, his primary concern was the safety of her passengers and crew. He had not heard any more gunfire since the initial moments of the assault, but he did not take this as a sign of the pirates' goodwill. Doubtless, they knew that once they started killing people, the fear of certain death might push some of the hostages to attempt a counter-attack. It was much more likely that the intruders would first concentrate on seizing the Sultan's treasures, and then simply scuttle the ship, sending all the witnesses to their crime to the bottom of the South China Sea. Kismet reckoned the best chance the hostages had lay with his finding the junk's radio and sending a distress call to the mainland. Hopefully, rescue boats would arrive in time to pluck the survivors from the water.

He dropped stealthily to the deck of the junk and darted once more into the shadows. With the folding knife again in hand, he crept around to the opposite side of the boat, hoping to place its superstructure between himself and any lookout posted on the cruise ship. He then stole forward, cautiously exploring the unfamiliar vessel to locate its radio room. It was impossible to know where to turn next. No two junks were alike and most were haphazardly thrown together in response to the needs of the moment.

As he rounded the superstructure, he got his first look at the demolition work carried out by the pirate crew. The detcord had carved through the ship's hull with surgical neatness, opening her to the despoilers. The bottom cut of the rectangular hole was almost perfectly level with the deck inside; the intruders had chosen their point of entry carefully, further evidence that their actions had been directed by someone among the crew. The pirates would be able to come and go with relative ease. Kismet knew he didn't have much time.

The sound of approaching footsteps sent him hastening once more for cover. A young Chinese man with an AK-47 slung over one shoulder, strolled by his hiding place a few moments later. Kismet breathed a sigh of relief that his presence apparently remained unnoticed, but then he heard something that caused his heart to freeze in his chest. It was the electronically reproduced melody of a cellular telephone ringtone.

Kismet's hands flew to his pockets, desperate to silence the phone's trilling, even though he knew it was already too late. The young pirate could not possibly have failed to hear the sound. His worst fears were confirmed as he saw the man stop in his tracks. Kismet's hand tightened on the twin handle halves of the Balisong, squeezing just enough to release the spring-loaded latch.

The pirate took his cell phone from his front trouser pocket and pushed a button to receive the call, silencing the ring tone.

The sudden adrenaline dump made Kismet feel like throwing up. His personal cell phone was in his luggage along with everything else that would have been useful right then, but in the grip of panic he had forgotten that detail. As the pirate commenced chatting with a distant, unseen party, Kismet sagged in relief, biding his time in his place of concealment.

His grasp of the dialect spoken by the young man was insufficient for him to follow the conversation, but it seemed like a fairly casual exchange; a curious relative or girlfriend perhaps. It took Kismet a few moments to grasp the real significance of the phone call.

They've got coverage out here!

He had caught a glimpse of the pirate's phone. It was a regular digital unit, almost small enough to disappear inside a closed fist, not a satellite phone receiver, which despite advances in miniaturization technology, would have been considerably larger. It seemed impossible that phone service existed in the middle of the South China Sea. Nevertheless, the young man carried on his conversation as naturally as if he were on a street corner in Singapore.

Kismet realized the cruise line must have established a satellite link for their passengers, allowing them to use their personal phones as they pleased—probably passing along a hefty surcharge for the privilege—which in turn had created a cell through which the pirate's call had been routed. The particulars of the arrangement didn't concern him; all he cared about was getting his hands on that phone.

FORTUNE FAVORS

The young Chinese man continued his conversation animatedly, speaking at seemingly random intervals as he leaned against the junk's starboard railing. The exchange lasted an interminable sixty seconds before the pirate eventually pulled the receiver from his ear and hit the 'end' button. He contemplated the bright blue backlit display for a moment, and then moved to return the device to his pocket.

Kismet leapt forward, wrapping his left arm around the young man's throat as he seized his right hand in order to prevent the loss of the phone. The pirate struggled in Kismet's choke hold, but the latter had the advantage of surprise and superior physical strength. After a moment of struggle, the pirate went limp in Kismet's grasp.

He quickly dragged his captive back to the niche where he had been concealed only a moment before. The young man was still breathing but had blacked out from the temporary disruption of the blood flowing to his brain through the carotid artery. Kismet hastily relieved the pirate of his weapon, and bound the man's hands behind his back, using the cummerbund from his tuxedo as an impromptu rope. As an afterthought, he tugged his black bow-tie free and stuffed it into the captive's mouth. Only then did he pluck the phone from the man's slack grasp. He still had no idea whom to call.

He contemplated the numeric keypad a moment longer, then hit the zero key, making the universal summons for an operator. As soon as the connection was made, he spoke a single word: "English."

The reply was incomprehensible, but a few moments later another voice came on the line, "May I help you, sir?"

"I need to make an international call from this phone, but I don't know the country code for this network."

"What country?"

"The United States."

"Sir, the country code is 'one.' Simply dial one, and then enter the number you wish to call."

Kismet thumbed the 'end' button then hastily entered the eleven digits that would connect him with the one person who would not only believe his wild tale of piracy on the high seas, but might actually be able to help. There was a long silence as his summons went out into the ether, then the ring tones sounded through a haze of scratchy static. After three trills, a voice from the other side of the world spoke: "This is Christian Garral. How may I help you?"

Kismet grinned at the familiar voice. "Hey, Dad. It's Nick. I need a big favor."

2

***THE STAR OF MUARA* WAS STILL AFLOAT** when Kismet lost sight of her. If it was indeed the intention of the pirates to sink her once their business aboard was complete, they did not remain to witness that outcome. Kismet hoped he was wrong about that prediction.

The raiders had returned to the junk and their various speedboats shortly after Kismet completed his call. He dared not look out from his place of concealment to observe them, but got the impression that they had taken only what could be easily carried; small relics, paintings, precious stones and so forth. Doubtless they had helped themselves to the cash and valuables of the passengers as well. Like all good opportunists, the pirates knew that the larger relics from the old Sultan's collection would be far too difficult to move—both literally and with respects to resale—to make their theft worthwhile despite their extraordinary value. The costume jewelry worn by the women at the party would represent a pittance alongside those ancient wonders, but a smart thief only took what he could fence.

Still, it seemed like an awful lot of trouble for such a modest score. Why hit the collection at all if they planned to leave most of it behind?

Kismet did not know what would result from his hasty distress call. He only had time to relate the particulars of the crisis to his father and make a few suggestions as to who might best be summoned to rescue the passengers and crew of *The Star of Muara*, and bring the pirates to justice. Christian

Garral was more of a world traveler than his adopted son could ever aspire to be; no doubt he would know exactly whom to contact in that part of the world in order to yield the quickest and most satisfactory resolution.

The junk had moved off, flanked by several of the cigarettes. The smaller jet boats languished under the burden of diminished speed, champing at the bit like thoroughbreds forced to trot alongside a pack mule. Kismet didn't know what port the junk finally put into, but at a top speed of about twelve knots, it had proved to be a long journey over a short distance. Fortunately, it appeared that no one had missed the young man Kismet had waylaid.

As he had expected, the cell phone signal had failed when the ocean liner dropped below the horizon. The junk had motored almost due east, correcting marginally as the destination came into view.

The pirate base was located on a small jungle island, a partially overgrown pillar of igneous rock sprouting from the South China Sea. The cigarette boats broke off their escort duty and surfed over the reef into the sheltered lagoon. The junk plotted a more cautious course, but eventually threaded the coral and basalt gauntlet, mooring at a long wooden dock which extended like a pointing finger into the lagoon. Kismet removed his shoes and slipped over the side before the offloading commenced, treading water near the stern of the boat, careful to keep the AK-47 he'd appropriated from the Chinese pirate high and dry. The black fabric of his tuxedo provided adequate camouflage in the inky darkness and no one noticed him.

The towering promontory glistened in the perfect water, outlined by a sliver of moonlight. There was a structure atop the rock mass, a walled fortress from Malaysia's colonial era, from which the silhouette of a roaming watchman was visible. Kismet took a deep breath and dove beneath the surface of the lagoon, stroking toward the wooden pier where he could rise without being spotted.

The scene above was a patchwork of modern technology and the traditional art of piracy. The crewmen streaming from the junk with crates of booty in their hands would have been right at home in the seventeenth century, but the four-wheeled all-terrain vehicles towing utility carts onto the rickety pier ruined the image. In minutes, the captured treasures were heaped onto the wagons and towed back toward the beach. A group of pirates followed on foot, barely visible to Kismet in his hiding place, but one figure stood out distinctly from the others.

The scarlet fabric of her evening gown served to accentuate rather than conceal the woman's figure and the mane of blonde ringlets that cascaded to the middle of her back revealed not only her gender, but also her identity. The woman being escorted from the pirate ship was none other than Elisabeth Neuell, former A-list movie star and currently the Sultana of Muara.

What Kismet knew about the actress' career and her marriage into one of the richest families in Southeast Asia, was solely the product of half-glimpsed supermarket tabloid headlines. He had seen her in one or two film roles—just enough to agree with the general complaint of critics that her talent was mostly underutilized by directors—but aside from that, he knew only that she was a lovely woman who had run away from one fairy tale kingdom—Hollywood—and into another, marrying her prince charming. There had been inevitable comparisons to the life of Grace Kelly, and indeed, in another age, Elisabeth Neuell might easily have launched her career as one of Alfred Hitchcock's blonde bombshells. In any event, once she had taken the hand of the young Sultan, her interest in making movies had waned, this in spite of the rumored infidelities of both she and her husband. Her questionable moral character did not presently concern Kismet. She was a hostage, a captive of the pirate raiders, and as such demanded his attention.

Her captors were either guilty of very poor judgment, or had effectively trumped a military response; Kismet couldn't decide which. Either the Sultan would move heaven and earth to recover his bride, or he would leave the pirates alone for fear that harm might come to the Sultana. Kismet decided to remove that wild card from the table.

There was no hesitation on his part. Attempting to rescue the hostage was a natural extension of the same immediacy of response that had prompted him to leave the cruise ship behind in the first place. That she was a beautiful woman did not matter one bit to Kismet; he would have done the same for anyone held captive by the pirates.

He caught a last glimpse of her crossing the beach toward the narrow jungle trail, of her shapely figure and blonde curls limned in moonlight.

Well, maybe it matters a little.

The tropical sea was a warm soup that sapped his energy as he lingered beneath the pier. He waited until all activity on the junk ceased and the last flicker of light from the shore party disappeared into the jungle before crawling stealthily onto the beach.

Despite its imposing shadow, the cliff reaching up to the fortress was not sheer. Foliage clung to its steep slopes, highlighting the protrusions of rock that formed a veritable stairway up the face. Moving with a confidence born of urgency, Kismet deftly picked his way up the cliff, slowing his pace only when the upper reaches of his climb were in sight. He paused just below the lip, listening for the telltale sounds of conversation or footsteps but heard only the noise of the breakers, rushing softly over the reef beyond the lagoon.

The last part of the climb required a dynamic exertion; Kismet could touch the lip of the precipice with his outstretched fingers, but in order to complete his ascent he had to simultaneously jump and heave himself up onto the edge in a single movement. If the sentinels of the fortress' night watch were looking his way when he did, things would get ugly. He exhaled softly as he immediately dropped low and rolled away from the edge, seeking cover.

The walls of the fortress were precariously near to the edge. Kismet cleared the distance to the base of the stone barrier in a few steps, and flattened himself there, trying to pick out the sentries on the battlement above. For thirty seconds he watched, fighting to keep his breathing soft and shallow despite the exertion of climbing in the thick tropical humidity. Then he saw it, the faint glow of a cigarette ember high above, to his left.

The smoldering red point of light hovered motionless for a long time, then flared brightly. A moment later, it soared out over Kismet's head and vanished into the jungle carpet. A barely audible thumping noise indicated that the sentry had resumed a walking tour of the battlement. Kismet counted twenty footsteps before going to work.

FORTUNE FAVORS

He stripped out of his tuxedo jacket and the dress shirt underneath. The latter garment he wrapped tightly around the hooks of the grapnel he had seized before departing the cruise ship. He played out two arm lengths of rope and began whirling the hook and line in a broad circle. When the hook had achieved sufficient momentum, he released it, stepping away as he did, lest it fall back on his unprotected skull.

It did not. The hook sailed over the parapet and landed with a muted thud. The thin layer of fabric wrapped around the metal prongs had effectively muffled the noise of impact. He pulled in the line until the hook caught, giving it a final tug to make sure it was set, then wrapped the line around his body. Almost as an afterthought, he donned the jacket over his naked torso.

His biceps screamed in protest as he began ascending the vertical surface. His stocking-feet slipped uncertainly against the damp upright poles that formed the perimeter of the fortress. Nevertheless, three minutes later, he was atop the palisade, peering up and down the length of the battlement for any sign that he had been noticed.

The only sentry, the man he had spied before, was poised with his back to Kismet on an adjacent wall. His posture suggested that he was urinating out into the jungle canopy. As quietly as he could, Kismet heaved himself over the wall. His landing was light, though to his ears the noise was certainly enough to arouse suspicion. He loosened the hook from where it had bitten into the wood, and drew in the line, coiling it once more over his shoulder.

The pirates had done a great deal of work in order to reclaim the old fort from the jungle, fully restoring several buildings and evidently erecting the three pre-fabricated huts that looked completely out of place in the setting. Kismet nevertheless got the impression that this was a temporary base of operations; a transition point where they could lay low and gradually filter back into the civilized world with their newly acquired wealth.

He moved quickly and quietly, keeping an eye on the less than vigilant sentry who still roamed the battlement, and dropped down into the compound. When he was certain that no eyes would see him, he darted toward one of the nearby structures, taking shelter beneath a large window, covered by a gauzy veil of mosquito netting. There was a light burning from within, but Kismet heard no indication that the room beyond the window was occupied. He cautiously raised his head and peered over the sill.

Elisabeth Neuell sat with her back to the window, gazing into a streaked vanity mirror as she patiently brushed her hair. She now wore only a flimsy negligee, which seemed to be made of the same stuff as the mosquito netting. There was no one else in the room.

Odd attire for a hostage, Kismet thought absently. He savored the role of peeping tom for a brief moment, and then cautiously pulled the veil aside.

"Your Highness," he whispered.

The Sultana's eyes found him in the mirror, and her hand froze in mid-stroke, but otherwise she did not react to his presence.

"I'm here to rescue you," he continued, hefting himself onto the window sill and stepping forward into the room. "Get dressed. We haven't much time."

She laid the brush aside and pulled on a robe of the same fabric as her chemise. It didn't increase her level of modesty dramatically, but it would have to do. She then looked him over, noting the sodden formal attire and his bare chest underneath. "Who are you?"

"My name is Nick Kismet." He extended a hand, unsure if that was the correct protocol for greeting royalty. "I got bored at the party and decided to go for a moonlight swim. Now, if you have no objection, I think we should get moving."

She regarded him warily, but took his hand and followed his lead. He rolled over the windowsill, dropping noiselessly onto the ground below then reached out to help her. She lowered herself into his embrace, intuitively understanding what was required. As her arms tightened around his body, he could not help notice how good she smelled.

He grudgingly relaxed his hold, allowing her to stand on her own. Elisabeth's posture seemed to flaunt her figure; she crossed her arms under her breasts, thrusting them up as if for inspection. In every other way, she seemed cool and detached, as if this were the sort of thing she did every day, and no longer found it even mildly stimulating. "Now what, Nick Kismet?"

Kismet shook his head to break the hypnotic spell cast by her breasts. "Now, we get out of here."

"Lead on," she replied, almost indifferently.

Kismet nodded. He glanced around, locating the lone sentry at the far end of the wall, apparently in the midst of another smoke break. He gestured in the opposite direction. "This way."

"I take it the Sultan sent you."

"Your husband," he replied, as if to remind himself. "No, nothing like that. Like I said, I was at the reception on the ship when these guys made their big debut. I snuck onto their boat and hid out while they loaded her up. I didn't even know they had you until I saw you disembarking here."

She looked past Kismet, as if distracted. "I don't recognize you. I thought I knew most of his friends, especially the Americans."

"I've never met him," Kismet explained, holding out his hand. She regarded it suspiciously than placed her own smooth palm in his.

"But you volunteered to rescue me? Just like that? How very heroic of you." If she was mocking him, Kismet could not hear it in her tone. She kept her voice kept low as they stole along the inside perimeter of the wall. "I'm lucky you came along. I don't think the Sultan cares enough to try to rescue me. The sapphire maybe—"

"I'm sure your husband is very concerned for your safety."

She smiled knowingly into the darkness. "You are a very naive man, Mr. Kismet. The Sultan's chief concern is the preservation of his lifestyle. I am but one of many playthings he has acquired. If he is concerned, it is because he does not like losing his toys."

Kismet paused at the base of the wall, pulling Elisabeth down as the guard began the return phase of his patrol. "Well, *I* am concerned for your safety."

"I'm touched," she replied, her voice ringing genuine. "But you are also here for the treasures, aren't you? You said you didn't even know I was onboard. You were following the treasures. I mean, that's probably why you came on the cruise in the first place."

It was Kismet's turn to smile unseen. "You have no idea. But I wouldn't trade my life—or anyone else's—for a few dusty relics."

"It's nothing to be ashamed of," she whispered. "I know where they're keeping most of it. I'm sure the sapphire is there."

Her statement, delivered in the same offhand tone that she had used since he stepped into her life, caught him totally off guard. "What?"

"I know where Jin will put it. I can get it, if you'll let me."

"Jin?" Kismet didn't recognize the name, but it was safe to assume that Elisabeth had named the leader of the pirates. He did not have to ask about the gemstone she kept referring to. The Zamaron Sapphire was one of the few pieces in the collection to be publicly advertised in advance of the floating exhibition. The prize of the Sultan's collection, it was in fact the "star" for which the cruise ship had been named. The enormous star sapphire, three hundred and twenty three carats, had originally been found in India a thousand years before Christ, and was reputed to have mystical powers. It had all but fallen out of history, hoarded by a succession of men who, like the recently deceased Sultan, kept such a marvelous and remarkable treasure hidden away for its own safety. Priceless or not, Kismet wasn't about to risk his safety—or anyone else's—for the gemstone. "Too dangerous. The Sultan can get it later if it's that important."

"Later?"

"After he shows up with the cavalry and levels this place. I'm sure he's already looking for you."

"What on earth are you talking about?"

"Never mind. Let's go."

"Wait." Her voice carried an urgency that compelled him to stop. "I am not leaving without that stone."

"Are you nuts?" he hissed. He turned to face her, but she was already moving away. He had to break into a jog to catch her. "What the hell do you think you are doing?"

"I'm getting the sapphire," she replied, her eyes glittering with anticipation. "When you walk out of here, you're going to get to show me off as your prize. Well, I'm going to have that stone. Trust me. I know exactly where it is. I can get it."

Kismet scowled, but knew that she was prepared to argue until she got her way, and that precious time would be lost in a futile effort to dissuade her. "All right, but hurry."

"Follow me."

As Kismet walked closely behind the actress, he once more found himself confronted with her beauty. Yet it was not only her physical form that alternately aroused and discomfited him. Her casual disinterest seemed to mask a passionate, win-at-all-cost spirit, and he found that almost irresistible.

What in the hell are you thinking, Kismet? She's a married woman.

Elisabeth led him unhesitatingly through the compound. "You seem to know this place awfully well for a hostage."

"I got the nickel tour when we arrived." She diverted him back into the compound, to the door of a large building that adjoined to the east wall of the fortress. The rusted iron latch parted with a tortured shriek, causing Kismet to wince, but evidently raised no alarm. "In here."

The expansive barn-style doors opened into an enormous room that might have passed for a medieval mead hall. The space was dimly lit with oil lamps hanging from wrought iron hooks in each corner, but otherwise unfurnished. A balcony extended out at the second story level, encircling the hall like a mezzanine. Though the floor was littered with straw, and the air reeked of animal odors, the building did not seem to be a barn in the strictest sense. Kismet saw several of the ATVs lined up against one wall, still shackled to utility carts.

"Wait here," directed Elisabeth, hastening through the interior.

"I'm coming with you."

She shook her head confidently. "It's better if I go alone." She blew him a kiss over her shoulder then disappeared into the dimness. "Wait here. I won't be a minute."

Kismet sighed, leaning against the wall. The sudden inaction frustrated him. He had been constantly moving, constantly doing; now he was just waiting. He paced out a small circle, making three orbits, before he could take it no more.

Elisabeth had surely been caught. He had to help her.

Leaving the relative shelter near the entrance, he ventured out into the open. The four corner lamps threw out semicircles of light through their streaked glass panes, light that fell impotently on the hay-strewn floor without offering any real illumination. Kismet strode the length of the hall, peering into the shadows at the far end for some indication of another exit.

As he stepped past the all-terrain vehicles, he noticed that the wagons they towed were still fully loaded with glass display cases taken from the cruise ship. The pirates had evidently been schooled in the importance of preserving the quality of the delicate artifacts they had seized, taking on the added labor of carrying the large and cumbersome cases, rather than simply smashing out the glass and heaping up the booty.

His curiosity got the better of him momentarily and he made a cursory inspection of the containers. He saw no glint of gold, nor any sparkling gemstones; doubtless the pirate leader knew better than to leave those items lying around in a barn. Nevertheless, what he saw verified all the rumors he had heard about the Sultan's collection. The raiders had grabbed Mayan idols, carved masks, Inca mummy cases and dozens of other art treasures from cultures long since extinct. Many of the less recognizable pieces appeared to share a unique style, leading Kismet to wonder if the Sultan had perhaps scooped the archaeological institutions by purchasing the entire catalogue of a dig uncovering an unknown civilization.

There was one relic that caught his eye in spite of its apparent ordinariness. He leaned close to the display case peering inside at the artifact, which rested on a bed of red velvet. It was a hexagonal piece of stone, carved extensively with rows of wedge shaped markings. Kismet recognized it as cuneiform writing from ancient Mesopotamia, thought to be the earliest form of written language.

The relic seemed out of place among the collection of art treasures. He did not doubt that it was an artifact of great value, but he had difficulty understanding why the opportunistic pirates would have bothered with it.

FORTUNE FAVORS

Why go to the trouble of hauling what looked, at least to the untrained eye, like a big rock?

It was a riddle for another time. Elisabeth had not yet returned. Kismet turned way from the cache of relics and moved toward the far end of the room.

There was something there, something glinting in the darkness.

His hand found the pistol grip of the Kalashnikov rifle he had liberated from the pirate on the junk. He stuffed the wooden stock into the pit of his shoulder and pulled the bolt back an inch in order to verify that a round was already chambered.

The night suddenly seemed less quiet; he could almost hear the timbers of the structure creaking in the wind. Once the Sultana's escape was noticed, things were going to get a lot noisier, and he didn't want to be in the fortress when that happened. He had to find Elisabeth and get out.

His search for the far end of the hall ended abruptly at a grillwork of iron bars. Like everything else, they had lost any metallic sheen they might once have possessed to the corrosion of humid, salty air. Nevertheless, they remained firm and impassable. He gripped a vertical bar in each hand and attempted in vain to move the barrier. Daunted, he took a step back and tried to discern what lay beyond the bars.

With an ear-splitting squeal, a section of the bars began to rise like a portcullis. Kismet's gaze riveted on the slowly ascending gate, and he suddenly felt very uneasy. Floating in the darkness beyond were two glowing embers that looked exactly like...

"Eyes. Uh, oh." He began slowly backing away from the cage.

Gentle laughter abruptly echoed in the great hall. Kismet glanced up quickly, instinctively, then forced his gaze back to the eyes of whatever it was that watched him from the now opened cell. "I should have known better, when you said to trust you."

"Yes," replied Elisabeth from somewhere above and to his left. "Are you always such a sucker for a pretty girl, Nick?"

39

"More often than you'd believe," he muttered, more to the mocking voice of his conscience, than to the actress. "So let me guess. This pirate, Jin, made you a better offer than the Sultan?"

"Oh, I certainly did," replied a different voice. Though masculine, the speaker's tone was high, almost flute-like, and his speech was deeply accented. "Lights!"

The hall was suddenly bathed in the glow from more than a dozen electric bulbs, all shining down from the balcony. Kismet did not look away from the eyes, which still seemed to be hiding in shadow, but in the periphery of his view, he saw at least a score of men moving above him. He knew without looking that Elisabeth and Jin, the leader of the pirate gang, were among that number.

"You seem to have trouble with the ladies," chuckled Jin. "Maybe you will have better luck with my other princess."

The hovering embers blinked then moved forward out of the darkness. Kismet was not surprised at all when the features surrounding the glowing points coalesced into a feline face, the largest member of the cat family, a tiger. Kismet locked his own eyes with the stare of the stalking cat, backing up slowly.

"Or perhaps not," concluded Jin.

Without looking away, Kismet fixed the place where Jin's voice seemed to be coming from. He vaguely remembered reading that Bengal tigers liked to attack their human victims from behind, that they would not approach if their prey seemed to be watching. This had prompted the men working in the Indian jungles to wear masks on the back of their heads, so that their "eyes" were always watching out from behind. Kismet had no idea if this was merely jungle lore, or if the tigers on the Malay isles were as gullible as their cousins to the west, but it seemed like a good idea. As the cat padded forward however, he could plainly see that the animal had been starved and abused; doubtless, it would not wait long to attack anyone trapped with it in the pit. With slow, deliberate moves so as not to provoke the tiger, he let go of the AK-47 and slung it across his back, and then removed the coil of rope from his shoulder, hefting the grappling hook.

"Ah," sighed Jin. "Perhaps this will be more entertaining than I first believed."

Kismet tight expression cracked in a wide grin. "You don't know how right you are."

His arm moved in a barely visible arc, the rope uncoiling like a striking serpent as his arm stretched upward. His gaze never faulted. The hook sailed up and struck something just out of view. He immediately pulled with both hands setting the hook and taking in the slack. An instant later, someone pitched over the balcony railing and crashed onto the floor in front of him.

"Nice of you to join us, Jin."

The pirate winced as he pushed himself to his elbows, dazed by the fall. Kismet gave the rope a shake, loosening the hook from Jin's clothing where it had snagged. Blood seeped from a ragged wound on the pirate's back and dripped onto the floor of the hall. Jin stared blearily at Kismet then his eyes opened wide as he whirled around to face his pet. The tiger had already sprung, and at that moment, all hell broke loose.

The entire promontory shuddered as a peal of what sounded like thunder rolled though the structure. The balcony was suddenly filled with chaotic shouting, mostly in Chinese, but Elisabeth's strident shrieking wove in an out of the din. A second tremor followed quickly on the heels of the first, and this time, the electric lights winked out as somewhere in the compound, the generator was knocked out. The fortress was under attack.

Kismet jumped back as the tiger pounced on its fallen master. Loud concussions echoed in the hall as at least one of the pirates on the balcony tried to distract the tiger by shooting at it. Kismet instinctively raised a hand to ward off flying splinters of wood as he rushed through the hall.

The pirates on the balcony were attempting to flee, but in their panic, they were tripping over each other. Elisabeth seemed to be struggling to stay on her feet as the human current changed unpredictably. With a grim smile, Kismet decided to rescue her for the second time that night.

Another mortar round crashed into the compound, causing the ground to heave. One of the doors into the building was blasted open. At least three of the pirates were knocked from the balcony, crashing stunned on the floor below, while others clung to the railing to avoid a similar fate. Kismet felt the debris from the nearby explosion harmlessly pelting him.

The tiger ignored the external attack altogether, gripping Jin's throat in its mouth and throwing the pirate across the floor. It was on him again in a second, swiping its claws across his face.

Scrambling away, Kismet utilized the grappling hook once more, hurling it onto the balcony high above. The line wrapped around a railing, the hook setting securely when he drew in the slack, and he quickly set about scrambling up the wall.

His arms screamed in agony. All of the exertions of the night seemed to return in a single burst of pain. Gritting his teeth, he planted his feet against one of the support pillars and tried again. Somehow, with his biceps quivering on the verge of total fatigue, he reached the level of the balcony floor. Swinging his body like a pendulum, he got one of his legs up, then the other, and managed to roll his torso onto the edge. Frantic pirates stumbled blindly over him as they fought with each other in order to escape. Only when he stood up in their midst did they identify him as a foe and turn their destructive attention toward him.

Kismet dodged the thrust of an old-fashioned cutlass, hearing the unmistakable sound of the blade piercing flesh behind him and the groan as a wounded pirate went down. His fist, still clenching the rope, hammered into the sword's wielder, and as the man staggered against the railing, Kismet guided him over. He plucked the heavy blade from the man's grasp as he went, and wrenched it free of the body of the unfortunate soul who had inadvertently been on the receiving end of the misguided thrust. Discarding the rope, he took the sword in his right hand and charged the pirate ranks, scattering them.

Elisabeth stood a head taller than most of the men on the balcony, and Kismet saw her hair flashing only a few feet away. With wild slashes, he mowed a path toward her. When she saw him, a tortured look crossed her beautiful face. "Damn you!"

"Did you get the sapphire, princess?"

FORTUNE FAVORS

Her eyes blazed as she raised her hand toward him, a small pistol locked in her grip.

Kismet lashed out with the cutlass. The tip struck the barrel of the gun and knocked her arm upward as the firing pin struck the shell. The muzzle flashed in his face, but the round impotently struck the ceiling. He quickly moved in closer, snatching the gun away with his left hand.

The wayward Sultana raised a fist, as if to strike him, but he was faster. Stabbing the cutlass into the floorboards, he delivered a roundhouse to her jaw that spun her around. Before she could fall, he snatched her up and threw her over his shoulder. He shoved the gun into the waistband of his tuxedo trousers and then worked the cutlass loose.

"Well this has been fun, Your Highness. But it's time to take you back to your husband."

If Elisabeth heard him, she did not reply.

Kismet fought his way through several more pirates, and found a staircase leading back down to the ground floor. He crossed the rubble strewn area, mindful of the tiger which continued to feast on its former master, and headed for the ATV quads. It took him only a moment to loosen the tow bar attachment and free one of the small motorized vehicles from its treasure wagon. He started it up and climbed aboard. Elisabeth still had not stirred.

The sounds of the shelling now filled the night. Much of the fortress was in flames, and the wall on the ocean side was breached in three places. On the threshold of the barn-like storehouse, Kismet had an unobstructed view of the assault.

Three helicopters—judging by their silhouettes, Kismet reckoned they were reliable old UH-1 "Hueys," repurposed after the Vietnam war—beat the air high above the pirate compound. Several thick lines dropped from the hovering aircraft like spider-silk, and human figures began abseiling into the midst of the compound, protected by covering fire from their comrades still aboard. In a matter of seconds, a dozen camouflaged warriors had fast-roped down and were spreading out to engage the confused pirates. Kismet surmised that the commando squad was there in response to his own summons, but the fortress was presently a free-fire zone; the only salvation lay in physically removing himself from the battlefield. He revved the throttle on the ATV and charged into the midst of the skirmish.

The pirates were attempting to muster a response to the overwhelming attack, but their numbers were already severely diminished and their arsenal of poorly maintained rifles and handguns was no match for the concussion grenades and assault rifles wielded by the attacking force. Most of the pirates simply threw down their weapons and fled into the jungle. Reasoning that the refugees would know the best way out of the fortress, Kismet swerved the quad in their direction, plunging into the darkness beyond.

The explosions did little to illuminate the dark woods. The canopy of overgrowth quickly eclipsed any ambient light, forcing Kismet to slow the vehicle to a crawl. He debated using the quad's headlights, but decided that doing so would merely make him a target. Instead, he switched off the engine and let the noise of the jungle settle over him like a blanket.

"Well," he sighed. "That didn't go too badly."

His grin faltered as he became aware of several shapes, nothing more than silhouettes, ringing his position. A flashlight blazed in his face, blinding him momentarily, but also revealing the jungle pattern fatigues worn by the group surrounding him. He raised his hands slowly, painfully aware of the fact that the Sultana of Muara was slung over his shoulder like a sack of potatoes.

"It's okay, I'm one of the good guys."

"Lieutenant?"

The voice was familiar, but even more so was the pronunciation of that single word. Kismet hadn't held military rank in nearly twenty years, but in all the time he had been an officer, he had only once heard the word pronounced as "Lef-tenant." He blinked in the direction of the voice—the man holding the light.

"Sergeant Higgins?"

Another shape interposed, stepping into the light. Kismet recognized the man from his publicity photos, but in most of those he was smiling.

"Release my wife," demanded the Sultan. His hand rested on the grip of a holstered pistol.

FORTUNE FAVORS

Kismet eased the semi-conscious woman from her undignified perch, setting her on the rear fender of the ATV. As he did, her eyes fluttered into focus. She looked first at Kismet, and then turned slowly to face her husband. Kismet expected her to launch into some kind of conciliatory plea, but when the former actress spoke, her tone was anything but contrite.

"What are you doing," she rasped. "He's one of them."

Kismet was still trying to make sense of her declaration when the Sultan drew his sidearm, thrusting it toward him. Kismet was taken aback. "Your highness?"

"I will have your head for this," raged the Sultan.

Kismet gaped, mouthing a reply. Judging by the Sultan's fierce expression, trying to explain the facts would do little to help the situation. He decided to try a different approach.

Although the Sultan's gun was less than a hand's breadth from his face, Kismet launched into motion. He wrapped an arm around the Malay prince's neck, and plucked the gun from his unprepared grasp. By the time the soldiers could react, Kismet had the muzzle of the weapon buried in the Sultan's ear. "Lower your guns and move back."

The commandos did not seem willing to relinquish their control of the situation, and Kismet could sense each man wondering if there was time to make a killing shot before the trigger could be pulled on the royal hostage.

"I mean it," he grated, screwing the barrel deeper into the Sultan's skull and eliciting a low cry. "Back off."

"Do as he says."

Kismet again recognized the voice and the distinct accent of a New Zealander. Evidently, Sergeant Alexander Higgins remained a figure of authority in whatever army he now served; as one, the commandos lowered their assault rifles until the barrels were pointing at the ground and opened a path of exit.

Kismet did not release the Sultan, but instead manhandled him away from the parked ATV and toward his intended avenue of escape. He did not offer words of thanks to Higgins; the night was still young and there remained ample opportunities for things to go wrong.

Once past the perimeter established by the ring of soldiers, he turned, backing away from them toward the tree line. The commandos hesitantly grouped together, watching him and cautiously easing forward. He took a final backward step, then propelled the Sultan into their midst. As they instinctively moved to assist the royal personage, Kismet bolted into the depths of the jungle.

The night came alive with the tumult of gunfire, and Kismet knew that the bullets zipping through the humid air, shattering bamboo poles and smacking into tree trunks were meant for him. Apparently Higgins' orders didn't carry that much weight after all.

He couldn't tell if the soldiers had elected to pursue him on foot, but after an initially fierce fusillade, their guns fell silent and the sounds of the jungle enveloped him completely.

There was no way he could have heard the barely whispered parting words as he vanished into the night.

"Good luck, mate."

3

BY THE TIME THE SULTAN OF MUARA arrived back at the cruise ship bearing the name and flag of his small country, repairs to her breached hull were well underway. Dead in the water since the sabotage of her computerized systems by pirate agents posing as members of the crew, the ship faced only minimal danger from the gaping wound. As a precaution, the chief engineer had dumped enough ballast to lift the holed section away from the waterline to mitigate the risk of inundation, and it had not been necessary to abandon the vessel. Nevertheless, most of the passengers had elected to depart, at least temporarily, the idea of a long ocean voyage having lost its appeal. The Sultan likewise decided to leave the ship, claiming that the act of piracy and the near-fatal kidnapping of his beloved wife had created a domestic crisis which necessitated his remaining in the Sultanate.

Over the next twenty-four hours however, the situation improved remarkably. The repairs were completed—not simply a patch to cripple the ship into port, but a seaworthy reconstitution of the hull. The only indication of the damage was the flat gray of the primer coat used to protect the welded steel plates from rapid oxidation in the salty air, and even that distinction was scheduled to be addressed by maintenance crews at the next major port of call. The sabotage to the engine room and the ship's computer were likewise repaired in short order, and the craft was deemed ready for service before the fall of the next evening.

There were many reasons why it was important for *The Star of Muara* to be restored to active status as quickly as possible. Several of the antiquities in the collection were too large or fragile to be moved while the ship remained on the high seas; it was this very fact that had protected them from the greed of the pirates. An overriding concern however was giving the appearance that no crime or act of terrorism could prevent the success of the exhibition. It was an important psychological message to the world; if the cruise could be thwarted, what next? Only by demonstrating that everything was back to normal, that the hijacking had been merely an inconvenience, could the sponsors of the Muara exhibition hope to return a profit. Of course that normalcy would be an illusion. The already impressive security force was tripled, even though at the time no one but the crew remained aboard, and they were all undergoing an intense, if somewhat tardy, vetting process.

The next step in establishing that everything was back on track was to begin returning guests to the ship. Fully two-thirds declined the invitation, despite a number of incentives. But for every current passenger unwilling to return, there were ten thrill-seekers from every part of the world who were eager to book passage on what the news media had begun calling "The Pirate Cruise."

The last of a long procession of helicopter shuttle flights touched down shortly after midnight. The pilot dutifully opened the rear door for his passengers, urging them to exit cautiously as they passed beneath the still spinning rotor blades, and then set about collecting their luggage. Burdened as he was with a double armful of suitcases and garment bags, he left the cargo door open and he hastened toward a pair of stewards who waited a safe distance from the aircraft. Neither the pilot, nor the stewards saw a dark-clad figure slip from the belly of the helicopter and melt into the shadows. Nevertheless, Nick Kismet's return to *The Star of Muara* did not go completely unnoticed.

FORTUNE FAVORS

From the moment he escaped into the jungle, Kismet had operated under the assumption that the Sultan's pronouncement of his death sentence ought to be taken at face value. As the sovereign ruler of the tiny kingdom, the man quite literally had the authority to call for a summary execution, and no amount of legal posturing would prevent a dutiful palace guard from carrying out the order. It was of course entirely possible that the facts of the matter had come to light but he wasn't about to risk exposure until he was certain of it.

His decision to return to the ship had been more a matter of convenience than a thoughtfully arrived at strategy. Escaping from Borneo by any other means would have meant days of hardship and fugitive wandering through one of the most untamed places on Earth. In contrast, the cruise ship was a bastion of twenty-first century technology where he would quickly be able to affirm his innocence and arrange asylum should the worst-case scenario play out. It also seemed like the last place anyone would think to look for him.

From the helipad, he made his way into the ship proper, ducking into one of the common rooms where he made a mostly futile attempt to brush away the stains and wrinkles that permanently marred the fabric of his dinner jacket. He considered stuffing the soiled garment in a refuse bin, but unfortunately he had left his shirt at Jin's fortress, still wrapped around the grappling hook.

Although it was nominally a party-ship, the atmosphere aboard was restrained. Where only a day before, wealthy debutantes had wandered the decks with cocktails in hand, this night found the ship seemingly deserted. As if observing an informal curfew, the passengers had retired early, leaving only a scattering of crewmembers roaming the decks. With the aid of a convenient fire-escape route map, Kismet plotted a course to a nearby lounge, intent on quieting the ravenous beast in his belly and soothing his strained nerves with a drink. Upon entering the salon however, he stopped dead in his tracks.

The small dining area was adjacent to one of the antiquities exhibits, and the lounge looked like the headquarters of a paramilitary operation. No less than a dozen men in navy blue fatigues and black berets, openly wearing holstered automatic pistols, were scattered throughout the room. Almost as one, their eyes swung to greet this latecomer.

His hesitation was only momentary, but when he started into motion again, he felt their scrutiny slice through him like laser beams. He fought the impulse to turn and flee, and instead strode to the bar. If he was indeed on some kind of watch list, then it was already too late; no sense in wasting the opportunity for a final drink before being hauled off in irons. But a second glance as he slid into one of the swiveling chairs revealed that the security guards had lost interest in him. Kismet breathed a sigh of relief and nodded to the bartender. "Macallan, neat. Better make it a double."

The server quickly decanted a large portion of Scotch Whisky into a tumbler and set it before him with a knowing smile. Kismet savored a mouthful of the peaty spirits then decided to press his luck a bit further. "This is kind of embarrassing, but I seem to have misplaced my key, and I can't remember what my room number is."

"No problem, sir." He picked up a telephone and punched a three-digit code. "Name?"

Kismet tried to sound casual as he supplied the information, then took another sip of his drink while the bartender relayed the information. After a moment, he hung up and turned back to Kismet. "Good news. The purser will bring a replacement key card for you, straightaway."

Kismet weighed the response and decided it concealed nothing sinister. "Thanks. Now, what are my chances of getting something to eat?"

Rather than wait at the bar for the purser's arrival, Kismet took up his Scotch and wandered toward the entrance to the exhibit. If his fugitive crisis was indeed over, he was going to have to turn his attention back to the matter that had brought him here in the first place. Oddly enough, he found comfort in the thought, as if in so doing he might somehow delete the events of the past day from memory.

Yet something about the incident nagged at him, like a tiny sliver of metal lodged in the skin of his subconscious. He could still see it in his mind's eye; a stone prism etched with tiny lines of cuneiform. Why had Jin's pirates chosen that piece?

The prism was almost certainly one of the pieces looted from Iraq in the days leading up to the 2003 invasion that had ousted the regime of Saddam Hussein. Shortly thereafter, Kismet, in concert with French authorities, had raided the operation of a former Iraqi intelligence officer who had opened a pipeline of looted antiquities during the 1990's to establish an alternate source of revenue to offset the crippling economic sanctions imposed by Western nations. The evidence gathered at the man's villa in Nice indicated that more than a few items had found their way into the Sultan's collection.

There was no denying that the piece had a reliable pedigree. The circumstances surrounding its removal from its country of origin might even have added to its value as a curiosity, but it remained just that: a curiosity. Kismet could not fathom why the pirates had elected to liberate it along with the other relics; had it simply been a target of opportunity?

The artifacts had been grouped according to country of origin, and as he neared the section which housed the art of Mesopotamia, he was dismayed to find that he was not alone in seeking out the prism.

The man was tall, and would have seemed gaunt if not for the luxurious silver mane that framed his angular face—a countenance that appeared too youthful for a man gone completely gray. His clothing was nondescript; the dark trousers and a blousy black shirt might have been the attire of an off duty waiter. His left hand held a notebook in which he was painstakingly copying lines from the prism, and the middle finger of his right, which held the pen, was adorned with a gaudy, gem-encrusted ring. Impulsively, Kismet tried to get a better look at the ring, and in so doing, drew attention to his presence. The tall man inclined his head in a polite nod, revealing eyes the color of gypsum, then returned to his labor.

"What's it say?"

The scribe looked up, a faintly perturbed expression flickering across his features. Kismet smiled, hoping to put the man at ease, but saw no change in the gray eyes. He risked extending a hand to the man. "I'm Nick Kismet."

The man's expression softened just a little, but he disdained the handclasp. When he spoke, his enunciation was precise, with just a hint of superciliousness but no discernible accent. "Dr. John Leeds, at your service."

In the corner of his eye, Kismet saw a man wearing the common uniform of a ship's steward enter the lounge. He felt an inexplicable compulsion to remain with the strange scholar, but the hunger and fatigue in his body argued that he should take his leave. "A pleasure making your acquaintance, doctor. Enjoy the cruise."

"It is the Epic of Gilgamesh."

The quiet voice froze Kismet in mid-step. He turned back. "I take it you're not a physician, Dr. Leeds."

The statement elicited a faint smile. "No. My field is comparative theology. I am also—if I may be so bold as to say it—an expert on mythology and the occult."

"Thus your interest in one of the world's oldest fairy tales."

Leeds laughed, but his icy eyes froze away any hint of mirth. "My interest is not purely academic. The quest of Gilgamesh is one that I happen to share."

"As I recall, Gilgamesh was looking for the secret of immortality."

"Even so."

For a moment, Kismet could only stare in mute disbelief at the other man. When he at last found his voice, he averted his eyes, gazing instead at the amber contents of his glass. "Gilgamesh never found it. What makes you think it's there to be found?"

"Actually, Gilgamesh did find it. In the legend, Uta-Napishtim, the only man to be given the gift of immortality, told Gilgamesh of a plant which could give him eternal life; a plant that grew at the bottom of the sea. Gilgamesh recovered the plant, only to lose it to a hungry serpent."

"I stand corrected." For some reason, Kismet got the distinct impression that Leeds didn't think of the Epic as a fairy tale. "So do you think such a plant really existed?"

"Straight to the point, Mr. Kismet? What if it was that simple; eat the fruit of the Tree of Life, and live forever? Would you not do so in a heartbeat?"

Kismet was already regretting having asked, regretted having even introduced himself to Leeds in the first place, but something about the man—maybe it was his self-confessed quest for immortality, or maybe just the fact that Leeds came off as an arrogant bastard who needed to be taken down a notch—compelled Kismet to stay. "Who wouldn't? But if such a plant, a Tree of Life, existed, someone would have found it by now."

"And why do you believe no one has?"

Kismet contemplated the prism for a moment. "So this...the Epic of Gilgamesh is factual?"

Leeds smiled again, a humorless grin that lowered the temperature in the air-conditioned salon by several degrees. "Theologians cannot help but recognize the similarities between characters in the Epic, and those mentioned in the Bible. Gilgamesh is certainly Nimrod, the king who would be a god. Uta-Napishtim the immortal who survived the Great Flood, is Noah. Genesis also speaks of the Tree of Life in the Garden of Eden; doubtless the same plant Gilgamesh sought. Its placement at the bottom of the ocean would be an allusion to Eden being lost to the Flood."

Kismet stroked his chin thoughtfully. He wasn't a believer, but he knew enough about both theology and mythology to hold his own in the conversation. "Okay, I'll buy that. Of course, the Bible records Noah's death, whereas Uta-Napishtim was supposed to be immortal."

"Noah lived to be nearly a thousand years old; the longest any man lived after the Great Flood. His son Shem apparently possessed a similar gift of longevity. To the rest of the world, they would certainly seem immortal."

"And it is your contention that they possessed some vestige of the Tree of Life from the Garden of Eden that kept them alive well beyond the limit of an ordinary life span?"

"Contention? Better to call it an hypothesis. I am a scientist Mr. Kismet, studying the religions of the world, ancient and modern, not so much to determine what is true, but to find the commonality that might educate us as to the origin of faith."

Leeds flipped to the back of his notebook as he spoke, and Kismet realized that the thick leather bound volume was actually a Bible. "In the Western world, it is generally accepted that, if there is a religious truth, it is expressed in the Judeo-Christian belief system. Now, if we are to accept the Holy Scriptures as essentially factual—and that is a leap of faith which many in our modern society are no longer willing to make—then the account of Genesis proves unquestionably that the antediluvians lived to extraordinary ages. Adam, Methuselah and Noah himself, all lived to be nearly a thousand years of age. These accounts were not meant to be taken as allegory, as so many today want to believe; the language is very precise. Those men living before the Great Flood had extraordinarily long life spans. What changed?

"The answer is here. Genesis chapter two: 'And a river went out of Eden to water the garden; and from thence it was parted, and became into four heads.'"

Leeds looked up from the pages and watched for a reaction, but Kismet could only shake his head. "I'm not sure I follow you."

"The rivers that issued out of Eden, the garden of life, were likely imbued with the properties of the Tree of Life, mentioned here in verse nine: 'the Tree of Life also in the midst of the garden.' Adam and Eve were not permitted to eat of the fruit of that tree. They were expelled from the garden for their transgression and barred from entering by the cherubs and the blade of a flaming sword. Nevertheless, the life-giving properties of the Tree of Life flowed out of Eden in the waters of those rivers; diluted to be sure, but still potent enough to enable those men to live to extraordinary ages."

"Then the Flood came and washed it all away," continued Kismet, making no effort to limit the skepticism in his tone. "So how did Noah and Shem manage to live on for so long afterward?"

FORTUNE FAVORS

"One explanation would be that both were born into the antediluvian world; both would have tasted the waters of life. But I postulate a different theory.

"Noah was certainly the favored of God, even as Uta-Napishtim was in the Epic of Gilgamesh. I believe that Noah may have carried pieces of the Tree, perhaps its fruit, plucked from the river waters before the Flood. He would have given these powerful items to his sons Japheth and Shem, though not to Ham, the accursed progenitor of the Negro race."

Kismet winced at the unexpected diatribe. He was liking Leeds less as the conversation progressed.

"Nimrod," continued Leeds, "was a descendant of Ham, and likely coveted the gift that Noah had passed to his superior offspring. Perhaps the quest of Gilgamesh is an allegory describing Nimrod's desire to seize that power from the children of his grandfather's brothers."

"Sounds like you've got it all figured out."

"There is much more evidence to support my claim."

Kismet wanted to leave; wanted to be away from the odious Dr. Leeds as much as he wanted to take refuge in his stateroom, but the unequivocal assertion held him rooted in place. "Evidence?"

"Earlier you asked why no one else had ever discovered the secret of immortality. In fact, an eighteenth century French nobleman, the Comte de Saint-Germain, reputedly discovered the secret of immortality in a substance he called 'the Philosopher's Stone'."

"I've heard the story," Kismet replied warily. "Various charlatans throughout history have claimed to be Saint-Germain, Cagliostro, the alchemist Nicholas Flamel...snake oil salesmen, one an all."

"Are you so sure that they were charlatans? If Noah or Methuselah could live to be nine hundred years old, why not these men?"

Kismet shrugged. He silently admonished himself for not having made his escape sooner. What he had first mistaken for charisma was, it seemed, just the persuasive passion of a crank. "Those stories failed to convince me then, and nothing I have heard here convinces me now."

55

"Then consider a different tale." Leeds gestured with the Bible. "Have you ever heard of the Sacred Heart of Jesus Christ?"

"Aside from the fact that hundreds of churches, schools and hospitals are named for it, not really."

"The Devotion of the Sacred Heart is a liturgy found in the catechism, though it is not explicitly mentioned in scripture. The doctrine itself has more to do with the symbolism of Christ's love for mankind, a love so passionate that it caused his heart to glow visibly in his chest.

"In the subtext of this tale however, I see yet another clue in the puzzle of the quest for immortality. There is a tradition among the Gnostics, who were in fact among the earliest of Christ's followers, and never accepted the pollution of the Roman church, that Jesus was in fact one of the Magi; a class of Rabbis devoted to studying the Kabbalah. During the forty days and nights, which Christ spent in the wilderness, he learned the secret of unlocking the powers hidden in the language of the Torah. I believe that he also found something else.

"Another supposition of scholars is that Shem, the son of Noah, was also Melchizedek, King of Salem, and there is no mention of Melchizedek's death in the scriptures; in fact, St. Paul alluded to Melchizedek's immortality in the Epistle to the Hebrews. It is my belief that Melchizedek bequeathed his vestige of the Tree of Life to Jesus Christ during the forty days of his meditation, and the Christ in turn used the knowledge of the Magi to incorporate it into his own flesh, making it one with his own heart."

"That is an interesting way of skewing the scriptures," remarked Kismet. "But it doesn't really support your idea of eternal life. Jesus didn't exactly survive to a ripe old age."

"Only because he was slain. And yet death could not hold him, for he rose three days later, as an eternal spirit." Through his discussion, Leeds' voice remained calm, never betraying the passions he evidently harbored on the subject. "Notice however the particulars of his crucifixion, mentioned in the Gospel of St. John: 'But one of the soldiers with a spear pierced his side, and forthwith came there out blood and water.' The spear of the centurion Gaius Longinus pierced the heart of Jesus. When that happened, the heavens darkened and the earth shook. The gospel of St. Matthew says that tombs were opened and the dead came to life. Imagine the power that was released when the Sacred Heart was pierced. The spear of the centurion became a powerful talisman, as did the chalice in which Joseph of Arimathea collected the heart-blood of Christ. Longinus himself received the gift of immortal life."

"I have heard those legends as well; the Spear of Destiny and the Holy Grail. I seem to recall that Longinus viewed his immortality as a curse."

"Only because of his guilt for having slain the Christ. He doubtless wished to kill himself, even as Judas the betrayer did, but he was denied the release of suicide."

Kismet shook his head, as if clearing away cobwebs. "Okay, so Jesus' powers to heal, raise the dead and everything else came from his possession of some magic fruit. We'll sidestep the fact that about every Christian on the planet would view that as blasphemy. How exactly is that going to lead you to the secret of immortality? You said it yourself: the Sacred Heart of Christ was destroyed when he was killed."

"True, but remember what I said earlier. Noah passed his gift on to Japheth also. There were at least two, and perhaps many more pieces of the Tree of Life. I believe they were seeds that survived the Great Flood. Shem, who later became Melchizedek, had the one which eventually became the possession of Christ and made possible his transcendence of the flesh. Japheth also took possession of one of the seeds, and I believe that this is the one which Nimrod, or Gilgamesh sought and eventually captured."

Kismet frowned. "You said a serpent devoured it."

"Indeed. But in this instance, the serpent was actually a metaphor for the priesthood of the cult of serpent worshippers. They seized the seed by violence, perhaps even slaying Nimrod, and fled."

Kismet nodded slowly. "So that is what you are after: the Seed that belonged to Japheth."

"The Japhetic Seed is still out there somewhere. There are too many legends of men who have discovered the power of eternal life for me to believe otherwise."

"Everyone wants to live forever," Kismet argued. "That's why the quest for immortality is central to religions and folklore. Some people are desperate enough to try crazy things to find the Garden of Eden, the Philosopher's Stone, or the Fountain of Youth."

"Curious you should mention that." Leeds flipped to the back of the Bible and withdrew a folded sheet of parchment. "The Fountain of Youth is rather a pet hobby of mine. There are in fact several legends of such a place on nearly every continent, though the quest of Ponce de Leon is perhaps the one with which people are most familiar. Did you know that most scholars reject the idea that Juan Ponce de Leon, the first Spanish governor of Puerto Rico, was actually looking for such a fountain?"

"I had a professor who maintained that Ponce de Leon was really looking for a cure for impotence, and not a true source of eternal life. Sixteenth-century Viagra."

If Leeds even heard him, he gave no indication. "There are of course contemporary accounts that verify his interest in finding a rejuvenatory pool, though in most, we find him looking for an island in the Caribbean. It is only in the memoir of a man named Hernando D'Escalante Fontaneda, written in 1575, that we find mention of Ponce De Leon searching for the Fountain of Youth in Florida. He wrote: 'Juan Ponz de Leon, giving heed to the tale of the Indians of Cuba and Santo Domingo, went to Florida in search of the River Jordan...that he might become young from bathing in such a stream.'

"Fontaneda was a remarkable man. He was, as a youth, shipwrecked on the Florida coast in the year 1549, and captured by Calusa Indians. The Calusa sacrificed all the other survivors of the wreck, but Fontaneda survived, and lived with them in captivity for nearly twenty years. He was eventually freed, and for several years thereafter, served as a guide and translator for Pedro Menéndez de Avilés, the Spanish governor of Florida. During that time, he spoke often of a great treasure pit in a Calusa village—gold and silver plundered from wrecked Spanish ships. Fontaneda boasted that, with a hundred men, he could seize the wealth of the Calusa leader, but just three years after winning his freedom, he returned to Spain to reclaim his ancestral lands. A few years later, he recorded the account of his time in captivity. On the subject of Ponce De Leon's River Jordan, he wrote: 'I can say, that while I was a captive there, I bathed in many streams, but to my misfortune I never came upon the river.'"

Leeds paused and Kismet wondered if that had been his cue to applaud. To fill the uncomfortable silence, he nodded and said, "Interesting."

"Even more interesting is this letter." Leeds removed a folded sheet of paper from between the pages of his Bible. "It was written by Andrés Rodríguez de Villegas, the colonial governor of Florida from 1630-32, to King Philip IV of Spain. Evidently, the letter was handed over to the Inquisition and eventually found its way into the Vatican's secret archives, which given its nature, comes as little surprise."

Kismet again noted how precisely Leeds spoke, as if reading from a teleprompter. He expected the silver-haired man to start reading the missive aloud, but to his surprise, Leeds proffered the document.

It was obviously a photocopy, printed on a crisp sheet of twenty pound bond paper. Someone had scrawled an English translation under each line of quill pen written Castilian Spanish. Kismet scanned the first few lines verifying that the translator had stayed true to the original text, and then focused his attention on the English translation:

"Most Powerful Lord,

"In my last letter to you, I wrote of the man Henrique De Moresco Fortunato, who has been residing in Saint Augustine for more than a year. I was suspicious of Fortunato since he could give no account of how he came by his extraordinary wealth. It was said by some that Fortunato might perhaps secretly be a descendant of Hernan Fontaneda, who as a boy was captured by Indians and later served my predecessor some sixty years past. Fontaneda often spoke of an Indian treasure hoard the location of which only he knew. It was my belief that Fortunato had learned of its location, and procured the treasure for himself, so I took it upon myself to investigate. Little did I imagine what Fortunato, drunk on wine, would reveal to me."

Kismet paused. His eyes flashed over the name that kept repeating. "Henrique Fortunato," he muttered. "Henry Fortune?"

"I beg your pardon, Mr. Kismet?"

He looked at Leeds, jarred out of his reverie. "Sorry." He looked down the letter reading silently until his eyes caught the place where he had left off.

"'I am not a son of Fontaneda,' he told me. 'I am the very man.

"'I, Hernando Fontaneda, was a captive of the Indians for seventeen years, and in that time I learned of many things, the mundane and the profane, which I dared not share with my fellow Spaniards. The treasure of Carlos, the Indian King, was the least of my discoveries.

"'You have heard of the pool of life, and the River Jordan, sought by Ponz de Leon but never found. It exists. I have seen it with my own eyes. There is a cavern where fire dances upon the surface of the water, as if at the very mouth of Hell. The water, if you dare touch it, will impart renewed vigor. An old man will grow young and vital. Do you not believe me? How many years do you think I have? Thirty? I was born nearly one hundred years ago.'

"All this and more, Fortunato revealed to me. I know not if he spoke the truth. If he is not Fontaneda, then how do I explain his great wealth? But if he is the man he claims to be, then he has committed the gravest of sins, seeking life eternal apart from the grace of our Lord. Worse, he has found it.

"'I ordered his arrest, intending that this was a matter to be investigated by the Holy Inquisition, but he fled, overpowering all who stood in his path with uncanny strength. He has since fled the city, escaping into the lands of the Indian. His property has been seized, yet the goods taken represent the barest fraction of the wealth I believe he possesses still.

"'With an additional five hundred arquebusiers, I may be able to hunt the man down; send me a thousand, and I assure you it will be done."

Kismet glanced back up to the middle of the letter and reread Fortunato's statements.

"What do you think of that?" inquired Leeds, his icy gaze probing.

Kismet shrugged. "You said that was in the Vatican archives? How'd it end up there?"

FORTUNE FAVORS

"I would surmise that the Church wanted to suppress any mention of the Fountain, for the very reason Rodriguez wrote in the first place. Eternal life, apart from the grace of God, would have been a most egregious sin."

Kismet handed back the letter. "So what are you doing here, chasing after Gilgamesh?"

"The letter is but one piece of a greater puzzle. I do not know if Fortunato was in fact Hernando Fontaneda kept unnaturally young by some mysterious pool. He may simply have been a drunkard, spinning a tall tale. I cannot stake my search upon a single questionable account. Nor can I entirely dismiss such an account out of hand.

"I do sincerely believe that the first step in my journey lies in understanding what became of the Seed after it was taken from Nimrod. Those who worshipped Nimrod would have pursued the priests of the serpent cult to the ends of the earth. They might have ended up in the Americas, but they could just as easily have taken their prize to Asia or deepest Africa. Serpent gods exist in almost every ancient culture and are universally viewed as a symbol of eternal life, except in the Judeo-Christian mythos, where they are associated with evil."

Kismet picked up his glass and took a meaningful step backward. "I would say you have a lifetime of searching ahead of you."

"Perhaps an eternal lifetime," replied Leeds without a trace of a smile.

"Well good luck to you. Thank you for a stimulating conversation. I hope you find what you seek."

Leeds inclined his head, and then returned to copying the prism as if the exchange had never occurred. Grateful for the tacit dismissal, Kismet hastened back to lounge where a plate of food and the key card to his room waited. Strangely however, hunger and fatigue had fled away, replaced by a poorly defined memory of a name that was uncomfortably similar to that of the 'drunken' braggart in Leeds' letter.

The taciturn occult scholar watched Kismet go without saying a word, but as the other man departed, a new arrival to the exhibit hall came over to join Leeds. Without preamble that latter spoke: "I just had a conversation with Nick Kismet."

The man's jaw dropped, revealing a single silver incisor in an uneven row of natural, but yellowed teeth. "Kismet," he rasped, as though the name were an oath.

"Patience, Ian. I doubt he suspects what we know." Leeds caught a final glimpse of Kismet collecting his dinner from the bartender. "But he knows something about the Fountain; I'm sure of it. And I think he will lead us to it."

Kismet exited the lounge and moved onto an open-air balcony overlooking the starboard flank of the ship. He clutched the deck railing and closed his eyes, as if in the grip of vertigo.

He kicked himself for having visibly reacted to the letter Leeds had showed him; the mention of the cavern had caught him totally by surprise. He racked his brain to remember where he had heard the name Henry Fortune, and if it had been in connection with a cavern featuring some extraordinary natural phenomenon. He couldn't think of anything specific, but the feeling that there was something more going on persisted.

The deck and number of his stateroom had been handwritten on the paper sleeve which contained his key card, and a consultation of the escape route map helped him navigate to his lodgings where, with a little luck, his luggage would be waiting. Nestled inside one suitcase was a rugged laptop computer with a satellite telephone modem that would enable him to access the GHC archives; if Fortune's name had appeared in any document received by his agency, it would be revealed through the miracle of modern technology.

FORTUNE FAVORS

He moved through the ship on auto-pilot, his mind still turning over the bizarre encounter with Dr. John Leeds. He instinctively disliked the man; perhaps that was the driving force behind his sudden compulsion to trump Leeds in his search. But beneath that lay a lingering suspicion that Leeds' admitted obsession with the legend recorded on the cuneiform prism was a little too coincidental when viewed in the light of recent events. The connection was too tenuous to even be considered circumstantial evidence, but it was enough to fuel Kismet's suspicions. As he slid the key card into the electronic lock and entered the stateroom, he decided he was going to have to do a little research on Dr. Leeds as well.

Abruptly his consciousness was jerked like a yoyo back into the moment. Someone was in the room. A figure shrouded in shadow sat opposite the open door and a haze of cigarette smoke hung in the air between them.

"Pardon me," he said quickly, retreating backward. "Must have the wrong room."

He knew better of course; the key cards made such an error virtually impossible. There could be only one explanation: the trap he had feared had finally sprung. The Sultan's security forces had caught up to him. Before he could escape however, the table lamp near the seated figure flicked on, illuminating the grinning visitor. "Took your sweet time getting here, mate."

Kismet nearly dropped his untouched dinner plate as he recognized the speaker. He had only gotten a glimpse of the man the night previously, and in the intervening hours had not really considered the possibility of a further reunion. "Sergeant Higgins?"

Then his voice fell as he caught sight of the other person in the room. He worked his mouth, trying to articulate his thoughts, but nothing came out. He gaped a moment longer as Higgins' companion drew closer.

"Hello again, Nick Kismet."

"Elisabeth." It was all he could say. Bile rose in his throat, choking off his utterance. He opened his mouth to speak again, but no curse he could muster seemed adequate to the moment. Failing that, he turned and stalked away.

4

HIGGINS CAUGHT UP TO HIM a few steps from the door, leaving the treacherous actress alone in the stateroom. "Wait. You don't understand—"

"What the hell is she doing here?" Kismet rasped. He turned to face the former Gurkha, getting his first real look at the man who had once stood with him in a battle they both thought would be their last. The burly Kiwi was a couple inches taller than he and built like a rugby player. His curly brown mop was longer now than when he had been in the regiment. Kismet saw no gray hairs, but the leathery creases in his countenance betrayed his age. Even under the best of circumstances, he would have avoided this reunion; he had no desire to relive the events of that night with his one time comrade in arms.

"You don't understand. She wasn't trying to betray you. If you would let her—"

"I can't even look at her. She nearly got me killed. Twice."

"Would you just listen to me?" Higgins grabbed hold of Kismet's shoulders, shaking him as one might a wayward child. Though the Kiwi outweighed him by at least a good thirty pounds, Kismet tensed as if preparing to defend himself. Higgins dropped his hands and took a step back. "Just listen," he continued, his tone more subdued. "There's a lot more going on here than you realize. The Sultan believes Elisabeth betrayed him. He's publicly divorced her—you know how easy that is to do in a Muslim country—and secretly put a price on her head. She's on the run, mate."

"Good."

"Will you let me finish? You don't know what really happened. Not in Jin's fortress and not with the Sultan."

Kismet leaned back and crossed his arms over his chest. "Okay. I'm listening, but this had better be good. I've already had a double helping of fantasy tonight."

"It would be better if you let her tell you."

"Humor me, Sergeant. And while you're at it, maybe you'd like to explain how you got mixed up this mess."

"All right." He drew in a breath. "I'll answer the last bit first. And it's just Al now; I gave up being Sergeant Higgins as soon as my hitch was up. Went into business for myself."

"You're a mercenary?"

Higgins shrugged. "We prefer the term 'independent contractor.' It's a dangerous world, especially hereabouts. A wealthy bloke like the Sultan needs a lot of security. It's been a decent paycheck. I've been working for the family for close to six years."

"And Elisabeth?"

"Among other things, I was her bodyguard."

"'Among other things,' Al? Is that a polite way of saying that you're screwing her?"

The Gurkha's intent expression cracked. "Don't I wish? I'm a bit unrefined for her tastes, but all the same, I've been looking out for her for a while now."

"I'd say you fell down on the job. Those pirates had help from someone on the inside. Come to think of it, Elisabeth looked pretty cozy with their leader."

"It is true that maybe she wasn't a hostage in the literal sense of the word, but there's a lot more to it than that. The Sultan is a cruel bastard. Their marriage hasn't exactly been 'happily ever after.' She wanted out; wanted to leave this whole bloody place behind. When Jin took her captive, she thought she'd fallen into some kind of damned romance novel. And then you showed up.

"She hoped to convince you to rescue her from both Jin and the Sultan, and thought that sapphire might help her start over. But after she left you, Jin's guards caught her, and she had no choice but to give the appearance of helping him."

"You actually believe all this?" Kismet could not control his ire. "You weren't there."

"No I wasn't. But ask yourself this; what does she have to gain by trying to earn your trust?"

"I don't know, but I'm sure I'll find out." Kismet ran a hand through his hair. "So what is she doing here? The Sultan came to his senses and threw her out. Why are you with her? What's your stake in this?"

A guilty flush darkened Higgins' already ruddy features. "He wants her dead. God help me, but I've been protecting her so long, I just can't stand the thought of her getting hurt. But I can't do it; I'd attract too much attention. That's why I thought of you."

"You knew I'd come here?"

Higgins grinned ruefully. "I figured you'd reckon this was the safest place to be. But to tell the truth, I had my...I've had one of my people following you from the moment you escaped."

Kismet shook his head in weary disbelief. "Listen, Al. I'm sorry this has got me so upset. I'm hungry. I'm tired. I haven't slept in a bed in God only knows how long. This is just a bit much right now."

"So you won't help?" The Kiwi made no effort to hide his disappointment.

"Just leave me alone for now." He tried to punctuate his request with an emphatic gesture, and only then realized that he was still holding the covered plate with his dinner. "Look, she's welcome to use my stateroom. I'll sleep in a deckchair or something. We can sort this out tomorrow."

Higgins nodded slowly, the defeated expression still in evidence. "Right, then. I'll let her know what you've decided."

FORTUNE FAVORS

"Damn it," Kismet muttered as he watched the big Kiwi disappear back down the companionway. "I was really looking forward to that bed."

○

Dr. Leeds was gone, as was the steward in charge of the bar, but the contingent of security guards seemed to be a permanent fixture in the adjoining gallery. Kismet did not venture beyond the salon, but instead settled at a table near the exit and commenced his long overdue repast. The food was lukewarm and flavorless, but he barely noticed.

He struggled to get Elisabeth out of his thoughts. His anger was already yielding to the arguments Higgins had presented in her defense. He knew better, of course. Higgins had not been there in the tiger pit; had not heard her mocking laughter…

He shoveled another forkful of food into his mouth, chewing vigorously as if to shake the memory loose. "So Dr. Leeds thinks he can find the secret of immortality," he wondered aloud, hoping that by articulating the thought, he might force his mind to switch tracks.

To some extent, it worked.

What intrigued him was the scope of Leeds' search. In one short conversation, the man had incorporated a mosaic of Judaism, Christianity, Gnosticism, and an obscure Mesopotamian myth, into a seemingly coherent philosophy. Despite his superior manner, Leeds expressed himself with a certainty that made a person feel foolish for doubting.

Kismet searched his memory for details of the Epic of Gilgamesh. Elisabeth's untimely intrusion had side-tracked him from his original plan to research the legend, but he still remembered his college course on mythology, where he had read translations of the tablets of *Shin-eqi-unninni*, largely considered to be the most complete account of the Epic. The tablets, recovered from the same library in the ruins of Nineveh as the prism Leeds was studying, had been tentatively dated to 2000 BCE, making them the closest thing to a contemporary account. Gilgamesh was generally accepted as an actual historic figure, king of Uruk, a city in Babylonia, though Kismet could not recall if he had ever been linked to the Nimrod of the Genesis account.

Leeds had focused on the latter third of the Epic, the final three tablets describing Gilgamesh's search for the secret of immortality. The character of Uta-Napishtim indeed bore a close resemblance to the biblical Noah; survivor of a global flood, preserving alive all species of animal life in a great boat, even right down to the detail of his sending forth birds to see if the waters had receded.

Gilgamesh himself was anything but heroic. He began the story as an oppressive king and demi-god, demanding, among other things, the right to share the bed of every virgin bride before her husband. The people of his kingdom called out to the gods for someone to deliver them from the oppressor, and their prayer was answered in the form of Enkidu, a shaggy wild man who lived in the forest and could talk to animals. At first, Enkidu and Gilgamesh fought, but soon they became fast friends. Together, they challenged and slew Humbaba, demon of the cedar forest, and in the process offended the goddess Ishtar. Humbaba's dying curse was fulfilled when Ishtar smote Enkidu with a fatal illness.

Following the death of his friend, Gilgamesh troubled by his own mortality, began the search for the immortal Uta-Napishtim and the secret of eternal life. Along the way, he was repeatedly advised to abandon his quest; even Uta-Napishtim tried to reason with Gilgamesh that human death was the will of the gods and the search for eternal life could only end in futility. The outcome of the tale, with Gilgamesh losing the plant that possessed the secret of immortality, seemed underscore this eventuality.

The story was told from Gilgamesh's point of view, a retrospect on his life, inscribed on the lapis lazuli stone foundations of his city. Gilgamesh's transformation from an oppressive jerk into Enkidu's fast friend and mourner seemed like the stuff of heroic fiction, not history. The kings of ancient times never recorded their own failings, or allowed their scribes to show them in less than favorable light.

FORTUNE FAVORS

Leeds' premise seemed to turn on the connection between Gilgamesh and Nimrod. If the two men were one and the same, it would seem to indicate that an epic quest for a life giving plant, what Leeds thought was a Seed of the Tree of Life, really did occur. Of course, that assumed the Bible account about Nimrod—and for that matter Noah, and the Great Flood— was historically accurate, despite very little supportive evidence.

Kismet pushed his plate away and asked the bartender if there was a place where he could get computer access. A few minutes later in the ships cybercafé, he accessed an online edition of the Authorized Version of 1611, better known as the King James Version of the Holy Bible. He clicked on 'Genesis' and began skimming through the lines of text until he reached the first mention of Nimrod. There were only three short verses:

"And Cush begat Nimrod: he began to be a mighty one in the earth. He was a mighty hunter before the LORD: wherefore it is said, Even as Nimrod the mighty hunter before the LORD. And the beginning of his kingdom was Babel, and Erech, and Accad, and Calneh, in the land of Shinar."

He set the book down thoughtfully. Erech was easily Uruk—the ancient name for Iraq—the city-state built and ruled by Gilgamesh in the parallel legend. In fact, both men were described as city builders and kings. It was a tenuous link, but a link nevertheless.

Still, a great distance separated Gilgamesh from the Fountain of Youth. He would have dismissed the matter as a crackpot scheme on Leeds' part if not for one thing. Though his recall remained faint, he kept coming back to the name Henry Fortune; and something about a cave where 'fire danced on the water.'

It had been almost exactly the same language as that used by a Spanish colonial three hundred and fifty years earlier, a man whose name curiously enough, translated into Henry Fortune. He felt certain that he had first encountered that pairing while perusing the archives of GHC and UNESCO correspondence.

Over the course of its seventy year history, the United Nations' cultural organization had received thousands of letters, often formal request from governments and preservation societies requesting that certain historically important places receive World Heritage Site status, but interspersed among them were inquiries from private citizens. Gaining access to that prodigious database had been Kismet's primary motivation for taking the job as Global Heritage Commission liaison; he was convinced that somewhere in those files, he would find a clue that would lead to the mysterious Prometheus organization, and answers about the mystery that had dominated his life.

Prometheus.

While the quest for Prometheus was never far from his thoughts, seeing Sergeant Higgins again had brought it all back to the surface. That night in the desert, so long ago now, had been his first and only real encounter with Prometheus. He had surmised that they were some kind of secret society devoted to scooping up sacred relics—he could only guess about what else they had their hands in—but could not fathom their interest in him personally. He still remembered the words of the Prometheus team leader, a man who had identified himself as Ulrich Hauser:

Kismet, if I killed you, your mother would have my head.

Two decades later, that remained the extent of his knowledge.

"The Fountain of Youth." It seemed ludicrous on the surface, but if, by some miracle, it really did exist, it was exactly the sort of thing Prometheus would want to control.

The information he wanted was only a few keystrokes away, but he didn't dare access the GHC database from an unsecure computer. That would have to wait until he could get his laptop from his stateroom. Still...

He typed the words he had just muttered into a search window.

"Nick?"

Kismet jumped when he felt the soft touch on his arm. He spun around to face the person that had startled him, recognizing her voice at the same instant he saw her face. Elisabeth's hand remained on his arm, her touch strangely appealing. Almost guiltily, he closed the Internet browser, even as the screen filled up with websites promising answers to his inquiry, and then stood, putting Elisabeth at arm's length.

He knew he ought to rage at her, but some instinctive need held him back. He was attracted to her...aroused by her. He managed to keep the conflicting emotions out of his voice, addressing her in a flat tone. "What do you want from me?"

She smiled, fixing his gaze with her own. "I think you know."

He forced his eyes away from hers. There was a purple discoloration on her cheek, just above the jaw, that her make-up could not quite conceal. He'd done that, but then she'd been point a gun at him moments before. He reached out with a finger, caressing the bruise gently. "You almost got me killed. Twice."

"Believe it or not, you almost got me killed twice, too."

"Is that supposed to make me trust you?" He could not entirely mask the bitterness in his tone. "You betrayed me to Jin."

"He caught me as I was taking the sapphire. Nick, I had to play along and hope for the best. If he had suspected that I was trying to escape, he would have killed me on the spot."

"It didn't look that way from where I was standing...in the tiger pit."

"I'm an actress, Nick. It's what I do."

"You were awfully convincing." He sighed, his eyes flashing back to meet hers. "You're pretty convincing right now. Is this just an act?"

She took a step forward, close enough that he could almost feel her body heat radiating against his skin. "Am I convincing enough?"

Kismet felt her hand take his. He drew back as if her touch was venomous, but her eyes did not waver. "Alex told me that I took your stateroom. I'm willing to share."

"What the hell do you want from me?" he repeated, his voice a dry rasp.

She extended a finger, caressing his cheek as he had hers a few moments before. Her eyes held his, their intensity forcing him to look away. "Can't you believe that this is what I want?"

Her mouth drew close to his, and though every fiber of his conscience screamed that this was wrong, when her lips touched his, he yielded. The kiss filled his mouth with a flavor of sweet tobacco; a lusty fragrance that he drank greedily. His hands moved involuntarily to pull her close, against his body.

"I'll probably regret this tomorrow," he whispered, his voice husky with rising passion.

"Only if you refuse."

○

From the end of the corridor, Alex Higgins watched as Elisabeth and Kismet entered the stateroom, arm in arm. The expression on his face was unreadable, but his eyes remained fixed on the closed portal for a long time. After several minutes, he turned away, entered his own stateroom, and firmly closed the door.

A second pair of eyes, unseen by Higgins was also watching; watching Kismet and Elisabeth lost in a strange animal passion for each other, and watching Higgins wage a conflict of friendship and jealousy. A faint smile crossed the face of the watcher, the seed of a plan, beginning to germinate.

○

Their lovemaking was frenzied; as if, by the ferocity of their passion, they might exorcise the demons that had haunted them from the moment he had appeared in Elisabeth's window. Their fire for each other burned hot, a vain attempt to cauterize the open wound of their mutual distrust; each struggling to give the other a fulfillment that neither really desired. In the end, their mutual volcanic release satisfied a physical craving, but only exacerbated the deeper emotional hurts.

In the aftermath, Kismet held her in his arms; afraid to pull away, but feeling acutely the discomfort of having taken something he neither deserved nor wanted. As he gazed at Elisabeth's beautiful face, he couldn't help but feel pity for her. At the same time, he could not quell the deep-seated embers of loathing that smoldered just beneath the surface.

FORTUNE FAVORS

His inner turmoil quickly subsided as he watched the gentle rise and fall of her breasts; in repose, she seemed so innocent that he felt a pang of self-recrimination. There was so much he felt he needed to say to her, yet he could not articulate a single syllable.

After a long while, her eyelids fluttered open. She was barely visible in the silvery moonlight that flooded through the porthole. Her smile surprised him; it seemed so genuine that he found himself wanting to apologize for having ever doubted her. He gazed into her eyes, and for a long silent moment they seemed to be daring each other to speak.

Kismet's lips parted, the beginning of a thought taking shape on his tongue. Then, he saw something that caused him to hesitate.

Something like the shadow of a hidden agenda flickered across her eyes. The heady fragrance of their lovemaking that had lingered in his nostrils was now overpowered by a vile, unclean odor.

Kismet's body reacted to the premonition faster than his mind could. He rolled over, throwing his hand up in time to arrest the downward plunge of the scimitar-shaped dagger. Its curved blade quivered a mere inch from his sternum. In that moment, as adrenaline began coursing through his body, his mind caught up.

The silent attacker, a leering man with Asian features ravaged by disease, bore down on the long knife, trying with all his might to impale Kismet. The assassin was not as strong as he, but it was all Kismet could do to hold the blade away from his heart. Refusing to accept the stalemate, the attacker rose up on his toes, trying to force the blade down.

Kismet heard Elisabeth scream beside him, and his gaze flickered toward her. A second figure was moving toward them, a second curved blade reflecting silver light. Above him, the sour-breathed laughter of the assassin beat at his face like a physical assault.

Unable to force back the knife-wielder, Kismet changed tactics. He contorted his body in order to get a leg up around the man's neck. Catching the killer's throat in the crook of his knee, he drew back, pulling the attacker into a scissors hold. As his left leg came up, trapping the surprised assailant behind the shoulders, Kismet heard the dreadful sound of snapping vertebrae and knew instantly that he had broken the man's neck.

The curved knife fell from the man's lifeless fingers and dropped directly toward Kismet's heart. He twisted, trying to avoid its downward plunge, and felt the sharp tip score his flesh before falling away.

There was an intense flare of pain, but Kismet ignored it, kicking the limp corpse away, even as he reached out to deflect the attack of the fallen man's accomplice. He grasped the second man's wrists, arresting his double-fisted stab, and redirected the man's momentum so that he fell forward, onto the bed and atop its occupants. Kismet drove his right elbow into the man's face, and twisted his wrists, forcing him to drop his knife.

The assassin fell from the bed, rolling onto the floor and howling in pain as he cradled his injured forearms. Kismet sprang over Elisabeth and launched himself at the man who looked up in time to see Kismet looming over him. He rolled away and Kismet fell flat on the floor.

The attacker was up in an instant, racing for the doorway. Kismet rose to hands and knees, but immediately realized that the assailant was beyond his grasp. He grabbed the wooden chair tucked under the writing desk, and pitched it across the room to strike the retreating assassin legs. The man fell backward, his weight snapping the chair like matchwood. Kismet leapt after him, intent on catching the man—maybe for questioning, maybe not; he hadn't decided yet—but the man recovered too quickly, extracting himself from the wreckage of the chair and throwing the door open. Light from the corridor spilled into the room, momentarily blinding Kismet, and in that split second, the intruder escaped.

Kismet took a step out the door, but went no further. He stood in the corridor, stark naked, feeling vaguely foolish. There was no sign of the attacker.

As he stepped back inside the stateroom, Kismet flipped on the overhead light. Elisabeth was sitting up in bed, the sheet pulled up around her breasts. She seemed to have regained her composure and was taking a cigarette from a metal case. Kismet walked around the bed to where the body of the first assassin lay. He knelt beside the fallen man and began searching the body for some clue as to what precipitated the attack.

"How did they get in?" asked Elisabeth, exhaling a stream of smoke.

"They must have been in here before we came in. Probably hiding under the bed."

"You mean they were here while we—" She didn't have to finish the question, or wait for his reply before grimacing.

"I thought I had managed to sneak on board without anyone noticing," continued Kismet, rolling the body onto its side to examine the man's back pockets. The search proved fruitless. He leaned back on his haunches and sighed. Then, his expression darkened as a new thought occurred to him. "Unless they weren't after me."

"What's that supposed to mean?" Elisabeth took another drag on the cigarette. For the first time, Kismet wondered how much of her cool demeanor was merely the result of her professional skills.

"Think about it." Before she could defend herself from the oblique accusation, Kismet rose and dug a fresh ExOficio shirt and a pair of cargo pants from his duffel bag. He also took out his Glock, loaded a magazine and chambered a round, and tucked it into his waistband at the small of back.

"Going somewhere?" asked Elisabeth.

"Our friend here is getting off before the next port." He lifted the assassin's corpse, looping the man's stiffening arm across his shoulders. As an afterthought, he picked up the curved daggers the attackers had wielded. A cursory inspection revealed them to be crudely made and not worth keeping. He tucked them both into the dead man's belt. The body hung awkwardly against him, sagging dead weight, but Kismet managed to shuffle him toward the door. As he did, he felt a flare of pain in his chest. Blood was welling up from the stab wound, and though it was barely larger than a pinprick, an area the size of his fist was aching just to the right of his heart. He didn't want to think about what sort of germs might be starting to colonize there, but disinfecting the cut would have to wait until he got back. "Be sure to lock the door."

Elisabeth watched him leave without saying a word. When he was gone she lowered her head to her knees and began shaking uncontrollably, but managed to pull herself together a few moments later, and finished the cigarette.

Nevertheless, she almost screamed when an unexpected knock came at the door.

○

As Kismet dragged the lifeless form through the halls, careful to avoid attracting attention, he wrestled with the puzzle of the attack. He knew that, at least throughout Southeast Asia, he was probably a wanted man, but he couldn't shake the feeling that there was something more to the situation. If the two assassins had followed him, why had they waited so long to show themselves? Had they simply been waiting aboard the ship, expecting him to reunite with Higgins? If that was the case, they would also have known that Elisabeth was using his stateroom. The more he pondered it, the more convinced he was that Elisabeth herself was the target of the attack. Remembering that a second assassin still roamed the decks lent urgency to his errand.

His feelings for Elisabeth remained problematic. The unquestionable physical attraction he felt for her was undiminished, yet he was certain that she was once again using him, or worse, setting him up for another betrayal.

He felt a pang of concern also for Higgins. Perhaps in helping the actress escape, his old comrade in arms had also earned a death mark. He had no doubt the big Kiwi could take care of himself in a fight, but the assassins had struck from out of nowhere. Kismet recognized that he owed his own escape, more than anything else, to sheer luck; if he had not glimpsed the movement of shadow in the stateroom, both he and Elisabeth would now be as dead as the man whom he was dragging toward the aft deck.

Leaning the assassin's body against the railing, he made a careful visual sweep of the deck and the portholes of the next deck up. No one seemed to be up and about on the ship. Kismet casually removed the chains that blocked the disembarkation gate and helped the assassin on the next step of his journey. The limp shaped was instantly swallowed by the dark water.

When he got back to the stateroom, he knocked, hoping that Elisabeth had followed his parting advice to lock the door. When she did not reply, he tried the latch. The portal swung open, revealing a vacant room.

Wisps of smoke hung in the air, drifting from a nearly extinguished cigarette in an ashtray on the nightstand beside the bed. The sheets curled around the memory of a female body, still warm from her presence, but Elisabeth was gone.

Despite his vigilance, Kismet's labors had not gone completely unnoticed. The second assassin, still gingerly holding his broken wrist, watched with growing anger as his brother's lifeless body was unceremoniously dropped into the sea.

He had no idea who the man—the former Sultana's lover—was. He and his brother had only been interested in collecting the bounty on Elisabeth Neuell, but right now the blood price was the last thing on his mind. Revenge was the first.

Injured and disarmed, he knew that a frontal assault was out of the question. His new target had already demonstrated unusual skill in hand-to-hand combat. No, he would have to take the man completely by surprise.

With his good hand, he removed his belt and fashioned a slipknot. He would drop the loop over the man's head and then pull the noose tight. Strangling was one of the easiest ways to kill an opponent with superior size and skill, provided of course the loop could be tightened before the victim had time to react. Once the garrote was set, he would just hold on for about thirty seconds until unconsciousness claimed his victim. He knew this from experience; he had killed this way before.

He shrank back into the shadows as his brother's killer passed by, and waited a few seconds more, gathering his courage, before emerging from his hiding place. With the garrote in his good hand, he took a deep breath and started forward.

Suddenly, everything in his world spun around crazily. Instead of his target's retreating back, he found himself almost nose to nose with another man—a man who now tightly held the assassin's head between his hands. It took a moment for his eyes to focus, a moment in which his head was filled with a sound like pieces of glass being crushed underfoot. Darkness began to swell at the periphery of his vision, eclipsing the features of the man who held him...the man who had twisted his head completely around, snapping his neck at the third cervical vertebrae.

"Sorry, chum." The killer's whispered voice was as harsh as the sound of breaking bones. "That one's mine."

If the assassin recognized his killer in that last fleeting second, the knowledge died with him. Less than a minute later, he joined his brother in an unmarked watery grave.

5

KISMET AWOKE TO AN INSISTENT KNOCKING. His chest was still smarting from the stab wound, but only a crust of dried blood remained to mark the spot. It took him a few moments to recall where he was or how that injury had occurred, but he rolled out of the bed, slipped into his trousers and stood up. All the while, the knocking did not abate.

With his gun in his right hand behind his back, he opened the door.

Alex Higgins stood at the threshold. His eyes registered only the slightest flicker of surprise upon seeing someone other than the woman he believed to be occupying the stateroom. "Morning, mate."

"Al." Kismet covertly tucked the gun into his waistband. "Come in."

Higgins stepped inside and looked around. Kismet saw him staring at the ashtray on the nightstand. Red lipstick painted the end of a single cigarette remnant. "Where's she gone off to?"

Kismet was awake enough to realize that Higgins must have had some clue as to what had transpired. Nevertheless, he could not tell from the former Gurkha's demeanor, just how he felt about it.

"She's gone. I don't know where she went."

"What did you...what did you say to her?" Higgins's voice was suddenly hard, with a bitter accusatory edge.

"It was nothing like that." Kismet picked his shirt off the floor and slipped it on. "We actually...Well, I'll just say that we came to an understanding. Then things got interesting." He briefly related the details of the attack, along with his suspicions about the motive behind it. "When I got back she was gone. There was no sign of a struggle. Her clothes and all her luggage were gone, too. If I had to guess, I'd say she left voluntarily."

"Why would she do that?" complained Higgins. "Especially if these bastards are after her. Doesn't she know we can protect her?"

Kismet shrugged. "I guess she got what she wanted from us."

"Why are you so quick to judge her?"

Kismet mentally threw up his hands. Higgins had a blind spot for the actress and couldn't see reason. Admittedly, Kismet too had been enticed by her charms, but the difference was that he had never quite been able to let go of his suspicions about the actress, and so had little difficulty getting over how she had used him. "It doesn't matter now. She's made her choice. And you know as well as I do, that she knows how to take care of herself."

Higgins frowned but said nothing.

Kismet pulled on his shoes. "Is it too late to get some breakfast?"

Higgins surprised him by chuckling. "Finally, something we can agree on."

Kismet had not slept well. He had spent nearly an hour looking for Elisabeth, fearing the worst. Only later did he recognize all the signs that pointed to her leaving on her own. After that, he had tried to sleep, but was haunted by the echo of her presence. He could still smell her on the sheets, and the arousing scent triggered vivid, disquieting memories of their lovemaking, and the brutal aftermath. Eventually, overcome by sheer exhaustion, he had succumbed to sleep. Now, all he really wanted was to leave the Malaysian misadventure behind and get started on the new endeavor which occupied his thoughts, something he intended to do just as soon as the beast in his belly was quieted.

FORTUNE FAVORS

After his third trip to the breakfast buffet, Kismet's mood improved dramatically. *The Star of Muara* hired only the best classically trained chefs, and the coffee, grown in Indonesia, was fabulous. Kismet downed several mugs full, savoring the full-bodied, faintly sweet flavor. With the caffeine coursing through his veins, he felt ready to tackle his new project. He opened his laptop computer and enabled a secure connection to the GHC server.

"Checking with your stock broker?" Higgins quipped.

Kismet smiled and gave a vague nod, but said nothing as he typed the words "Henry Fortune" into the search engine. A few seconds later, he had his answer.

Higgins voice intruded again. "Seriously, mate, what are you looking at? Internet porn?"

Kismet realized that almost ten minutes had passed. "Sorry, it's a work thing."

"You're here because of all these relics, right?"

"Right. I work for the UN. We're trying to help get everything back where it belongs." He knew, even as he said it, that his answer sounded evasive. Worse, he felt a pang of guilt at deceiving the man who had once faced certain death at his side. Maybe it was time for a leap of faith. "This is something different though. Sometime in the 1960's a man named Henry Fortune reported the discovery of a new cave system somewhere in the southern United States. His letter attributed some unique properties to the cavern; in his words: 'Flames dance on the surface of the water' of a 'pool possessed of magnificent properties.'"

"Was it true?"

"I don't know. As near as I can tell, no one ever looked into it."

"That's fifty years ago. What's changed? What made you decide to go looking for a cave in America, while sitting here on a cruise ship in the South China Sea?"

Kismet drew a breath. The more he talked about it, the more he wondered about that himself. Earlier, in the privacy of his own thoughts, the idea of beating Dr. Leeds to the prize, or maybe finding something that might draw Prometheus out of the shadows seemed so much more desirable. But really, what was he looking for? The secret of eternal life? Yet, as preposterous as that sounded, there was no denying the eerie similarity between the cavern Fortunato had described to Rodriguez, and the one Henry Fortune had written of more than 300 years later.

The letter was addressed with an anonymous:

To whom it may concern:

For many years I have kept to myself a fabulous secret; a concealed knowledge which I have believed the world unready for. The time has come however, to share my discovery with the scientists of our modern era. The treasure of which I speak has for years been secreted away in a cavern, or perhaps it would be better to say that it is a part of the cavern for the treasure is a natural wonder unlike anything else on the planet. Within is an underground pool, where flames dance on the surface of the water. Moreover, the pool is possessed of magnificent properties, which cannot be adequately explained until witnessed directly. It would not be too much to say that it seems to defy the very laws of creation. I have held back this secret for too long. The world is in need of such a wondrous thing.

Kismet read the letter aloud and finished with the signature. "'With deepest regards, Henry Fortune.'"

"Sounds like something for the bloody X-Files," scoffed Higgins. "What do you suppose he was on about?"

"What he described might be something as commonplace as luminescent lichens or methane discharges. Still, the chance to find and map a previously unknown cave would be enough to make any spelunker salivate."

It was then that he realized his search had returned two results. He didn't remember a second letter, but according to the database, someone had attempted to follow up on the report. He clicked on the file and gazed at the second scanned document. Though it shared the same return address, general delivery to a postal office in Charleston, South Carolina, the handwriting was very different.

"This is interesting. Listen: 'It is with great sadness that I must inform you of the death of Mr. Henry Fontaine. He took his secret to the grave. With regrets, Joseph King.'" Kismet reread the letter, noticing the different spelling for Fortune's last name. It seemed to accentuate the link between Fortune and Hernando Fontaneda.

"Well, that's that," sighed Higgins. "Another one for the blokes who write books about unsolved mysteries. But, you never answered my question: why are you interested, now after all these years?"

Kismet stared back at the burly Kiwi. "There was something in the Sultan's collection that made me think this might be important. It's a complicated story and if I tried to explain it, you'd think I was crazy, but I am starting to believe that I need to find this cave."

"Important? How important?"

Kismet spread his hands. "Maybe a matter of life and death. Maybe even bigger than that."

"That's how it always is for us, isn't it?" A smile flickered across the big man's hard face. "Listen, I did some caving as a lad, and I know a thing or two about caves. The southern United States is honeycombed with karst—interconnected limestone caverns, most of them underwater. You could spend a lifetime—ten lifetimes—splashing around and not find a damned thing."

"An eternal lifetime," Kismet murmured, thinking about Leeds' words from the previous evening. "What if Mr. Joseph King of Charleston knows more than he's telling?"

"That was fifty years ago. What are the chances he's still alive?"

Kismet knew the Kiwi was probably right, but it was his only lead. "I'm going there. The sooner I get off this tub, the better. I'll leave from our next port, whatever that is."

"Macao."

83

"Good enough. I'll start making the arrangements now." He looked at Higgins again, thoughtfully. "What about you?"

"I'm for the unemployment line, I suppose. I doubt His Royal Highness would take me back, and I can't say I'm terribly interested in working for him anyway. And Elisabeth..." He let the sentence trail off.

"How would you feel about working for me?"

"You serious, mate?"

"You said you'd done some caving. I could use your expertise."

"My expertise is in killing people, Nick. Cave exploration was something I did at summer camp one year." But something about Kismet's offer softened him after a moment. "Oh, what the hell? I could use a change of pace."

Kismet was heartened by the Kiwi's enthusiasm, but deep down, he knew the reason he had made the offer to the former Gurkha had nothing at all to do with his ability as a spelunker. He took another deep breath. "Listen, there's something you need to know about.

It's possible that some people—some very bad people—might think there's a connection between this cavern and the Fountain of Youth—"

Higgins registered a blank expression. "Fountain of Youth?"

"In the year 1512, a Spanish explorer named Juan Ponce de Leon was told by natives in the West Indies about a pool of water capable of rejuvenating the old; literally, restoring their youth. The natives told him that the Fountain could be found on island called Bimini, somewhere to the north of what is now Cuba. Ponce de Leon got permission from the king of Spain to go looking for this Fountain."

"There's a legend like that in the South Pacific, too. Captain Cook searched for it. I take it this de Leon bloke never found it?"

"Since he is no longer with us," remarked Kismet, "I would say that's a safe bet."

"Do you think such a thing could really exist?" Higgins seemed alternately skeptical and intrigued. "I mean, if it did, wouldn't everyone know of it by now?"

FORTUNE FAVORS

Kismet nodded. "Most historians believe what Ponce de Leon was really after was the gold of the New World, which makes more sense. It's doubtful that Spain, in the grip of the Inquisition, would have sanctioned any kind of a search for eternal life. The very thought of it would run contrary to the dogma of the Church—no salvation except through Christ. Whatever his reasons, he did explore the Caribbean, found Florida and established the first permanent Spanish settlement in what would become the United States."

Higgins leaned back in his chair. "So you think that the 'fire on the water' described by Henry Fortune has something to do with this Fountain of Youth?"

"Ordinarily, I would call that a wild leap of deduction. But last night I read a letter written almost four hundred years ago, describing the exact same thing, in almost exactly the same words, dictated by a man named Henrique Fortunato."

"Fortunato sounds an awful bloody lot like Fortune. But this letter from Joseph King says that Fortune died. Would that be possible if he had access to a Fountain of Youth?"

"I don't know. It's a place to start." Kismet leaned forward to catch Higgins' eye. "But that's not why I want you along. I don't know if this cavern really exists, and the odds of it actually being the site of the legendary Fountain of Youth..." He shrugged. "But there are people who believe things like that are real, and worth killing to protect."

The light dawned in former Gurkha's eyes.

"I see. Once more into the breach." Higgins raised his mug to toast the venture. "Just like old times."

"God I hope not."

The tiny speaker in the earpiece of the cell phone trilled as the call was sent. It rang three times before the person on the other end initiated the connection without speaking. The person making the call spoke immediately.

"We are the chains of God. ID number 145211212." The voice, sent electronically through the ether was in no way recognizable, thanks to the small auto-tuning device that had been affixed to the mouthpiece. The device randomly altered the pitch and cadence of the speaker, making any kind of positive identification impossible.

The call would most certainly be monitored by the American National Security Agency's Echelon program—their computers eavesdropped on every phone call in the world, listening for keywords that might hint at some possible terrorist plot or act of espionage—but the caller wasn't worried. Nothing would be said to raise an alarm, and even if something did cause the call to be flagged, there would be no evidence left behind. In a few minutes, the phone—a throwaway purchased months earlier but not activated until this very call—would be sitting at the bottom of the ocean.

After a brief pause, the person at the other end, his voice similarly disguised, spoke again. "Was your mission successful?"

"Not exactly, but there's been an important development."

"Go ahead."

"Nick Kismet. He's here."

Another pause and a strange noise that might have been a sigh. "That's very interesting."

"There's more. Guess what he's looking for."

The person on the other end listened in rapt silence as the information was relayed. When the caller finished, he asked, "Do you think he will find it?"

"If it really exists. He may have information that we don't."

"This could lead to the Source. We cannot risk letting him get too close. Find out what he knows, and then dissuade him from the search. I leave the question of 'how' to your discretion."

"Does that mean the first order has been revoked?"

The man at the other end laughed. "Are you asking for my permission to kill him?"

"Well, yes."

FORTUNE FAVORS

The man at the other end thought for a moment, then in a voice that, despite the effects of the modulator, was still icy and grim, said, "Do what you have to."

Alex Higgins had a lot on his mind.

He stood on the forward observation deck, staring out at the sun-dappled water, trying to make sense of everything that had happened in the last few days.

Nothing was ever certain in a soldier's life, and despite the fact that he had been retired from the military for more than a decade, he was still very much a soldier. Recent events had, like a well-placed explosive device, completely obliterated everything familiar, but it was a soldier's duty to regroup and get the fight. The only problem was, he didn't know what to fight for.

His mind turned over Kismet's proposal. It had seemed simple enough when he had agreed to it. Tramp around for a while in the United States, looking for a cave that probably wouldn't ever be found, and some crazy Fountain of Youth that certainly didn't exist. As he had intimated to Kismet, it might even be fun. He wasn't that concerned about the project itself. No, the thing was eating at him, like a grain of sand embedded under his skin, was being with Kismet himself.

Seeing the American again had opened an old wound, and he was only now starting to feel it. They had fought together, been captured by the Republican Guard and brutally interrogated, and by some miracle that he had never really comprehended, Kismet had gotten free, rescued him, and hauled his ass across the desert to safety. He owed Nick Kismet his life.

And maybe that was the problem. The life debt was something he could never repay. *When you owe someone a debt that can't be repaid, you feel like their slave.*

It didn't help that Kismet had shagged Elisabeth.

He couldn't very well blame Kismet for that. Higgins was a believer in the notion that "all's fair in love and war." If Elisabeth fancied Kismet over him, then so be it. But it was so bloody obvious there was no chemistry there. Kismet could barely conceal his contempt for the former Sultana, while Elisabeth was plainly just using the American for…comfort? Sex? Who knew what she really wanted, but whatever it was, Higgins would have willingly…eagerly given it to her.

Why didn't anyone care how he felt?

"Bitch," he muttered, and then instantly regretted it as he spied the source of his turmoil leaving the observation deck in the company of a silver-haired man dressed entirely in black. Higgins had almost missed her.

"Beth!" When he had been her bodyguard, she had insisted that he call her that, at least in private.

Elisabeth Neuell stopped and slowly turned to face him. A quick smile greeted him. "Alex!"

The black clad figure at her side continued moving, never looking back. Higgins felt an almost overwhelming curiosity about the man's identity, but Elisabeth commanded his full attention. He rushed forward, as if to embrace her, but stopped short an arm's length away. She however did not hold back. She wrapped her arms around him, pulling his head down to hers and quickly kissed him on the cheek. It seemed an innocent enough gesture, a token of affection between two friends, but Higgins felt the blood rushing to his face.

"What happened to you?" He finally managed to say. "You just disappeared."

Elisabeth's smile slipped a notch. "Oh, Alex. I behaved so awfully. I realized that I was using you, and Nick, to protect me. When I saw that clearly, I knew I had to stand on my own."

"But we—I was so worried. I wish you had told me."

She smiled again, and Higgins felt his volition melt. "Alex, I can take care of myself. In fact, I realized that I had to. You risked so much for me. I do appreciate it, too." She reached out, looping her arm through his, and tugged him into motion.

FORTUNE FAVORS

"The truth of the matter is," she continued, in a less serious tone. "I met the most extraordinary man...no, it's not what you're thinking."

"I don't understand. You met someone? When?"

"Right after Nick and I were attacked. You do know about that, don't you?"

"Yes. But—"

"His name is Dr. Leeds. He's a fascinating man." Something almost like embarrassment tinged her cheeks. "I know this will sound silly, but he's a...well, he has these special abilities. Psychic abilities. I didn't believe it myself at first, but then he proved it."

Higgins gaped, struggling to process what he was hearing.

Elisabeth seemed not to notice. "Dr. Leeds is looking for something unbelievable, and he has asked me to be a part of it."

Higgins recalled that Kismet had mentioned that other people might be looking for the cavern—looking for the Fountain of Youth. Was this who he had been talking about? This psychic?

"You must hear all about it. It is wonderful. It could change the world." She loosened her hold on his arm. "I have to go now, but I will arrange for you to join us tonight for dinner."

"Beth, I—" Before Higgins could even begin to articulate what he was thinking, the actress slipped away. He watched her until she turned a corner and disappeared from view.

Her presence was too much to digest. After losing her once, he could not believe his good fortune at finding her once again. But had anything really changed?

As Higgins reached the door of Kismet's stateroom, he tried to figure out how he would broach the subject of his encounter with Elisabeth, and her apparent alliance with the psychic Dr. Leeds. His instincts told him that Kismet would not be pleased by the news, and Higgins wasn't sure how to feel about that. He was about to knock when he saw that the door was slightly ajar.

A loud thump and the sound of a struggle issued from inside, and his troubled thoughts evaporated in a flash of adrenaline. He burst through the door, ready to join whatever battle was being fought within.

○

It hadn't taken long for Kismet to exhaust all legitimate avenues of research. There was plenty of information available about the Fountain of Youth legend, but all of it was either from a historical perspective, written with a view to debunking even the notion that Ponce de Leon had been looking for it in the first place, or so ridiculously fantastic as to further underscore the foolishness of the quest. His thoughts had eventually turned to Dr. Leeds.

He had been surprised to learn that Leeds was almost as much of a celebrity as Elisabeth. He came from old money in the American South and was by all reports comfortably wealthy, though not perhaps beyond dreams of avarice. From a very young age, he had been interested in the supernatural. Eschewing a place in the family business, he apprenticed to a well-known stage magician, and soon was a headlining performer. While best known for mind-reading and hypnotism acts, he was quite adept at illusions on a grand scale.

Unlike many of his peers, Leeds seemed to honestly believe in paranormal phenomena, and even as he played psychic adviser to movie stars and politicians, he formalized his studies of comparative religion and the occult, earning a PhD and his preferential title.

But the reviews and biographical articles didn't tell the whole story. Leeds had enemies, and in the darker corners of the Internet, Kismet found accounts of the man's involvement in black magic, renegade Masonic rites, and devil worship. Some of the conspiratorial rumors were laughable, but Kismet saw a grain of truth in many of them, particularly those which characterized the occult scholar as a rabid white supremacist, and possible a neo-Nazi. Some reports linked him to unexplained acts of violence, even the unsolved murders of some of Leeds' rivals and harshest critics.

If even half of what was said about the man was true, Leeds was not someone to be trifled with.

By late afternoon, the long hours of physical idleness had left him feeling drowsy. He considered heading to the salon for a drink, but then decided instead to have a sip from his personal supply which he kept in a stainless steel hip flask. The container, adorned with a distinctive red star, was a memento from his recent trip to the former Soviet Republic of Georgia. After freeing some Russian sailors from captivity, one of them had given him the container as a gesture of gratitude.

He hadn't thought much about it at the time, but looking back, it was a hell of a lot more useful than flowers and a Hallmark Card, especially since he'd replaced the flavorless vodka with some smooth, 127 proof Booker's Bourbon whiskey.

The spirits compounded his drowsiness and he was just starting to nod off when he felt an unexpected draft on his cheek.

Through the veil of his barely parted eyelashes, he saw someone creeping through the doorway. The figure was indistinct; he could not hope to see the person clearly without opening his eyes and turning to face the intruder. He intuited that it was not Higgins. He did not believe the big man could move as stealthily as the person now closing the door and moving toward him.

Was this another wave of bounty hunting assassins, taking revenge for his part in Elisabeth Neuell's defection from her husband? Was it Dr. Leeds taking preemptive action against a rival Fountain hunter?

Kismet resisted the impulse to hold his breath. The only way to turn the tables on the intruder was to lull him into believing that his entry had gone unnoticed. He measured the person's footsteps with his inhalations. Each breath seemed to bring the intruder closer.

The approaching steps halted right beside him. In his mind's eye, Kismet could see the shadowy form hovering above him, a knife or cudgel gripped loosely in one hand. He concentrated on the barely audible sounds of the person moving, trying to anticipate when the unseen weapon would be raised for use, all the while keeping a steady rhythm of breathing. Inhale...Exhale...Inhale...

Kismet blew out his breath in a burst of motion. Twisting his body, he propelled himself off the bed, striking the intruder in the abdomen. His right hand flew to the nightstand, fingers brushing but failing to grip the butt of the Glock resting there, while his left sought the other person's throat.

Both Kismet and the intruder hit the floor together an instant later. Kismet heard the breath driven from the other's lungs as his full weight came down. He tried to identify the face, looking for some similarity to the syphilitic assassins that had attacked the previous night, but a stream of fiery light from the afternoon sun struck his sensitive pupils, momentarily blinding him.

He felt the intruder's hands, first trying to pry loose Kismet's choke hold, then beating ineffectively against Kismet's chest. The blows gave no evidence of superior physical strength, but their determination made up for the lack of raw power. Kismet added his right hand to the stranglehold. "You lose."

"What the hell?"

Kismet heard the exclamation from behind him—Higgins' voice—and turned to look. His eyes, still flashing with burned-in retinal fireworks, gradually focused on the big Kiwi, standing in the doorway of the stateroom. Kismet did not relax as his grip one bit as he spoke, "Looks like we've got an unexpected visitor."

Higgins seemed to ignore him, focusing instead on the intruder. "What on earth are you doing here?"

Kismet looked down for a moment, and then felt the figure beneath him shift. Suddenly, his left arm gave out as the other person struck directly at a pressure point in his elbow. Kismet toppled forward, and the intruder squirmed from beneath him, flipping him over, and straddling his chest.

Instinctively, Kismet fought back. The weight on his torso was hardly enough to pin him down; it was as if the intruder was a mere child. He drew back a fist, ready to pound his attacker senseless. Then his burning eyes focused on the stranger's face, and he understood why Higgins had reacted as he had.

FORTUNE FAVORS

The face of the intruder staring down at him belonged to a young woman. Her short hair and elfin features could not hide the obvious family resemblance. Kismet's assailant looked enough like Higgins to be his—

"Daughter?"

The waif grinned down at him. "Want to try for best two out of three?"

PART TWO
AUDIENCE WITH THE DEAD

FORTUNE FAVORS

6

"WHAT ARE YOU DOING HERE?" repeated Higgins, a hint of anger creeping into his tone.

The girl straddling Kismet fixed him with a disdainful look, then gracefully dismounted and faced him with her hands on her hips. "Good to see you too, Dad."

Higgins extended a hand to Kismet and helped him up. "I see you've met my daughter."

"I'm afraid we skipped past the introduction and went right to groundfighting." He turned to the girl and sized her up.

She looked to be in her mid-twenties. Taller than he had first realized, her willowy frame—thin, but more like a marathon runner rather than a fashion model—was clad in designer blue jeans and a long-sleeved striped t-shirt. Her short dark hair—the same color as Higgins'—was pulled back in a stub of a pony-tail. She wore soft pink lipstick, but no other makeup that Kismet could see; Higgins' daughter was obviously a tomboy. He extended a hand. "Nick Kismet."

"Yes, I know." There was no mistaking the twang of her New Zealand accent.

Realization dawned and he pulled his hand back abruptly. "You never answered his question. What the hell are you doing in my room? Why did you attack me?"

"As I recall, you attacked me." A defiant smile curled the corners of her mouth, and then she stuck out her own hand. "The name's Annie, by the way. Annie Crane."

Higgins pushed between them. "Damn it, girl. I told you to get your arse back to Auckland."

"Don't have a hissy fit, dad. The Sultan called off his dogs. He's already got more bad publicity than he can handle right now."

Kismet threw a questioning look at Higgins, and the latter rubbed the bridge of his nose as if he was getting a headache. "Annie is my...call her my administrative assistant."

The girl laughed, but did not interrupt.

"She was at my office in the palace when the shite hit the fan. I told her to get out quick. Obviously, she listens to me about as well as her mother ever did."

Kismet turned to Annie again. "So why are you here? In my room?"

"Dad told me he was going to be working with you. He's mentioned you a time or two over the years. Always figured you'd look younger somehow." The smile again, eyes full of mischief. "Anyway, I thought I'd come see what all the fuss was about."

"Sorry to disappoint you," Kismet replied stonily.

"Who says you did?" she retorted, but Kismet had already returned his attention to Higgins.

"Look, if you have to deal with this, and can't help me out, I'll understand."

The former Gurkha's brow furrowed. "Actually, I think I may have some new information about our—" He glanced at Annie—"Our project. I ran into Elisabeth. She's hooked up with someone who I think may be looking for it as well."

Kismet's breath caught in his throat. "Dr. Leeds?"

"Figured you might know about him. Anyway, she invited me to dinner tonight...to meet this bloke. I thought you might want to tag along."

"Dinner?" chirped Annie. "Fabulous. I'll need to buy a dress though."

Kismet sighed. Elisabeth Neuell and Dr. Leeds together. Wonderful. But his curiosity was more powerful than his disdain. "I suppose I'll have to go shopping as well. I need a new tux."

Despite his apprehension about what the evening would bring, Kismet felt a little more centered as the appointed hour drew near. Part of that was due to Annie's revelation that the storm originating from the Sultan's palace had more or less blown out. The knowledge that the death mark had been rescinded relieved him of one source of stress; he just hoped the surviving assassin lurking somewhere on the ship had gotten the message.

The main dining hall of *The Star of Muara* was resplendent, and as Kismet entered he realized that it was the first time he was experiencing what most of the passengers had come for in the first place. Formal dining wasn't something he typically went out of his way for, but at just that moment, he understood the appeal. He turned to Annie, who was bookended between him and her father, and smiled.

The tomboy was gone, or at the very least, sublimated. Higgins' daughter looked extraordinary in an oriental-style gown of jade green silk. Her rather plain hairstyle had been transformed into a crown of wavy curls, laying bare her finely sculpted neck, adorned with a string of pearls. She bore little resemblance to the waif that had sneaked into Kismet's stateroom and nearly gotten herself killed.

Kismet had learned quite a bit about the girl over the course of the afternoon. Although she was the offspring of a relationship that had never quite gotten off the ground, Higgins doted on his daughter, and she in turn was fascinated by his world of travel and adventure. When he had called her his "administrative assistant," he had been downplaying her role. Higgins had taught her everything about his trade, and while her own education supplied her with the skills to manage his business affairs, she had also done a fair amount of hands-on work. She proved as much when she had tracked down

Kismet's location on the ship and thwarted the electronic lock on his stateroom. She also evidently knew a thing or two about hand-to-hand combat.

Though he carried his dazzling daughter on his right arm, Higgins could not have looked more uncomfortable in his formal wear. The ship's tailor had gotten his proportions exactly right, but Higgins acted as if the suit were choking the life from him. Kismet resolved to get a drink into his friend before dinner, and asked the maître-d' to send two Macallans to their table. Annie asked for a cosmopolitan. The man nodded, and then gestured to the seats they were to have for the night. Kismet's smile fell when he saw who was waiting at the table.

Elisabeth looked stunning. During the course of their time together, Kismet had not exactly seen her at her best, but tonight she looked ready for an Academy Awards red carpet walk. A strapless evening gown of black velvet clung to her enticing figure, accentuating every curve and displaying every asset. Her long blonde hair cascaded in waves down her bare shoulders and back. Her full lips were seductively painted and her smile was, as ever, hypnotic. And yet, while her beauty was almost enough to make him forget about her mercurial nature, it was not sufficient to distract him from the other person seated at the table.

Kismet almost did a double take. Unlike nearly every other man in the room, Leeds had disdained formal attire, and was instead wearing what looked to Kismet like the black cassock of a Catholic priest, though instead of a clerical collar, the garment continued up, almost to the underside of his jaw. Stranger still was the black skullcap that completely hid his steely gray hair.

Leeds did not rise to greet them, but held Kismet's gaze contemplatively as the latter held a chair for Annie. Kismet matched the stare, but did not comment until he and Higgins were seated as well. "I didn't realize this was a costume party. Let me guess: Nostradamus?"

If Leeds took offense, he did not let it show. He simply folded his hands on the table in front of him. "This is my professional attire."

Kismet was tempted to continue testing the other man's implacability, but the glint of a gem encrusted ring on Leeds' right hand distracted him.

"Dr. Leeds is going to conduct a séance after the meal," intoned Elisabeth. "It promises to be very exciting."

"No doubt," remarked Annie, disdainfully appraising the other woman.

Elisabeth flashed a perfect smile that somehow lowered the temperature in the room. "My goodness, if it isn't Annie. You certainly cleaned up well. Has Nick told you all about our adventures together?"

Annie matched her smile. "Why no, he didn't. It must have slipped his mind. Perhaps it didn't make that much of an impression."

"A séance?" Kismet interjected, trying to steer the conversation away from his indiscretions. He focused on Leeds. "That sounds a bit lurid for such a highly-regarded religious scholar."

"I am a student of the mysteries of the human mind and spirit," Leeds replied. He shifted his hands again, steepling his index fingers together in front of his chin. "There is only so much that can be learned from books. Precious little, in fact."

Kismet tried to match Leeds' stare, but his eyes were drawn to the ring. He now saw that, the precious stones were set in distinctive pattern which he recognized as an Ouroboros—a snake devouring its own tail—an ancient symbol of immortality. "Whereas the dead have all the answers?"

"For thousands of years, wise men have inquired of the spirits of the dead. More than three-quarters of people living today believe that the soul lives on after death, and if it indeed does, then certainly the departed would have insights into matters beyond our comprehension. Contacting them, of course, has never been a simple matter."

The waiter arrived with the drinks they had ordered. Kismet gulped down the contents and nodded for another. He had once again made the mistake of getting Leeds started, but as before his curiosity got the better of him. "And who will you be contacting tonight?"

"Why, Hernando Fontaneda, of course."

"And he will lead us to the Fountain of Youth!" chimed Elisabeth. "Isn't it marvelous?"

Kismet could not imagine why Leeds had taken Elisabeth into his confidence; he had not expected the man to be so open about his intentions. "The

Fountain of Youth? So you think it's real? Just on the basis of that old letter?"

Leeds continued turning the ring so that, in the prismatic depths of the gemstones, the light seemed to dance. It gave the illusion that the Ouroboros was alive and writhing on his finger. "It seems imprudent not to make the effort."

Kismet wanted to answer him, wanted to accuse him of being foolish, but the words would not come. He was entranced by the undulating snake on Leeds' ring and stared deeper into the image, as if doing so might reveal some secret truth to him.

"The Fountain of Youth?" Annie looked around at her dining companions. "Are you off your nut?"

Leeds smiled without turning to look at her. "Miss—?"

"Crane. Annie Crane."

"Miss Crane, consider this. If you heard a rumor that a buried treasure was concealed in your back yard, would you fear to dig it up because the rumor might prove false?"

"Of course not. But a fountain that can make someone young again?"

"If it does exist then it is certainly worth discovering. Mr. Kismet and I discussed this at some length. Isn't that right?"

Kismet nodded slowly, unable to tear himself away from the light show of Leeds' ring.

Leeds continued. "I would have thought he would have shared the particulars with you. There are countless tales of men who have received the gift of extreme longevity. Dozens of men in the Bible lived for many centuries."

"The Bible?" Annie did not attempt to conceal her disbelief. "What does that have to do with the Fountain of Youth?"

"Oh, a great deal. It would require a source of, dare I say, divine power to turn ordinary water into Waters of Life. That source is a Seed of the original Tree of Life, described in Genesis.

"After the Great Flood, the priests of the Serpent cult captured the Seed and fled their home in Mesopotamia. They escaped across the oceans, perhaps traveling across a bridge of ice from what is now Russia, to the

North American continent. They took their prize as far as they could, and placed it at the bottom of a pool, transforming the waters into a Fountain of Youth."

Kismet heard every word Leeds uttered, but his attention kept returning to the twisting image on Leeds' finger. *Serpent*, he thought. *Serpent cult. Immortality.*

"Is it any surprise that snake worship, in one form or another, is so ubiquitous in ancient American cultures?" asked Leeds, as if sensing Kismet's fascination with the Ouroboros. "They would most certainly be the descendants of those original Serpent priests. The ancient Maya and Aztec worshipped snake gods—Quetzalcoatl, or Kukulcan—with human sacrifices, hearts cut out of still living victims."

Annie mouthed: *Eew! Gross!*

"So this Seed," intoned Higgins. "And the Fountain of Youth, are probably in Mexico?"

"Not at all. Those cultures arose thousands of years after the theft of the Seed. The object of my quest might be anywhere in the Americas. However, the next clue in our search is the legend of the Fountain of Youth itself. Those natives who instructed Ponce de Leon sent him to the north of Cuba. And Hernando Fontaneda, one of his contemporaries, may have actually found it. You know something about that don't you, Mr. Kismet?"

Distracted by the serpent's dance in Leeds' ring, Kismet did not even hear himself answer. "Fortune talked about a cave. But he's dead now."

"Dead?" Leeds asked the question sharply, and for a moment, the turning of the jewel stopped. Kismet blinked and started to look away, but the rhythmic motion commenced anew. "Well, perhaps it could happen. But he did make contact? He wrote you? Mentioned the cavern?"

Leeds' voice seemed to cushion him, enabling him to float on the ether as he returned to the fugue, descending deeper into the kaleidoscopic labyrinth. "He took his secret to the grave."

"Who told you that?"

FORTUNE FAVORS

Kismet opened his mouth to answer, but a sudden sharp pain in his thigh, like the sting of a wasp, distracted him. He closed his mouth and tried to swat the imaginary insect away.

"Who told you of Fontaneda's death?" prompted Leeds again.

In his mind's eye, Kismet saw his hand, brushing at the invisible pest that stung at his thigh. But his hand did not move, and no effort of his will could make it comply. He tried to ignore the sting, but it persisted, growing into a throbbing ache. Beads of sweat broke out on his forehead as the irritation blossomed into unbearable pain.

"What was his name? You told me, but I can't seem to remember."

"King," whispered Kismet. Perspiration trickled into his eyes, stinging them. He wanted to blink, but found himself deprived of even that small act of voluntary movement.

"Of course," replied Leeds, his voice soothing. "Now I remember. And he wrote from...Where was it again?"

As Kismet opened his mouth to speak, the pain in his leg redoubled. He gasped, and the intensity of the sensation broke his concentration. As the spell gave way, so did his ability to tolerate the pain. His hand flew to the place on his leg where the sensation was most intense, encountering not an insect, but a hard, unyielding object. He looked down to identify the source of his agony.

Annie was staring at him, her eyes wide in disbelief. Her fingers were gripping a dinner fork, the tines of which were buried in the fabric of Kismet's trousers, piercing through to his skin. With an abrupt movement, he wrapped his hand around hers and extricated the fork from the meat of his thigh. He half expected to see blood dripping from the prongs; it felt like she had penetrated through to muscle.

When their eyes met, she relaxed her grip, allowing the fork to fall the floor. He also relaxed, suddenly realizing why she had acted as she had.

"Kismet?"

Kismet turned to look at Leeds again. The other man continued to turn ring with his thumb. At his side, Elisabeth looked on hungrily. Kismet locked

103

his gaze on Leeds' eyes, refusing to be sucked in again. "I'm sorry. Suddenly I'm not feeling very well."

Leeds' visage was hard as ice, and did not crack with disappointment. "How unfortunate. We shall have to conclude our discussion at another time."

Kismet pushed away from the table, rising to his feet. He did not have to exaggerate his motions; nausea clenched at his stomach. Annie quickly rose, wrapping a protective arm around his waist. "I'll help you to your stateroom."

Higgins also rose, looking uncertainly from Kismet to Elisabeth. The actress was on her feet instantly, darting around to take Higgins' arm. "Oh, Alex, you simply must stay. You don't want to miss the séance."

Kismet nodded weakly. "I'll be fine."

As soon as Annie helped him away from the table, Kismet began feeling better. He said nothing however until they were outside the noisy dining hall. "What the hell was that all about?"

"I was going to ask you? I think that nutter Leeds hypnotized you."

Kismet shook his head. "Impossible."

"He was asking you all these questions about some man who found the Fountain of Youth—"

"Fontaneda?"

"That's it. Only you kept saying 'Fortune.' You told him Fortune was dead. Then he asked you about another man. I think you said it was the king."

Kismet nodded slowly. "Joseph King. He wrote the second letter, telling us that Henry Fortune, who also might have been Fontaneda, was dead. But why on earth would I tell Leeds about him?"

"Well, you did. When I figured out what was happening, I knew I had to break the spell somehow."

Kismet stopped walking, and fixed her with an accusing stare. "You stabbed me in the leg. With a fork."

"Good thing I did, too. Who knows what else Leeds would have gotten out of you."

FORTUNE FAVORS

"You're right," sighed Kismet. "I can't believe I let him do that. I owe you one."

"Yes, you do." She smiled, then took his arm again and pulled him along. "Come on. Let's get back to your stateroom and see how much damage I did to your leg."

He laughed. "It takes more than a fork in the leg to slow me down."

"Is that a fact? Well, I will have to try harder next time."

Kismet found that he liked the feel of her hand on his arm. It had been a long time since he felt that way. He didn't have the best track record in affairs of the heart. His single-minded pursuit of the Prometheus group always seemed to get in the way. His last relationship, with a young woman that had accompanied him on an expedition to the Black Sea, had ended almost as soon as it had begun. His attraction to Elisabeth had been more of a primal thing; animal magnetism at work. He had taken little comfort in their time together, and got no joy from the memory of her touch. What she had done wasn't that much different than Leeds' attempt to violate him hypnotically. The thought caused him to start, like an electric shock.

Annie could not help but notice his reaction. "What's wrong?"

"Al," he said after a long pause. "We left him alone back there. What if Leeds tries to pump him for information?"

"I think he has more to worry about from that tramp Elisabeth." Her reaction brought back his smile. "However, I think you should give Dad some credit. After all, you were the one who let yourself be hypnotized."

He grinned ruefully. "Even so, I don't like the idea of leaving him alone in there. I don't trust Leeds for a second. Or Elisabeth."

"Really? I got the impression you two were sort of chummy." There was no mistaking the acid in her tone.

Kismet's grin became a grimace. "Ancient history. She almost got me killed. Twice—No, make that three times. It's kind of hard to define our relationship."

Annie laughed aloud, and the intensity of her expression melted away. "I think I understand. As I recall, you tried to kill me."

"And I see you won't be letting me forget that, either." Kismet paused as they rounded the end of the corridor, leading to their stateroom. "That's peculiar."

"What?"

He led her forward a few steps to the stateroom door; it stood slightly ajar. Kismet reached out and gently pushed the door, swinging it wide open. Beyond it, he saw a man wearing what looked like a crewman's uniform hunched over the computer on the desktop.

Not sure why they even bother with the key cards around here, he thought, and turned to Annie. "Friend of yours?"

Though his tone was half-joking, he steeled himself for a confrontation with the intruder. He noticed Annie similarly tensing at his side

"I'm afraid not."

The stranger stopped moving, aware he had been caught. Though Kismet could only see the man's back, he judged him to be perhaps six inches taller than himself, broadly built like a football lineman. Kismet pushed forward ahead of Annie and entered the room. "I suppose you're going to tell me that there's a perfectly good reason you're here."

The man remained motionless for a second then sprang into action. His first act was to clasp his hands together and bring them down like a hammer on the keyboard of the laptop computer. There was a sickening crunch of plastic breaking, and several of the keys flew away like pieces of shrapnel. Then the intruder whirled to face them. Kismet's estimate of the man's size was right on the mark, but the fellow apparently did not wish to rely on the advantage of his larger physique. Kismet saw his own pistol locked in the man's grip and point directly at his chest.

Kismet's eyes drew into narrow, defensive slits. "I guess not."

The intruder smiled, revealing crookedly spaced, yellowed teeth, with a single peg of silver replacing a lower incisor. The man's face and head were clean-shaven, but dark stubble clung to his rough features like a permanent stain. His face, craggy and leathery from exposure to sun and wind, looked vaguely familiar to Kismet, probably someone he had passed by earlier in the cruise. The man thrust the gun forward, as if doing so might intimidate the people who had caught him.

Kismet was not intimidated. He crossed the room in two leaping steps, brandishing his fists as he closed on the intruder. The other man's grin fell as his opponent, flying in the face of reason, ran headlong toward the Glock. He tried to pull the trigger, but Kismet was there first.

He struck the man's wrist with the edge of his left hand, knocking the gun away. In the same motion, he lashed forward aiming his right fist at the intruders jaw.

The man reacted faster than Kismet expected, reflexively raising his right knee and driving it into Kismet's solar plexus. Kismet's fist glanced off of the intruder's jaw, doing little more than annoying the big man. With the wind knocked from his lungs, Kismet staggered backward.

Kismet fell back against the wall as the intruder dashed past him, intent on fleeing the stateroom. He tried to will his feet to chase after the man, but the message got no further than his bruised diaphragm.

As the escaping intruder passed through the doorway, his head suddenly snapped to the side. The force of the unseen blow drove him against the bulkhead, but he recovered quickly, shrugging off the effects. He swatted at the source of the blow with the back of his hand, as if at an irritating fly, and then took off running.

Kismet's breath returned in a sudden gasp, and he lurched into motion, running after the man. He found Annie, laid out on the carpeted floor of the hallway. She sat up, massaging the knuckles of her right hand. Kismet knelt for a second beside her, confirming that she had suffered no injury more serious than bruised pride, and then resumed the pursuit.

"Stay here," he shouted over his shoulder.

Annie struggled to her feet. "Not a chance."

Kismet quickly closed the distance to his quarry. He caught sight of the man at the far end of hallway, looking back over his shoulder to see if he was in the clear. When he spied Kismet, he put on a fresh burst of speed. The intruder darted to a stairway and ascended quickly. Kismet reached the foot of the stairs as the other man reached the top.

Kismet's foot left the final step in time to see the intruder pulling the large double doors to the dining rooms shut behind him. Kismet charged the door, bursting through without stopping. The man had not lingered to keep him out, but was already crossing the busy dining room. As Kismet stumbled headlong, trying to regain his balance after crashing through the doors, the big intruder glanced backward.

In that instant, he collided with a waiter carrying a tray of desserts. Artfully decorated pastries flew into the air in a confectionery cloud. The shock of the impact spread throughout the dining room, shouts and gasps rising into a cacophony. The intruder quickly regained his feet, his clothing streaked with buttercream frosting, and maneuvered through the minefield of broken plates and desserts on the floor.

The collision with the waiter allowed Kismet to close the distance to his prey, but the gain was short lived. Vaulting over the fallen waiter, Kismet's leading foot set down on the remains of a piece of cake, and slid away from beneath him, dropping him on his backside.

Before he could recover from the indignity of his fall, he heard the pitch of the room change from amused confusion to outright chaos. Amid the strident screams of a dozen women, Kismet discovered Annie standing in the doorway of the dining hall, brandishing his Glock.

"I told you to stay put," he shouted.

He did not belabor the point, but rose to his feet and picked his way through the splattered desserts before she could even attempt to answer. The fleeing intruder had reached the exit doors at the far end of the dining room, and was rapidly increasing his lead. Kismet leapt clear of the dessert wreckage and renewed the chase.

The doors opened onto an exposed deck, and Kismet caught a glimpse of the man's back as he ran sternward. However, when he reached the place where the man had been, there was no sign of him. Kismet stopped running, cocked his head to the side, and listened for the telltale sound of footsteps. Out of the corner of his eye, he saw Annie exiting the dining hall, still hefting the gun. He scowled at her but said nothing.

FORTUNE FAVORS

Then his ears caught the staccato beat of footsteps nearby. He took a deliberate step forward, trying to isolate the sound. It was coming from above. In a flash of insight, he realized where the intruder had gone. He darted forward at a full run until he reached a metal staircase ascending to the uppermost deck of the ship. He vaulted the banister landing on the third step and raced up the stairs, taking three at a time.

He emerged onto the ship's highest observation deck. His quarry stood at the far end of the deck, gripping the railing, gazing out at surface of the ocean twelve stories below. The only way off was the way they'd both come. The intruder was trapped.

Kismet approached at a walking pace, stopping when he was close enough to hear the other man's labored breathing. "Let's try that again. Who the hell are you, and why you were in my stateroom?"

The man's silver tooth flashed as he grinned. Kismet did not comprehend the reason for his sudden attack of humor until, a moment later when the man reached into the depths of his jacket, and drew out a long knife with an ornate, wavy blade. Kismet recognized it as a *kris*, an ancient Indonesian ceremonial dagger. It was probably a replica the man had picked up as a souvenir, but that didn't make it any less dangerous.

One of his army combatives instructors had once told Kismet: "Always rush a gun, but run away from a knife." The logic behind this was simple; a gun could reach out and hurt you even if you ran away, so your best chance of survival lay in trying get close enough to deflect the barrel or take the gun away. But the closer you got to a knife, the more likely you were to get cut.

The silver-toothed man laughed, weaving the knife back and forth. "I was hoping I'd get a chance to stick this in you."

Kismet couldn't quite place the accent. Something from the Commonwealth; it might have been Aussie or it could have been from Liverpool. That didn't concern him as much as the fact that his assailant seemed to be making this personal. Kismet raised his hands halfway, more as a placating gesture than a sign of surrender. "If you've got some problem with me, let's talk."

The movement of the blade stopped abruptly, and the man looked back blankly. "Oh, Kismet. You really have no idea. It's almost a pity that you'll die ignorant."

"I don't think you're going to kill me." Kismet's mind raced to figure out the puzzle of who the man was and what he wanted. "You were looking for something in my room, and you obviously didn't find it. If you kill me, there's a chance you'll never find what you are after."

"Bah! Killing you is something I've wanted for a long time."

As he edged closer, Kismet heard the sound of another pair of feet ascending the stairs. He knew without turning to look that it was Annie. A few moments later she was running across the deck, hefting the Glock.

In the moment that the knife-wielding intruder saw Annie, Kismet made his move. The big man recovered quickly from the distraction, thrusting with the blade, but Kismet anticipated the attack, and sidestepped. The *kris* stabbed the air impotently to Kismet's left, and as the man's momentum carried him forward, Kismet stepped closer, slipping his right arm around the man's shoulder and hooking a hand behind his neck in a half-nelson. The knife clattered to the deck, but then he wrenched himself free and spun around, lashing out with a foot to sweep Kismet's legs from under him.

Kismet landed hard on his side. The silver-toothed man dove for his knife, but even as his hand took hold of the ornate haft of the weapon, Annie shouted a warning for him to stop. She didn't have a clear shot—she was just as likely to hit Kismet as the intruder—but it was enough to give the man pause. He straightened up without recovering the *kris*, and shook his head sadly. "Gonna shoot me, little girl?"

"She doesn't have to." Kismet struck as the man turned to face him, landing a roundhouse that sent the intruder crashing into the waist-high rail that ringed the observation deck. The man flipped over the barrier, but succeeded in wrapping one arm around it to arrest his fall.

"Should have let me shoot him," Annie remarked, shaking her head.

Kismet ignored her, stalking toward the hanging intruder. "One more time. Tell me who you are."

FORTUNE FAVORS

The man showed no sign of surrender. Even as he struggled against his own failing grip, Kismet saw the defiance building in his eye. "I don't think so," was the grated reply.

The man abruptly let go with his right hand. Kismet saw a glint of light, the reflection a familiar emblem engraved on a golden ring standing out from the man's fist, for just a fraction of a second before that fist hammered into his face.

Kismet's head snapped to the side with the force of the blow. It took a moment for his vision to clear, but when it did, he rolled back to the railing and leaned over, looking for some sign of his assailant.

Annie was at his side an instant later. "My God, are you all right?"

"Where did he go?"

"He must have fallen in."

Kismet shook his head, instantly regretting it as the pain of the man's parting blow flared anew. He gingerly probed his aching cheek and saw blood on his fingertips. The man's ring had sliced through the skin under his left eye. While it had not been as gaudy as Leeds' ring, the symbol was the same: an Ouroboros.

He pushed away from the rail and retrieved the *kris*, testing its edge with a thumb. Annie stepped in front of him. "Nick. Would you please tell me what's going on?"

"No," he replied, thinking about the image of the snake devouring itself. "But I think I know who can."

Alex Higgins tore his gaze away from Elisabeth and watched with a perplexed expression as his daughter left the dining hall with Kismet at her side. Something was wrong; some unspoken tension between Dr. Leeds and Kismet had reached and passed a climax. But Leeds gave no indication of what the problem might be. He merely stared at the table, silently waiting. Several seconds passed before he abruptly stood and nodded to Elisabeth.

"Delightful!" She reached out and took hold of Higgins' hand. When he felt her touch, every vestige of apprehension melted away. The feel of her skin set his heart pounding and the faint scent of her perfume led him like a ring through his nostrils. "It is time for the séance. This will be tremendously exciting."

Dr. Leeds made a casual gesture toward some of the other guests in the dining hall. Half a dozen people left their meals unfinished and rose to follow him from the room. In the euphoria of his intimate contact with Elisabeth, Higgins scarcely noticed the route he and the rest of Leeds' entourage took and was hardly aware as he was guided to a seat at a large round table, draped with a voluminous blue tablecloth. The room was dark except for a score of small votive candles that offered little in the way of illumination but certainly contributed to the mood of the occasion. Elisabeth sat beside him, and in short order, the other guests filled in around the circumference until only one seat remained.

Dr. Leeds seemed to glide into the room; his long cassock hid his feet from view. He smoothly took his seat and gestured to the audience. "Please, link hands."

Higgins' felt Elisabeth's hand in his; he barely even noticed another guest take his other hand.

Leeds spoke again, his tone both hushed and commanding. "We wish to know more of our quest. There are many answers that may not be found on this terrestrial plane, but beyond it, in the spirit realm. Hernando Fontaneda was the keeper of the secret, but he has passed beyond this world. Will you reach out with me, to contact him?"

There was a murmur of ascent and Dr. Leeds seemed satisfied. "He may not remember at first. Your concentration and assistance is crucial. Leave off all doubt now. Close your eyes and focus your thoughts."

Higgins did as he was told, but found he could not concentrate in the way Dr. Leeds wanted him to. His thoughts were swirling, not around the spirit realm, but the heaven of Elisabeth's touch. He gripped her hand, as if to squeeze his emotions into her, barely cognizant of Dr. Leeds' mumbled incantations.

FORTUNE FAVORS

"Alex," Elisabeth whispered urgently. "Open your eyes. Look!"

He obeyed, looking into her eyes, but she nodded toward the center of the table. Higgins nearly fainted when he saw the figure there, hovering in the mist above the table's surface.

Though it was only a few inches in height, Higgins had no trouble making out the apparition; the details of its face and dress were vivid. He was unquestionably looking at the likeness of a Spanish conquistador. The crescent helmet concealed the face of the specter, but he knew that it must be Hernando Fontaneda.

"*¿Quien estoy?*" whispered Dr. Leeds, his voice strangely altered. "*Diga me. Quiero saber.*"

"He is speaking Spanish," gasped one of the men at the table. "He wants to know who he is?"

No one seemed willing to answer. Realizing that Dr. Leeds was acting as a medium Higgins, in a trembling voice, supplied the name.

"*Si. Recuerdo.*" whispered Leeds. "*A ver, ¿a dónde estoy? Me parece que es bien oscuro.*"

"He remembers," translated the same man. "He wants to know where he is. He says he it is very dark there."

"You died," replied Elisabeth. "Don't you remember?"

"No." The voice issuing from Leeds' mouth switched to deeply accented English. "How did I die? Do you know?"

No one could give him an answer, not even Higgins.

"Tell me more. I might remember. There was a man...King was his name. I was with him, but I can't remember..." Leeds' eyes fluttered open and he stared directly at Higgins. "You know," he said, still speaking in the Spaniard's voice. "Tell me. Where did I die?"

Wide-eyed and trembling, Higgins stared at the apparition. Elisabeth's gentle touch on his arm prompted him and he opened his mouth to answer.

The dining area was a shambles from Kismet's pursuit of the knife-wielding intruder. Icing from destroyed pastries seemed to be everywhere. Moreover, some of the passengers acting in blind terror had overturned their tables, spilling plates, silverware and food, and were crouched down behind them. The waiters were conferring with the ship's officers about the cause of the mayhem. One of them spotted Kismet and identified him as one of the perpetrators. The officers moved to question him, but stopped short when they saw the prodigious blade of the serpentine knife held in his right fist.

Kismet dismissed them with an exasperated gesture. "Where are the people who were sitting there?" He pointed to the table where he had left Higgins, in the company of Dr. Leeds and Elisabeth Neuell.

"In the conference room," replied a waiter, before anyone could think to silence him. "For the séance."

"Sir," interjected one of the senior officers, trying to be calm and authoritative. "I must ask you to surrender your weapon."

Shaking his head, more out of frustration than defiance, he pushed through the group and headed for the exit.

The conference room was dark, lit only by a few candles. The perfect place for an ambush, Kismet decided. He spied Higgins at a table, with Elisabeth and Leeds. The latter was mumbling something, while in the center of the table, projected onto a cloud of mist was the likeness of a gaudy conquistador; a product of amateurish make-up and costume, smoke and mirrors. He stalked over to the table, unnoticed by all except of the architect of the charade himself.

Leeds' icy gaze defied his stare, but Kismet was unmoved by Leeds' parlor tricks. Higgins opened his mouth to speak, to reveal the location from which the final correspondence with Henry Fortune had originated, but Kismet cleared his throat, breaking the spell.

The gathering looked up in surprise and Elisabeth breathed a vehement curse. Dr. Leeds folded his arms casually across his chest. "You are disturbing the spirits, Kismet".

FORTUNE FAVORS

"Perhaps the spirits can answer my questions. I'd like to know why the man that ransacked my room and tried to kill me was wearing a ring with an Ouroboros. Kind of like the one you're wearing, Dr. Leeds."

Leeds remained impassive. "You're imagining things, Kismet."

"I didn't imagine this." Kismet thrust the knife out, over the center of the table, and then stabbed downward, into the heart of the apparition. The blade sliced through the vapors, shattering a mirror concealed underneath, and causing the ghost to dissolve. The gathering dispersed, frightened by the display of violence, but Kismet wasn't finished. Grabbing hold of the table and shoving it out of the way, he advanced on Leeds.

Leeds did not cower, but instead threw something to the floor, a glass vial that shattered and began spewing thick smoke. A screen of dense fog suddenly rose up around Kismet. He waved his hand to fan away the acrid fumes, and pushed forward undaunted, thrusting his hands out to the place where Leeds was sitting.

His hands closed on empty air. Dr. Leeds and Elisabeth Neuell had vanished.

7

UNFAIR THOUGH IT WAS, KISMET offered no protest when the captain ordered him off the ship. He was eager to be done with *The Star of Muara*, eager to put the whole sordid affair behind him, and most of all, eager to take up the search for Henry Fortune's wondrous cavern.

In the early hours of the morning following the disastrous séance, Kismet, along with Higgins and his daughter, boarded a helicopter for the mainland. A few hours later, they were on a trans-Pacific flight to Los Angeles, and because of a trick of geography, arrived in the United States on the evening of the calendar day before they left. They spent a night in a hotel near LAX, but early the next day were back in the air.

The long flights gave Kismet time to think, but his mind was not occupied with fantasies of discovering the source of immortality. Rather, he kept replaying what the man with the silver tooth had said: *You really have no idea. It's almost a pity that you'll die ignorant...Killing you is something I've wanted for a long time.*

Kismet knew of one very good possible explanation for the man's hostility: Dr. Leeds and his thug were part of the Prometheus group. And if Prometheus was after the Fountain of Youth...or the Seed from the Tree of Life or whatever else...then Kismet was determined to beat them there.

But as much as he wanted to believe that Dr. Leeds would somehow lead him to the answers he had been seeking for half his life, he knew that the explanation wasn't a perfect fit. In his only meaningful encounter with Prometheus, he had been led to believe that he was somehow protected, or at least that Prometheus had no interest in taking direct action against him. He had never been able to fathom the why of it, aside from a cryptic intimation that his mother might somehow be a player in the drama, though even that information was suspect. In any case, his prior knowledge of Prometheus' goals certainly didn't square with Leeds' silver-toothed goon's lethal grudge. So where did that leave him?

After collecting their luggage from the carousel at La Guardia Airport, Kismet hailed a taxi and the three of them crowded into its rear seat. Little was said as the hired car fought traffic through Queens and across the Williamsburg Bridge; the three had virtually exhausted every avenue of discussion during long hours spent in airport lobbies.

Much of the conversation had focused on Elisabeth Neuell. Higgins, who knew her better than any of them, and was clearly smitten in spite of everything that had happened, was loathe to admit that she might be up to no good, but he was at least willing to allow that Dr. Leeds was not to be trusted.

Then they had turned to the issue of how they would proceed in their search for the cavern. The whole adventure hinged on finding Joseph King, or possibly his heirs, and hoping that he, or they, knew something about Henry Fortune's—or rather Hernando Fontaneda's—explorations. The rest of the time had been wiled away in an endless and mind-numbing succession of card games and similarly pointless distractions.

Though he was not easily given to sentiment, Kismet felt a wave of relief as the taxi turned on to Central Park West. The familiar foliage of the park, brightly verdant in the summer humidity, was a welcome sight after the disastrous cruise. A few minutes later, they pulled up in front of the American Museum of Natural History, where Kismet's kept an office.

"I booked you rooms at the Carlyle," Kismet told the others as he got out. "It's just on the other side of the park."

Annie gazed breathlessly out the window. "New York. I never dreamed I'd be here."

"We can probably squeeze in a couple days of sight-seeing if you like." He was about to give the cab driver their next destination when Higgins abruptly got out.

"Just across the park, you say?" The former Gurkha nodded toward the verdant urban greenspace just across the street. "If it's all the same, I think I'd like to stretch my legs a bit."

Kismet shrugged and with the driver's assistance, retrieved their luggage from trunk. Higgins and Annie traveled light; one small carry-on bag apiece, containing the bare minimum for an overnight stay. Neither of them had anticipated traveling abroad. Kismet hauled his own duffel bag out as well and paid the driver.

"The hotel is on 76th and Madison Avenue," he explained as they shouldered their bags. "If you go up to 81st—" He pointed to a street intersection a couple blocks north of the museum—"and stay on the Transverse Road that cuts through the park, it will bring you out a couple blocks north of where you want to be. Go east one more block to Madison and head south to 76th."

"No worries," Higgins answered.

"And what will you be doing?" Annie asked.

"I'm going to print up everything we've got so far, and hopefully get some contact info on Joseph King."

The young woman glanced at her father and then at Kismet, and he sensed that she was trying to decide which man to accompany. Kismet put her at ease. "I'll meet you for dinner in an hour or so at the hotel and get you caught up," he said. "Enjoy your walk."

Although they had indeed spent nearly two days sitting in airport lounges and even more uncomfortably, airplane seats, Higgins was not entirely sincere in stating his motives for choosing to walk through Central Park. As the taxi had cruised up Central Park West, he had caught a glimpse of a familiar face near the park entrance opposite the museum, and felt compelled to investigate. He didn't want to reveal this to Kismet, and was unsure if he even wanted Annie to accompany him. *Probably just a look-alike*, he told himself, unconvincingly.

But as he and Annie crossed the street, the face he had glimpsed appeared again, looking right at him...beckoning him. Annie saw as well.

"What the—?" She glanced sidelong at her father. "That's her, isn't it? How the hell did she get here?"

Less than fifty yards away, Elisabeth Neuell was leaning against the stone half wall that lined the border of a footpath into the park, casually smoking a cigarette. Her extravagant formal wear had been replaced by a yellow mid-thigh length tunic dress. Despite the garment's simplicity, she made it look glamorous. Higgins was a bit surprised that she had not already been recognized by a passerby; maybe her star had dimmed a bit in the years since leaving her career to become Sultana. As they drew closer, Elisabeth dropped her cigarette and stubbed it out with the toe of her sandal.

He sensed Annie starting to outpace him, perhaps intent on some kind of confrontation, and he quickened his step to head her off. "Beth!" he called, jogging ahead of his daughter. "What on earth are you doing here?"

"You must have hired a Concorde jet to get here ahead of us," Annie supplied, with a hint of scorn. "But how did you know to find us here?"

The former Sultana gave a tight smile. "That's not important right now."

"I think it bloody well is," Annie retorted, advancing with her fists balled.

Higgins blocked Annie's way with a restraining arm, but kept his attention on Elisabeth. "It's a fair question, Beth. Especially after what happened back on the ship."

"I'll explain everything, but right now you just need to trust me. Can you do that?"

Higgins glanced at his daughter, reading her answer in the set of her jaw, but then he nodded.

Elisabeth reached out and took his hand and led him into the park. Annie scowled, but followed after them. They didn't go far however; Elisabeth guided them to one of Central Park's famous horse drawn carriages, one of several that were parked on the street near the intersection with the footpath.

The driver dismounted as they approached and offered his hand to Elisabeth, helping her step up into the covered *Vis-a-Vis* style carriage. As Elisabeth took her seat, Higgins saw that the coach was already occupied.

Annie leaned past him and looked inside. "Dr. Leeds. What a surprise."

Leeds had foregone his elaborate skullcap and cassock in favor of black slacks and a charcoal gray turtleneck shirt. He looked almost ordinary. "Please," he said, offering a hand. "Ride with me and I will explain everything."

Annie's body language made it clear that she didn't want to get in, but Higgins' curiosity impelled him forward. "Come on, Annie girl. Won't hurt to listen to what the man has to say."

"Wanna bet?" Annie grumbled as she climbed inside, sitting next to Higgins on the rear facing seat.

Leeds folded his hands in his lap and did not speak until the carriage lurched into motion. When he did start talking, it was in a low but faintly pleading voice. "I don't know quite how to tell you this. Nick Kismet is not who you think he is."

Annie rolled her eyes. "What the hell is that supposed to mean? Especially coming from you."

Leeds offered an inscrutable smile. "Did Kismet tell you about Prometheus?"

As the printer whirred to life, Kismet accessed a commercial peoplefinder website and typed in "Joseph King Charleston SC." The response was prodigious; there were a lot of discrete references to Joseph King floating around the Worldwide Web, and no way to really tell which one was the one he needed. It was going to be a tedious process and he wasn't in the mood for that right now. He sent the search results to the printer as well. He was about to check his email when his eye caught on one of the advertisements at the top of the webpage.

He almost laughed aloud. "Surely it can't be that easy."

He logged off the computer and scooped the sheaf of paper from the printer tray, then headed for the exit, eager to share his discovery with Higgins and Annie.

He only got as far as the front steps of the museum when he was stopped dead in his tracks.

Powerful hands seized him in mid-step. Two men flanked him, pinioning his arms and immobilizing him. A third materialized out of the crowd and stood directly before him. It was the man with the silver tooth. Kismet struggled uselessly against his captors. They had lifted him off the ground, and he was unable to find any leverage that might break their hold.

Silver Tooth just grinned.

Kismet saw the blow coming, but could do nothing to protect himself. The man's fist burrowed into the pit of his stomach, and his body curled around the impact like a worm on a fishhook. A wave of nausea racked his body.

"To answer your earlier question, the name's Ian MacKay." A second blow hammered into Kismet's gut, and then he felt the papers torn from his hand. "And this is what I was looking for. Thanks ever so much."

A third punch took his breath away and brought him to the brink of unconsciousness. When the darkness receded, he found himself lying supine on the steps, surrounded by a throng of people who were only just beginning to wonder why he was writhing in agony.

○

"Prometheus," Leeds began, "is quite simply a cabal of intellectuals intent upon remaking the destiny of our planet."

Annie rolled her eyes again, but their host ignored her open incredulity.

"They took their name, rather hypocritically, from the Titan in Greek mythology—a figure renowned for his wisdom and his love of mankind. It was Prometheus who stole fire from the gods of Olympus and gave it to man, and it was he who made sure that Pandora's Box also contained hope. But this modern Prometheus obscenity is more like Zeus, intent on locking the mysteries of our world away, hoarding the secret knowledge for their own schemes. And like the gods of Olympus, they delight in playing games with people's lives, controlling them as a puppet master works the strings of a marionette. They are playing just such a game with your friend Nick Kismet. He is, unknowingly I believe, their greatest experiment."

"Experiment?" asked Higgins. "What kind of experiment?"

Leeds brought his fingers together in a steeple beneath his chin. "I'm not sure they even know. They unleashed him on the world, and then sat back to see what sort of havoc he would wreak. And they have been protecting him. I believe you have witnessed their interference first hand, Mr. Higgins. How else would you explain your miraculous escape from the Republican Guard in Nasiriyah?"

"This is ridiculous," scoffed Annie.

"It is the truth," Leeds answered, unperturbed. "And without his even realizing it, Kismet has become their bloodhound, tracking down the world's last remaining mysteries—mysteries like the Seed of the Tree of Life—so that Prometheus can hide them away...or perhaps use them for some nefarious purpose."

Annie leaned close to her father, and *sotto voce* said: "What's 'nefarious' mean?"

Higgins ignored her. "How do you know all this?"

"I have given my life to searching for the very mysteries Prometheus wishes to conceal. One cannot wade too deep into those waters without hearing whispers of the conspiracy...or of the Nick Kismet experiment."

Higgins glanced at Elisabeth, who seemed to be hanging on Leeds' every word. "Why are you telling us? What are we supposed to do about it?"

"Kismet must not be allowed to uncover Hernando Fontaneda's secret. I do not wish any harm to come to him, but if he finds the Seed, then Prometheus finds it, and they will not share its magnificent power with the world. They most certainly won't share it with us."

Leeds smiled again. "So, what I want from you, put simply, is this: join me in my quest. Abandon Kismet, for his own good, and help me find the Seed before Kismet or Prometheus."

Annie bit back a caustic reply and instead watched her father's reaction. She felt a surge of disappointment when she realized that he wasn't going to reject Leeds' offer out of hand. "He won't stop looking, you know," the former Gurkha said, after a long pause.

"No, I don't imagine he will. That is the very reason that I seek a partnership with you. Time is of the essence. I have resources which can expedite our search, but you...you possess the information that can point me directly to the goal."

"You already pumped us for that information," Annie retorted. "What else do you think we know that you didn't get from that phony séance?"

Leeds inclined his head in a conciliatory gesture. "It may be that you have some crucial piece of knowledge, the importance of which none of us realizes. And it may also be that your contribution to the endeavor will arise, not from what you know, but from what you will do."

Annie stabbed an angry finger at Leeds. "You know what? You can go fu—"

Higgins cut her off, gripping her knee in his left hand. "I need to discuss this with my daughter. Privately."

Leeds' smile returned. "I know just the place."

Kismet rolled over onto hands and knees. His gut seemed twisted around the bruises forming in his abdomen. Nevertheless, he climbed to his feet and began pushing through the crowd toward the street.

He scanned the boulevard in both directions, and then looked over at the park entrance. The men who had accosted him were gone. He couldn't fathom how MacKay had managed to reach New York ahead of them in order to lay an ambush, but his aching insides told him that the silver-toothed thug had not made the trip alone.

He charged down the steps, dodging traffic, in a beeline for the 81st street intersection with the Transverse Road. It hadn't been five minutes since he parted company with Higgins and Annie, but MacKay and his team had evidently been watching all along, and might have already made a move on his friends.

One of Central Park's famous carriages—a red and yellow *Vis-a-Vis*, drawn by a single chestnut gelding—was parked just beyond the entrance. The driver, wearing a formal jacket and an old-fashioned top hat, nodded in his direction as he passed, prompting Kismet to pull up short. "I think my friends may have come through here a few minutes ago; a big guy with dark hair, and a tall, skinny girl with short brown hair."

The driver nodded. "Saw 'em. They caught a ride with my buddy, Jack."

"A ride? A carriage ride?" Kismet frowned. "Just the two of them?"

"Not sure. But I know Jack's route if you want to follow 'em."

"Do it." Kismet swung into the coach, settling into the front facing seat. "There's a big tip for you if you can catch them."

"That's what I wanted to hear," answered the driver with a grin and he climbed up onto his seat, perched about the front wheel. He gave the reins a shake, and horse and carriage lurched into motion together.

Kismet drummed his fingers impatiently on the carved wooden sides of the coach. The animal's hooves and the clatter of the metal rimmed wheels on the paving stones started a low tremor, which passed through every molecule in the cab. Kismet gritted his teeth against the annoying sound, absently wondering how the starry-eyed lovers that frequently made use of the carriages could endure the din.

The horse drew the cab along the gradually curving Transverse Avenue. Children played on the edge of the pond off to the left, oblivious to the anxiety he was experiencing. Unable to simply sit idle, Kismet leaned forward, peering over the driver's shoulder to catch a glimpse of the other carriage.

"Can you push it a little," he shouted over the rumbling, trying not to sound rude.

The driver shrugged and cracked his buggy whip over the horse, urging the gelding into a trot. The clatter of hooves and wheels on the asphalt was like a blaring siren ahead of the carriage, warning pedestrians to get clear. They did so grudgingly, voicing their opinions with characteristic New York politeness.

"Hang on, back there," the driver shouted over his shoulder. "I know a shortcut."

Despite the warning, Kismet was jounced violently as the carriage turned sharply to the right, just a few hundred yards past the East Drive underpass. The metal-shod wheels banged over the curb, and then the ride got a lot smoother and a lot quieter as they headed out across a manicured lawn. The hooves and wheels left a pockmarked trail of divots in their wake, but when Kismet glanced around to gauge the reaction of other park visitors, he saw no one. They were moving into the Ramble, the park's thirty-eight acre manufactured wilderness.

A stand of trees lay directly ahead and Kismet knew the driver would have to slow down in order to go through the wooded area, but to his surprise and dismay, as soon as they reached the tree line, the driver pulled back on the reins, stopping altogether.

"What the hell kind of shortcut—?" Kismet fell silent as he saw the dismounted driver peering into the covered passenger area. He had removed his top hat, but the most conspicuous thing about him was the semi-automatic pistol in his right fist.

"This is where you get out, sir. Don't worry about that tip. It's been taken care of."

In the sudden quiet, Kismet heard the rumble and clank of a piece of machinery emanating from the woods. He stared at the driver, meeting the man's gaze rather than looking at the gun. There was a hardness there; this man believed he was capable of pulling the trigger. "Tell me something; are you one of Leeds' true believers, or just hired help?"

The gunman ignored the dig. "Get out."

Kismet complied, keeping his hands elevated. The driver maintained a standoff distance of about ten yards, enough to ensure that he would have time to pull the trigger if his captive tried anything. He gestured with the gun, pointing toward the tree line. Kismet knew that his odds of surviving this trap would be greatly reduced if he complied, but he there seemed to be little alternative. Without taking his eyes off the gunman, he moved into the trees.

He emerged into a clearing—a secluded meadow ringed by trees—and immediately discovered the source of the machine noise. Parked in the middle of the open area was an enormous gasoline-powered industrial wood chipper. In principle, it was no different than a backyard mulch machine, but this device was designed to chew up entire tree trunks. It was so big it had to be towed by a truck. A six-foot long chute, lined with a series of rollers, led to a pair of spinning wheels which would grab anything that touched them and thrust it into a nest of rotary knives. Another metal chute, like a square-pipe, curved up out of the body of the machine like a snorkel, and was positioned above a pile of woodchips in the back of a small flatbed truck parked alongside the chipper. The gasoline engine was running, and all the wheels and knives were turning, but nothing was being fed into it and nothing was issuing from the output chute.

"You're so bloody predictable, mate."

Kismet tore his gaze away from the chipper and turned to the source of the voice. Ian MacKay stood a few feet to his right.

"Oh, I think you'll find I'm full of surprises," Kismet said.

MacKay just laughed, his hands resting on his hips. Kismet did a slow sweep and found another man positioned to his left. This fellow, one of the pair that had grabbed him on the front steps of the museum, held a long metal pole topped with a vicious-looking pruning saw. The ersatz carriage driver brought up the rear, still wielding his pistol.

"You really went to a lot of trouble," Kismet remarked. "I'm touched. What did you do with the work crew? Kill them?"

"Naw. Just gave 'em the afternoon off with pay, so to speak." MacKay's eyes took on a hard edge. "I don't suppose you'd save us all a lot of trouble and just jump in. Won't hurt for more than a second or two I reckon."

FORTUNE FAVORS

"Where are my friends? If you've hurt them..." He didn't complete the threat; he knew how hollow it sounded.

"Least of your worries, mate." MacKay nodded to his cohorts, and the man to his left immediately thrust the pole-saw at him.

Kismet hurled himself out of the way, diving into a shoulder roll that took him to the middle of the clearing. As he came back to his feet, he spun around to face the trio of attackers. He now saw that the carriage driver had put his gun away, and now held a small gas-powered chain saw, which he triggered menacingly as he advanced. MacKay just stood with his hands, balled into fists, resting on his hips.

Kismet didn't know why they hadn't simply shot him. Maybe they were afraid of leaving telltale forensic evidence or had it in their heads that they could somehow make his death look like an accident. He wasn't about to ask.

The three men spread out, trying to establish a perimeter and prevent him from escaping. As noisy and intimidating as the chainsaw was, Kismet was more concerned about the man with the pole-saw. If he was going to survive this, he was going to have to take the initiative, and quickly.

He took a step sideways, closer to the rumbling chipper. Then, as his assailants moved to take the ground he had ceded, he lunged toward the man with the pole-saw. It was a feint only; he caught himself before putting his weight on his outstretched foot, but it was enough. The man reacted instinctively, stabbing the saw blade at him again, and this time Kismet was ready. Turning just enough to avoid the thrust, he wrapped an arm around the sturdy aluminum pole and yanked it forward. The saw wielder was pulled forward, off balance and his impromptu weapon twisted out of his grip as he slid face down across the grass.

Kismet spun around and whipped the pole toward the man with the chainsaw. The man parried, triggering the chain reflexively, and the cutting tool met the pole in a shower of sparks. The vibration traveled through the hollow metal rod like an electric shock and Kismet felt it slipping from his grip before he could even think about trying to hang on tighter. His opponent immediately advanced, raising the chainsaw overhead as he did, and slashed down with all his might.

Kismet stumbled backward and the whirring teeth on the chain sliced through the air where he had been. The saw narrowly missed him and plunged into the soft ground, throwing up a spray of dirt and grass. Kismet barely saw any of this though; his foot struck the man from whom he'd taken the saw, still supine on the ground and struggling to rise, and he tripped backward, flattening the man a second time.

It felt like it took an eternity for him to fall, an obscenely bloated moment in which he flailed his arms, unsuccessfully trying to restore his balance. Yet, even as he fell, his mind was turning over possible courses of action. He twisted, trying to land on his side, so as to grapple with the fallen assailant. Doing so would give MacKay and the other man time to advance, but it would reduce the odds that were stacked against him by a third.

Before he could act on his plan something slammed into the back of his head and a curtain of darkness fell. He was still conscious, but for a few seconds could do nothing but lay motionless in a daze. Except he wasn't on the ground and he wasn't motionless. Strong hands had reached under his arms and hauled him more or less erect. His heels dragged across the ground for a few yards and then he felt himself being lifted into the air. As his vision cleared, he caught a glimpse of Ian MacKay's silver toothed grin of delight, and then there was another burst of pain as he was slammed down on the chipper's feed chute. The roller wheels offered no resistance as MacKay gave him a shove and he began sliding headfirst toward the machine's gaping maw.

Annie leaned against the stone battlement, gazing out from the mildly crowded observation deck of Belvedere Castle, across the landscaped expanse of Central Park and the city skyline beyond, but her brain registered none of it. Her thoughts were consumed by the gravity of Leeds' revelation, and even more so by the fact that her father was evidently contemplating the requested alliance. While it was certainly true that she barely knew Nick

Kismet, and had no particular obligation to him, the simple fact of being asked to be disloyal a friend galled her. That her father would consider, even for a second, betraying the man that, by his own admission had once saved his life, was even more disturbing, and she told him as much.

"Annie," Higgins sighed. "You don't understand. What he said…"

"About some diabolical secret society? Puppet masters pulling our strings? It's complete bollocks and you know it."

"Annie, I was there that night. I know what he's talking about."

"Yes, you were there. You know that Nick isn't part of some conspiracy."

"For twenty years, I've tried to understand what happened. None of it ever made any sense until today. As crazy as it sounds, what Leeds said…it fits. Why we were there, why we got captured, and how we escaped. We were in…" Higgins' breath seemed to catch in his throat, and when he tried to continue, he had to force the words past clenched teeth. "In the goddamned Republican Guard torture chamber, and Kismet just walked us right out; like Daniel in the lion's den."

Annie's retort died on her lips as she saw the pain of reliving the memory twist her father's features. When she spoke again, it was in a more subdued tone. "Nick wasn't responsible, dad. Even if everything Leeds said is true, he's not a bad man."

"I know, Annie girl."

"So, we're going to tell Leeds to sod off, right?"

Higgins stared at her for several seconds before slowly nodding an affirmative.

Almost a hundred yards away, Dr. John Leeds listened intently to the exchange. He couldn't make out all the nuances—the tripod-mounted Detect Ear parabolic microphone wasn't that discriminating—but the amplified audio feed, in conjunction with his visual observations, courtesy of a pair of Minox 10X44 binoculars, was sufficient to tell the tale. For just a few moments, he thought perhaps he had succeeded in winning the father over, but it seemed the daughter's passionate defense of Kismet was going to prove insurmountable. Perhaps with more time and persuasion, he might be able to...

He lowered the binoculars as one of his hirelings approached. The man was a mercenary, some acquaintance of MacKay's; Leeds found the whole arrangement rather distasteful. He didn't trust people whose loyalties could be bought or traded. Still, hirelings had their uses.

The man proffered a bundle of papers. "Ian told me to bring this to you."

Leeds took it without comment and began thumbing through the pages. He committed the words of the letters—the first from Henry Fortune himself, and the second from Joseph King—to memory. Then he saw that the remaining papers were phone and address listings for every Joseph King in the greater Charleston area. Leeds breathed an ancient Sumerian curse.

"There's nothing here we didn't already know."

"Maybe you shouldn't have been so quick to get rid of Kismet," observed Elisabeth. The actress stood a few steps away, smoking a cigarette.

Leeds cast a baleful glance in her direction, but did not comment. The mercenary stared back at him, expressionless.

Leeds sighed. "I believe we may safely assume that Kismet doesn't, or I should say didn't, know anything more than this. Which reminds me..." He unclipped a Motorola Talkabout from his belt and keyed the send button. "Ian, report."

There was a long silence at the other end, and then finally a burst of squelch, followed by a terse: "It's done."

Leeds smiled and keyed the walkie-talkie. "Excellent. I'm sending two more your way."

FORTUNE FAVORS

Kismet turned his feet outward and managed to hook his toes on the chute's angled side-guards. His death-slide stopped mere inches from the spinning feeder wheel; he thought he could feel the molded steel teeth tickling his hair.

MacKay's grin fell a notch when he saw that Kismet had stopped moving. His puzzlement lasted only a moment, but it was enough. As the big man grabbed Kismet's ankles, preparing to shake him loose, Kismet levered his torso forward, sitting up, and thrust his arms out as far as he could reach. His hamstrings screamed as he folded his body almost in half, but he fought through the agony and found something to hang onto: MacKay's ears.

The silver-toothed killer howled in agony as Kismet's nails dug into his flesh. As MacKay tried to bat his hands away, Kismet wrenched his body sideways, rolling up and over the side-guard.

As he hit the ground alongside the chipper, he caught a glimpse of movement and instinctively rolled away, under the chute, narrowly avoiding a swipe from the chainsaw. He kept rolling, and for a fleeting moment, was hidden from view. It was an opportunity he dared not waste.

The chipper was mounted on a dual-wheeled trailer rig, and Kismet made good use of the twin tires as a stepladder. He scrambled onto the top of the chipper engine cowling, and hurled himself, feet first, at the man with the chainsaw.

His feet connected squarely with the man, one to the jaw and one squarely in the chest, catching him completely unaware. The idling chainsaw fell from his grasp as the double-kick knocked him senseless. Kismet pushed off from the stricken man, tucking and rolling to soften the blow of his own landing, and was on his feet again, dodging behind the chipper before MacKay and his remaining comrade knew what was happening. He paused there to catch his breath, and then ducked his head around the corner to see where the next attack would come from.

He didn't see the gun in the hand of the phony driver until the man triggered a shot. He jumped back, startled, and collided with MacKay. Even though the big man had been intent on flanking him, Kismet's abrupt retreat caught him off guard, and for a moment, both men simply regarded each

131

other without moving. Then MacKay threw a wild punch that missed Kismet and connected instead with the chipper's housing. Kismet seized the advantage and planted a foot in MacKay's chest, but his foe stood firm. Instead of sending MacKay reeling backward, it was Kismet himself that rebounded back, landing on his back, out in the open. Reasoning that he stood a better chance against MacKay than against a bullet, he scrambled for cover behind the chipper once more, and right into MacKay's grasp.

The big man got one hand around Kismet's throat, and suddenly that was the only thing that mattered. Even as he fought the chokehold, Kismet felt MacKay dragging him again toward the chute.

"Put that damn thing away," MacKay bellowed. "And give me a hand."

Darkness was falling over Kismet's eyes. He tried tearing MacKay's hand from his throat, tried also kicking at the man who was choking the life out him, but couldn't tell if he was making contact. His extremities no longer felt connected to his body.

What seemed like only an instant later, he felt the stranglehold loosen just a little, and in that moment felt the hard rollers of the chipper chute beneath him. Frantic, he blindly thrust arms and legs out, hooking them awkwardly over the side-guard, knowing full well that he was mere inches from being ground into sausage.

"Damn it," MacKay muttered. He still held Kismet by the throat, but the grip was tentative, as if fearful that he might get pulled in along with his victim.

A small engine revved off to his right, obscured by the hovering darkness and he heard the carriage driver shout: "I'll cut him up."

Kismet reacted instantly, instinctively. He threw his weight to the left, rolling up and over the side-guard. He felt MacKay's grip tighten, but the big man was too slow by a fraction of a second. Kismet hung on the edge of the slanted steel guard, his mass pulling him one way and only the hand around his throat held him back from a fall.

Suddenly MacKay's grip grew impossibly strong and Kismet felt himself being pulled toward the machine. He struggled to find something to stop his plunge but MacKay's hold was irresistible.

FORTUNE FAVORS

Then he heard a scream. It lasted only a second before being drowned out by an even more terrible sound.

The chipper engine changed pitch as something entered the maw and the blades made contact. The stranglehold abruptly relented, and through the dark haze, Kismet caught a glimpse of the hand that had held him vanishing beneath the chipper's feeder roller. A spray of red erupted from the outflow chute and sprayed the pile of woodchips. The machine continued grinding a few seconds longer, and then returned to a quiet idle.

The man with chainsaw seemed paralyzed by the horror of what he had just witnessed. Kismet could only surmise that when he had made his desperate bid to escape, his captor had inadvertently been caught by the feeder wheel and pulled inside, but the phony carriage driver had witnessed everything. Kismet seized the opportunity and hurtled himself over the feeder chute, flattening the stunned man with two-footed kick. He pitched the chainsaw out of reach and then relieved the unconscious man of his pistol.

As the adrenaline surge began to recede, it was all he could do to keep from throwing up. He rocked back on his haunches with his head down, and tried to make sense of what had just happened. After a few seconds, he remembered that Higgins and Annie had probably been taken, but before his could even think about his next move, he heard a disembodied voice say: "Ian, report."

It took him few seconds to find the walkie-talkie; its now-deceased owner had stashed it next to a tree. Despite the fact that he had heard only two slightly distorted words, Kismet had no trouble identifying the speaker. He considered taunting Leeds, but then thought of a better use for the radio. He keyed the talk button and did his best to mimic MacKay's gravely brogue. "It's done."

8

ANNIE FELT STRANGELY DISAPPOINTED by Dr. Leeds' reaction to their decision. He had merely inclined his head, as if in surrender. "That is unfortunate." He gestured to the carriage. "The driver will convey you to whatever destination you desire."

And with that, the silver-haired occult expert had turned away. Elisabeth, who had remained just out of earshot, followed in his wake, but glanced over meaningfully over her shoulder. Annie didn't know what to make of that. She shook her head and turned to her father. "What now? Should we go back to the museum and tell Nick what happened?"

Higgins expression was unreadable. "He's probably already on his way to the hotel. We should get there as well."

Annie noted that her father had not answered the second part of her question. She climbed into the carriage with him, but before she could repeat her inquiry, another man got in as well. Judging by his athletic build and short haircut, Annie immediately pegged the man as someone with military experience, but it was the way he held the pistol that really gave it away.

He kept the gun was low so as to be inconspicuous to passersby, but the barrel did not waver in the man's grip; it was aimed at Annie's abdomen. The man's eyes however were locked on her father.

"Let's not make a fuss," the man said in a low voice.

FORTUNE FAVORS

The coach lurched into motion and by the time Annie was able to tear her eyes away from the gun, they were on the Transverse Road and heading east. Annie searched the faces of pedestrians walking along the roadside, hoping to spy a police officer, but their captor quickly divined her intent.

"Don't even think about it. I'd prefer not shoot you, but I will if I have to."

Annie swung her gaze back the man, matching his stare. "I think you're planning to kill us anyway. Why should we make it easy for you?"

The man regarded her for a moment, as if sorting through possible replies, but then just snarled, "Shut the hell up."

Higgins remained silent, but Annie knew her father was anything but paralyzed with fear. The former Gurkha had survived scrapes worse than this and she had no doubt he was just biding his time and waiting for the right opportunity to make his move.

They abruptly left the road and headed out across the manicured lawn at the edge of a large wooded area. There was no one around to witness the evident breach of park rules, no one to report the strange action to the authorities and perhaps summon help. After only about a minute, Annie saw a second carriage, waiting idle and evidently abandoned, on the edge of the woods. Their driver steered directly for the second coach and pulled up alongside it.

"Here's how this is going to work." The gunman gestured meaningfully with the gun, his eyes never leaving Higgins. "She's going to get out first. You stay put until I tell you to move. We're all alone out here, so I won't hesitate to pull the trigger if you try something. You might get the jump on me, but not before she goes down. Got it?"

"I hear you." Higgins voice was flat, betraying no emotion.

"Good." The man's gaze finally moved to Annie. "Now, out."

It was the moment she had been waiting for, the moment when the man's attention would have to leave Higgins. She felt certain that her father would act decisively as soon as she became the focus of their captor's scrutiny. She turned in the bench seat, confident that salvation was only a

135

heartbeat away, and extended her feet onto the step that extended from the underside of the carriage.

Higgins might have been planning something like what she imagined, but when salvation came, it wasn't at her father's instigation. There was a blur of motion in front of her as someone—*Kismet!*—darted out from behind the second carriage and leaped into theirs, pouncing on the gunman.

Despite the man's stated readiness to kill Annie, his reflexes were too slow. Kismet went for the gun hand first, thrusting it up and out of the way so that, when the man squeezed the trigger, the pistol discharged harmlessly into the canopy. With his free hand, Kismet punched directly at his opponents jaw, instantly rendering him unconscious.

Higgins was jolted into action. He pushed Annie back into her seat with one hand, while the other wrapped around the senseless gunman's fist to prevent him from pulling the trigger again. Before he could attempt to wrest control of the firearm however, everything went wrong.

Kismet's decisive attack had removed the immediate threat, but the element of surprise had been his only advantage, and that was spent. Before he could do or say anything, the driver reached down from his perch and grabbed Kismet by the shoulders. With a single mighty heave, he hauled Kismet through the opening in the canopy and pitched him out ahead of the carriage. The driver then thrust a stubby object through the aperture; Annie recognized it immediately as a sawed-off double-barrel shot gun. "Sit down," he snarled. "I don't have to even aim this to splatter you to both to Kingdom Come."

Higgins released his hold on the pistol and let the man's hand drop to the floor of the carriage. The driver kept the shotgun trained in their general direction, but half-turned forward and coaxed the horse into motion.

Kismet hit the ground hard. His wind was knocked from him and for a moment, he could only writhe in agony. The violent throw had left him disoriented, unable for a moment to tell which way was up, but as the turmoil in his inner ear subsided and the world stopped spinning, he realized that he was face to face with one of the coach's metal-shod wheels.

And then it started to move.

His brain immediately calculated that it would tread across his body, crushing him if he didn't get out of the way. That realization broke the barrier between thought and action. He threw himself sharply to the right, rolling underneath the wagon as it advanced. He reached up and wrapped his right arm around the axle of the rear wheel and was immediately dragged along as the carriage picked up speed.

Although the grass beneath him was relatively soft, the burn of friction quickly reached a feverish intensity. Kismet got his free hand around the axle and hugged it to his chest so that only his feet were in contact with the ground. His boots offered considerably more protection than the fabric of his cargo pants, but the tradeoff was the intense exertion of holding himself up. He struggled simply to remain there for a few seconds longer, gathering his energy for what he knew had to come next.

A glance forward, past the front axle and the flashing hooves, revealed that the driver was making for the Transverse Road. Kismet knew he had only a few seconds left before the discomfort of being scoured by grassy earth turned into something much less pleasant. He let go with his right hand and began probing the underside of the carriage for handholds. His fingers found a metal frame, part of the leaf-spring suspension, and as soon as his grip was secure, he unwrapped his left arm and shifted it to the frame as well.

His situation was only marginally better; he was now a few inches further away from the ground—nowhere near where he needed to be—and his arms were burning with the exertion. From his new position though, he was able to get a better idea of what to do next. Directly above him was a small step, designed to hold bags and other cargo. Gritting his teeth in anticipation, he slowly relaxed his arms, allowing his body to drag once more on the ground, in order to bring the step within reach.

Kismet was dimly aware that, as he made contact once more with the ground, the pistol stashed in his waistband was jarred loose and went skittering away, but he couldn't worry about that. He twisted around, taking the punishment on his knees, and managed to get his feet under him. He estimated that the carriage wasn't moving faster than about fifteen miles an hour—maybe less—considerably faster than a walking pace, but not beyond the realm of possibility for a flat out sprint. As soon as the soles of his boots made contact, he started running.

He needed only a few steps to gather his momentum, and for that brief time, he was actually running faster than the horse that pulled the carriage. Yet what he saw in that brief instant as he ran forced him to revise his strategy. He only caught a glimpse of the driver and the shotgun he held trained on the captives in the coach's front facing seat, but that was enough for him to realize that just climbing onto the step wasn't going to be good enough.

Kismet ducked down again before the driver could glance back and spy him. He needn't have worried; the man's attention was momentarily focused on making the transition from the grassy ground of the Ramble to the hard macadam of the Transverse Drive. He slowed the carriage to a crawl as he neared the concrete curb, and Kismet knew that once on the paved road, his ability to keep pace with the horse would quickly evaporate.

He had noted that the driver was sitting sideways on this elevated bench seat, turned to the right so that he could keep the shotgun trained on the passengers while maintaining a view of the road ahead. As the horse stepped down onto the pavement, Kismet dashed along the left side of the coach, in the driver's blind spot, and vaulted up onto the driver's perch.

There was a great deal of risk to his friends—a reflexive trigger squeeze would shred the father and daughter in the back seat, but Kismet was counting on the man to react by trying to bring the gun around to meet the new threat. He was half right.

As soon as the driver realized he had company, he did indeed start to turn, but before he could, Higgins pounced forward, grabbing the short barrel of the gun and thrusting it up into the overhead canopy. The gun thundered in the semi-enclosed space, and a load of double-ought buckshot tore through the fabric. Higgins' hand went instantly numb from the eruption and the gun barrel slipped from his grasp, but he did not let it slow him down. Even as Kismet drew back to deliver a cross-body punch, Higgins reached through the narrow opening and planted the heel of his left hand in the small of the driver's back. The blow, delivered at almost exactly the same instant that the front wheels of the carriage dropped down from the curb, pitched the man from his seat. He rebounded off the horse's hindquarters and bounced like a pinball from the rigging, before crashing onto the pavement. The carriage lurched twice as first the left front wheel and then the rear wheel were lifted a few inches off the pavement. The driverless horse continued out to the shoulder lane and veered to the right, heading east.

Kismet didn't look back. His attention was focused on gathering in the reins, which the driver had taken with him in his fall, in order to get control of the carriage. He clambered over the raised footboard and cautiously reached a foot down onto the rigging. With his left hand gripping the carriage, he extended his reach as far as possible and managed to snare the trailing strap. A few seconds later, he settled back onto the driver's seat and pulled back on the reins, bringing the coach to a halt.

He turned and peered into the passenger area. "Are you guys okay?"

"What?" Annie shouted, evidently deafened by the close proximity of the shotgun blast, but Higgins, who was cradling his right hand, just nodded.

Kismet took a deep breath and allowed his mind to process everything that had happened. About fifty yards behind them, the motionless form of the fallen driver was starting to attract the attention of motorists traveling through the park on the Transverse Road. They had to keep moving, but even as Kismet turned to relay this decision to his friends, he saw Annie brace herself against the backrest of her seat and then with both feet, shove the unconscious form of the man who had earlier held them at gunpoint out of the carriage. The gunman crashed unceremoniously onto the pavement, hidden from the view of traffic by the carriage itself. As soon as they moved, he too would become a spectacle, drawing more unwanted attention.

"Good riddance to bad rubbish," Annie shouted, still unable to gauge an appropriate volume level.

Kismet rolled his eyes at her impulsive action. They needed to abandon the conspicuous carriage and exit the park on foot. But before he could put this decision into words, he heard the hissing sound of a car slamming on its brakes and skidding to a halt beside them. It was a non-descript sedan, marked with a sticker identifying it as a rental car. It might have been just another curious rubbernecker, aghast at the sight of what appeared to be a dead body laying in the road, but somehow Kismet knew they weren't that lucky. The windows reflected the scenery, denying him a look at the occupants, but he didn't need to see inside to know that trouble had arrived.

"Leeds!" he rasped, as if the name was a curse. "Hang on!" He snapped the reins, urging the horse once more into motion even as the doors of the sedan popped open.

The car immediately began rolling forward again, but one of its passengers disembarked and began sprinting after the carriage on foot. Kismet glanced over his shoulder, saw that the runner was cut from the same cloth as the man that had been waiting with MacKay in the Ramble—*mercenaries*, he thought, unable to keep his face from contorting into a snarl—and then saw Higgins brusquely plant a foot in the man's face as the latter caught up to the coach. That dealt with the immediate threat, but the sedan represented a problem on a different order of magnitude. Kismet shook the reins again, shouting for the horse to move faster. Grudgingly, it did.

Speed alone, however, would not suffice to save them. Another backward glance showed the sedan charging forward, angling to pull alongside them. Kismet reacted immediately by swerving the carriage toward the center of the road. Traffic flowing the opposite direction was starting to back up, but as soon as Kismet saw a break in the stack, he cut the carriage across the lane. Leeds' driver did not hesitate to follow but the sedan was not quite as agile as the carriage and in the time it took him to force his way through the gap, the carriage picked up some momentum and stretched their lead by more than a hundred yards.

Still not enough, Kismet thought.

A tunnel loomed ahead. Although the crest of the hill through which it passed was shrouded in trees, Kismet recognized it as the East Drive crossing, part of the great park loop that was inaccessible from the Transverse Road. Or rather, inaccessible to automobiles.

Kismet hauled on the left rein, steering the horse onto the grassy embankment. The gentle slope passed through a scattering of trees, and then opened onto a sidewalk that ran parallel to the road. Behind him, Leeds' driver did not hesitate to follow. As the carriage completed its ascent, the sedan jumped the curb and started up the hill behind them.

Kismet got a brief glimpse of the sedan sloughing back and forth across the embankment as its tires tore up turf in an effort to find purchase, but then he turned his full attention to driving the carriage. He steered right, pulling into the bike lane on the right hand side of the road, and headed south.

Leeds' car crested the rise less than a minute later, a minute in which Kismet was able to coax the horse to a fast trot and put almost three hundred yards between them and their pursuer. But the horse was not bred or trained for speed and the bike lane was not exactly carriage friendly. Cyclists and skaters had to be shouted out of the way and most did not go without protest. Although the carriage was probably little more than a speck in the distance to Leeds and his men, the disruption left little question about which way Kismet and the others had gone.

"Bugger!" Higgins stuck his head through the opening. "There's two of 'em now. Looks like Leeds got himself an army."

Although he didn't doubt the former Gurkha's word, Kismet looked back to verify that a second sedan had climbed the embankment and joined the chase. Vehicle traffic on East Drive was one-way in the opposite direction, but that didn't seem to bother the drivers. Both cars pulled onto the bike lane and charged after the fleeing carriage.

"We've got to get off the road!" Kismet wasn't sure if he was shouting to inform his passengers, or to help him decide what to do next, but it was sound advice. Traffic and laws notwithstanding, Leeds' cars would be able to close in on them in a matter of seconds. The only way to outdistance their pursuers was to find an escape route where the cars could not follow. Unfortunately, that was easier said than done. Dense stands of trees lined either side of the road, denying passage not only to automobiles but also to the carriage, and Leeds' men were too close for them to abandon the horse-drawn vehicle and make a run for it.

The road ahead curved gently to the left and then in a few hundred feet arched back to the right. Just past that vertex of the curve, on the far side of the road, Kismet spied a break in the trees. "That might work," he muttered.

He cautiously steered the horse into oncoming traffic. Because the speed limit for cars on East Drive was only 25 mph, there was little risk of a collision, but the carriage nevertheless cut a swath of chaos across the road, with cars skidding to a halt, turning sideways or veering into the bike lane. Then, just that quickly, they were through.

Kismet slowed the horse to a walk and guided it toward the gap in the tree line, and then the forest enfolded them, falling like a curtain on the mayhem behind them.

The carriage emerged from the stand of trees at a point directly opposite the famed Alice in Wonderland statues on the edge of the Conservatory Water. Kismet turned the horse onto the footpath that ran along the edge of the reservoir, once again heading south. He glanced over his shoulder again, half-expecting to see one of the sedans emerge from the trees, and gave a relieved sigh when that did not happen.

Higgins clambered around the frame of the damaged canopy to join him. "I think we lost them. Now what?"

"No pun intended, but I don't think we're out of the woods yet. Leeds might just have the resources to watch every exit from the park. I'll breath easier when we're out of the park...hell, when we're out of the city."

Higgins nodded but said nothing more. Kismet followed to the trail south until it curved toward an intersection with a paved road—Terrace Drive, which exited the park and turned into East 72nd street. Kismet approached the road cautiously, but there was no sign of Leeds' sedans. He continued east to the junction with Fifth Avenue, and then halted just inside the park's boundaries. They left the carriage there, the gelding tethered to the wrought iron fence and in plain view, and trekked out to the main thoroughfare. Kismet allowed a few taxis to pass by before hailing one at random. As they got in, he told the driver their destination.

"Rockefeller Center."

The driver cocked his head sideways, probably wondering who would hire a cab to reach a destination that was within easy walking distance, but then dropped the flag and waited for his chance to pull into traffic. Higgins could just make out the distant shriek of sirens as police cars from all over the surrounding area closed in on the park.

"It's only a few blocks away," Kismet explained. "But it's always busy. We can get lost in the crowd until we figure out what to do next."

As expected, the ride was short. After Kismet paid the driver, he led his companions through the crowd of tourists milling in the artificial canyon between the glass and concrete towers where the corporate and media empires shaped the future of the world. They drew to a halt on the balcony overlooking an ice skating rink, but Higgins' gaze was drawn to an enormous statue—a gilded bronze figure in repose.

He hadn't exactly received a classical education in the Regiment, but Alexander Higgins recognized this image.

Kismet sank wearily onto a vacant bench. "Okay," he said finally. "Spill it. What in the hell happened back there?"

"They were waiting for us," Annie said quickly, almost too quickly.

"Yeah, I kind of figured that part out. It's the 'how' that's still a bit murky. They just abducted you off a crowded New York City sidewalk?"

Higgins felt his daughter's stare burning into him, but couldn't seem to tear his own gaze away from the statue. Prometheus, bringing fire to mankind. *Coincidence? Not bloody likely.*

"He said he just wanted to talk," she said, after a long pause. "He wanted us to work with him to find...well, you know. It all sounds a bit daft, really."

"Except he seems to think it's worth killing for." Kismet glanced at the still silent Higgins for a moment. "It's pretty obvious what Leeds is up to: divide and conquer. He must think I've told you something. The joke's on him, since right now, he knows just as much as I do."

Higgins nodded slowly, but Leeds' words echoed in his head. *How else would you explain your miraculous escape...?* He finally met Kismet's stare. "Right. We told him to bugger off. Of course, I hope you do know a bit more, or otherwise we might as well all just go home now."

A wry smile curled the corners of Kismet's mouth. "It's not so much what I know as what I think I know. Joseph King said that Fontaneda—Fortune, rather—'took the secret with him to the grave.' He used those specific words. I think that's a clue, and I think I know what it means." He briefly outlined what he had discovered in his Internet search for Joseph King. "Unfortunately, if Leeds is half as clever as I think he is, he'll pick up on this, too."

"So you're saying the clock is ticking," Annie ventured.

Kismet nodded.

Higgins brought his palms down on his thighs with a slap. "Then what are we sitting here for?"

He even managed to smile. But as he followed Kismet and Annie out of the crowded plaza and back toward the street, his mind was six thousand miles away...

And more than twenty years in the past.

FORTUNE FAVORS

INTERLUDE
DELIVERANCE

FORTUNE FAVORS

INTERLUDE

Nasiriyah, Iraq—January 1991

PAIN.

Higgins floated in and out of consciousness, but it was nearly impossible to distinguish the difference.

His chest was burning. *Ribs*, he thought in one of his brief lucid moments. *Separated, maybe broken.* A whimper escaped his lips, but even the breath drawn to replace that agonized exhalation cost him dearly, and he slipped once more into blackness.

Another blossom of torment brought him back, this time not just from his injured torso. His right arm felt like it had been stabbed through with shards of broken glass, and the pain intensified as the limb moved—was moved, without his intention or permission—and then his entire body was wracked with white hot fire.

Abruptly, he felt the ground fall away beneath him. His shoulders screamed as his weight fell against them. The pain in his wounded arm threatened to send him back into oblivion, but the need to gain even the smallest measure of relief anchored him to consciousness. Instinctively, he flexed his left arm, trying to ease some of the burden, but this merely served to further inflame his injured ribs.

Even screaming was unendurable.

"Wake up."

FORTUNE FAVORS

The command barely reached him, but the ability to comply or resist had long since been torn away.

Nevertheless, he tried to open his eyes. His right eyelid parted, only just, but his left did not so much as twitch.

Through the sliver-thin opening he, beheld the face of his tormentor only a few inches away. The olive-skinned man with jet-black hair wore a camouflage uniform, but Higgins couldn't make out any insignia or badges of rank.

Higgins lips moved but he made no utterance. He couldn't breathe.

He had been hung by his arms, stretched out so that, even absent the damage to his chest, the simple act of drawing a breath would have been exhausting. His toes scraped the floor beneath him, close enough to touch, but too far to permit him to gain purchase and relieve some of the strain.

His torturer glanced away and said something incomprehensible, another language, Arabic perhaps. A moment later, the bonds holding Higgins by the wrists shuddered as he dropped a few inches. The pain was transcendent, but he felt the floor grow solid against the balls of his feet. He pushed up, and managed a shallow inhalation.

"You are American?"

Higgins answered with a whimper.

"You are alone now. The man captured with you died while I was interrogating him." There was a long pause, perhaps to let the gravity of that simple declaration draw the captive deeper into despair. "But you can spare yourself that fate. He told me a great deal about your mission before he expired, and all I require now is confirmation.

"You are badly injured my friend. You need medical attention, and I will see that you get it. Our countries are at war, but we are civilized men, are we not? You will receive the best medical care we can provide. In a way, you are very fortunate. Our forces will soon scatter the carcasses of your countrymen on the sand as a feast for the birds, but you will live. You will be treated with respect, and one day, when your cowardly leader grovels in defeat, we may deign to return you to your home...to your loved ones.

"Or perhaps not. That is for you to decide. It is a decision you must make now."

Another whimper trickled from Higgins' lips.

The man spoke again in Arabic, and the ropes holding Higgins went slack, dropping him to his knees. Already at his threshold of endurance, Higgins savored the small measure of relief that followed.

"I believe it's customary to begin with your name and rank."

He grasped at the question like a lifeline, but the words that slipped from his mouth were garbled. His tongue was thick in his mouth; his lips were split and swollen from the beating he'd received when captured.

"Sergeant, is it? Not American, though. British, I should say." The man sneered contemptuously. "America's lap dog. Your countrymen would do well to abandon the sinking ship of your former colony. But we are soldiers, are we not? Sent off to fight and die at the whim of our imperial leaders."

Another pause.

"And why is it that the Americans sent you to die here tonight? Were you to reconnoiter our missile emplacements? Gauge our troop strength?"

"Don't know," Higgins mumbled.

That was the tragedy of it.

Like any other soldier, Higgins had long known of the possibility that an enemy might capture him, imprison and torture him. And as easy as it was to contemplate such eventualities from the safety of the barracks or over a pint with his mates, no man could know how they might respond when tested, what his personal breaking point might be.

But that was moot, right now. It was not within his power to answer or refuse to answer because he simply didn't know.

Random bits of information flashed in his head like the pieces of a shattered stained glass window. The American officer...Kismet...dead bodies, strewn about on the floor of a half-buried ruin...a car, erupting in flames...his fellow Gurkhas, ripped apart....*See you in the next life.*

"Don't...know."

The interrogators face drew into a frown, then he spoke in Arabic again.

FORTUNE FAVORS

Higgins felt the rope go taut and before he could draw a breath, his arms were wrenched upward again. There was a bright flash of pain, and then the darkness took him.

○

The pain was still there when he awoke again, but tolerable now. The strain on his shoulder was gone; he could even feel a throbbing in his fingertips as his circulation was restored.

"Don't know," he mumbled.

"It speaks." The voice was soft, reaching through the layers of his misery with a promise of comfort, a promise that he couldn't bring himself to trust. But there was something familiar there; it didn't sound like his tormentor.

"Lef...Kis...?" His good eye opened a crack and he glimpsed the face of the American with the improbable name. The man bore little resemblance to the lieutenant who had accompanied Higgins' squad on the nighttime infiltration. Kismet's combat uniform had been stripped away, and his face and shoulders were a mass of bruises and weeping abrasions.

"Yeah, it's me. Don't try to talk. And try not to scream."

A fresh wave of agony radiated from his right arm, but then almost immediately subsided into a dull ache.

Kismet spoke again. "I think I've set the bone, but hold still while I find something to splint it with."

Higgins eye opened a little wider and his surroundings gradually came into focus. He was lying supine on the floor of a featureless concrete room. An incandescent bulb hung overhead, the only source of light, but there was little for it to illuminate. He saw that he, like Kismet, had been stripped naked, and as this visual message filtered through his brain, he felt the rough floor against his skin.

Kismet moved into view again, and bent over Higgins, ministering to his broken arm. "I hope you feel better than you look, my friend."

"Said...dead..."

"You must mean Colonel Saeed. He told me you were dead, too." Kismet made a rough noise, and it took Higgins a moment to realize that it was a chuckle. "I'd say he was half right. For both of us."

"Where...?"

"He's gone. They're all gone." Kismet glanced around furtively. "I don't know what's going on. I searched the whole building...hell, the entire compound. There's no one here. It's like they abandoned it. This is probably some elaborate ploy, but what choice do we have?"

Higgins felt a throb of discomfort as Kismet wrapped a length of cloth around his right forearm, but nothing like the agony he'd earlier experienced.

"There," the American said. "That's best I can do with what I've got. Any other serious injuries I should know about?"

Higgins impulsively shook his head and immediately regretted it.

"That's what I thought," Kismet replied, commiserating. "Come on, let's get you on your feet."

Kismet's guarded enthusiasm was contagious. Tapping into a fresh vein of resolve, Higgins felt his strength returning and with only a little assistance from the American, was soon standing more or less on his own; Kismet kept a steadying hand on Higgins' left biceps.

Kismet stopped abruptly before they reached the exit. "Well I'll be damned. Look at that."

Higgins strained to focus his good eye, and followed Kismet's pointing finger to a tabletop just to the right of the door. Lying there, as casually as one might leave their coat draped over the back of a chair, were a pair of unsheathed *kukri* knives. Kismet scooped them up and pressed one into Higgins' left hand.

As his fingers curled around the carved wooden hilt, he felt a strange mix of emotions: pride, that he would have yet another chance to die as hundreds of Gurkhas before him had, with his blade in hand; weary resentment, at the fact that circumstance had denied him relief from his suffering, and instead conspired to place him once more in harm's way; and a singe grain of desperate hope. The blade was a symbol of all those things, but for practical purposes, it was next to useless. He couldn't hold it in his dominant hand,

and was nearly blind to boot... if fate brought them once more into contact with the enemy, it wouldn't be much of a fight.

But as Kismet had indicated, the building in which they had been held captive was abandoned. They found a storeroom that contained, among other things, uniforms with the red triangle insignia of the Republican Guard sewn on the shoulders.

With no little help from Kismet, Higgins donned a uniform and even managed to stuff his feet into a pair of unlaced boots. As a disguise, it wouldn't pass even the most cursory inspection, but he felt less vulnerable with his nakedness covered.

With Kismet leading the way, they ventured outside the building. Dawn had broken, but there was no activity whatsoever in close proximity to the structure. *Looks like something from a bleedin' Mad Max movie*, Higgins tried to say, but his cracked lips wouldn't form the words.

Kismet nevertheless seemed to understand. "Yeah, I don't like it either." Hefting the *kukri*, he turned slowly, scanning in every direction for some indication that their captors were waiting to spring a trap. If they were there, they were well hidden.

A dust-streaked Toyota Land Cruiser was parked nearby and the two men headed for it. Kismet opened the door for Higgins and offered a steadying hand as the latter slid into the passenger seat, and then circled around to the driver's side. The American searched all the usual places for a spare key, and finding none, shifted the transmission into neutral and popped the hood. He was away only a few moments before the engine turned over and rumbled to life.

"Handy trick," Higgins managed to say.

Kismet nodded as he slid into the driver's seat. He reached over the steering wheel and insinuated inserted the tip of his *kukri* into the gap between the wheel and the steering column. There was an audible click as the locking pin released, and the wheel moved in his hands. "Now we run the gauntlet."

Higgins nodded weakly. There was no way this was going to work, but then there was also no reason for the Republican Guard to have abandoned their compound. Events were now so far beyond his control, the only reasonable course of action was to keep moving toward whatever was going to happen.

But nothing did happen.

Kismet wandered through the walled enclosure until he found an open gate leading out onto a paved road. The guardhouse beside the gate appeared empty as well, but beyond that, there was at least some evidence that the world had not come to an end without them. Kismet swung the Land Cruiser out onto the road and headed south, away from the city.

Much of what followed was a blur for Higgins. Several hours and perhaps hundreds of miles slipped by in a pain-induced fugue. He awakened from time to time, mostly when Kismet stopped to top off the petrol from the spare cans mounted to the vehicle's bumper, but if anything more dramatic than that occurred, it escaped his notice.

In the years to come, Higgins would marvel at the miracle of their escape; it seemed like a religious mystery, something comforting that was meant to be accepted on faith, and which would only be diminished by too many questions.

It would be more than two decades before he would have reason to think about it differently.

PART THREE
GRAVE SECRETS

9

THE SUN WAS JUST STARTING TO BRUSH the tops of the trees that lined the west fence as Joe King finished his last pass with the big riding mower, and steered the machine onto the gravel path leading back for the shed. No sooner had he dismounted to throw open the wooden doors when the automated sprinklers activated and droplets of water began falling on the immaculate—and freshly cut—emerald green turf.

Just made it, he thought as he got back on the mower and coaxed it forward a few more feet, into its parking spot. It had been a busy day. His plan to get an early start on the north lawn had been derailed when, on his way out, he'd noticed some fresh graffiti—the third time in as many weeks. He'd spent the better part of the morning scouring paint off the weathered marble and picking up the litter—fast food wrappers and beer bottles—that had been left behind by the vandals. The first time it had happened, he had called the police, but aside from taking the report and suggesting that maybe some additional security measures were in order, the officer had been of little help. Joe understood. From their point of view, it must have seemed like a victimless crime. Indeed, aside from being put off his schedule a few hours, what harm had been done?

But it wasn't so much the fact of the vandalism that concerned Joe, as the tone and message of the graffiti: swastikas, triple-Ks, and a variety of slurs ranging from the old classics to some Joe had never heard before and only barely grasped.

What did you expect? He had thought to himself as he scrubbed the last bits of paint from a tombstone. *Keepin' one of the oldest cemeteries for black folks in the county. 'Course the rowdies are gonna make it all about color.*

In the end, he'd managed to get the north lawn cut before the sprinklers came on, and now the defaced graves were the furthest thing from his mind as he pulled the shed doors closed and shackled them with a padlock. He knew it had been a slow day up at the office—folks weren't, contrary to the old joke, dying to get in, at least not into a plot at the Ashley Rest Memorial Gardens, which suited Joe just fine—and that meant plenty of time for Candace to whip up one of her spectacular suppers. He quickened his pace, skirting along the edge of the stately manor that now served as the chapel, and aimed for the adjoining building, a small but adequate single story house that he and Candace called home.

That was when he saw the visitors.

At first, he thought nothing of it. In an age where people could look up their ancestors on the Internet, it wasn't unusual for folks to come by the house, asking for directions to the last resting place of a distant relation. But as he drew closer and got a better look at the pair standing on the porch, he felt a tingle of apprehension. A tall man with silver-white hair, dressed entirely in black, and a shapely, poised blonde woman.

White folks almost never came asking for directions.

As he got within earshot of the porch, he slowed to listen in on the exchange and heard the male visitor speaking.

"Good evening, ma'am." Joe thought the man sounded rather abrupt, rude even, but it might have owed to the fact that there wasn't the least trace of an accent in his voice. "I am looking for Mr. Joseph King."

Joe could just see the top of Candace's head, her wispy gray hair bobbing in the space between the two visitors. "Joe's my son," she answered. "Unless of course, you looking for Joe's granpappy, Mr. King senior. You'll find him out in the gardens, if you take my meaning."

"He's dead."

FORTUNE FAVORS

Joe felt a chill at the way the man said it, and lurched forward again, gathering his courage to shoo this pair away before they could cause any real trouble.

"That's right," Candace continued smoothly, with a confidence and courage borne of her years. "So if your business is with him, then I'd say you came about ten years too late. Now, if they's nothing else, I'll bid you kind folks good evenin'."

The tall man seemed to stiffen, and Joe saw him take a step forward. "Actually, ma'am. Maybe there's something you can help us with."

Joe broke into a sprint, bounding up the steps, but whatever demand he had been preparing died on his lips when he caught sight of the small automatic pistol the blonde woman now held pressed against Candace's abdomen.

The silver-haired man half turned to acknowledge him. "Ah, this must be the junior Mr. King. Perhaps you can help as well."

Joe drew up short and raised his hands in a gesture of supplication. "Don't want no trouble now, sir."

"Nor do I. I just have a few questions, and then I'll be on my way." The man offered an icy smile as he gestured for Joe to enter the house. "For your sake, I hope you know the answers."

"What do you want to know?"

Even as he asked the question, Joe realized the answer, but he still did his best to look surprised when the silver-haired man said simply: "Tell me everything you know about Hernando Fontaneda."

○

"Stop!"

Kismet immediately shifted his foot from the accelerator to the brake pedal, bringing the rented Ford Explorer to an abrupt but controlled stop. They had turned off the main road and onto a long graveled driveway only a few seconds earlier, so there wasn't much risk of causing a collision, but

Higgins' sudden command nevertheless filled him with apprehension. "What's wrong?"

Higgins, from the front passenger seat, pointed forward, down the length of the landscaped drive to a cluster of buildings dominated by an immaculate white antebellum manor house. "They're here already."

Kismet tried to sharpen his focus, scanning the foreground, perhaps a quarter of a mile distant. A silver sedan was parked in front of the manor—nothing too suspicious about that. Then he caught a glimpse of motion...a flash of golden hair, illuminated by the porch light, disappearing into the doorway of a smaller structure, just as old as the manor house but considerably less elegant, extending out from it like an architectural postscript.

Annie leaned over his shoulder, curious about the unexpected stop, and saw it too. "That bitch," she snarled.

It was an opinion Kismet shared. He eased off the brake and guided the SUV off the road surface, then turned to his companions. "So, how do we play this?"

Higgins didn't answer, but instead got out and circled around to open the Explorer's rear hatch. A moment later, Kismet saw him peering through the scope affixed to a long, matte black bolt action rifle. The business end of the gun was pointed at the porch of the distant house.

"They're inside," Higgins announced after a few seconds, lowering the gun. The Kimber Model 8400 Advanced Tactical rifle, equipped with a Trijicon AccuPoint 2.5-10X56 30 millimeter scope, was the former Gurkha's favorite new toy.

"Why don't you go conduct a little recce?" Higgins answered at length. "See what our friends are up to. We can cover you from here."

"We?" Annie protested.

Higgins patted the polymer stock of the rifle. "Wasn't talking about you, Annie girl."

Kismet suppressed a laugh, but then addressed the young woman in a more serious tone. "Actually, I think I should go alone. Your father will watch my back, and you can watch his."

FORTUNE FAVORS

Annie frowned, but nodded, grasping the tactical rationale behind the decision.

Kismet slid out of the Ford to retrieve his own combat gear—a MOLLE compatible shoulder holster rig which he'd adapted to hold his *kukri* sheath on the side opposite his Glock. He slipped the nylon web straps around his shoulders, checking one last time that everything was secure, and then covered it all up with a loose leather bomber jacket. He tossed a nod to the others, and then set off down the drive toward the house.

He didn't know what sort of resources Leeds had at his disposal, but judging by the reception committee the occult scholar had arranged in Central Park, he thought it best to stay below the radar. It seemed well within Leeds' ability to monitor the airports, so instead of a ninety minute flight he opted for the twelve-odd hour long overland route.

Despite the need for urgency, Kismet wasn't going to let Leeds take him off guard again, so before leaving New York in the rented Ford, he had taken Higgins and Annie on a little shopping spree. He'd grimaced a little at the price tag of Higgins' weapon of choice; even more costly had been the time spent finding a shooting range where the rifle could be properly zeroed.

"You have to let me zero it," Higgins had persisted. "Otherwise, what's the point of buying it?"

Kismet had wondered that very thing when the initial purchase was made, but he was pleased that Higgins seemed to finally be treating Leeds as a real threat. There had been more than a few times when he'd wondered where Higgins' loyalties lay. He still didn't know what to make of Higgins' reaction to the statue of Prometheus at Rockefeller Plaza.

In all the time since that fateful night in Iraq, the one thing Kismet never had cause to question, was the role of the soldiers who had accompanied him. He had always just assumed them to be unwitting pawns in someone else's game, but Higgins' reappearance, so close to a trove of priceless artifacts...so close to what might be a connection to the secret of immortality itself...made him question all his assumptions.

His choice of Rockefeller Plaza as a rallying point had been deliberate.

161

In the early days of his quest to unmask the Prometheus conspiracy, he had quite naturally wound up there, staring at Paul Manship's gilded bronze statue of the mythic Titan delivering his gift of fire to mankind, wondering if this place...this confluence of corporate power, the home of not one, but several television networks and twenty-four hour news agencies...might not be some kind of beacon for his newfound foe. Perhaps even their headquarters.

His investigations had yielded nothing, and not just at Rockefeller Center, but he had become quite familiar with the place, and had even started to think of the balcony over the ice rink as a sort of sanctuary.

He hadn't failed to notice Higgins staring at the statue of Prometheus, but the old soldier's reaction had been impossible to gauge. There was a look of recognition to be sure, but no different than what could be seen in the goggle-eyed gaze of hundreds, perhaps thousands of first time visitors. Prometheus wasn't exactly the Statue of Liberty, but it wasn't unreasonable to think that Higgins might have heard about it. What he didn't question was the look of delight in the soldier's eyes when he'd picked up the Kimber rifle.

Kismet reached the front porch of the house a few seconds later, but instead of climbing the steps, he crept around its perimeter to see if there was a back entrance that would permit him to go in unnoticed. As he ducked under the broad picture window at the front of the house, he could hear loud voices from within.

"Liar!" raged the occultist. "Fontaneda told your father, and your father told you. I know he did. Now you tell me, or I will cut your heart out."

The threat was palpably real, even through the double-paned insulated window. It occurred to Kismet that, in all his encounters with Leeds, he had never witnessed the man losing his temper.

"Please sir," came the hoarse reply, barely audible. "He didn't tell us anything."

Kismet paused a beat. Had it been a woman's voice? He started forward again, rounding the corner, and spied a back door to the house. He tried the knob; locked.

FORTUNE FAVORS

With a dismayed frown, he stole back to the front of the house. As he ducked under the window, he heard Leeds threaten again. "Do you love your son? If you don't tell me about Fontaneda, I'll cut his throat."

"Please," begged the weak voice. Leeds had used the word 'father'...was this Joseph King's daughter? "Please. I've told you what I know. There's nothing else."

Kismet could sense that something terrible was about to occur inside. He crept onto the porch and touched the knob, turning the handle slowly so as not to betray himself with the click of the latch mechanism. Pistol in hand, he pushed open the door.

There was a short vestibule just beyond the door, and past that a right turn into the sitting room. Kismet could plainly see four figures. He immediately recognized Leeds and Elisabeth, even though their backs were turned. The blonde actress stood with a gun pressed against the temple of a young African American man, while the silver haired occult scholar menaced an older woman, presumably the young man's mother...and evidently, Joseph King's daughter. Something glinted in Leeds' hand...a blade of some kind, a straight razor or a scalpel.

With a disdainful grunt, Leeds thrust the old woman away and wheeled on Elisabeth's hostage. The blade came up in a glittering arc and then held there, poised above the young man's neck like the Sword of Damocles.

Kismet threw caution to the wind and charged forward, brandishing his pistol. "Back off, Leeds!"

Elisabeth gasped in surprise, but recovered with unexpected speed. She brought her own pistol around, aimed at Kismet's chest, and in the same fluid motion, stepped between him and Dr. Leeds, placing herself directly in his sights, and at the same time, spoiling his shot at the occultist.

Leeds seemed not to have notice the intrusion. There was a strange hunger in his eyes as he stared down at the captive, contemplating him like the victim in some bloody ritual sacrifice. In a rush of understanding, Kismet realized that was exactly what the young man was about to become. This wasn't about torture or coercion any more.

He tightened his finger on the trigger, felt it start to move. He could see the hesitation in Elisabeth's eyes. She wasn't going to shoot, not intentionally at least, but she wasn't going to move either. "If you think I won't shoot you—"

Before he could finish the threat, Leeds' blade hand began its final, horrible descent.

As soon as Kismet started down the drive, Annie and her father picked up and began moving as well. They didn't approach the house; it was only about four hundred meters, and with Higgins' scope and the pair of spotter's binoculars Annie had grabbed from the back of the Ford, they didn't need to be any closer to see what was going on. They just needed a better line of sight. They hiked across the road and out across the manicured cemetery lawn, careful not to trip on any of the low headstones—or step on any graves—and took a position facing the large front window of the house they'd seen Elisabeth Neuell enter.

Annie did a quick three-hundred-sixty degree scan, to ensure that none of Leeds' hirelings were creeping up behind them, then turned back to the house and peered through the binoculars. The window was partly obscured by slat blinds, but when she moved her head sideways, ever so slightly, she found that she could see right through them.

She easily picked out the familiar figure of Elisabeth Neuell. Annie's breath caught in her throat as she realized that the actress was holding a gun to someone's head. The rest of the tableau resolved quickly. Dr. Leeds, tall and silver-haired, was menacing another captive…an old woman.

"Bollocks. Dad, they're—"

"I see it," Higgins cut her off. His voice was taut, and in the silence that followed, she could hear his breathing, deep and steady, just the way he'd taught her. Take a breath, let it out, find your target, take a breath, let it out…

FORTUNE FAVORS

She braced herself in anticipation of the shot, but it didn't happen. Her father continued to breathe rhythmically, his right eye glued to the scope. In the interminable silence, Annie realized why he hadn't yet pulled the trigger. He had been a soldier, a steely-eyed killer, but was he that person any more? Could he kill this way—not some enemy soldier on a foreign battlefield, but someone he knew?

She forced herself to do another quick sweep of their surroundings—still no sign of anyone else in the cemetery—then peered through the binoculars again.

Something had changed.

Elisabeth was now pointing her gun toward some unseen target...Kismet! And Dr. Leeds was now standing over her former hostage, his upraised hand gripping a blade.

"My God! He's going to cut him, Dad!"

The hand with the knife started to descend.

Higgins let out a breath...

And squeezed the trigger.

10

THERE WAS A LOUD CRACK as something punched through the window.

Just over Elisabeth's shoulder, Kismet saw Leeds' hand explode in a spray of red flesh and broken steel. Bits of the blade flew across the room, embedding in the wall in the same instant that the sound of the shot buffeted the fractured window pane.

Dr. Leeds stared down at the ravaged flesh where his right hand had been, a look of amazed detachment on his face. The bullet had blasted through the small bones of his hand, virtually severing the appendage through the middle of his palm. His fingers dangled uselessly from the bloody ribbons of flesh that had survived the trajectory of the thirty-caliber slug.

Elisabeth held her stance, blocking Kismet's way, but looked back at her associate in mute horror, unsure of what to do.

Leeds just stood there for a moment, dumbfounded. Then, he began to laugh.

Kismet bolted forward, ducking under Elisabeth's gun barrel, and snared her wrist, twisting it until the pistol fell from her nerveless fingers. She gave a yelp, then wrenched free of his grip, fleeing to take refuge behind the wounded occultist. Leeds continued laughing, seemingly oblivious to the pain.

FORTUNE FAVORS

Kismet advanced, holding the Glock trained on his adversary, but before he could close the distance, the occultist brought something from his pocket. Kismet pulled the trigger, but Leeds was already moving, and as the bullet flew harmlessly past his head, he hurled the object—a glass ampoule filled with some kind of gray powder—to the floor.

Brilliant white fire exploded in the center of the room, blinding Kismet momentarily. He triggered the pistol again into the expanding miasma of black smoke, then checked his fire; there were at least two people in this house he didn't want to kill, and blinded by the flash and smoke, there was no way to tell the difference.

Holstering the pistol, he plunged forward to where he thought the young man was. His ears were ringing from the discharge of the pistol and the detonation of Leeds' flash grenade, but he could hear shouting, the voice of the young man, calling out a name.

"Candace!"

"I'm here."

As the fumes cleared, he saw the two now-freed captives huddled in front of a sofa, but there was no sign of Elisabeth or Leeds, save for a trail of blood leading outside. He knelt in front of them, and for just an instant, flashed back to a night more than twenty years earlier, when he had attempted to offer comfort to victims of violence. This time at least, he'd been able to do more than just ease their passage.

"It's okay," he said in his most soothing tone. "I'm here to help."

"What do you want?" demanded the young man, his eyes fixed on the Glock in its holster, visible beneath Kismet's open jacket. He didn't sound nearly as distraught as Kismet would have expected.

"Well, I guess I want the same thing that other guy did," he answered honestly, leaning back in an effort to hide the gun from view and look a little less intrusive. "But I'm not going to threaten you to get it."

"Figures," was the disdainful reply.

"Joe!" This sharp interjection came from the old woman. "You mind your manners, now. This man just came to our rescue. The least we can do is hear him out."

Joe didn't seem terribly impressed with the old woman's exhortations. "Don't take that tone." He seemed poised to continue in that vein, but a noise in the vestibule instantly silenced him.

Kismet drew his pistol and spun on his heel, but before he could take aim, Higgins and Annie stepped into view. He eased the gun back into its sheath and glanced back at the householders. "It's okay. They're with me."

The young man—Joe—gave a snort.

The old woman spoke again, with the same reproving tone. "Joe. These folks helped us."

Kismet turned to Higgins. "Leeds?"

"Gone," Annie announced with some satisfaction. "They made it to their car and took off out of here like they were on fire."

Kismet shook his head ruefully as he turned again to the pair—mother and son, if he'd overheard correctly. "He'll be back."

Joe stood, raising the woman to her feet, and then sagged onto the sofa. "All right. Just who in the hell are you, anyway?"

Kismet paused a beat. Given the violence that had just occurred, the man's distrust was warranted, and unless he did something to change the mood, it was unlikely that he'd get any kind of meaningful cooperation. *Start at the beginning*, he thought.

He looked intently at each of them in turn. "Joe, right? And Candace? I'm Nick Kismet. I work for a United Nations cultural agency. Several years ago, a man named Henry Fortune contacted my agency about...an unusual discovery." He thought he detected just a hint of a reaction, but whether it was to the mention of Fortune's name or the 'discovery,' he couldn't say.

"When we attempted to follow up on it, we got another letter from a Joseph King." He gestured toward Candace. "That would be your father?"

She nodded slowly.

"Mr. King indicated that Fortune had died, and that seemed to be the end of it."

"Henry Fortune died in the 1960's," the woman said. "You're chasing after something that happened fifty years ago?"

FORTUNE FAVORS

"Some new information has come up." Kismet scrutinized the woman's face. "Did you know him?"

"I remember Henry," she said, her tone not quite wistful. She exchanged a knowing look with the young man, almost as if asking permission to elaborate.

Kismet thought he was gaining a measure of trust, and decided to give them a moment. He turned to Higgins. "Al, why don't you try to establish some kind of secure perimeter?"

The former Gurkha seemed to understand what Kismet was really asking, and beckoned his daughter to follow him back outside. "Come on, Annie girl. Let's go keep an eye out for unwanted visitors."

When they had left, Kismet eased into an adjacent chair and turned to the old woman. "The man that assaulted you wants Fortune's discovery. You've already seen what he's willing to do to find it. Whether or not you actually know anything doesn't matter to him right now; you're in danger. You need to leave here. At the very least, you should call the police."

Calling the police ought to have been their first reaction as soon as they had ascertained that the danger was past, and yet strangely, the pair hadn't shown the slightest inclination to do that.

Joe glanced at the wall. The spatter of blood and metal fragments was the only real evidence that the whole thing hadn't been just a bad dream. "Ain't callin' the police," he said quietly after a moment. "Call them, an' then we'd have to answer questions that I ain't inclined to answer."

He turned back to Kismet. "You saved us. I suppose that counts for something. So let's just cut to the chase. We know what you're lookin' for."

Candace gasped apprehensively. "Joe, you sure about this?"

The young man nodded. "It's been a secret too long. Is it Henry Fortune you're looking for? Or the Fountain of Youth?"

Elisabeth sucked greedily at the cigarette, holding the nicotine-laced smoke in her lungs for several seconds before exhaling out the open car window. The breeze of their passage down the Savannah Highway snatched the fumes away, but a lingering trace of the odor permeated the car. During their time together, Leeds had forbade her from smoking in his presence, but right now she didn't give a damn what he thought, and besides, he seemed to have other things on his mind.

She'd only gotten a brief glimpse of the wound in the moments following their escape from the cemetery. Leeds had quickly wrapped his injured hand in a now thoroughly blood-soaked cloth, but she'd seen enough to know that the pain must have been debilitating. The unseen sniper's bullet had torn off half his hand. Nevertheless, Leeds had calmly led her from the smoke filled house and back to their rented sedan where he'd gotten in the passenger's side and instructed her to drive, supplying her with a destination as soon as they were outside the cemetery gates.. Except for the telltale beads of perspiration on his brow, Leeds seemed completely indifferent to the experience.

Maybe not completely indifferent, she thought. *He's not bitching about me smoking.*

She tossed the cigarette butt out the window and took the exit Leeds had earlier indicated. As she negotiated the main streets, he spoke again, guiding her through turns and into a residential neighborhood like some kind of living GPS device.

"Stop here," Leeds announced after directing her to turn into a typically nondescript suburban cul-de-sac.

Elisabeth eased the sedan to the curb and Leeds promptly got out, protectively cradling his injured right hand, but otherwise moving with his usual self-assuredness. She hastened after him, catching him just as he turned up a concrete path to the front door of a rambling ranch-style home that had seen better days. Without preamble, Leeds stabbed a finger at the doorbell, then impatiently rapped the knuckles of his left hand against the doorframe.

A dog began barking from somewhere inside the house, followed by gruff commands from its owner. The door swung open a moment later to reveal a stocky middle-aged man who studied them carefully through the screen-door—Elisabeth noted that his gaze lingered appreciatively on her—before speaking. "Can I help you folks?"

"I am Dr. John Leeds." There was, at last, the barest hint of discomfort, or perhaps it was urgency, in his tone. "This is Elisabeth. I have been told that you are a physician. I have been injured..." He held up his right hand, and the movement caused a fat drop of blood to spatter on the concrete at his feet. "I require medical attention."

The man's eyes widened. "Well, goddamn...Why did you come here? You should get to the emergency room!"

Leeds pitched his voice low. "This is a bullet wound. I cannot seek treatment through the normal channels. I was assured that you could help me...Dr. Ayak."

The man went instantly pale. For a moment, he appeared unable to do anything but stare at them, but then he furtively opened the screen and stepped out, pulling both doors shut behind him. When he spoke again, it was in a low hiss. "Now what the devil are you playing at, here? You folks reporters?"

For the first time since she'd been with him, Elisabeth saw Leeds taken aback. "I—we are not."

"Read about 'Ayak' on the Internet, did you?"

Elisabeth couldn't tell if the man was taunting them, or making a sincere inquiry.

Leeds inclined his head. "It would appear that I was misinformed. I apologize for disturbing you."

The man snaked a hand out abruptly and snared Leeds' shoulder before he could turn. He held the occultist, staring into his eyes for a moment, and then seemed to reach a conclusion.

"We don't use that secret language bullshit no more. It's the goddamned twenty-first century, you know." He gave a weary sigh, and then beckoned them to enter the house. "Unless that's cherry pie filling you're dripping on the ground, it's plain to see you're hurt. Come on in and I'll have a look."

As they followed him inside, the man called out, "Louise, there's some folks come to speak with me in private. Why don't you go watch the 'Wheel' in your bedroom."

There was a sound of movement from somewhere in the house, and an abrupt silence when a television set was switched off, but the man said nothing more as he led his guests through a formal dining room, and into a neatly arranged kitchen.

"Put your hand over the sink, and let's see what bit you."

Leeds complied, and gingerly began unwrapping the cloth. Elisabeth gasped involuntarily as she saw the ragged wound—raw red, speckled with grisly bits of yellow and white, surrounded by swollen purple skin. It looked as though his hand had been nearly amputated, just above the palm. His fingers flopped uselessly across the back of his hand, one of them still adorned with the gaudy Ouroboros ring.

Their host also looked a little shaken by what was revealed. He shook his head. "There's not a lot I can do for you. You don't go to the hospital, and those fingers are as good as gone. Not even sure they can save 'em for you."

"Then I have no further use for them," Leeds replied, his earlier dispassion once more in evidence. "'If thine hand offends thee, cut it off.'"

The man gave a disbelieving chuckle. "Well. You're a God-fearing man, then. Let me get my bag."

As the man headed for the exit, Leeds called out to him. "Time is of the essence, doctor. Before you proceed, I must ask that you put me in contact with the Circle."

The doctor froze in mid-step, and turned around, his face twisted with the same suspicion that had originally greeted them. "Mister, I don't know who you think I am—"

"You are part of an ancient and honored rite of brotherhood, a circle of men who stand in defense of the Invisible Empire. As am I. In the name of our shared bond, I call upon you in my hour of need."

Elisabeth thought Leeds' pronouncement sounded rehearsed, but then she felt that way about him most of the time. As an actor, she had an ear for such things, and to her, Leeds seemed always to be playing from some carefully prepared script. Yet, as she listened to what he was saying, the full impact of his words hit home.

The Circle…oh, God, what have I gotten into?

"Mister…what did you say your name was?"

"Dr. John Leeds."

"Dr. Leeds, then. You obviously know a thing or two about me, and in the name of whatever it is you think we share, I'm gonna do what I can to fix up your hand. But let me set you straight about something. Any 'brotherhood' I might belong to? That's got nothing to do with ancient rites or any of that mumbo jumbo. I wear the sheet—yes, I'll admit it—but only because I'm not about to stand idly by while the country I love is being taken over by a bunch of Jews and niggers and spics."

Elisabeth winced visibly at the slurs, and immediately felt a flush of fear at having betrayed herself with the reaction.

Leeds again seemed uncharacteristically rattled by this development, but quickly recovered his composure. "It just so happens that a particular nigger is responsible for my injuries. I was hoping that you and your brothers could help me with…a little payback?"

The man stared back through narrowed eyes. "Mister…excuse me, *Doctor*, this here's the twenty-first century. We don't do that lynch mob shit no more. We can't afford to, if you take my meaning." He paused and took a breath. "However, I may know a few good ol' boys who aren't as, shall we say, scrupulous? They don't care nothing about rites or ancient mystic brotherhoods neither, but for the right price, I reckon they'd do most anything you want."

Leeds gripped the man's forearm with his good hand. "Make the call."

Joe stood up and crossed to what looked at first glance like a side table. He removed the various decorative accouterments, and Kismet saw that the table was actually an old steamer trunk. Joe unlocked it and threw back the lid to reveal several stacks of leather bound books.

"Here," Joe said without looking at Kismet. "Is everything we know about Hernando Fontaneda."

It had not escaped Kismet's notice that Joe had been consistently using the Spanish form of the name. He rose from his chair and went to stand beside the young man.

"These are Fontaneda's diaries."

The volumes might have been from a museum exhibit on the history of bookbinding. Those in the stack on the far left looked rough, hand sewn, while those on the right appeared to have been fashioned using modern—or at least twentieth century—techniques. Kismet gently picked up a book from the left hand stack and opened it.

The old binding creaked in his hands. The thin vellum pages were brittle and the ink had gone blurry in places. There was no question that the book was hundreds of years old, but if he needed any further evidence of that, he found it on the first page; a date:

Anno Domini 14, Junio 1645

The book was written entirely in Castilian Spanish, a language that normally would have posed little difficulty for Kismet. The script however was elaborate and spidery, and like so many writings of that era, the text was rife with grammatical errors and inconsistent spelling. The prose was rambling and disjointed, as if the author had been having trouble keeping the sequence of events straight. Nevertheless, it took only a few minutes of reading for him to begin painting a picture of the life of Hernando Fontaneda and his four hundred and fifty year old secret.

In the year 1549, the ship carrying young Hernando De Escalante Fontaneda wrecked on the Florida coast. The survivors were captured by Indians who proceeded to sacrifice them all, except for Fontaneda, who somehow learned enough of their language to be useful. During the seventeen years that followed, he learned several native dialects and served as a translator for the Calusa king, Carlos.

Kismet was already familiar with much of the story; Fontaneda's memoir of his captivity was a matter of public record. But the book he now read contained a slightly different recollection of those events.

During his time with the Calusa, Fontaneda heard many rumors of a magical pool capable of healing grievous injuries and extending life indefinitely—the very thing he claimed had brought Ponce de Leon to the Florida peninsula. But the pool…the Fountain…was far from Carlos' territory. Fontaneda, a slave and prisoner, had no opportunity to ascertain its location, but he never stopped thinking about it. He even wrote about it in his memoirs, calling it the "River Jordan" and claiming he had never found it. He had even spoken mockingly of the many natives who had believed the legend over the years. 'So earnestly did they engage in the pursuit, that there remained not a river nor a brook in all Florida, not even lakes and ponds, in which they did not bathe; and to this day they persist in seeking that water, and never are satisfied."

The claim, written for publication in Spain, was disingenuous. It was true that Fontaneda hadn't actually found it, but he knew exactly where it was.

Risking the last of his inheritance, he set out once more for the New World, and this time, he brought with him a small army, mercenaries all—outcasts and fugitives, *conversos* and Moriscos fleeing the persecution of the Inquisition, freed Negroes desperate to make their own fortune and avoid being returned to a life of servitude. The expedition debarked at Saint Augustine sometime around the turn of the 17th century. Fontaneda would have been about seventy-five, far too old to be tramping around the fetid swamps and jungles of the Florida peninsula, especially at a time when surviving to fifty years was an accomplishment.

At first, the expedition traveled through lands inhabited by peoples known to Fontaneda, and whose languages he spoke. But the Spaniard had not come seeking peaceful relations. His forces attacked the village where Carlos' hoard was kept, and they took the treasure with them as they continued on, intent on finding an even greater prize.

For several days, as they traveled deeper into the interior, the surviving Calusa harried them but after a while, the Indians turned back, content to let the wilderness finish what they had begun. Some of Fontaneda's men fell prey to wild beasts—panthers, alligators and poisonous snakes. On more than one occasion, the voyagers would awaken to discover some of their number missing, carried away in the night by unseen attackers. Later on, they would find the headless corpses of their comrades, a warning to the survivors.

A warning that went unheeded.

Eight days after the massacre of the Calusa village, their party now reduced by half, they discovered a village of natives living near the shore of a great lake. In the middle of their village, bubbling up from the ground, was a spring of water. The purity of the water and the abundance of healthy plant and domestic animal life, as well as the vigor of the villagers bespoke a single truth; they had found the Fountain.

Yet this spring was clearly not the source. Its potency was diluted; its power nothing like that of which they had heard. The villagers still grew old and died. Fontaneda knew they must continue their search. They entered the village, and demanded to know the source of the waters. When the natives were not forthcoming, the Spaniards slaughtered them and took to living in the village. Soon after, they located a cave entrance in a place revered by the slain villagers, and Fontaneda led the expedition into the dark entrance. The cavern was holy ground for the natives; no human had entered its depths in centuries. Not far inside the cavern, they discovered a miraculous chamber, where fire danced upon the surface of a shimmering pool. The merest taste of the water from the pool invigorated Fontaneda magically stripping away the years and healing his wounds.

Natives who had survived the village massacre fled into the forest, spreading the news of the Spanish atrocities. Ancient tribal feuds were forgotten in the face of the new threat, and several tribes combined their forces to make war with Fontaneda's army, most of whom died when the attack finally came. Fontaneda and six other survivors fled back into the cavern.

FORTUNE FAVORS

They fortified their position, setting up traps to protect themselves, although none of the natives dared enter the sacred cavern. After a long period of time, they decided to venture from their refuge, only to discover that the village had been burned to the ground, and overtaken by an unnaturally dense thicket of foliage. A few of the survivors claimed that the ill fortune of the expedition was evidence of God's judgment upon them; they were being punished for partaking in such an unholy quest. Had they not been warned, before ever embarking on their endeavor, that the search for life eternal apart from Christianity, was the search for the profane; the will of the Devil, not the will of God? Now, they knew it was true.

The discovery of the Fountain had indeed given them youth and virility, but at great cost. The restoration was useless as long as they were imprisoned in a foreign wilderness. Moreover, many that had drunk of the Fountain's water had perished. The Fountain had not proved to be the source of life eternal for them, but had instead caused death, and quite possibly, damnation.

The decision was finally made; they would return to the shore of the ocean and wait there for ships from the island colonies to arrive. Upon returning to civilization, they would confess their crimes, and remain silent before all others concerning the profane Fountain.

They attempted to reach the coast, but were attacked several times, and forced to retreat once more to the fortified cavern. In the end, only Fontaneda and two comrades, all of them badly wounded, reached the safety of the Fountain chamber. The sparkling waters were a constant temptation; they had only to drink of the unholy water and be healed. His companions held out, refusing the easy path of sin. Hernando however vacillated. Drinking from the Fountain, he immediately felt his body restored to health. His comrades died, cursing his weakness.

For untold years Fontaneda lived alone, at times lapsing into madness because of the virility burning with no outlet, inside him. His magically begotten youth would fail him from time to time, blessing him with long spans of lucidity, but in his weakness he would always return to the cavern, and the restorative waters of the Fountain.

As the Spanish increased their presence in the New World, Fontaneda gained the courage to return to his countrymen. The presence of fellow humans gave him an outlet to his carnal frustration, and his first return was blessed with over a decade of normal existence, married and living as he was accustomed thanks to King Carlos' treasure stash, but never revealing who he really was, or the secret of the Fountain.

It was at this point that Fontaneda's account ceased to be a reminiscence of days past, and instead became a day to day record of his life. Kismet, lost in the story, began skimming the sometimes brief entries and soon reached the point in the tale where Fontaneda had made his drunken boast to the colonial governor. The account was not quite verbatim with what he had read in the letter, but sufficiently close to convince Kismet that the author of the diary was the same man that Andrés Rodríguez de Villegas had written of.

Hernando Fontaneda born sometime around 1535, was still alive—still robust and vital—a hundred years later.

Kismet weighed this assertion carefully. He didn't doubt that he was reading a contemporary account, written by someone living in the mid-seventeenth century. But it didn't necessarily follow that the account was the whole truth. Fontaneda...or Fortunato...might have been a con man, just like many of the alchemists and mystics that roamed Europe, claiming to be immortal. Where was his proof?

He went back to reading, curious to see what Fontaneda had done next. Not surprisingly, after fleeing Saint Augustine, he returned once more to his refuge in the cavern where he had found the Fountain of Youth.

From that point forward, through the end of the volume, the entries were nothing more than the meandering thoughts of a fugitive living in self-imposed exile. Kismet closed the book and reached for another, but then hesitated. It would take weeks to read through them all. He needed to get this collection away, find somewhere safe, away from Leeds' relentless machinations. Unless...

Kismet turned to his hosts. "You've read these?"

Joe shrugged noncommittally.

FORTUNE FAVORS

"You said you knew about the Fountain," Kismet pressed.

"He told us about it," Candace volunteered. "I mean, back before he..."

She trailed off, but her meaning was clear. Fontaneda, the man who had later reinvented himself as Henry Fortune, had told Candace and her father, Joseph King, about the Fountain. Why he had chosen to unburden himself remained as much a mystery as his death, and Kismet was burning with curiosity about both of those questions. There was something more to all of this, something he was missing, but it seemed unlikely that he would get answers from this pair. "Did he tell you where to find it? Is that information here?"

His hosts exchanged a meaningful glance, and then Joe spoke again. "No. But there is a map."

Kismet felt a thrill of anticipation, coupled with frustration at the young man's evasiveness. "Where is this map?"

Joe smiled cryptically. "Like that letter said, he took his secret to the grave."

"The map is buried with him? In his coffin?"

"Well it ain't quite that simple—"

Before he could complete the thought, Annie burst into the room, visibly alarmed. "Someone's coming!"

11

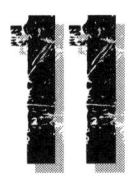

KISMET GESTURED FOR THE OTHERS to get down and then moved to the side of the big window and peered through the blinds. Headlights were visible, at least three different vehicles, rolling up the drive toward the house. If it had been only one car, he might have been inclined to disregard its significance; someone visiting the grave of a loved one perhaps, or coming to make arrangements for a funeral. Three vehicles though...definitely not a coincidence.

"Annie, get your dad back in here." He turned to Joe and Candace, but before he could say another word, a loud crack reverberated through the house, followed by an equally loud report. More shots followed, and suddenly the window exploded inward in a spray of glass shards. Kismet hit the floor as bullets began tearing into the wallboard opposite the window and continued slamming into the exterior.

Higgins appeared from an interior doorway, having evidently broken in through the back door and made his way through the house. "We're surrounded." He shouted. "A dozen or so men on foot flanked us before the trucks showed up."

A dozen? Kismet wondered where Leeds had managed to pull together an army on such short notice.

The incoming fire slacked off momentarily, and almost too late, Kismet grasped the significance of this. He spun around to face the vestibule area, just as a pair of figures came through the front door, brandishing shot guns. Both were clad in long gown-like white garments that appeared to have been stitched together from bed sheets, replete with full-head masked cowls.

Kismet did not let his disbelief stop him. As the lead figure lowered the gaping muzzle of the shotgun, aiming it in his direction, Kismet squeezed off a controlled pair with the Glock.

The white robed figure staggered back into his trailing comrade, the second man's shroud now spattered with fine droplets of red. Kismet brought the pistol up and triggered another round, but the second man was already scrambling back, out of the vestibule. A moment later, the fusillade resumed.

As he backed away, Kismet saw Joe staring in disbelief at the motionless form that lay sprawled across the entry, and he knew the young man wasn't transfixed by the sight of a dead man, but rather by his distinctive apparel. There was a look of terror in the young man's eyes. *Like he's seen a ghost*, Kismet thought.

"We don't know what this means," he shouted, trying to break the spell. "Focus. We need to get out of here!"

The attack had come so swiftly that Kismet was only now beginning to think strategically. Leeds needed the information that these people possessed if he ever expected to locate the Fountain. The unrestrained fury of the assault had to be a ploy—a shock and awe tactic just like the white robes—designed to crush their morale and force a surrender...

Something crashed through the tattered remains of the blinds and hit the floor in the front room. The odor of gasoline filled the room and an instant later, the burning rag stuffed into the end of the Molotov cocktail ignited with a whoosh.

Okay, maybe not a ploy.

For a few seconds, the flames were concentrated in the area where the firebomb had landed, consuming the spilled fuel, but the blaze quickly spread, blossoming out in a circle from the point of ignition...a circle that blocked all access to the steamer trunk with Hernando Fontaneda's diaries. Even as he started toward the chest, he saw that it was too late to retrieve them, and if they didn't do something quickly, it would be too late to do much of anything.

"There's another way out," Candace shouted over the din of gunfire, her voice stronger than Kismet would have thought possible given her years. She crawled to the hearth and then gripped the bricks. To Kismet's surprise, the elevated platform rose a few inches, as if on a hinge. Joe reached her side a moment later, adding his strength to hers, and the hearth swung up to reveal an empty space, like a waiting sarcophagus.

"Here!" Joe shouted, waving to Kismet urgently. He then helped Candace climb into the newly created opening and disappeared into it after her.

Even from across the room, Kismet could see that the space was more than just a recess; the hole concealed by the hearth was a passage to…what exactly, he didn't know, but it had to be a be better than the alternatives of being shot or burning up.

"Annie! Al!" He shouted, trying to locate them through the growing curtain of smoke. "Fire escape!"

Higgins emerged from the miasma, dragging Annie by the arm, and unceremoniously dropped her into the dark void.

A wall off flames rose up behind Kismet, blocking the path to the front door. The incoming gunfire ceased immediately, and over the roaring of the fire, Kismet could hear Leeds' voice, stridently raging at the ineptitude of his accomplices. He knew what was coming next.

A white-robed shape appeared across the room, emerging from the interior of the house, evidently having entered through the back just as Higgins had done. The figure was hazy through the smoke, but he evidently saw Kismet and brought his gun around.

Kismet fired the Glock into the smoke cloud, driving the man back long enough to clear a path to the hearth, and then dove headlong into the dark unknown.

It was like falling into another world. The darkness was almost absolute; a square of dim light—fire partly obscured by smoke—from the opening directly over his head was the only illumination, and the only way for him to even begin judging the dimensions of his surroundings. He could tell that the opening was about eight feet overhead, though he could have guessed that from the plunge. As for the rest, it might have been a wide open cellar or a tunnel—there was no way to tell. In the faint orange glow, he could make out Higgins and Annie, no more than a few steps away. The old Gurkha seemed ready to face whatever fate threw at him next, but Annie looked visibly anxious, almost distraught.

"Come on!" Joe shouted from the darkness. "Get away from the opening."

There was a flicker of light from the direction of his voice, as a battery operated fluorescent lamp warmed up, and Kismet finally got a look at their refuge.

The space was cramped, the rough-cut dirt walls only about six feet apart. Upright beams stretched from concrete footings up a to wood-slat ceiling that sagged in the middle as if holding back a tremendous weight, and barely allowed six inches of clearance. The one dimension that didn't seem to be closing in on them was its depth; beyond where Joe and Candace stood, holding matching electric lanterns, the underground space was indeed a tunnel, stretching away into the impenetrable darkness for at least fifty feet, and probably more.

Joe continued urging them deeper into the passage but Annie hesitated, clutching at her father's arm as if unable to breathe. "I can't," she whispered, turning involuntarily back toward the entrance.

Kismet shook his head and tried to turn her back into the tunnel. Even though she didn't fight him, he could feel the resistance in her muscles as he grasped her arm. She was clearly in the grip of some irrational panic.

Claustrophobia. Hell of a time to learn about that.

When they were about ten feet down the passage, Joe turned called for Kismet to stop.

"They can still follow us. Here." He pointed to a thick rope, which ran vertically from the floor alongside one of the support pillars. The rope was anchored to an eyebolt set in one of the footings, and ran up to the ceiling, where it functioned as part of the support system for the wooden slats.

Kismet noticed a second line on the opposite side, and realized that these two ropes were holding back the collapse of the entryway.

"Cut the rope," Joe urged.

Kismet felt a moment of hesitancy. The ropes were the only thing restraining uncountable tons of earth; if they cut them, the ceiling would cave in and their way out would be blocked permanently.

No, not the way out. The way for their enemies to come in, to follow them.

Kismet drew his *kukri* and hacked at the rope. The dry old fibers parted with an audible twang and the slats on that side dropped partway down, allowing a torrent of dirt and gravel to spill forth into the tunnel behind them. The ceiling beyond that point remained intact. He darted across to where Joe waited, and with another sweep of the blade, sliced the anchor rope in two.

The ceiling fell hard, as if in a single mass, and hit the ground with such violence that Kismet was nearly knocked down. The tremor shook the rest of the tunnel, forcing Kismet and Joe to scramble away lest more of the ceiling come crashing down.

An eerie silence flooded the tunnel as the collapse sealed them off from the noise of the attack and the fire. The only audible sound was of Annie gasping for breath.

"My God!" she whispered, on the verge of fainting. "We're buried alive."

The loose cluster of white robed figures scattered like pigeons as Dr. John Leeds strode fearlessly through the smoke filled house. Leeds, looked like a raven in his black cassock, a stark contrast to the soot-stained white garments favored by their new accomplices, or for that matter, to the thick mitten of gauze wrapped around his maimed hand.

He picked his way through the charred timbers and found a group of men deploying a battery of small fire extinguishers to battle back the blaze that one of their number had recklessly started. The small extinguishers were designed to combat small fires, and even in concert, there simply wasn't enough of them to completely snuff out the spreading fire. At the perimeter of the room, the fire continued to spread, licking at the walls.

Elisabeth, following cautiously behind him, knew that the only reason Leeds hadn't flown into a rage was that doing so would have been an admission that he had erred in enlisting this bunch of good ol' boys. In New York, such arrangements had been handled by Leeds' aide, Ian MacKay, but the Scotsman with the silver tooth had not been heard from since the abortive attempt on Kismet's life in Central Park, and they could only assume that he had not survived the encounter.

Given that Nick Kismet was involved, that outcome was not altogether surprising.

Leeds may have been a genius when it came to mysticism and the occult, and as adept at manipulating people in face-to-face encounters as any carnival fortune teller, but he had zero organizational skills. In Hollywood, he would have been a great executive producer but a complete failure as a director.

The men with the extinguishers stood in loose formation around the hearth of a brick fireplace in the front room. The top of the platform had been lifted out of the way revealing a dark opening with a heap of freshly turned dirt a few feet down.

"Some kinda escape tunnel," growled one of the hooded men, nodding to the fireplace. "Completely caved in. They got away."

"Then all is not lost," growled Leeds. "In spite of your failure."

"Two of my friends are dead," hissed the man, incredulous. "And you're happy 'cause those niggers survived?"

"Your attack was poorly engineered. You relied far too much on your ability to frighten them into submission."

The man tried to respond, but his words were lost in a fit of smoke-induced coughing. A section of the rear wall collapsed inward, releasing a fiery cloud of sparks. Even Leeds was forced to take a step back.

"We have to get out of here," insisted one of the men. "This whole place is coming down."

Without waiting for a reply he started for the door. Elisabeth felt an overpowering urge to follow, but Leeds stood his ground a moment longer. "A tunnel has two ends. This is one; find the other."

○

In the settling dust of the cave-in, Kismet finally took a moment to survey their refuge.

The tunnel had been dug through dense clay soil, a task that had surely taken several years, especially since it seemed unlikely that powered digging equipment could have been employed. . The walls remained bare dirt, but the ceiling had been shored up by beams and posts, placed every ten feet of so. The ceiling was low enough that he actually had to duck to pass under the beams, but the tunnel was almost wide enough in some places for two people to walk abreast.

Annie was huddled into a ball, sitting with her back to the dirt wall. Her father knelt beside her, one arm around her shoulders, but his attempts to offer comfort did not seem to be meeting with success. Kismet took a knee as well.

"It's okay," he said. "I think we're safe for the moment."

"Safe?" gasped Annie. She seemed to be fighting to get the words out, as if in the grip of an asthma attack. "We're trapped. Buried alive."

"We're not trapped," Kismet insisted. "This is a tunnel. King dug it, it must lead somewhere."

"I can't breathe."

"That's just in your head. There's plenty of air down here." Despite his assurance, Kismet was suddenly very conscious of the close quarters and the fact that the air did seem to be getting a little stale. He shook his head to clear away the rising paranoia. "Look Annie. The tunnel does end, but we have to get moving if we're ever going to get out."

FORTUNE FAVORS

That seemed to motivate her. Annie looked up, a single mote of hope floating in her pool of misery. He offered her a sip from his flask, and she gratefully downed it.

"Did you dig this tunnel?" Kismet asked when they caught up to Joe and Candace.

Joe shook his head, his eyes, and perhaps his thoughts, unfocused. "The tunnel was dug back before the War...the Civil War, that is."

Then the young man straightened perceptibly. "Actually, it was Fontaneda that dug it, way back when. He was an Abolitionist. He'd give runaway slaves a place to hide until they could catch a ride on the Underground Railroad. Dug this tunnel so they could come and go."

The idea of the Spanish Conquistador as a Southern gentleman in the years before the Civil War, and an Abolitionist no less, was mind-boggling. If everything he thought he knew about the man was true—including the claim that he had discovered the Fountain of Youth—then Fontaneda would have been about three hundred and fifty years old at the time of the Civil War. It was difficult to conceive of how four or five lifetimes of experience might have changed the man. Had his decision to support the anti-slavery movement been a way of atoning for past misdeeds...like the slaughter of the native village that had protected the Fountain in the first place?

Kismet thought about the dead fall that had blocked the entrance and wondered if that had been Fontaneda's doing as well.

The tunnel followed a straight line for at least fifty yards before coming to an abrupt and unexpected end. The walls were hidden behind stacks of mildewed cardboard boxes and old splintered wooden crates. If not for the secret entrance under the hearth and the long separating distance, it might have seemed like nothing more than a storage cellar, but in light of those two details, Kismet was inclined to believe that boxes were nothing more than window dressing. His suspicion was confirmed when Joe started shifting some of the boxes out of the way to reveal an eight-foot folding ladder, resting on its side.

Joe wrestled the ladder out of its hiding place and then propped it up in the center of the tunnel. Kismet realized that the ceiling was higher here, and as Joe extended the legs of the ladder, Kismet saw a dark opening directly above where the ladder had been positioned. Joe rocked the ladder a couple times to ensure that it was stable, then retrieved his lantern and climbed up until his upper body was above the top step and mostly inside the opening. After a few moments of fumbling with something overhead, he resumed his ascent and disappeared completely through the hole in the ceiling. Kismet approached the ladder, and saw Joe staring down out of a well-lit open space high overhead.

"It's a little cramped up here. Mister...Kismet, was it? I think you should come up first. There's something I want to show you."

Kismet glanced at the others. Annie was still on the verge of hysteria. Higgins offering his daughter what comfort he could, simply shrugged. The old woman, Candace, gave him an encouraging nod and gestured for him to go up the ladder. He did.

The overhead space was much smaller than the confines of the tunnel; it was about the size of a walk in closet, but part of the space was dominated by what looked like an enormous chest. It was a crypt, he realized, and the chest was a sealed casket.

Joe gestured to the funerary container. "There it is. What you came for is in there."

It took Kismet a moment to realize what Joe was saying. "This is Fontaneda's tomb?"

"He built an empty vault to hide the tunnel exit. When he died, it seemed like the best place to lay him to rest. No one else was using it." Joe laid his palms flat on the top of the casket, staring at the smooth surface with an almost wistful expression. "So, you want me to open it?"

Kismet swallowed. "How do you even know what's in there?"

"I know," Joe said, as if that was the final word on the subject. "He took his secret to the grave. That's what Joseph King told you in the letter, right?"

Shoving aside a final hesitant attack of conscience, Kismet nodded. There was a faint hiss as Joe broke the seal. Kismet felt a stir of expectation and dread as the cover was thrown back. A mixture of strange smells wafted from the casket; some kind of perfume fragrance—sandalwood, perhaps—

that couldn't quite mask the odor of embalming fluid. But there was no smell of rot or decay; if there was a body in the casket then it had remained perfectly preserved. Kismet picked up Joe's lantern and held it above the shrouded figure that lay in repose within.

There was indeed a body, a man, with a thick unkempt mane of black hair and a bushy beard that could not quite hide his youthful features. His skin had the pallor of death, but looked firm, with no hint of decomposition. The motionless figure in the casket could have merely been sleeping, or just recently deceased, instead of having been dead and buried for more than fifty years. In fact, he looked a little too good.

If the Spaniard's youthful features were a testament to the power of the Fountain, if his life and health and vigor had been preserved for nearly four hundred years beyond its normal span, then what had happened at the end? He clearly had not died of old age.

Kismet saw Joe staring at the face of the cadaver with a mystified expression. "What's the matter?"

"The hair. And the beard? I don't..." He took a breath. "I can't believe Joseph King would have laid him to rest in such a state."

Kismet looked more closely, studying not only Fontaneda's face, but also his hands. The fingernails were long, unnaturally so, like the talons of a raptor. It was a popular misconception that hair and fingernails continued to grow after death; what actually happened was that, as the skin gradually became desiccated, it shrank and pulled back, which created the illusion of longer hair and nails. But nothing like that could account for what he was looking at. The dead man's beard and fingernails would have had to be growing for several months, years perhaps, to achieve the length and density it now possessed.

"He really found it," Kismet said, almost in a whisper. "The Fountain of Youth. Maybe whatever kept him young, kept these cells alive long after the rest of him died..."

Morbid curiosity prompted him to check the lid of the casket. He half-expected to discover claw marks, but the silk headliner was intact. Fontaneda had evidently been very dead when his body had been placed inside. What had actually killed him was anyone's guess.

"You said there was a map?"

Joe took a deep breath, then leaned over the cadaver and tore open the dead man's shirt. The action took Kismet by surprise, and it took a moment for him to realize what he was seeing. Etched into the pale skin, partially obscured by a tangle of chest hair, was an intaglio of lines and symbols. Fontaneda's map to the Fountain of Youth was tattooed on his chest.

It was not a map in the traditional sense. It more closely resembled a childishly drawn landscape, with triangles that might have been mountains and rounded, irregular shapes that Kismet took to be lakes. There were other markings as well, animals shapes, similar in form to petroglyphs found all across the Americans, and perhaps most distinctive, a small Christian cross. The image was marred by what looked like a jagged white scar, almost directly over the Spaniard's sternum, but the blemish didn't significantly alter the picture. There were no names or orienting marks, but vertical lines stretched various points—the centers of the "lakes," the heads of the animal shapes, the peaks of the "mountains," all at very deliberate angles, like the rays of a web, to converged on the head of another animal shape, a long squirming snake outline that almost completely bisected the image. The tip of its tail was in the center of the man's chest, a few inches above the scar, and its head was just above his navel.

"This is meaningless," Kismet growled. "There aren't any mountains like that in Florida."

He drew his *kukri* and began scraping the edge of the long blade across the exposed skin, shaving away the hair to more completely reveal the image. The snake shape was unquestionably the focus of the reference lines, the requisite "x" to mark the spot. That suggested something, a landmark of some kind that would provide the final clue when they arrived there. He looked more closely at the mountains, and decided they were not mountains at all, but rather resembled squat pyramids.

"Pyramids in Florida?" he muttered. Something about that seemed familiar, too.

"That mean something to you?" Joe asked.

Kismet frowned. He wasn't sure he wanted to share this revelation. "I don't know. I'll have to do some more research. I need some paper to copy this."

"I don't have any," Joe said. "I think there's only one way to take this map with you."

Kismet immediately grasped what Joe was saying, and tried just as quickly to dismiss the idea. There had to be a better way to record this image. Maybe Higgins or Annie had a scrap of paper he could use…He could take a picture of it with his phone…

But if he took a reproduction of the map with him, he'd need to destroy the original in order to prevent Leeds finding it. As revolting as the idea was, given the circumstances and the very short list of alternatives, Joe's suggestion had merit.

"All right," he growled, not meeting the young man's gaze. "Might as well get this over with."

He laid a hand on Fontaneda's chest, feeling the dead man's skin for the first time. It was cool to the touch, but supple like the leather of his bomber jacket. Thinking about it in those terms helped him dissociate from what he was about to do. It was just a piece of hide, no different than the calf-skin used to make vellum parchment or driving gloves.

He placed the tip the *kukri* above his hand, and cut a straight line across the Spaniard's torso.

The skin parted and immediately spread open to reveal purple-blue viscera beneath. There was no blood, but the cut did release an invisible cloud of formaldehyde vapor that stung Kismet's eyes and nostrils. Blinking away the effect, he turned the blade for another cut, this time down Fontaneda's right side. Two more such cuts outlined the map in a square. With each cut, the skin had spread apart as if under tension, and now the map—he tried to think of it only as such, ignoring the grisly reality of what he was doing—was outlined by a dark square.

He inserted the tip the *kukri* underneath the epidermis, working at it until he succeeded in peeling a corner away from the underlying dermis.

Then, gripping that corner between a thumb and forefinger, he began to pull, as if trying to peel a piece of wallpaper away from a wall without tearing it. The skin was tougher than he expected, and tearing it wasn't a problem, but separating the layers of tissue was not as easy as he'd hoped. Finally, after several minutes of tugging at the corner of the map, worrying the blade further and further under the skin, he succeeded, and it came away with a hideous sucking sound.

He laid the map back on the cadaver's chest and meticulously wiped the *kukri* clean before sheathing it. Only then did he inspect his handiwork.

The map was intact, but separated from its human frame, the canvas of skin had shrunk considerably, condensing the tattooed lines and pictures into a dark but still legible image. The obverse side was covered with a grotesque gray film, thankfully dry to the touch. Suppressing one last shudder of revulsion, Kismet rolled the map up and tucked it into the inside pocket of his jacket.

Joe had watched the whole process without speaking, and now he simply nodded and lowered the lid of the casket, returning the Spaniard to his final rest. "Now you know what he knew," he said simply, without a trace of judgment.

Kismet gestured to the door of the crypt. "That's our way out?"

The young man nodded. "There's a good chance they're still out there."

Kismet was sure of it. Leeds and his white robed goons were probably already digging up the cemetery trying to find the tunnel exit. Getting back to the rented Explorer didn't seem like a viable option; what did that leave?

"You said this tunnel was used by runaway slaves? Where did they go from here?"

"There was a trail leading to Charleston harbor. It's several miles, an all night walk. From there, they'd travel north in the holds of merchant ships owned by Northern Abolitionists. But that was a long time ago. Everything has changed. There's a few acres of woods, but beyond that it's mostly neighborhoods now."

Change wasn't necessarily a bad thing, Kismet thought. They didn't need to walk all the way to the port; they only needed to find a place where they could hide out and maybe call a taxi.

Of course, Leeds would know that. His new allies would be watching the roads.

"There's a rail line about a mile to the east," Joe continued. "You get to that, and you can follow it north into the city."

The way Joe said "you" set off alarm bells. "You're coming with us, right?"

A strange smile touched Joe's lips. "I think Candace and I will just stay put. You're gonna need to move fast if you want to get away, and Candace...well, her runnin' days are long gone."

"Will you be safe? What if Leeds discovers this crypt?"

"We can take care of ourselves," Joe answered confidently. "An' no offense, but the sooner you're gone, the better off we'll be."

Kismet wasn't so sure about that, and he didn't relish the idea of abandoning the pair to such an uncertain fate, but the young man seemed to have made up his mind. "Then there's something I need to know."

Joe cocked his head sideways. "Somethin' more?"

"You knew about all this. You had the diaries, you knew about the Fountain and even the map. So why are you here?"

"Well..." Joe let the word hang in the air for several seconds. "The truth is, I'm kind of scared of that Fountain. It don't seem natural, somehow."

"And old age and death are natural?"

"Everybody gets old and everybody dies. Ain't nobody that never died, not even him." He gestured to the casket. "What did he accomplish with all those extra years?"

Joe frowned, as if he had meant to say something else but couldn't find the words. "Living like that...how is it any different than getting addicted to a drug? You live for the next fix, you keep it a secret and don't share because you're afraid that if you do, it won't be special no more."

"So, eternal life just leads to misery?" Kismet didn't mean for the question to sound rhetorical, and quickly added: "What about Candace? Wouldn't you like to spend a few more years with her? And not just as an old woman, but young and full of energy? Wouldn't the world be a better place if the oldest and wisest of us had a few more years?"

"Mr. Kismet, I think that if folks learn about the Fountain, there's going to be plenty of misery for everyone. Powerful people will control it. And poor folks...black folks...they'll just be in the way in a world where everyone lives forever."

The argument surprised Kismet, not in the least because of how difficult it was to refute. "Everyone has something to give, Joe, something worth preserving."

"I don't think so. If you want to go find it, that's you business. Me and Candace are going to stay where we belong."

Kismet looked at King thoughtfully. "And this is where you really belong? Are you sure of that?"

"More than you might think, Mr. Kismet." Joe smiled sadly. "If I could talk you out of looking for it I would. I think when you find it, we'll all be in a world of hurt."

12

ANNIE CRANE HUGGED HER ARMS AROUND her chest and squeezed her eyes shut, but try as she might, she could not convince herself that she was somewhere else. Somewhere she wasn't buried under tons of earth.

Claustrophobia, she thought. *An irrational fear of being trapped in an enclosed space, and I've got it. How am I only learning this now?*

Right up to the moment when she had plunged into that dark hole, Annie would have believed that she wasn't afraid of anything. She was Al Higgins' girl. She could shoot as well as any man she knew, was an expert rock-climber, flew paragliders and jumped out of airplanes…oh, there were still a lot of things on her bucket list—scary things—but not a one of them filled her with the kind of overwhelming primal terror she felt now.

Of course, now that she thought about it, there were a few things that had never held much appeal. Her dad had invited her to go caving once or twice, but the timing had never been good. Or had she just found excuses to avoid doing something that scared her more than she realized?

"Annie!" Her father's voice was a welcome intrusion on her private hell. "Let's go, girl. Time to get moving."

If 'moving' meant getting out of this living tomb, she was all for it.

With the eagerness of someone trying to escape a snake pit, she scrambled up the ladder. Just knowing that she wasn't underground anymore was a marginal relief, but the cramped little cube of cut stone in which she found herself wasn't much better, particularly when she realized what function it served.

Kismet stood with his face pressed to the door of the crypt, a door which she now saw was open just a crack. He turned back to the rest of them after a moment. "Let's go."

Annie didn't resist as her father bustled her forward, through the door which Kismet threw open to the night. If anything, she fairly ran to get through it.

The transition from tomb to open air was like a resurrection, but her euphoria was fleeting. She caught a whiff of smoke on the wind, and spied flashes of light—the beams of electric torches—crisscrossing the air above the endless sea of grave markers, and realized that, while they had escaped her underground nightmare, the danger which had prompted them to seek refuge in the tunnel was far from past. Leeds' white robed goons were still looking for them.

Kismet tugged on her arm, pointing toward a maze of larger vaults that were clustered together near the crypt they had just exited. "This way."

As she started to run behind him, a backward glance revealed that the crypt door was closed again, and the couple from the house—Joe and Candace—weren't with them. She wanted to ask about this, but it was clear from their haste that questions and explanations would have to wait.

○

Joe descended the ladder and found Candace waiting patiently at the end of the tunnel.

"So you just sent them on their way?" she asked, a faintly accusatory tone in her voice.

"Didn't seem like they'd have it any other way," he answered. "Sooner they're gone, the sooner we can get back to normal."

"Normal," Candace scoffed. "It's done, Joe. There ain't no going back to what was, and you know it."

FORTUNE FAVORS

Joe leaned against the ladder and hung his head. She was right, of course. Oh, they could wait down here as long as it took; the hooligans in white robes—whether they were Klansmen or just a few rowdies using the sheets to misdirect suspicion, he didn't know—probably wouldn't linger until sunrise, especially if they caught the scent of Kismet and his companions. But what then? Their home was destroyed, and with it, the life they had so carefully constructed for themselves.

Candace moved to stand next to him, but said nothing. Joe intuited that something more was troubling her, and he thought he knew what it was. "You think I should have told them everything, don't you?"

"They saved us," she replied, without directly answering him.

"I told them where to find what they're looking for."

"Yes."

He could tell from her tone that she was holding back. "Then what's the matter? That Kismet fellow knows what he's doing. They'll be fine."

"They need to know the truth."

Joe sighed. Maybe she was right; maybe Kismet did deserve to know everything. But the Fountain had a way of keeping its own secret; who was he to interfere?

○

They managed to get as far as the edge of the cemetery before they were noticed.

As they clambered over the fence that marked the border, Kismet heard distant shouts and saw flashlight beams playing along the tree line, seeking them out, and knew that now it would be a race.

He'd briefed Higgins and Annie on the plan as they had darted between the headstones. If they got separated in the darkness, they would find each other again at the rail line Joe had told him about. Now, as they started running headlong, no longer making an effort to conceal their movements, he would have to trust them to make that rendezvous.

The sparse woods offered some concealment, but there was little doubt that Leeds' men were giving chase. When he glanced back, he could see their flashlights through the boughs. They had a good lead, maybe it would be enough. But as the minutes passed, ticked out by the pounding of his heart and the rhythm of his breathing, he heard an ominous sound in the distance and knew that fate had thrown a monkey wrench into the gears of his plan. A low rumble and the squeal and clatter of steel wheels on iron rails...there was a train on the line.

At least it will be easy to find, he thought.

As he broke out of the woods, he caught his first glimpse of the train. He could make out the squared-off silhouettes of box cars, or maybe shipping containers, as well as tankers, and flatbed cars with unusual shapes secured to them. It stretched in both directions as far as he could see, at least a mile long, moving south, away from the heart of the city at what seemed like a glacial pace. They could still follow the rail line back to the city, but if their pursuers caught up to them, there would be nowhere to go, not while that serpentine behemoth blocked the way.

Maybe...

He glimpsed Annie emerging from the woods behind him. She seemed rejuvenated after her paralyzing and unexpected bout of claustrophobia in the tunnel. Her breathing was steady, as if the desperate flight through the woods had been no more challenging than a jog to the corner store. Her father trotted out a few seconds later, panting just a little, but clearly still in fighting shape. Kismet noted with some satisfaction that the old Gurkha still had his Kimber rifle, now slung across his back. He waved, urging them to join him as he started running again, slower now so they could catch up, and headed straight for the train.

He paused at the edge of the raised gravel rail bed and beckoned them close. The ground rumbled beneath his feet as thousands of tons of steel rolled by just a few yards away.

He pointed up at the line of cars. Higgins seemed to grasp what he was silently suggesting, for a look of disbelief twisted his visage. "Mate, you are not bloody serious."

FORTUNE FAVORS

Annie's gaze switched between them until she too seemed to understand. "Oh."

"I think we can do this," he shouted back. "It's not going that fast; maybe only twenty miles an hour."

It was a guess, but a good one. Out in open country, a train might cruise along at fifty or sixty miles per hour, but here, close to populated areas with a lot of road crossings, trains had to observe speed limits just like automobiles.

Okay, it might be more like thirty miles per hour, he decided, but didn't voice this aloud. "We can do this," he repeated. "It's our best chance. We hop this train and get off a few miles down the line. They won't have a clue where we are."

Higgins glanced at his daughter, and then nodded with only the barest hint of reservation. Annie was a little more reticent with her assent, but Kismet was pleased and a little surprised at how quickly they accepted his crazy plan. He realized it was probably because they had no idea just how dangerous what they were about to do really was.

There wasn't time to work out the finer points. They would have to run alongside the train, as fast as they could manage, pick out a good handhold as the cars passed by, grab on and pull themselves up. An Olympic sprinter, running all out, could easily reach twenty miles an hour and sustain that pace for a few hundred meters. None of them were in that kind of shape, but with adrenaline pumping, he didn't doubt that they could come close, at least for a minute or so. The train would be moving at about five to ten miles an hour faster, so grabbing on would, in theory, be a little like reaching out from a standstill and snaring someone running by.

Higgins went first, with Annie only a few steps behind him. Kismet too started running along, giving the others a little bit of room. He paid scant attention to their progress, keeping his focus on the task at hand. Further complicating matters was the fact that in order to reach the train, they would have to dart up the sloping side of the rail bed at the last minute, effectively running right at the lumbering train as it moved by. A stumble or an error in judgment of even a few degrees, and they might very well be crushed to death or sliced in half beneath the clattering wheels.

He caught a glimpse of Higgins making his move. The old Gurkha found a previously untapped vein of energy and dashed up the rail bed to grasp the front edge of a flatcar as it rolled by. His grip was fierce enough that the train pulled him off his feet, and for a moment, he was dragged along, his boots bouncing off the gravel, but then with a superhuman heave, he hauled himself up onto the platform where he immediately rolled onto his belly and reached out with both hands to his daughter.

Annie made it look easy. Her lithe form and the vigor of her youth enabled her to almost match the pace of the train for a few seconds, long enough to catch her father's hands. He lifted her onto the flatcar with the grace of a ballet dancer lifting a ballerina over his head, and then they were gone, whisked from Kismet's line of sight as the train rolled on.

He quickened his pace, lowering his head as he broke into a full sprint along the base of the rail bed. A container car, with no easy handholds, passed him by, moving almost twice as fast as he. He kept running, biding his time. A second container car passed, and then another.

Not good.

He glanced over his shoulder, afraid that he might be running out of train, but positioned as he was, he just couldn't tell. Then he saw his chance; a flatbed with some kind of vehicle or large machine was coming up next. As its front corner passed him, he charged up the gravel slope and reached out.

In that moment, the sheer lunacy of what he was doing hit him like a physical blow. He'd done some crazy things in his life, sometimes without any kind of safety net, but this time it felt different. Maybe it was because he was running, exerting himself to the physical limit at a time when he most needed his judgment to be pitch perfect. The exacting nature of what he was attempting filled him with uncertainty, a dread reminder of just how precise his timing would have to be, right at a moment when he most needed to be sure of himself. The thunderous passage of the train car right beside him didn't help his focus any.

Then his outstretched hand felt something that wasn't smooth unyielding metal. It was a heavy nylon web belt, one of the tension straps that held the flatbed's cargo in place. He curled his fingers around it...

FORTUNE FAVORS

And was yanked off his feet.

For an instant, he panicked, struggling to gain his footing while at the same time trying to keep his legs from being swept under the car. In desperation, he flung his other hand up to grasp the strap, even as his feet started to drag and bounce along the gravel slope.

Damn it, he thought. *Now I'm screwed.*

He dared not let go, but how long could he endure the punishing assault of being dragged by the train. He had to pull himself up, but was he strong enough?

He flexed his biceps, pulling with all his might, but almost immediately, something like liquid fire began to burn in his muscles and he felt them start to fail. In desperation he kicked at the ground moving beneath his feet, trying to propel himself up, just a few inches...

It was enough. He pulled his torso up against the strap and felt the edge of the flatbed against his hips. The instantaneous respite from being dragged restored his confidence, and savoring his success for just a moment, he began working his hands up the length of the strap until he could haul himself the rest of the way up onto the flat bed, where he finally collapsed in exhaustion.

After a few relieved breaths, he rolled onto his side to get a look at his new surroundings. The first thing he saw was an enormous black donut shape more than three feet in diameter—a truck tire—and then he realized that there was another right beside it, and a few feet down, separated by an external fuel tank, there was another pair. As his eyes continued to adjust to the darkness, he made out more details of the strange looking vehicle. It had been a while since he'd seen one, but he recognized it right away. It was an M977 A2 Heavy Expanded Mobility Tactical Truck, the ten-ton capacity, eight-wheel drive, diesel powered workhorse of the US Army.

The train was transporting military hardware, probably vehicles that had been shipped back to the States after seeing action in the Middle East or Afghanistan. It now occurred to him that the other flatbeds he had seen, including the one that Higgins and Annie had mounted, were likewise loaded with HEMTTs or possibly Humvees, all on their way to a motor pool somewhere halfway across the country. The details didn't really matter much, but the vehicles would be a lot easier to negotiate around than container cars that now separated him from his companions.

He glanced in the direction the train was traveling. There were at least two container cars between him and his friends. Easy or not, it was time to get moving.

He rose and moved alongside the HEMMT, stepping over the tension straps and chains that held it secure to the flatbed, until he reached the front end of the flatbed. In the darkness, he could just make out the heavy steel knuckle that joined this car to the next a few feet below where he stood. About six feet away, across a gap bridged by that coupling, was the container car. He now saw that the container was secured to a flat car just like the truck. Although its massive bulk almost completely filled the moving platform, there was a narrow ledge—about six inches wide—around its perimeter. The ledge was tempting, but the sheet metal walls of the container afforded little in the way of handholds.

He stepped cautiously down onto the coupling, maintaining two-handed contact with the edge of the flatbed car until both feet were firmly planted. Then, with only a single quick step forward, he reached across to grasp hold of the shipping container. From there, it was an easy thing to pull himself up and onto the ledge.

Instead of attempting to traverse along the ledge, he instead used the vertical rods of the containers external door latch like a climbing ladder, and deftly pulled himself up onto the roof.

The wind of the train's passage blasted him with surprising intensity, ripping at his jacket and stealing the moisture from his eyes. The train was probably only going about thirty miles an hour, but the rush of air was relentless. He stayed low, hugging the slick metal and crawling forward, even though the chance of being blown off his perch was effectively nil. After a few minutes of inching his way along, he reached the far end of the container and another long gap between cars.

With a running start, he probably could have easily leapt to the next roof, but there seemed no pressing reason to tempt fate. Instead, he lowered himself slowly down to the ledge and again stepped cautiously over the coupling.

As he did, something flashed through the air above his head.

He did not see it so much as sense it, and as soon as he looked and saw nothing, his rational mind tried to dismiss the experience. It could have been anything...probably was nothing...but the animal part of his brain—that evolutionary holdover instinct that raised gooseflesh on the back of his neck and set his heart to racing—was unconvinced. Although still moving with painstaking care, he felt a new urgency as he began climbing up the container door.

As soon as his head rose above the roofline, he saw the figures—two of them, white robes whipping furiously about their bodies—striding forward down the length of the car, bent forward in defiance of the headwind. Evidently, Leeds' goons had seen them hop the train, and at least a few of them had managed to follow suit.

"Damn!" The wind snatched the muttered curse from Kismet's lips. He inched up onto the roof, staying flat, and drew his Glock from its holster, as the two creeping figures reached the far end of the car. Higgins and Annie were up there somewhere, waiting for him and completely unaware of the trouble headed their way.

He was about to rise to his feet, intent on giving chase, when a strong hand grabbed one of his ankles and yanked him from the roof and into the crushing darkness between the cars.

Annie widened her stance as the train rocked into a curve and nearly caused her to lose her already tentative footing. She gripped the side of the military truck secured to the flatcar which she and her father had boarded only a few minutes earlier and waited for the sensation to pass.

She gazed once more into the darkness, down the serpentine line of cars behind them, and wondered aloud. "What's taking him so long?"

They had both seen Kismet make it aboard the train…or to be more precise, they had seen him charge up the sloped rail bed before vanishing from sight. They had continued watching, but he had not reappeared, which probably meant that he was aboard, but could also mean that he had slipped and fallen onto the rails, and been subsequently sliced apart by the steel wheels.

No, she told herself. *He made it. We made it, and it wasn't that hard…so he made it too.*

But if he had made it onto the train, where was he?

"We should go look for him," she decided, shouting to be heard over the din.

Her father gave a perturbed look, but then nodded his assent. With one hand still resting against the exterior of the truck, Annie began moving toward the rear of the train, intent on finding Nick Kismet. She had only gone a few steps however when a strange white shape appeared atop the shipping container on the car behind them. It took a moment for her to register what she was seeing, a moment in which the cloaked figure abruptly launched into the air, white robes fluttering like moth wings, and came down squarely on the flatcar, just a few steps away.

Higgins saw the unexpected arrival and immediately brought the barrel of his rifle around, but before he could attempt to aim the unwieldy weapon, the intruder raised a handgun of his own and let lead fly.

The report of the pistol was muted by the rush of air, sounding about as loud as a door slamming. Annie hit the flat deck and hastily rolled under the tall wheels of the military transport. She expected to hear her father's rifle thundering as he returned fire, but to her surprise, he hit the deck and rolled beside her, shaking his head in frustration. He gripped her shoulder and then pointed to the forward end of the car. "Go!"

She didn't argue. Scrambling away on hands and knees, she quickly reached the end of the car. The rush of air moving past caught away most of the sounds from behind her, but there were at least two distinct voices shouting to each other; the gunman wasn't alone. She gazed ahead, to the next car in the train—another flat car—and mentally rehearsed what she was going to do next.

Like a sprinter off the block, she sprang to her feet and launched herself forward, over the gap between the cars. There was no hesitation in her stride; perhaps on some level she was trying to compensate for her earlier episode of claustrophobia, but she was confident of her ability to make the jump, even working against the train's forward acceleration. She touched down lightly and caught herself with outstretched palms against the front end of another military truck. She skirted around the vehicle and made for the next car in the line, intent on putting even more space between herself and the gunmen.

A rush of movement and a faint tremor beneath her feet alerted to the presence of another person on the car, and she shrank instinctively against the truck as if trying to melt into its exterior.

"It's me," Higgins rasped. "Can't get a shot. Keep moving."

He didn't need to explain it to her. The Kimber was a devastating weapon, but its long barrel made it unwieldy in close quarters, and to make matters worse, it only had a five round magazine. The only option that made any sense was to fall back and find a more defensible position, where the rifle's lethal accuracy and potency could be used to best advantage. On a linear battlefield like the train, that meant just one thing: get as many cars as possible between themselves and their attackers.

And Nick?

The thought was there before she could stop it from forming, but she pushed it away. Either Kismet was still alive and still in the fight or he wasn't, but there was nothing she could do to help him right now. She pushed away from the truck and started moving again.

She leapt to the next car and this time kept going, nearly at a full run. She danced over the tie-down straps, but as she reached the forward end of the car, she saw that the next car was different. It had a rectangular silhouette, but there was a platform at its rear surrounded by what looked like a low fence. Adjusting her stride just a little, she made the jump, catching herself on the barrier, and then clambered over it onto the platform. In the darkness, she could just make out a door, but in the moment that she grasped the latch handle, she heard something hit the rail behind her.

She whirled to find her father, clinging to the fence and struggling to regain his footing. Gripping his shoulders, she managed to steady him and then helped him over. When he was safely beside her, he turned and aimed the rifle into the darkness, looking for a target. With a nod, she fell back to the door and tried the handle. The door swung open, spilling light from the interior.

"Got it," she cried. "Come on."

Not waiting for a reply, she charged into the car, Higgins right behind her...

The car was full of men—armed men—and as she skidded to an abrupt halt, half a dozen gun barrels swung up to greet her.

○

Kismet's next thought was of pain.

He had flung his arms out instinctively, desperate to grab ahold of something to keep from falling into the gap between the cars or perhaps simply to regain some sense of which way was up. Then, he hit the heavy steel coupling and for a moment, experienced a supernova of pain. The metal knuckle caught him in the abdomen, punching the wind out his sails.

At some primal level, his initial instinctive response saved him, for even as the impact knocked his breath away, his arms curled around the coupling with the intensity of a vise. There was no conscious involvement; agony superseded all voluntary actions. Yet, even as the torment began to recede, a new eruption struck. A blow, then another, not as intense as his crash onto the coupling, but more focused...someone was hitting...no, kicking him.

The unseen assailant that had pulled him from the container was now trying to finish what he'd started.

Even as Kismet made this deductive leap, his desperate grip faltered. He didn't fall, but under the relentless assault, he felt the metal junction slipping away. He rolled sideways, the metal scraping against his arms as his own weight pulled him down. There was yet another rush of pain as the metal scraped against the insides of his clenched arms and legs, and simultaneously he felt something—the ground probably—slapping at his back, through the thick leather of his jacket.

He caught a breath, finally, and with it came a rush of purpose. He flexed his arms, drawing himself up closer to the coupling and away from the abrasive washboard of railroad ties and gravel. But even as that torment ended, he felt his assailant's boot strike a glancing blow on his forearm.

In desperation, he let go with his right arm and threw a hand up, hoping to deflect the next kick. His fingers grazed something soft and yielding—fabric, a pant leg perhaps. He grabbed onto it like a lifeline and pulled.

Perhaps because he was in such a dominant position, the move caught his attacker completely off guard. The fabric Kismet grabbed, the white sheet the man had donned both as a way of terrorizing his intended victims and masking his identity, became his death shroud. As Kismet hauled in on the sheet, the man was pulled off balance and pitched forward, into the gap between the cars. Kismet felt something brush against him as the man fell past, and then the sheet was violently ripped from his fingers.

For a moment, he could do nothing more than hang there, struggling to draw each breath but savoring the unexpected victory. But he couldn't stay where he was; just holding on was sapping his strength fast, and if he didn't move soon, he'd be joining his vanquished foe. Moreover, he knew that if one of the robed hooligans had made it onto the train, then others probably had as well. In fact, he was almost certain that the noise he'd heard just before the attack had been another of Leeds' men, jumping between the cars and already moving up the train, looking—he assumed—for Higgins and Annie.

He didn't hold back the roar of pain and exertion that accompanied his attempt to get back on top of the coupling; any noises he made were drowned out by the squeal and rattle of the train's wheels against the rails. The effort seemed futile; he would struggle to exhaustion and then simply fall into the darkness when his muscles failed. He might even survive...

No! He kept at it, shifting and squirming until, after a few agonizing seconds stretched out to eternity, he found himself once more atop the coupling. He quickly shifted his grip to the exposed ledge surrounding the shipping container, and began methodically working his way up onto it.

Escaping the jaws of death was like a tonic. The pain in his ribs was nothing more than a dull ache and his fatigued muscles felt revitalized. He quickly shinnied up the latch rods once more, this time keeping his head on a swivel to avoid being taken unawares a second time. When his head breached the plane of the rooftop, he checked in both directions, but the coast was clear so pulled himself the rest of the way up. Then, against his better judgment, he stood, and faced into the relentless wind of the train's forward passage.

The lead locomotive's headlamp cast a cone of illumination out ahead of the train. But the light also revealed dark silhouettes—two human shapes—moving in the foreground, along the top of the train, perhaps a hundred yards meters ahead. He couldn't tell whether the figures were his companions or more of Leeds' goon squad, but they were well past the point where Higgins and Annie had boarded. There was only one possible objective in that direction—the locomotive—but he couldn't fathom why the pair—be they friend or foe—would be headed there. Then he looked behind him, and it all made sense.

From his elevated position, he could easily make out the rear of train, at least two hundred yards back. Further back, perhaps another two hundred yards he saw the headlights of a vehicle, moving alongside the tracks and bobbing crazily as the driver negotiated the rugged terrain alongside the rail bed.

Reinforcements, he realized with a growing feeling of dread. Some of their pursuers had made it aboard, but evidently the rest had called for help. There was no way the driver of the approaching vehicle—probably a 4X4 pickup or SUV—would be able to get close enough for his passengers to cross over; he was having a hard enough time just keeping pace.

That, Kismet realized, was what the two figures advancing toward the locomotive were trying to accomplish.

FORTUNE FAVORS

Hunching over into the rushing air, he began moving as fast as he dared. He reached the end of the container and deftly climbed down to leap onto the flatbed. The urgency of the situation enabled him to sublimate his instinctive fears, imbuing him with a surefooted decisiveness as he negotiated the obstacles and unhesitatingly crossed between the cars, picking out handholds, climbing onto roofs as if they were merely a maze of obstacles on a child's playground.

In a matter of only seconds, he was past the flatcars where he was sure his friends had boarded. There was no sign of them, and he hoped that meant they had found somewhere to hide. He couldn't take the time to look; if Leeds' men succeeded in stopping the train, then all hope would be lost. He kept going.

A long series of box cars sped him along. He was able to jump from one roof to the next without breaking stride. Yet, even as he raced forward, the two figures he pursued dropped out of sight. He kept going, and reached the place where they had vanished a few seconds later.

The last boxcar in the line was hooked to a locomotive, one of a pair that worked together to pull the train. Kismet hopped over to the platform that ran along the side of the engine, following it to a short stairway that fed into the cab. The interior of the control room was dark and unmanned; the locomotive had been slaved to the lead engine. The engineer would be in the forward locomotive, and that was where Leeds' men would be headed. A narrow door led out the front of the cab and onto another small ledge, surrounded by a guardrail.

As he vaulted the rail and landed on the deck at the rear of the lead engine, he caught a glimpse of white fabric, fluttering in the wind, moving along the exterior of the locomotive, just ahead of him. Without slowing, he reached for his holster, but found it empty. His gun was gone; he had probably dropped it during the fall. His *kukri* however was still sheathed on the opposite side, and he drew it, switching it to his right hand and holding it in a fierce grip as he ran, determined not to lose his last remaining weapon.

Kismet rounded the corner, gathering his momentum to tackle the sprinting figure...

Something slammed into his back and sent him reeling. He staggered, rebounding off the blistering hot engine hood and fell back against the protective railing that lined the walkway. In that instant, he caught a glimpse of assailant, a hulking form beneath a now-grubby sheet that had somehow gotten behind him, and was now advancing with undisguised malevolence.

Kismet tried to get the *kukri* up but was a heartbeat too slow. The man closed the distance and thrust out his hands, wrapping them around Kismet's throat, squeezing the life out of him even as he bent him back over the waist high guardrail.

Kismet's reaction was automatic. He brought his hands up, intending to fight the chokehold, but the hilt of the Gurkha knife was still locked in his right fist. The blade glanced harmlessly off the attacker's forearm, but the mere reminder of its presence emboldened Kismet. He broke off his defensive struggle, and immediately went on the offensive with a backhand slash across his foe's exposed torso.

The man fell back, his howl of rage audible even over the deafening rumble of the diesel engine. Kismet slashed again, a miss, but enough to drive the man back, staggering, his will to fight evidently leaking away along with the blood that seeped from his wound.

Kismet broke off the attack and wheeled around, resuming the pursuit of the lone remaining attacker. There was a flash of light as the cab door ahead was thrown open, and then it was gone as the white-robed figure eclipsed the source. He was there a moment later, but instead of charging in blind he stopped to appraise the situation inside the cab.

The door was still open, and beyond, a shrouded figure brandishing an enormous large bore revolver—possibly a .44 Colt Anaconda or a S&W .500. With a hand cannon like that loose in the cab, he didn't dare rush the man from behind; a single shot, even a glancing wound to an extremity from one of the Magnum rounds, would be lethal. He didn't think the gunman planned on killing the train's engineer, but there was no telling what might happen if he spooked the man.

"Stop the train," the man ordered, shouting to be heard over the rumble of the diesel. He shook the pistol meaningfully. "Now!"

FORTUNE FAVORS

*Then again...*thought Kismet, hefting the *kukri*.

He stepped past the metal threshold and got within an arm's length of the unsuspecting gunman. Over the man's shoulder, Kismet saw two men in work clothes—the train's crew—standing with their hands raised, transfixed by the sight of the enormous gun barrel pointed at them. Kismet's unexpected appearance was enough to draw the gaze of one man, but probably because he had no idea whether Kismet was friend or foe, his terrified expression did not change. The other man turned to comply with his captor's orders.

Kismet drew a deep breath into his battered rib cage, and then with as much forcefulness as he could muster, shouted: "Drop the gun!"

The white-robed man started to turn, the reaction automatic, his instinctive curiosity greater than his fear of an unknown threat. Kismet had been expecting exactly this reaction, and as soon as he saw the barrel of the revolver waver a few degrees away from the train crew, he brought the butt end of the *kukri*'s hilt down squarely on the back of the gunman's head.

The hilt, two dense pieces of hardwood, riveted through the thick steel tang and capped at one end with an eighth-inch thick layer of metal, slammed into the man's skull like a hammer, and he crumpled beneath his sheet, deflating to the floor like some kind of fairy tale ghost banished by a happy thought. The heavy Magnum pistol, still clutched in one fist, thumped to the deck without discharging.

Kismet heaved a relieved sigh and lowered the knife. He made eye contact with each of the men in turn, offering a reassuring nod, then opened his eyes to tell them that they were safe, and that they should under no circumstances stop or even slow the train.

But the words never left his mouth. Before he could speak, heavy hands clapped down on either shoulder and yanked him back, through the narrow doorway and once more onto the catwalk where he stumbled uncontrollably toward the rear of the engine. A foot lashed out and swept his legs from under him, depositing him in a painful heap on the metal grill of the ledge. Flat on his back, he looked up into the blank white of his attacker's disguise. He couldn't see the man's eyes through the ragged holes in the sheet, but the bloody horizontal slash across the man's chest identified him as the man Kismet had earlier struggled with; evidently the man had regained his nerve and wanted back into the fight.

Kismet brought the knife up, and at the same time braced his feet against the walkway, propelling himself backward, away from his foe. The man closed with him, but the distance gave Kismet time to get back to his feet, slashing at the air in front of him to drive the man back. It worked, for a few seconds at least, and then the man reached under his shroud and drew his own blade, a big Bowie knife—easily fifteen inches in length—with brass knuckles on the hilt.

With his nerves already alight from his earlier brush with death, the sight of the heavy blade—a veritable short sword to rival the *kukri*—didn't give Kismet the slightest pause. He had survived more than one knife fight in his life—hell, he'd he survived more than one just in the last week—and he doubted very much the redneck under the sheet could make such a boast.

But then something happened that took the fight out of Kismet. At first it was just a strange sensation, like being pushed forward even though no one was behind him. Then he heard the ominous shriek of metal against metal, and knew what was happening.

Up in the cab, the engineer, recognizing that something very bad was about to happen, was doing the one thing Kismet desperately needed him not to do. He was stopping the train.

Kismet launched himself forward, hacking the air in front of him repeatedly and driving his foe back a step before the man even knew what was happening. The man under the sheet was big—football linebacker big—and surprisingly light on his feet, but Kismet could tell by the way he held the Bowie that his first hunch about the man was right; the only thing this man knew about knife fighting was what he saw in movies. He even tried, at one point, to parry Kismet's blade, like some kind of pirate, fencing with a cutlass. Kismet easily swatted the Bowie down, using the *kukri*'s forward curve like a hook, and then lashed out with a foot. The kick connected squarely with the man's gut and sent him reeling backwards where he tripped on the steps and fell halfway through the door to the cab.

FORTUNE FAVORS

Kismet leaped forward intent on shouting for the engineer to keep the train moving forward, but before he could utter even a syllable, a kick from the supine knife-wielder drove him back. The man was back up in an instant, charging forward with the knife out ahead of him like a lance. Kismet twisted to the side and managed to avoid the blade, but the force behind it—the man's bulky body—slammed into him and both men crashed into the engine hood and tumbled in a tangled mass of limbs and blades on the walkway.

Kismet thought he felt something sharp against his arm—a steel edge cutting through the leather sleeve of his jacket, probably the blade of his own *kukri* which had been torn from his grasp in the collision—but in the desperate unfocused struggle, the only sensation that meant anything at all to him was the persistent shift of his center of gravity as the train squealed to a stop beneath him.

The hand wielding the Bowie knife suddenly came into view above his head; the man had wrestled his arm free and now had the blade poised right above Kismet's throat. Both of Kismet's arms were pinned, immobile beneath the man's body. All he could do was wrench himself sideways as the knife point came down. Something tugged at his shoulder as the blade ripped through the leather, gouging a shallow furrow in the flesh beneath, but then the blade hit the metal of the walkway and stopped cold. The man had put so much force behind the thrust that the abrupt impact caused the hilt to twist out of his hand. Kismet was only peripherally aware of this fact, but he knew he'd avoided being skewered. Twisting again, he heaved himself and his assailant sideways. As the man resisted, Kismet thrust forward, ramming his forehead into the man's chin.

The stab of pain that shot through Kismet's skull was a small price to pay in exchange for the satisfying crunch of his assailant's lower jaw cracking and probably breaking. But that minor triumph did little to change the situation. Without his knife, the hulking attacker was left with only the weapons nature had given him—his fists, his body mass, his evidently superior strength—and unlike the knife, he was clearly more familiar with how to use those. Agonized and enraged, the man started raining blows in the direction of Kismet's exposed face. Kismet, his hands still trapped, could

213

do nothing but raise his head, staying as close to the other man as he could in order to limit the effectiveness of the punches.

The gamble worked. His assailant, frustrated by his inability to pound Kismet senseless, changed tactics and instead pushed away in an effort to extricate himself from the grappling match. Kismet got his arms free, but just as quickly wrapped his legs around the man's middle, trapping him in close combat, the same way he'd been instructed all those years ago when learning ground-fighting techniques in the army. Kismet got his right arm around the man's neck, then caught his right forearm with his left hand and began ratcheting his grip tighter.

The man continued to struggle ineffectually for a moment, but then seemed to realize what Kismet was doing. He stopped thrashing and instead tried to slide his beefy hands in between his vulnerable throat and Kismet's headlock.

The battle seemed to have come to a standstill, with neither man moving an inch. Kismet felt his foe's squirming fingers working into the notch of his elbow and realized that the man was about to succeed. In desperation, he began twisting his own body back and forth, trying to shake the man, the way a predator shakes its prey in its jaws to break its neck.

The man roared in fury, a roar that was all the louder for the fact that the squealing of the train's brakes had subsided to a low rasping. The agonized howl took the last bit of fight out of the man, and a moment later, his struggles ceased as asphyxia bore him down into dark unconsciousness. Kismet held tight a moment longer, fearing that that the sudden capitulation was a ruse, and then heaved the still figure away.

At that instant, the train lurched to a full stop.

Lights flashed and bobbed in the darkness alongside the train, heralding the imminent arrival of Leeds' men. Over the deep rumble of the idling locomotive, Kismet hear the distinctive report of gunfire and knew that, despite his victory in the close-quarters struggle, things were about to get a lot worse.

On hands and knees, he groped for his knife, found it, and was about to stand up when he became aware of another white-robed figure looming over him. The man that had reached the cab first, the one he'd cold-cocked with the *kukri*, had evidently recovered from the blow...and recovered his pistol as well. The gaping barrel of the Magnum was pointing straight at Kismet's face, and as the latter stared back, helpless in defeat, the shrouded man thumbed back the action and tightened his finger on the trigger.

A shot, then several more...too many too count...thundered in Kismet's ears.

But the revolver hadn't discharged.

The man with the big gun flinched as bullets ripped into him and then fell against the guard rail.

In disbelief, Kismet turned toward the source of the shots. Brilliant white light, the beams of a half-dozen or more high intensity LED flashlights, left him nearly blind, but he could just make out the shapes of the advancing group. The men were poised for action, carbines held at the high, ready and trained on him, but they weren't wearing the makeshift disguises of the bunch that had attacked them at the cemetery. This group wore a different uniform; helmets and body armor, tactical vests with spare magazines and other equipment, all in the distinctive gray and off-white digital camouflage pattern of the United States army's advanced combat uniform.

13

FOR THE NEXT TWO HOURS, Kismet barely moved.

Most of the soldiers had swarmed over the locomotive, ensuring that there were no other hostile elements lurking nearby, but two of their number had remained with him, keeping their M4 carbines raised and ready the whole time. He stayed quiet, and except for a few terse commands, so did they.

Once the security sweep was complete, an army medic in full battle-rattle arrived on the scene to begin assessing casualties. Ignoring Kismet, he went first to the man that had been carrying the revolver. He used a pair of trauma shears to cut away the man's disguise, revealing the bland face of a younger than middle-aged man with unkempt hair and a short beard. Kismet surreptitiously watched as the medic checked for a pulse, listened for breath sounds, and then repeated the process twice more before glancing up to the stone-faced riflemen and shaking his head.

The man that Kismet had choked out was luckier. Once again, the mask was stripped away, this time to reveal a much younger man, and the medic successfully found a pulse after a few seconds. He moved to the man's side, giving his security element a better line of fire in case the man came to, and went to work checking for other injuries.

"Broken jaw," he mumbled, as if dictating to an unseen secretary. He probed some more, repositioning the kid and mopping up blood to see if minor wounds concealed more severe injuries. "Superficial laceration to the upper chest...a lot of bruising..." He looked up again, addressing one of the other soldiers. "He'll live, but we should evac him to a local facility."

The soldier nodded and, still keeping his carbine raised with one hand, keyed a radio clipped to his vest and relayed the message.

The medic regarded Kismet with evident apprehension. "I need to check you over."

Kismet nodded, but said nothing. As far as the medic and the soldiers were concerned, he was a potentially hostile combatant; any attempt to put them at ease would probably just make them even more suspicious.

The medic ticked off the list of Kismet's injuries, mostly bruises and abrasions. He daubed Betadine onto a few of the deeper cuts and used butterfly sutures to close the wound on Kismet's shoulder. When he was finished, the medic addressed Kismet with a little less reservation. "You should probably get checked out in the ER as well, but Major Russell wants to talk to you first. You okay with that?"

Kismet nodded again. "I'll live. And the sooner I get to tell my side of this, the better."

The medic cocked his head sideways in a knowing gesture, and then went to work preparing the unconscious man for transport. Once the patient was borne away on a field litter, the long silence resumed, and Kismet waited some more.

The night air was just starting to get uncomfortably chilly when another soldier climbed up onto the walkway. This man had removed his battle armor but still wore a holstered semi-automatic pistol on his hip. There was a gold oak leaf badge on his patrol cap and the name tape on the front pocket of his uniform blouse read "Russell."

Despite being sore, tired and frustrated by the long period of inactivity, Kismet did his best to present a cooperative demeanor. "Major Russell."

The officer cut him off with a brusque wave. "It's Kismet, right?" He spoke with a clipped but precise style, accentuating his faint southern drawl. "Do you have any idea what you have done here? I have got a ten mile section of railroad that's now a crime scene, and now all train traffic on the eastern seaboard is at a dead stop."

Kismet bit back an equally rancorous reply and focused on what the major had, perhaps unintentionally, revealed. "I hope the fact that you know my name means that you've talked to my friends already. Are they okay?"

Russell's mouth twitched a little, as if fighting away a smile. "They're fine and in a lot better shape than you."

"So I assume they've already told you that we aren't the bad guys. The only reason we were even on this train is because we were being chased by the guys in white sheets. We were just lucky that this train happened to be transporting military equipment."

"*You* were lucky," Russell scoffed. "Regulations require an escort when our equipment is transported by civilian carriers, but it's just a preventative measure. If the crazies know that there are soldiers guarding the trucks, they'll think twice about hijacking them. Never in my wildest dreams did I believe someone would actually try."

Kismet thought the officer's manner seemed more irritated than confrontational. "I don't think your cargo had anything to do with this."

"No, I suppose not." Russell put his hands on his hips and sighed. "That bunch in the pickup lighted off like jack rabbits when they got a look at us. Local law enforcement is tracking them down now. Probably not part of any organized group—the local Klan chapter was quick to deny any involvement and I am inclined to believe them."

"Does it matter?"

Russell actually laughed. "More than you might think. If this was an organized attack, and not a bunch of rowdies jacked up on meth and moonshine, then it's domestic terrorism, and that means we break out a can of bureaucratic alphabet soup."

"It wasn't just 'rowdies.'"

"That's what your friends said."

Kismet tried unsuccessfully not to frown. What exactly had Higgins and Annie told this man? Had they mentioned the goal of their quest? Their protestations of innocence would surely be undermined by the revelation that they were really nothing more than treasure hunters. He tried changing the subject. "Can I see them?"

Russell crossed his arms over his chest, his expression at once perturbed and thoughtful. "I guess that depends on whether you can give me one good reason not to simply turn you over to Homeland Security. I'd just as soon do that, and let them sort this mess out."

"I don't know what more I can add." Kismet was choosing his words carefully, but at the same time trying to avoid sounding evasive. "My friends and I are looking for something...call it a historical research project. There's a man out there named John Leeds who wants to beat us to it. We were in the middle of an interview with someone when Leeds and this bunch of 'rowdies' drove up and tried to kill us. We ran into the woods and saw the train. They followed. End of story."

Russell didn't seem remotely convinced, but he didn't turn away. "Tell me more about this project you're working on. If this Leeds fellow is willing to kill, it must be...what, worth a lot of money? Or is it something else?"

Kismet couldn't tell if Russell was sincere. As both a former army intelligence officer and an attorney, he knew a little about interrogations and leading questions. But it wasn't like there was any trap to fall into; Leeds was the bad guy, they'd done nothing wrong, and if push came to shove, he'd argue that in court, never mind how preposterous it sounded. But Kismet didn't really get the sense that the major was trying to trick him. Maybe he really didn't know; perhaps Higgins and Annie had discreetly stayed mum regarding the more fantastic aspects of their mission. He was still trying to figure out how to explain it when Russell's expression abruptly hardened.

The officer frowned as he took a mobile phone from his pocket and glanced at the illuminated display. "Excuse me," he said, and then stepped down from the locomotive and retreated several paces away before taking the call.

Kismet could hear the major's voice and make out a few words—he distinctly heard the man say "yes sir" several times—but the topic of the conversation remained a mystery.

At length, Russell lowered the phone and dropped it back in his pocket with an almost quizzical expression. He addressed the soldiers who had been holding Kismet at gun point, ordering them to stand down then he turned to Kismet. "Let's go find your friends."

Alex Higgins was still trying to process the abrupt change in the demeanor of the soldiers who had been guarding them when he saw Kismet and Major Russell enter the car.

For two hours, he and Annie had been held at gunpoint, separated at different ends of the decades old steerage class passenger coach. Russell had interrogated them each in turn, relentlessly asking the same questions over and over again. For his part, Higgins had kept his answers short, cautious about revealing too much information, and resisting the impulse to ask about Kismet. He knew his daughter well enough to believe that she would do the same. Though obviously dissatisfied with their answers, the officer had eventually left the car, with he and Annie still sequestered.

Then, in response to a radioed message, everything had changed. The soldiers had relaxed their guard and allowed them to sit together, and a few moments later, Kismet appeared looking considerably worse for wear, but moving freely, without any sign of duress.

Annie burst from her seat and threw her arms around him. Kismet winced but gamely returned the embrace. Higgins too rose to greet him, but felt a surge of anxiety at the sudden shift in mood. Something about the whole situation bothered him.

Kismet looked to Russell. "Are you letting us go?"

The major turned away for a moment to converse with another soldier, but then gestured for the three to sit. "You're not in custody," he began. "Of course there are still a lot of questions to be answered, but no one thinks you've done anything wrong."

A long line of soldiers began filing into the car.

"Are we leaving?" Higgins asked.

Russell nodded. "I've been ordered to get this train to its destination, ASAP."

"So much for a ten-mile long crime scene," Kismet muttered. "By the way, I lost my Glock somewhere between here and where we got on. Might be...ah, something else on the tracks too."

"Something else?"

"Something or someone."

"Shit." Russell rubbed the bridge of his nose as if trying to ward off a migraine, then shook his head. "Someone else's problem now."

"But you're taking us along?" Annie said.

Russell's stare remained fixed on Kismet. "It seems this man, Leeds, has attracted some attention at the highest levels. He's a person of interest in a crime spree that occurred in New York's Central Part a couple days ago..."

Annie broke into a coughing fit.

"And there are a few other red flags associated with him. He's got indirect ties to a number of hate groups. Homeland believes he might be involved in some kind of terror plot. And obviously, he's targeted the three of you."

"So when we get where we're going, you'll hand us off to Homeland Security?" Kismet asked.

Russell drummed his fingers on his knee. "You work for the United Nations, right? It would appear that affords you a rather unique status. A sort of diplomatic immunity."

Kismet frowned suspiciously. "I've never heard of anything like that."

"Be that as it may, someone above my pay grade has made it clear that I am not to interfere with you, or whatever it is you are doing, in any way. You are, to put it simply, free to go. In fact, if you really want to, you can hop right off this train and go on your merry way."

"Leeds is still out there," Annie intoned. "Still after us."

"Is that the plan?" Kismet pressed. "Cut us loose in order to draw Leeds into the open?"

Russell managed a wry grin. "That possibility was discussed. However, my orders are to give you safe escort...to wherever it is you are going, and for as long as you need it."

Higgins kept a stony expression and watched carefully as Kismet digested the major's statement. Did Russell know what they were looking for? Did the offer hide some ulterior motive—an attempt by the government to seize control of the Fountain of Youth, if it existed to be found? Or was there some other player at work?

It was just like Iraq; one minute they were up shit creek, and the next...?

Kismet shook his head. "Let me get this straight. You've been ordered to provide a military security escort for us? I think the Posse Comitatus Act makes that illegal."

"Ordinarily, it would require special circumstances—a declared state of emergency, for example—for regular army troops to be deployed domestically. We, however, are a Georgia National Guard Unit, which means we can also be activated by the governor. There's a reciprocity agreement that allows us to operate most anywhere in the US. I don't pretend to completely understand the finer points, but my orders are clear." He paused a beat, and nodded meaningfully. "Whatever you need."

Higgins thought again about what Leeds had told him in Central Park. *Prometheus...*

Kismet has become their bloodhound, tracking down the world's mysteries so that Prometheus can hide them away.

Was that what was happening now?

○

There was no further discussion on the subject of their ultimate destination or purpose. Russell excused himself in order to attend to the responsibilities of command, leaving Kismet and his friends alone as the train began moving again.

Kismet felt a numbing exhaustion settling over him, and was on the verge of nodding off when Higgins voice reached out to him.

"I've got a bad feeling about all this, mate."

Kismet managed to prop his eyelids open and regarded the former Gurkha thoughtfully. He had his own reservations about the situation, and about the unusual offer Russell had made—an offer that was evidently sanctioned by the major's chain of command. On its surface, there was a certain logic to it. Dr. Leeds was by his own admission, a white supremacist, and while not every racist was a terrorist, Leeds had repeatedly demonstrated a propensity for violence and a disregard for the law, so it made sense that he would be on the radar of law enforcement agencies. It was just dumb luck that they had fallen into Russell's lap, and he had to believe that the offer of cooperation had nothing at all to do with the object of their search. Homeland Security wanted to take Leeds down, and Major Russell's Guard unit happened to be in the right place at the right time to accomplish that.

Still...

"I'm with you," he told Higgins. "Sometimes a coincidence is just a coincidence, but it always pays to stay on your toes."

"Do you think that all of this—" Higgins gestured to the train car full of lounging soldiers—"could be...maybe your government trying to get its hands on the..." He trailed off, as if afraid to even utter the words "Fountain of Youth."

Kismet had already considered this, too. "I don't see how they could even know about it. I didn't tell them; did you?"

Higgins and Annie both shook their heads negatively.

"It's still possible that they found out while investigating Leeds; maybe he posted 'Looking for the secret of eternal life' as his Facebook status. Regardless, the Fountain, if it even exists, is on American soil, so the government doesn't need to seize it; it's already theirs."

"You know it's not that simple."

"Maybe not. But better the government than Dr. Leeds." He held Higgins' gaze. "You're with me on that, right Al?"

"Of course we are," Annie intoned, sounding almost insulted.

Higgins nodded too, but Kismet felt a sliver of doubt about his old comrade's motives. He too had a bad feeling about the situation, and it had nothing to do with Major Russell's offer of military assistance.

○

The train reached Atlanta the next morning where the cargo was unloaded and turned over the drivers from the receiving military unit. Most of Russell's men remained there, completing their original mission to guard the shipment, until the transfer was complete, a process that lasted well into the afternoon. The major however, made good on his promise of assistance, offering them lodging at nearby Fort Gillem, a mostly decommissioned army base to the southeast of the city.

"We can put you up there as long as you like," Russell suggested. "At the very least, you can get a decent night's sleep."

Kismet was still undecided about whether to accept the major's offer to provide security for the ongoing search, but as he couldn't remember the last time he'd slept in a proper bed, the immediate invitation was one he couldn't refuse.

The afternoon was spent attending to details such as buying some clothes to replace their tattered, lived-in apparel and arranging for their abandoned vehicle to be released from impound in Charleston and returned to the rental agency. Kismet also took the opportunity to do a little research on their ultimate goal, and that evening, over a meal and few pints of beer at a local brewpub, he told the others what he had learned.

There had been no opportunity earlier for Kismet to share what Joe had revealed to him in Fontaneda's crypt, and despite his willingness to keep them in the loop, it was with some apprehension that he produced the tattooed map he'd cut from the Spaniard's corpse.

Annie's forehead creased in mild revulsion as he recounted the story of how the map had been procured, but he kept the discussion focused on what the map revealed.

"Fontaneda made this for himself," he explained. "He wanted to be able to find the cavern with the Fountain, and probably didn't trust his own memory. He didn't have GPS...hell, there weren't even any proper maps until a couple centuries later, so he would have had to come up with a way to mark its location using reference points that would be easy to find.

"These round shapes are probably lakes. There are a lot of them in the area west of Saint Augustine and unfortunately they aren't a very reliable reference because the geography has changed a lot since then. In fact, it changes almost constantly. "

He tapped the cluster of strange mountain-shapes. "I think this is the key. There aren't a lot of landmarks in Florida, and certainly nothing that could be confused with a mountain."

"They look more like pyramids," Higgins offered.

"That's what I thought as well. And it just so happens, that there are pyramids in Florida."

Despite their unfamiliarity with the region and its history, both father and daughter met this statement with raised eyebrows.

"The technical term is actually 'earthworks,'" he continued. "More than a thousand years before Europeans discovered the New World, several civilizations of mound builders arose in eastern America. The practice of creating earthworks seems to be universal; they are found all across Asia, and the early American cultures probably brought the knowledge with them when they emigrated across the Bering Strait. Most of the American earthworks sites are found in the Mississippi River valley, but there are quite a few in the Deep South as well. They made enormous pyramid-shaped and conical earthworks, as well as some mounds that resembled animals. The most famous of these is the Serpent Mound in Ohio."

Higgins tapped the snake image on the map. "Is that what this is?"

Kismet shook his head. "Fontaneda was definitely on the Florida peninsula. I think he may have found a different serpent mound, one that hasn't been discovered yet, or was possibly flooded or destroyed in the centuries since. But I think these other earthworks—the pyramids—might still be around today. There are several mound sites throughout the state, but I think the best candidate is the Lake Jackson Mounds on the panhandle."

He produced a Florida highway map and unfolded it on the table. He drew a circle near the city of Tallahassee, just north of the inverted V shape of Apalachee Bay. He then laid the tattoo map alongside it, orienting it so that the serpent was pointing down.

"The mounds are our starting point," Higgins observed. "Which way from there?"

Kismet touched another point on the tattoo map in the upper quarter opposite the pyramids, where a tiny cross had been inscribed. "I think this is supposed to represent Saint Augustine." He drew another circle, and then connected it with a straight line to the first, then approximated the converging lines of Fontaneda's map to form an off-center downward pointing triangle. The lines crossed southeast of Gainesville in the Ocala National Forest.

"The entrance to the cavern is where these lines converge." As he circled the X at the convergence of the lines on the highway map, he took another look at what lay in the center of the triangle. The mark was almost exactly on the south shore of Lake George, but what caught his eye was the St. Johns River, flowing north out of the lake and meandering across the landscape all the way to Jacksonville. The undulations of the river course almost exactly matched the curves of the tattooed serpent on Fontaneda's map.

Kismet recalled something Dr. Leeds had told him during their first encounter, that the snake was an ancient symbol of life. In the Bible, a snake had tricked Eve into eating from the forbidden fruit, an action which had led to banishment from Eden and the Tree of Life. In the Epic of Gilgamesh, a snake had devoured a similar plant with the same properties, depriving the hero of the prize of eternal life.

Now it seemed they would be the one's snatching the prize of life from the serpent's devouring jaws.

FORTUNE FAVORS

Despite Kismet's reluctance—and Higgins verbalized objections, there seemed little choice but to accept Russell's offer. The major would be able to provide them with resources that might help them pinpoint the location, but more importantly, the soldiers would keep Leeds off their back. That would be of particular importance if they actually found the Fountain, though when he discussed it with the major over coffee the following morning, he omitted mention of their ultimate goal, saying only that they were looking for a cavern that might be an important archaeological site. Russell seemed to accept the explanation without question as he arranged for a convoy to take them south. The major and his three guests rode in the relative comfort of a government issue passenger van, while a platoon of soldiers from Russell's battalion, part of the National Guard's 78th Homeland Response Force, bracketed them in Humvees.

About an hour into the five-hour journey down the Interstate however, the officer finally indulged his curiosity. "So, I've played along this far. Care to let me in on the big secret?"

Kismet gazed back at him, impassive. "What do you want to know?"

"This is a treasure hunt, right? Your 'archaeological' site..." He made air quotes. "I get that people are willing to kill for money. What I don't buy is that you want it bad enough to take that chance. So what's really going on?"

Kismet felt Higgins' eyes on him as well as Russell's. He glanced off into the distance at the scenery flashing by.

They had just passed Macon, Georgia, which Kismet had been surprised to learn in his research had once been inhabited by the same mound building culture that settled near Lake Jackson. Had those early settlers brought the secret of the Fountain of Youth to American? Were they the "Serpent priests" Leeds had spoken of, carrying the Seed of the Biblical Tree of Life, or something like it?

He put on his best poker face and answered. "I haven't deceived you, major. I'm following up on a lead that someone sent to my office, regarding an otherwise undiscovered cave—a natural wonder—that may also have special historical significance. You'll have to ask Dr. Leeds why he thinks it's worth killing for."

Russell continued to watch him, unconvinced, but did not press the point. "You served, right? Army?"

"Yes." Kismet was nonplussed by the change of subject. "Army intelligence during the first Gulf War. It was ages ago. Didn't end well. Why?"

"Basic military wisdom: know your enemy. Now I know who the enemy is, but without knowing why—his motivation—I can't very effectively defend against him. I think you know more than you are telling. Now, my orders don't require me to know the 'why' but I think that, sooner or later, you're going to have to tell me what makes this cavern so important."

It was early evening when they arrived in Gainesville, where they spent the night at a budget motel just off the Interstate. Russell's men set up a rotating guard schedule that not only maintained security on the vehicles but also watched access to their rooms.

The following morning, they headed east, into the Ocala National Forest. A remote campsite near Juniper Springs was selected, and while the soldier went to work erecting four GP, Small tents, Kismet reviewed topographical maps of the nearby lake country to establish parameters for their search. If the entrance to the cavern lay at the "snake's mouth" as Fontaneda's map suggested, then they would have to concentrate their search at the point where the St. Johns River flowed into Lake George. On the map, the tributary looked eerily similar to a serpent's forked tongue.

In another site, not far from the lake and just to the north of the army encampment, another group was establishing a campsite for the night. To a curious observer, they appeared to be clients of a commercial fishing tour operator, but there were two people in the party who looked completely out of place among the plaid shirts and ball caps that were *de rigueur* among the rest of the group. One was an attractive blonde woman in her early thirties, who might have been lovely were she not so bedraggled by days of travel at an exhausting pace. The humidity had caused her golden hair to frizz about her head like a halo, and she seemed to be attracting more than her fair share of interest from flies and mosquitos, despite the fact that she maintained an almost constant cloud of cigarette smoke around her. The winged insects weren't her only problem either; she was the only woman in a group of men that ordinarily wouldn't have even been in the same zip code as someone with her pedigree, and like a forbidden fruit ripening on the tree, she had unfortunately attracted their attention. Only one man in the group seemed to be immune to her charms and despite her initial ambivalence about him, Elisabeth Neuell now found herself irresistibly attracted to Dr. John Leeds.

She had felt a similar attraction to Kismet, though for much different reasons, and for a long time thereafter, she considered what might have happened if she had stayed with him. That of course hadn't been possible; too much had gone wrong between them. Kismet had always been, at best, nothing more than a means to end.

She had felt similarly about Dr. Leeds at first, but perhaps because he, unlike Kismet, had not succumbed to her repeated seductions, she now found herself obsessed with the idea of having him. Him, and the thing he sought—the secret of Eternal Life.

They had worked well together. It had been she, and not the occultist, who had recognized the clue in Joseph King's letter to Kismet's agency, and realized that it was a literal reference to a cemetery. Without Kismet's interference, they would almost certainly have learned the Fountain's location from Joe and Candace King. And while it was Leeds' money that was paying for their army of redneck renegades, it was her feminine presence that had staved off desertion and mutiny, particularly following the twin disasters at the cemetery and again on the train. Three had been killed and several more wounded. One of them had been arrested and had probably already spilled his guts to the authorities. Her flirtations were about the only thing that kept the rednecks from bolting.

More important even than that, it was she that knew where Kismet and his military escort were going next. "I've got a few secrets of my own," she'd told Leeds. "People in high places who are willing to do whatever I ask."

That explanation wasn't strictly speaking the truth in this case, but it was close enough.

Elisabeth envied Leeds' power, but she too had power, the power to control men—to command them with nothing more than a subtle promise of sexual reward. She rarely fulfilled that promise; to do so would break the puppet strings from which her servants dangled.

But her particular brand of power was a slippery thing. This adventure was proof of that. Dressed in jeans and a man's t-shirt, unable to regularly bathe, check her makeup or keep her hair under control, her visual appeal was diminishing.

There were ways to mitigate that, but it made her think about the real enemy, the irreversible hand of time. Her natural beauty had launched a successful movie career and attracted the notice of one of the wealthiest men on earth, but all of that had been years ago. Botox injections, collagen treatments, even human growth hormones and cosmetic surgery...none of these extraordinary measures could sustain her beauty...her power...more than a few years, a decade at most. The Fountain of Youth would change all of that. It would sustain her power indefinitely.

She hadn't believed in the Fountain at first; she had other reasons for aligning herself with Leeds. It was not Leeds' persuasive certitude that had eventually convinced her that it might be real, but rather the fact that Nick Kismet was looking for it too...and seemed poised to find it first.

She found Leeds, dressed as always in black and seemingly impervious to the oppressive humidity, standing at the edge of the camp, gazing south in the direction of the other expedition. His arms were folded across his chest, but she could see a steel hook, barely visible beneath his left elbow, where his right hand had once been.

Leeds had been disdainful of his doctor's attempt to save his maimed extremity, and as soon as the wound had been stitched, he had asked to be fitted with an artificial hand. The doctor had tried to explain patiently that the injury would have to heal completely—a period of several weeks if there were no complications—before they could begin the equally lengthy process of crafting a custom prosthetic and teaching him how to use it. Leeds rejected the advice, and in the end, the doctor had fitted a simple cuff with a fixed hook over the swollen stump.

Even his disfigurement, and the lethal hardware, Elisabeth found strangely appealing.

Noting her approach, he turned to face her. "Everything is in place," he observed, a tight smile visible on his face. "You know, my dear, I do believe we would have saved ourselves a good deal of effort by simply leaving Kismet alone, and letting him lead us to the Fountain."

"Are you admitting to a mistake?" she asked, incredulous. Could it be that the ever implacable and well-rehearsed Dr. Leeds, was cognizant of his human fallibility. If so, perhaps he had other human weaknesses and appetites to which, despite all evidence to the contrary, he was vulnerable.

Leeds' smile frosted over, but did not vanish. "All things considered, no. He is an unpredictable, dangerous variable. As long as he lives, he threatens the success of our venture. Yet, as fate seems to have given him the lead, I am content to wait."

"And if he finds it first?"

"My dear, why do you suppose I have been so diligent in trying to exterminate him? At every step he has proven more resourceful than I would have believed." His voice dropped to a murmur. "It's enough to make me believe the things they say about him are true."

Then he shook his head as if the thought irritated him. "It does not matter. I am everywhere. Kismet cannot find the Fountain unless I permit him to, and when he does, I shall be there to take it away."

The next morning, the search began in earnest.

Fontaneda's map gave Kismet a good approximation of where the cavern lay, but even if it was precisely accurate, there was a lot of ground to cover, and no indication at all what they should be looking for. The entire region was little more than a thick layer of limestone known as karst, shot through with innumerable wormholes, most of them flooded sinkholes and cenotes. Did the Fountain lie in one of them? Fontaneda's diary seemed to indicate a dry cavern, but that account had been written more than three hundred years earlier; who could say how the topography had changed. To find it, they would have to employ a brute force approach.

They organized in the fashion of a military patrol. The platoon deployed in an echelon formation, spread out in a line that ran north-south, while cutting across the area described by the map from west to east, and then back again in overlapping search lanes. The soldiers carried their M4 carbines, but on Russell's orders, the weapons weren't loaded. They were in a national recreation area, and while they could explain away their presence, even equipped for battle as they were, as a training exercise, live ammunition would raise suspicions and draw unwanted attention to their presence. If they ran into trouble, the weapons could be loaded in a few seconds. Kismet hadn't been able to replace his Glock, but Russell had provided him with an army-issued M9 Beretta. His *kukri* had also been returned.

The first pass followed the edge of Lake George, from the point where it began to curve north and ended at the St. Johns River. The ground was saturated and in some places, they had to wade through knee deep brackish water. Enormous waterlogged cypress trees blocked their path at every turn, throwing the carefully organized search into disarray. To make matters worse, because Kismet had no idea what exactly they were looking for, it was necessary to stop and investigate every sinkhole or depression or unusual lump in the ground to see if it was a clue left by Fontaneda. By the third pass, they were unable to see the lake and the only way to stay on course was by constantly consulting a GPS device.

With the sun settling in the west, they finished their last pass of the day and hiked back to the campsite, tired and dispirited. Russell dispatched two of his men to make the drive into town and bring back pizzas, while Kismet laid out a topographical map of the area and used a highlighter pen to record their progress.

"Doesn't look like we've accomplished much," Annie observed, looking over his shoulder.

Kismet regarded her thoughtfully. She seemed a very different person than the wisp of a girl he'd wrestled with back on *The Star of Muara*. He knew that her bout of claustrophobia in the tunnel under the cemetery had left her feeling embarrassed and vulnerable, but there was something else. She seemed to be clinging to her father, as if afraid to let him out of her sight. Though Kismet was only now realizing it, she had been like that since the incident in Central Park, and he wondered again what had happened to them that day.

"You're right," Kismet admitted. "I think all we did today was eliminate the most unlikely location."

"Why do you say that?"

"Look at where the lines cross." The previous night, he had transferred the information from the highway map to this smaller scale map, doing his best to accurately pinpoint the trajectories Fontaneda had used. The result had been a diamond shaped area, the northern tip of which lay out in the midst of the lake. Most of the diamond covered the inflow of the St. Johns River and its maze of tributaries. Only a very small portion of the diamond fell within the search grid they had employed. "We should have been looking here: in the serpent's mouth."

"In the river?"

Higgins shook his head. "And me without my gummies."

Russell surveyed the map as well. Though he had not been made privy to the original map tattooed on Fontaneda's skin, Kismet had seen no advantage to keeping him out of the loop regarding the area of the search. "We can use boats," he suggested. "I'll make the arrangements."

"Beats the hell out of tramping through the woods," Kismet said.

"Or wading through the muck," Higgins added.

Russell took a long look at the map, as if committing it to memory, then clapped Kismet on the shoulder. "Tomorrow, we'll find it. Whatever *it* is."

SEAN ELLIS

The next morning, Kismet was surprised and a little dismayed to learn that the boats Russell had arranged for were inflatable three man rafts. The rubber boats were more portable than hard-shelled craft like canoes, but more vulnerable to hazards hidden just below the surface, such as fallen tree branches. Eager to get on with the search, he kept these concerns to himself.

They hiked to the lake shore and inflated the boats using portable battery operated pumps. There were six boats in all, accommodating eighteen of them altogether—the rest of the platoon would remain at the camp. Kismet and his friends were assigned to separate boats, each with a two man escort, and the entire element was split into two groups to double their effectiveness.

Russell's boast of finding the goal that day proved overly optimistic. Kismet's concerns about the risk of using inflatable soft boats however, proved prophetic.

It was a little after four o'clock when Kismet and his escort were just paddling out of a minor creek—so tiny that it did not even appear on the detailed topographical map—when the little boat snagged on something.

At first, Kismet thought they had merely grounded on a submerged rock, but the audible hissing noise warned that the situation was far more critical.

"Damn it," raged the soldier at the front of the raft. "I missed that."

Kismet felt a shudder pass through the boat they back-paddled away from the snag. A submerged root shifted beneath the murky water, visible for only an instant as the water came alive with bubbles of air escaping from the ruptured air cell.

Kismet didn't think the raft would sink. The inflatable air cells were all independent, so one leak would not compromise the craft's buoyancy. At the very worst, it would lose some rigidity and take on a little water. Unconcerned, he was about to resume paddling when the soldier nearest to the leak panicked, scrambling away from collapsing cell.

FORTUNE FAVORS

Water suddenly poured into the boat as the undamaged section of the raft became overloaded. The shift caused everyone to pitch forward, and the hasty soldier tumbled into the creek. As he struggle to avoid being likewise dislodged, Kismet realized that the something was moving in the water all around them.

"Snakes!"

"Son of a bitch!" The soldier who had fallen in screamed at almost the same instant, splashing frantically. Amid the froth of white water, Kismet saw a dark, writhing mass fall away from the man's wrist.

Water moccasins!

Kismet's heart lurched into overdrive as he became aware of more of the squirming shapes. He couldn't tell what was a snake and what was just a shadow, but for a moment, they seemed to be everywhere.

Something moved near his foot.

The other boats in the party were already paddling over to help. Russell had his pistol out and was searching for a target, but Kismet barely noticed. At least one of the deadly vipers was in the stricken raft with him, squirming in the water just inches from his leg. Meanwhile, all around the boat, the water was alive with dark wriggling shapes. Before he could move, the man in the water was attacked again.

"Help him!" Annie cried from another boat. She started paddling furiously, as if she might, all by herself, somehow reach the struggling soldier and save him.

Russell fired into the water, dangerously close to both the ailing man and Kismet's raft. One of the squirming shapes exploded in a spray of viscous blood, but the animal continued to thrash violently. Russell fired again and again, emptying the magazine into the water.

Kismet did his best to ignore the tumult outside the raft. With painstaking slowness, he drew his *kukri*, but even that slight bit of movement caught the viper's attention. It coiled and struck...

The dripping fangs closed around the steel of Kismet's knife, and as it squeezed down, the razor edge sliced deep into its head.

With a flick of his wrist, Kismet hurled the mortally wounded snake back into the swamp.

While Russell and his men drove off the rest of the snakes, Annie's boat crew arrived to pulled the wounded soldier into their raft. The man was already clenching his teeth in agony and swearing at his ill luck.

Kismet heard Annie asking: "Will he be all right?"

Actual deaths from snake venom were rare, especially in the United States, but the grim expression of the unit medic as he hastily administered an antihistamine injection filled Kismet with dread.

The man—Specialist Jeremiah Olson—was still alive and conscious when they reached the hastily arranged rendezvous with the rest of the platoon and the Humvee that was waiting to take him to the hospital. There was every reason to believe that the man would survive, but the tragic incident had dealt a savage blow to the morale of the expedition, crushing all hope of finding their goal.

○

Russell waited until they were back at the camp, in the tent and more or less out of earshot from his men, to vent his rage. "I am done with this shit, Kismet. You will tell me what in the hell you are looking for, or I will leave you here, right here, right now, orders be damned."

Kismet sighed. He understood how the major felt; it was a soldier's job to follow orders, even if those orders didn't make sense, and it was the commander's job to send men into harm's way, without knowing the reason for the sacrifices that would be made. But that didn't make it any less of a burden.

On the other hand, would learning the truth about the mission—about the mythical nature of the their goal—put Russell at ease, or make the accident on the water seem even more senseless?

FORTUNE FAVORS

"All right, Major. You probably are going to wish I hadn't told you this, but here goes. You probably know the story of how Florida was discovered, right?"

Russell's eyes narrowed suspiciously. "Spanish explorers, looking for the Fountain of Youth...Wait...is that what you are looking for?"

His tone was incredulous, yet there remained an undercurrent of hope that belied his skepticism.

Kismet gave him a short version of events, starting with the correspondence from the man who had called himself Fortune, and leading up to the discovery of Fontaneda's diaries. He spoke of Leeds only as a rival explorer, omitting mention of all that had happened on *The Star of Muara*. Finally, he showed Russell the map, cut from the Spaniard's own skin.

"You don't seem crazy," Russell finally concluded. "But is any of this even possible? Eternal youth?"

Russell's question, strangely enough, was the one part of the mystery Kismet had not allowed himself to dwell on. From the moment the search had begun, his one thought was to beat Leeds to the prize. He had accepted Fontaneda's account on faith, focusing on finding the cavern, without indulging in "what if" fantasies about living forever or saving the world. He spread his hands, shrugging. "I'm no biologist, but it seems conceivable that some natural property of the water from this Fountain might stimulate new cell growth."

"It could heal wounds?"

"According to Fontaneda, almost instantaneously. But I'm sure if it exists, there's a rational scientific explanation. It's not magic."

"I understand now why this Dr. Leeds is willing to risk so much to find it first. And why we have to make sure he doesn't." Russell leaned over the map table. "So, where do we go from here?"

Before Kismet could answer, Russell's radio squawked. Kismet expected to hear a report from the medic who had gone with the injured soldier to the hospital, but instead he heard the voice of the platoon leader—Lieutenant Pierson—who had gone with Higgins in the second search team, eagerly announcing: "Sir, I think we've found something."

Although there were only a few hours of daylight remaining, Kismet, Annie, and Russell, along with a security detail, set out in the two remaining rafts and paddled for the GPS coordinates Pierson had supplied. About forty-five minutes later, they spied the rafts beached along a low delta that barely protruded from the water's surface.

Higgins was waiting for them, and anxiously guided them to an elevated clearing surrounded by cypress trees where the rest of the group was waiting.

"Well?" Russell asked. "What did you find?"

Pierson almost chortled. "You're standing on it, sir."

Kismet looked down, and then let his eyes roam the shadowy edges of the clearing, expecting…no, hoping, to see a marker of some kind, a petroglyph perhaps…the ancient equivalent of a sign that would point the way to their goal. Then he realized that Pierson had been speaking literally. The clearing in which they stood was almost perfectly square, about ten yards on each side, and was a good thirty-six inches higher than the rest of the land mass.

"It's a mound!" Kismet realized aloud.

Higgins nodded. "Just like your bloody pyramids. Only this one wasn't marked on the map."

"No, but Fontaneda spoke of a village near the…" Kismet glanced at the waiting soldiers and censored himself. "Near the entrance to the cavern. He wrote that, after they had exterminated the inhabitants, the village was overgrown. I think this mound was a part of that village. They probably built up the land here to escape the effects of seasonal flooding."

He clapped Higgins on the shoulder. "This is an important clue, Al. Well done."

"Can you use this to find the cavern entrance?" Russell asked.

"I won't make any promises, but I think we just got a lot closer."

FORTUNE FAVORS

Russell seemed satisfied with that. "Let's head back while we've still got light."

The officer then took something from his pocket. At first, Kismet thought it was the GPS unit, but a second glance revealed that it was a satellite phone.

Russell caught Kismet's apprehensive glance. "Orders. I have to check in daily with headquarters. I should have called as soon as we sent Olson to the hospital, but then all of this happened. At least now there's some good news to go with the bad."

Kismet nodded, but was still a little disturbed by the revelation that Russell had been maintaining regular contact with his superiors. In hindsight, he should have realized that the major would be required to do so, but now he regretted having revealed the true nature of their quest.

Later that evening, Russell's sat phone rang again. He recognized the number on the caller ID display, and answered with a simple, "Hello."

"You've done well, Major." The voice on the other end belonged to the same person that had spoken to him a few nights earlier, after the abortive attack on the train. Now as then, the caller came directly to the point. "The mission has changed. I have new orders for you."

14

They resumed the search the next day from the mound Higgins group had discovered.

Using the rafts to shuttle between land masses, they expanded the search outward in concentric circles and found still more evidence of ancient human habitation.

Kismet kept track of the mound locations on the map and soon had a rough plan of what the native village would have looked like in Fontaneda's day. On paper, it seemed to point like an arrow toward the lake.

"Do you think that's where we'll find it?" Russell asked.

Kismet shrugged. "I'm cautiously optimistic."

The officer considered this answer for a moment. "After what you told me last night..." He paused and glanced around to make sure that none of his men could overhear. "About what it is you're really looking for..."

He stopped again, as if trying to figure out how to broach a very sensitive subject. "Don't get me wrong. I have absolute trust in my soldiers. I've served with a few of them for more years than I can count...But something like this is...well, let's just say I don't think they have the security clearance for it."

Kismet held the other man's gaze. "I appreciate your help so far, Major. But this is not and has never been a military operation. Your men don't need security clearance. And if this turns out to be the real deal, then it won't matter if one of them leaks it to the press or posts it on Facebook. I'll be telling the world anyway."

"Until you do, I think the fewer people who know the exact location—when we find it that is—the better. I'm going to have Lieutenant Pierson pull back and establish a perimeter. I'll stay with the three of you and we'll keep looking."

"The search might go faster with more sets of eyes looking."

"I'm not so sure about that, especially as none of us really knows what to look for anyway." With that, Russell moved off to brief the platoon leader, and a few minutes later, the soldiers departed.

Kismet climbed into a raft with Russell, Higgins and Annie took another, and they began paddling toward the lake.

Lake George was clear and shallow, averaging only about eight feet in depth. At the south end, where it was fed by the St. Johns River—the channel through which the search party had just entered—there was a fan-like accretion of sediment. Throughout Florida's history, the river had been an important commercial route, necessitating occasional dredging which altered the natural flow regime. With the decline of steamboat traffic, the river and lake remained popular with recreational boaters. Management practices were now less intrusive, but frequent seasonal storms that hammered into the peninsula, coupled with the steadily rising sea level due to global climate change, meant that Lake George today bore little resemblance to the lake Fontaneda had discovered. That, Kismet believed, was the reason why they hadn't yet found the cavern; the geography had changed, the entrance to cavern, which had been on dry land when the Spaniard first entered it, was now out there, under the waters of Lake George.

They decided to start close to shore, rowing back and forth, making a visual sweep of the area. Kismet was contemplating ways to expedite the survey—SCUBA gear, or even something as simple as a depth finder—when Annie called out, directing their attention to something on the shore.

It was another mound, a bank, waist-high earth lushly covered in vegetation jutting from between the trees and sloping away into the water. But unlike the other mounds, which had been rectangular, suggesting platforms on which houses might once have been built, this elevated earthwork was narrow and deliberately sinuous, undulating back and forth as it disappeared into the woods.

"Is this it?" Annie whispered, her voice full of nervous tension. "Have we found it?"

Before Kismet could answer, the distinctive crack of a rifle shot echoed across the tops of the trees.

The shift to a defensive stance was immediate, but after a few seconds, when the sound did not repeat, Russell took out his radio and keyed the mic. "Pierson, give me a sitrep."

The only response was silence. Russell tried again, and with each failed attempt to make contact, the furrow between his eyebrows deepened. Finally, he turned to the others. "I don't know what's wrong with the comms. We should still be in range...I'm going to investigate. You three stay here."

"Is it wise to separate?" Kismet asked.

Russell shrugged, but then managed a wan smile. "Probably not. Don't worry. I won't take any chances. And I think you three can take care of yourselves." He nodded to Higgins and his big Kimber rifle.

Before climbing into the raft, he marked the location on his GPS. "I'll meet you back here in, say an hour? Any longer than that, and..." He shrugged and then pushed off, paddling in deliberate strokes for the river channel.

Kismet watched for a few minutes before turning to his companions. "Al, what do you think?"

The former Gurkha shook his head. "Something's wrong."

Annie folded her arms across her chest. "Do you think it's Leeds?"

Kismet didn't want to believe that the occultist had somehow tracked them down once again. Moreover, as ruthless as Leeds was, Kismet had trouble believing that man would go up against the army.

"So what do we do?"

Kismet frowned. They were close; he could feel it.

FORTUNE FAVORS

"This mound is shaped like a serpent, just like the one on Fontaneda's map. The snake wasn't just supposed to represent the river; it also showed what to look for." He pointed into the woods. "The head of the snake is where 'X' marks the spot. So, we find it...fast. And then get the hell out of here until we can figure out what's going on."

Father and daughter nodded in agreement, and Kismet, borrowed pistol in hand, led the way into the woods on the back of the snake. The trees seemed to fold over them, shutting out the light of day and plunging them into a world of shadow and silence. The ground to either side of the snake mound was saturated, and in some places there were deep, reeking pools of stagnate water, buzzing with mosquito larvae. About twenty yards in, Higgins gestured for an abrupt halt, and then pointed down into the murk. At first, all Kismet saw was the dark water and the browns and greens of the forest floor, but as he stared, he saw the statue still form of an alligator—at least eight feet from tip to tail—patiently waiting for something to come within reach of its powerful jaws. They gave the beast a wide berth and pushed forward, but a few moments later, they emerged from the trees and found themselves staring once more out at the waters of Lake George, about a hundred feet east of where they'd gone into the woods. The mound continued out into the lake and disappeared like the first.

"It's a loop," Annie exclaimed.

Something was nagging at Kismet's subconscious, trying to bubble to the surface. The snake, writhing, but ultimately coiling around in a circle to meet itself—"Of course!" he exclaimed. "It's an Ouroboros. Like Leeds' ring, the snake, devouring its own tail."

"Then the entrance is...where? Out there?" She pointed to the lake, approximating a point midway between the ends of the earthwork serpent.

Kismet was about to answer in the affirmative when a nearby tree branch exploded in a spray of woodchips, followed almost simultaneously by the report of a gun.

In unison, they dove for cover, practically tumbling onto the slope of the mound, even as more shots started to thunder from the woods. Clods of earth and splinters of wood showered down on them, and the air was filled with the smell of fresh cut wood and cordite. The shooters were close.

Too damn close, Kismet thought.

It had to be Leeds' men, though he couldn't imagine how they had slipped past the soldiers, or how they thought they were going to escape. It didn't seem possible that the entire platoon could have been wiped out; they'd only heard a single shot...

The shot had been a signal. As soon as he realized that, the other pieces began falling into place, even as the forest around them continued to explode with violence.

A signal to Russell, letting him know that the trap was laid.

Was it Leeds' men shooting at them? Or was it the army?

"Al! We can't stay here."

"Agreed." The Gurkha was on his belly, the rifle cradled in his arms as he scanned the top of the mound in all direction, trying to figure out where the fire was coming from. "But I think they've got us boxed in."

"Then we swim."

Higgins looked at him in astonishment and then glanced at the water. About thirty feet of murky swamp was all that separated them from the open waters of the lake. They would be exposed, but it was the only avenue of escape that didn't require them to run a deadly gauntlet of enemies.

"Give me the rifle," Kismet shouted. "I'll cover the two of you."

"Like hell you will. I'm a much better shot than you, and you're a better swimmer. Take my daughter and get the hell—"

Suddenly the dark water at their feet erupted, as something long and scaly burst onto the slope. Kismet barely had time to turn his head to look before the beast's jaws closed on the meaty part of his calf, and then, as quickly as the attack had begun, it ended with the alligator snatching its prize back into the swamp.

As the water closed over him, the spike of pain through his right leg recalled to Kismet's mind everything he knew about alligators—about their powerful jaws, about how they liked to drown their prey and leave them submerged, sometimes for days, before eating them.

FORTUNE FAVORS

He also recalled watching gator wrestlers subdue the thickly muscled creatures, almost effortlessly holding those powerful jaws because while an alligator's bite strength was almost unparalleled in the natural world, it had almost no muscles for opening its mouths.

As the scaly black monster thrashed deeper into the swamp, dragging him toward the deeper waters of the lake where the killing would surely occur, Kismet wondered if that bit of trivia would be enough to save his life.

○

Annie was still gaping in disbelief at the suddenness of the attack that had snatched Kismet away when more scaly shapes broke from the murk below them. Despite the bullets scorching the air overhead, she instinctively climbed higher, away from the reach of the slavering reptilian jaws. A pair of alligators waited below them, one still half submerged, but the creatures did not advance. The water was their element, and they were nothing if not patient.

Kismet's pistol had slipped from his grasp during the attack and now lay a few feet away from Annie. She scooped it up and was about to fire down at the nearest gator, when the Kimber boomed in her ear and the top of the beast's head exploded. It thrashed violently in its death throes, forcing the other alligator to retreat.

"Save your bullets," her father admonished. "That pistol won't even slow them down."

Helpless, Annie looked past the mortally wounded animal to where Kismet was locked in a struggle to the death with another, while dirt and debris stirred up by the constant barrage of gunfire continued to rain down around her.

○

Kismet felt the vise around his leg loosen almost imperceptibly, but enough. The blunt, peg-like teeth tore through the fabric of his trousers and the skin underneath as he wrenched free. Part of him desperately wanted to put as much distance between himself and the alligator as he could, but he resisted that urge; in the water, the alligator could move like lightning. Instead, he did the only thing he could think of to keep it from seizing him again: he wrapped his arms around its snout and hugged the beast to his chest.

The reptile was a writhing mass of power, stronger than any man he had ever fought. To make matters worse, he had no leverage in the water. It took all his strength to hang on as the animal thrashed, trying to dislodge him. The vestigial legs, which could propel the creature through the water with unbelievable speed, began clawing at him. The raised, scaly ridges on the alligator's back scraped against his chest as the beast twisted completely around in his grasp. It used its immensely powerful tail to throw itself, and its human attacker, from side to side, slamming Kismet against the lake's marshy bottom. Kismet could do nothing but hold on.

Abruptly, the creature stopped fighting him and instead started swimming for open water. Before Kismet knew what was happening, the alligator rolled over and dove for the lake bottom. He struggled for several breathless seconds before realizing that the creature was deliberately trying to drown him.

He didn't dare let go, but beyond that, he wasn't sure what to do. He loosed one arm from around its neck and began pounding at its pale gullet and underbelly, trying to drive it back to the surface. His blows were slowed by the water and bounced ineffectively off the tough scales of the reptile. The alligator continued sweeping its tail, swimming further out into the lake where Kismet would have no chance at all. He felt a pressure change in his ears; the beast was diving, taking him deeper, away from life sustaining oxygen.

He kept hammering his fist against the creature's scaly throat, while with his left arm he kept its mighty jaws pinned shut. The gator seemed impervious to his attack, and was patiently waiting for him to give up and die; it had the luxury of time on its side.

Kismet's lungs were on fire. He shook with involuntary spasms as he fought the impulse to inhale. He had to let go...he had to get to the surface.

He loosed his left arm and felt the monster twist away, its mouth falling open. The creature, perhaps believing that its prey had at last succumbed, stopped thrashing and twisted around to take him in its deadly jaws.

But Kismet hadn't given up. He found the hilt of his *kukri*, and despite the fact that water slowed his movements, thrust the boomerang-shaped blade into its pale belly. The thick hide nearly stopped the knife; only its tip penetrated, but then Kismet got his free hand on the hilt and jammed it deeper, twisting as it penetrated.

The alligator tried to squirm away, but succeeded only in disemboweling itself. Something blunt and hard—the mortally wounded creature's thrashing tail—struck Kismet in the back, forcing the last breath from his agonized lungs. The primal need to breathe overruled all other concerns, and kicking his legs, he broke the surface an excruciating three seconds later, inhaling as much water spray as air.

The gator had dragged him about thirty feet from the shore. He could just make out Higgins and Annie, pinned down near the edge of the woods by the relentless gunfire. Wary of encountering more gators and fully aware that even if he reached his friends there wasn't a hell of a lot he could do, Kismet stretched out his arms and started swimming back to shore.

As he reached the swamp at the edge of the lake, there was a pause in the fusillade. Several seconds passed without a shot being fired; it was as if the attacking gunmen had all emptied their guns at the same moment. In the midst of the eerie quiet, Kismet rose and scrambled toward his friends. He dropped to the ground when the barrage started up again and crawled the rest of the way to Annie. He saw that she was still clutching the Beretta he had earlier dropped.

"Are you all right?" he rasped, his voice barely audible over the constant thunder of gunfire.

Annie nodded, but said nothing.

"Hope you've got a plan, mate!" Higgins shouted.

Kismet didn't.

"This is no good, Nick! We've been here before. You know how it ends."

Higgins' defeatism fanned a spark of rage in Kismet, and before he even knew what he was doing, he ripped the gun from his companion's grasp. "If that's how you feel, then you might as well let me use this."

Higgins gaped at him. Darkness clouded his face; a mixture of embarrassment and seething rage that had nothing to do with the danger they were facing.

Somehow, Kismet couldn't bring himself to worry about the other man's hurt feelings. If they survived the next five minutes, there'd be time to make nice. Shouldering the rifle, he crawled up the side of the mound and risked a quick peek into the woods beyond.

A round hit near his head, spitting a spray of dirt at him and forcing him back down, but in that moment, he glimpsed a target—a man wearing woodland camouflage pants and a gray T-shirt—resting in the lowest limbs of a tree, about two hundred feet away on the other side of the mound. He readied the rifle, and this time when he popped into view again, it took him less than a second to find the man in the reticle of the Kimber's scope and pull the trigger. He was back down, behind cover, before the sniper's lifeless body hit the ground.

He racked the bolt, ejecting the spent casing, and advancing another round into the firing chamber. The magazine held only five rounds, and he had no idea how many Higgins had already used. Annie had his Beretta, with a fifteen round magazine...maybe...if they made every shot count...

He felt a hand on his shoulder. It was Higgins. "I've got an idea—"

"A little late for that!" growled Kismet, pushing him away. Higgins, thrown off balance by the push, nearly fell back down the slope. As he went down, he continued shouting for Kismet to listen, but Kismet paid no heed.

"When I give the word, we're going to go right down the middle," he said, directing his words mostly at Annie. "Right down their throats!"

FORTUNE FAVORS

Kismet didn't wait for either of them to acknowledge. It was a desperate gamble, and survival was unlikely in any case, but their chances would only diminish with hesitation. "On three..."

"One," He took a breath, thinking about how he was going to do this. *Come up, take a shot, move...*"Two."

Annie shouted something unintelligible but he was too focused on the task at hand to even notice. "Three!"

He started to rise, but then a firm hand clapped him on the shoulder, pulled him back and spun him around. It was Higgins.

His old mate's face was twisted into a mask of bitter determination, but that was not what stoppered Kismet before he could give voice to his own ire. Rather, it was the Beretta in Higgins' right hand, the business end pointing at a spot right between Kismet's eyes, that stopped him cold. Instead of rage, Kismet's tone was unnaturally subdued. "What the hell, Al?"

"Drop the gun," Higgins ordered.

"Dad!" Annie gasped. "What are you doing?"

"Drop the gun," he repeated, his voice almost quavering. "We're surrendering."

"Like hell we are," Kismet answered, his tone unchanged.

Higgins drew back a step, as if sensing that Kismet might try to make a grab for the pistol, and thumbed back the hammer. "I'm serious, Nick."

As his initial ire cooled, Kismet realized that Higgins *was* serious. He wouldn't hesitate to kill Kismet in order to save his daughter. With a bitter snarl, he lowered the rifle. "You don't think they'll just let us walk away, do you?"

Higgins took the Kimber from Kismet's loose grip and tossed it to his daughter. "Annie girl, find a rag or something, and tie it the end of the barrel. Run up the white flag."

As if aware of the drama being played out by the three, the shooters in the forest ceased their assault. Higgins took the makeshift truce flag from his daughter and waved it in the air. "Leeds, are you listening?" he shouted in the sudden stillness. "You once asked me to work for you, help you find it before Kismet. Well, I'll take that deal now."

The silence continued, broken only by Annie's whisper. "Dad?"

The betrayal stung, but somehow, it wasn't a complete surprise. Kismet had always wondered where Higgins' loyalties lay. "Why, Al? What did he promise you? Oh, let me guess…Elisabeth."

"Shut it," Higgins snarled. "You don't even know what this is really about. They don't even need to work for it anymore. They just turn you loose and you find whatever they want."

Kismet was taken aback. "Okay. I really have no idea what you're talking about."

"Oh, I rather think you do."

Kismet looked up to the top of the mound, where his nemesis, Dr. John Leeds, dressed as always in black, stood like a triumphant general surveying a conquered kingdom. Elisabeth stood right behind him, and a dozen men, sporting an arsenal of rifles, shotguns and pistols—every one of which was aimed down at them—stood to either side.

Kismet put on his best defiant grin. "Left your sheets at home I see. Too bad. I'd prefer not to have to look at your ugly, inbred faces." He ignored their muttered jibes and profanities, and turned to Leeds. "I like the hook. It suits you."

Leeds cocked his head to one side, his icy expression cracking just a little. "One more debt I shall soon repay."

He turned to Higgins. "Mr. Higgins, what makes you think my offer of a partnership—an offer you rejected—still stands?"

"You want the Fountain, right?" The former Gurkha was breathing rapidly; just getting the words out was an effort.

Leeds waved his hook in a dismissive gesture. "The Fountain is here. I don't need your help to find it. So, my question stands?"

"You were right." Higgins shook his head, as if embarrassed by the admission, but then looked up at the occultist, almost pleadingly. "Everything you told me…Prometheus…It's happening again. They've been calling the shots all along. Helping him without his even realizing it. So you see, this is the only way I can make it right?"

Prometheus.

When Higgins had said it, Kismet felt his own breathing start to quicken. *What the hell?* "Al? What do you know about Prometheus?"

Higgins tore his gaze from Leeds. "I know everything, Nick. How they use you to find these treasures so they can hide them away or use them to rule the world. And then, when you get in the thick, they swoop in and pull you out at the last second, never mind who gets hurt along the way. Like me and the lads in Iraq. Sacrifices for Prometheus."

The raw pain in Higgins' words stunned Kismet. The Gurkha had been carrying this burden for twenty years; it was a festering wound, filled with anger for something that he could barely comprehend.

That was something Kismet understood intimately.

"Al, I don't know what he told you, but I'm not working for Prometheus. I'm trying to stop them."

"Bollocks. You're helping them just by being here. By hunting these treasures and mysteries." He glanced up at Leeds, perhaps looking for confirmation. "How else do you think you got the army on your side? Things like that don't just happen, mate. Not unless there's powerful people pulling the strings from offstage."

Kismet found it hard to refute the accusation because the willingness of the army—or whoever it was that had given Russell his orders—had struck him as suspicious from the very beginning. He tried to change the topic. "Speaking of the army..." He looked past Higgins to lock stares with Leeds. "How did you get past them?"

"They didn't have to," announced another familiar voice; Russell stepped into view, taking a place alongside Elisabeth.

Higgins was visibly stunned by this revelation, the import of which seemed to undermine his accusation. "But...How?"

"You've just got your fingers—" Kismet put added emphasis on the word, "in everybody's pies, Leeds. I hope you know what you're doing, Al."

"I wish I could take credit for this," Leeds said. "Fate put you on that train. But it was my dear Elisabeth that took care of the rest."

The former actress spoke up immediately, as if she had been waiting for that cue. "When we learned that you were in army custody, I made a call to an old friend who owed me a favor—" She flashed a mischievous smile. "And just like that, the major was working for us."

Kismet shook his head in disbelief and fixed Russell with a withering stare. "And I suppose you're going to tell me that you're just following orders?"

The other man's refusal to meet his gaze was the only thing about the situation that gave Kismet any cause to be optimistic. If Russell was as honorable as Kismet believed him to be, then he would surely recognize that, orders or not, he was on the wrong side. He only hoped the major would figure it out and call for his troops before it was too late. He decided not to press the point; if Leeds even caught a hint of dissent, he'd probably have his goons kill Russell without a second thought.

Instead, he turned to Higgins. Despite the betrayal, he got the sense that the old Gurkha sergeant actually believed he was doing the right thing. "Al, he's lied to you. If anyone's with Prometheus, it's him."

The occultist's smile fell like the blade of a guillotine. "I most certainly am not. They are the very essence of evil; controlling the world like puppet masters, squandering the power of the ancients, hiding the truth about who we are and where we came from. They believe they are gods among men, and seek the power of the gods for themselves."

"So, they wouldn't let you join and you're pissed off?"

Though at some level, he thought it must be true, Kismet had tossed the quip out as a defensive mechanism to hide the real impact of Leeds' assertions. This man—this charlatan...this vile racist...this murderer—knew about Prometheus. He had the very answers Kismet had been seeking for more than half his life.

Leeds ignored the barb. "I am pleased that you've seen the light, Mr. Higgins. But I'm sure you understand that my trust is something you will have to earn, especially after refusing my earlier invitation. You may begin by surrendering your weapon."

Higgins lowered the pistol, easing the hammer down and thumbed up the safety. He then took a cautious step up, onto the mound, and handed the pistol over to Leeds, who took it in his good hand and studied it with evident curiosity, as if he'd never before touched a gun. He turned it over several times then gestured to his men.

Several of them advanced and took physical control of Kismet and Annie, pushing them down, frisking them with perverse enthusiasm.

"Leave my daughter alone," Higgins rasped. "That's my price for helping you."

"No deal, Mr. Higgins. You are also a prisoner."

"Dad, why?" Annie's voice was barely a whispered, and although he couldn't see her face, Kismet knew she was weeping.

"Then let me prove it to you," Higgins said. "Give me that gun and I'll finish this. I'll kill him."

Someone let out a low gasp, but Kismet couldn't tell who. A cold wave of adrenaline had washed over him and set his heart pounding in his ears like a jackhammer. He didn't believe for a second that this was what Higgins wanted; it was a bluff, had to be. But he knew it was a bluff that Leeds would call.

He was surprised to hear Elisabeth Neuell speaking out in his defense. "John, we don't need to do this."

Leeds ignored her. "You would kill your friend?"

"Friend?" Higgins spat the word out like a curse.

The occultist smiled again, but this was his customary cool, insincere smile. "Very well. I accept your terms."

The pronouncement left Kismet stunned, paralyzing him long enough that, by the time it occurred to him that there was nothing to lose by making a break for it, two of Leeds' men had already seized his arms, bending them back so that any movement was impossible. He struggled anyway.

Leeds tossed the pistol to Higgins, who caught it one handed. With practiced efficiency, the former Gurkha pulled the slide action back halfway, checking that a round was chambered. He then turned, and without a trace of hesitation, crossed to where Kismet lay face down, took the trigger in a two-handed grip, and pointed it at Kismet's head.

Only then did Higgins stop, glancing up at Leeds to see if a reprieve would be offered.

Finally realizing the futility of the struggle, Kismet stopped thrashing and twisted around to meet Higgins' gaze. "Al..."

There were a dozen things he could have said, a score of pleas he could have made, and every one of them flashed through his head, but he kept quiet. Anything he might say would accomplish nothing more than a futile sacrifice of his dignity.

But he did not look away from Higgins.

"Do it!" Leeds' voice was eager, hungry.

Kismet could see the tendons in Higgins' hand bulge slightly as he started to exert pressure on the trigger—heard the faint rasp of metal sliding against metal—and then, the loudest sound in the world.

PART FOUR
DEPTHS OF A LEGEND

15

CLICK.

For a moment, no one moved. Higgins stood stock still, as if he had expended the last of his motive force in pulling the trigger, and now hadn't the energy to even lower his arm. The sound of the hammer striking the evidently impotent bullet seemed to echo in the silent stillness. Then a sound intruded; the sound of Dr. Leeds laughing.

"Shit," blurted one of Leeds' gunmen, stepping forward and racking a round into the chamber of his pump-action shotgun. "I'll do him."

"No." Leeds didn't raise his voice; he didn't have to. The man quickly relented, backing away as Leeds continued. "No, I've had my little joke. You didn't think I'd hand you a loaded gun, and take the chance that you would shoot me with it?"

Higgins sagged a little.

"When your end comes, Kismet," Leeds continued, his voice still dripping with menace, "it will be far more...imaginative...than the swift release of a bullet in the brain." He turned to his subordinates. "Tie them up."

"Wait," protested Higgins, recovering a little of his nerve. "I meant what I said. You have to believe me."

"I don't have to do anything," countered Leeds. "As it happens, I haven't figured out what to do with you. I'll admit; your change of heart, if sincere, surprised me. Right now, I haven't the time to figure out where your loyalties really lie, but soon...Well, I'll have an eternity."

One of Leeds' men produced a roll of silver duct tape and commenced wrapping several thicknesses around Kismet's wrists—joined behind his back—and ankles. He repeated the process with a scowling but quiet Annie, but then, following a gesture from Dr. Leeds, allowed Higgins to remain free. The former Gurkha chose not to look Kismet or his daughter in the eye, but sank to the ground, and sat with his head resting against his knees as if exhausted or perhaps nauseous.

Kismet still wasn't sure what to make of the earlier scene. He still couldn't believe that Higgins had betrayed them; there had to be some other explanation, and yet, he had pulled that trigger. If not for Leeds' sleight-of-hand, rendering the weapon harmless, Higgins would have taken his life.

Kismet drew comfort from a single fact: he and Annie were still alive; anything was possible.

As soon as Annie was bound fast, Leeds waved his men off and knelt in front of Kismet. "Now, where is it?"

"Where is what?" Kismet replied with mock innocence.

Leeds calmly extended his maimed right arm and placed the tip of the hook in Kismet's left nostril. Despite his determination not to give the occultist the satisfaction of a reaction, Kismet instinctively tried to lever his body up and away from the pinpoint of pain that radiated across his face.

"It's out there," Higgins said, pointing the lake. "Just offshore. That's all he knows."

Leeds stared at Higgins for a moment, weighing the veracity of the admission, or perhaps just trying to decide whether or not to continue tormenting his prisoner, then gave the hook a twist and let Kismet's head fall away. The occultist rose disdainfully and began snapping orders to his confederates. When he finished, all but two of the men vanished back into the woods. Leeds and Elisabeth remained behind, as did his two newest recruits—Russell and Higgins.

Kismet could taste blood in his mouth, trickling down the back of his throat from the scrape in his nostril, minor though it was, the fresh wound somehow hurt more than the dull throbbing in his leg where the alligator had grabbed him. He spat a bright red gobbet in Leeds' direction, not quite close enough to invite a reprisal, but nevertheless a gesture of contempt.

"I'm curious about something, Leeds. How exactly do you plan to keep control of the Fountain once you find it? I don't care how persuasive Lizzy there is, I don't think the government is going to put you in charge. Or are you and the 'white power' boys going to launch the next Civil War from here?"

Leeds cocked his head sideways thoughtfully. "The Fountain? You disappoint me Kismet. I would have thought you'd have figured it out already. The Fountain of Youth is nothing more than an intermediate goal; a means to an end. I thought I explained all this. The Fountain is just a by-product of something far more important."

"You want the source," Kismet said, thinking out loud. "A Seed from the original Tree of Life. Take that and you can make a Fountain of Youth anywhere you like."

"Yes. But it is so much more than that. It is the source of…of everything. Unlimited power."

"Oh my God," Annie whispered.

Leeds licked his lips hungrily. "Indeed."

She blinked at him and then seemed to regain a little of her steel. "I meant, 'oh my God, he's a nutter.'"

Leeds just laughed.

Kismet and Annie, still bound, were bodily carried along the top of the serpent mound to an idling pontoon boat. The craft, a commercial model used for chartered fishing trips, could comfortably seat a dozen passengers and crew, but as they were dropped unceremoniously on the deck, Kismet saw that much of the available space was filled with bright yellow air tanks and other pieces of SCUBA equipment. Four of Leeds' hirelings crowded aboard; the rest melted back into the woods.

Kismet mentally arranged the boat's occupants like pieces on a chessboard, testing different strategies for escape. Leeds' thugs were pawns, but deadly ones, who would probably kill without hesitation. But what about the rest? What about Russell, could he be turned with an appeal to reason? Was Higgins beyond redemption, or would he choose to put his daughter's safety above all else, even as he had apparently done when deciding to surrender in the face of overwhelming odds? With Russell and Higgins on his side, they might be able to overpower the four hired guns; Leeds and Elisabeth didn't pose much of a physical threat. If Kismet tried to escape with Annie, would the two men try to stop him, or would they throw in their lot with he and Annie?

When the last of the group had crowded onto the boat, the skipper—one of Leeds' men—nudged the throttle on the outboard and steered toward the spot where they deduced the entrance to the cavern would be found. The boat had been equipped with a very sophisticated sonar DownScan Imaging Fishfinder; the video screen painted an image of the bottom—and what lay beneath the soft accretion of sediment—in stunning hues of color. But as amazing as the technology was, it only served to verify that Kismet's earlier conclusion about the site was dead-on; at the exact spot where the serpent mound's tale and head would have met, the sonar identified a large round hole in the limestone of the lake bottom—a submerged cenote.

There were probably dozens just like it in the lake. Northern Florida was shot through with limestone caves like the holes in a wheel of Swiss cheese. Nevertheless, Kismet knew that this was the one; this was the entrance to the cavern described in Fortune's letter, the place where Hernando Fontaneda had discovered the Fountain of Youth.

Leeds seemed to recognize it as well. He ordered his man to keep the boat directly above the opening. As they circled the site, Russell took off his uniform, unselfconsciously stripping down to his underwear, and then pulled on a "shorty" wetsuit. Meanwhile, Leeds addressed Kismet.

FORTUNE FAVORS

"Do you know why I didn't just let Mr. Higgins kill you?" Kismet got the sense that it was a rhetorical question, and before he could even begin to formulate an answer, Leeds continued. "I probably should have. Ian said I should kill you—"

"The big guy with the silver tooth?" Kismet replied innocently. "I noticed that he didn't seem to like me very much. What did I ever do to him?"

"Ah, under different circumstances, your ignorance would be amusing. Whatever happened to Ian anyway?"

"Search me. Maybe he was jealous of the magician's new assistant and decided to hit the pavement."

Leeds' eyes narrowed a little. "You're alive because you have the devil's own luck. No, strike that. Luck has nothing to do with it. You have a touch of the divine in you."

The comment hit Kismet like a slap.

"They never told you, of course," Leeds continued. "You are their grand experiment. If you knew what you are truly capable of, it would skew the data, so to speak."

Kismet felt like screaming at him. *Who? Who is running this experiment? How do you know all this? Who in the hell is Prometheus?* He shrugged, saying nothing.

"Ah, and that's what I'm doing right now, isn't it?" The occultist chuckled. "It's fitting really. They have used you to locate the ancient mysteries so they could hide them, and in so doing, hid your own true nature from you. It's appropriate, don't you think, that I should reveal their secret in order to use you for my own ends."

Russell finished pulling on the SCUBA gear and promptly stepped out over the side of the boat, dropping flippered feet first into the lake. He bobbed there for a few seconds, making final adjustments to his mask and regulator, then swam close to the boat. There was a reel of heavy nylon line attached to his belt and Russell secured the loose end to a grommet on the deck of the boat using a small carabiner.

"'I'm ready," he announced.

Leeds was still looking at Kismet. He shook his head. "Listen to me, prattling on about irrelevant things. I was talking about why I haven't killed you. You are still alive because you have a...a talent...yes, that's the word. You have a talent for delivering the goods.

"We both know it's down there, so by all rights, I should kill you now just so you don't queer my plans with that devilish luck of yours. But no, I think it's better to use your gift to my own advantage." Leeds clapped him on the shoulder. "Cheer up, Kismet. If you really are what they think you are, then you'll probably be the first one to see the Fountain of Youth."

"What does that mean?"

Leeds nodded to his nearest hireling, and the man stepped forward, brandishing a cheap-looking switchblade which he used to slice through the tape holding Kismet's hands together. Kismet flexed his arms for a moment, trying to restore the circulation to stiff muscles, but also stalling for time—time in which to figure out how to transform Leeds' reprieve into an opportunity to turn the tables.

"So, you want me to dive down and find the entrance?"

Leeds' man put away the switchblade and then bent over the pile of diving equipment. A moment later, he produced a weight belt which he buckled in place around Kismet's waist.

"Something like that." Leeds smiled his death's head grin. "Once you are inside the cavern, should you succeed in reaching it, you will be on your own for a few moments. My man will follow behind you, and if he does not signal back promptly, I shall feed Miss Crane to the alligators. Understood?"

Annie seemed confused by the exchange and glanced at Kismet. He was trying to think of something to say, some words of assurance, but before anything came to him, a shove from Leeds' goon pitched him over the edge of the boat and into the water beside Russell. Unlike Russell, who wore a bib-like buoyancy compensator, Kismet's only equipment was a twenty-two pound weight belt. He sank like a stone. The last thing he heard was Annie's scream of outrage, before water filled his ears.

The ballast pulled him into the cenote faster than he would have believed. The pressure built in his ears rapidly; his head felt as if it were about to burst. The unexpected shove had caught him completely unprepared. He'd gasped in the instant that he hit the water, but had inhaled almost as much water as air. He flailed uselessly to get control, coughing up great clouds of bubbles from his saturated lungs, as his involuntary descent continued unchecked.

He struggled for the clasp of the weight belt; it was fastened at the small of his back, and try as he might, he could not seem to loosen it.

He saw a blur of illumination floating nearby—Russell, just a few feet away, inverted and kicking with his flippers to match Kismet's rate of descent into the dark hole. He couldn't believe that the officer would just let him drown, but Russell made no move toward him. His attention seemed to be fixed on the shadowy recesses of the cenote.

Kismet felt his chest start to convulse, both from the water he had ingested and the need to inhale. His ears popped, briefly relieving the agony of pressure against his skull, and in that moment, he crashed into something.

The sides of the cenote were dark and ominous, and just barely out of reach, but jutting out from the submerged face was an outcropping of slimy limestone. He had slammed into the protrusion, but was now beginning to drift away from it. He stretched out his fingers, touching the stone, but was unable to grip the slippery surface. His fingernails scraped through a layer of algae, then slipped free.

He dropped rapidly again, the pressure building in his ears. His outstretched fingertips scraped against the vertical surface of the sheer rock face, but there was nothing to grab onto, nothing to halt or reverse his descent. He tried paddling with his hands and kicking with his bound feet, to get closer to wall and find some sort of handhold.

The pressure in his head became unbearable. He gave up trying to swim. A primal, instinctive response forced him to grip his ears with either hand. He snorted through his nose, but the air pocket inside his head resisted. Suddenly he had no more breath with which to combat the increasing pressure. His lungs were empty; his diaphragm was quivering in his abdomen with the need to draw breath.

The pressure barrier broke of its own accord. Kismet opened his mouth to cry out as water rushed painfully into his ear canal, but there was nothing with which to form a scream. His head felt as if it had been ripped apart by the sudden release, and his ears were filled with an agonized ringing.

Then, miraculously, his hand caught on another ledge. A horizontal fissure split the rock face directly before him. The lip to which he was clinging was the bottom of that fissure, but he could make out no details as to what lay inside the impenetrable shadows of the recess.

He tried to reach into the fissure, but again the weight belt pulled him away. His handhold failed and he tumbled away from the ledge. The darkness of the lake bottom seemed to rise up to greet him into its eternal embrace.

When he hit the lake bottom, Kismet immediately sank up to his knees in deep muck, while the resulting cloud of silt completely shrouded him in blackness.

Impotent rage consumed him. He wrenched with his legs, trying to free them from the suction of the submerged mud. An involuntary gasp brought a trickle of water into his windpipe, triggering a violent paroxysm, yet there was no air in his lungs with which to cough. In desperation, he plunged his hands into the mud, tearing at his boots, trying to pull his feet free, but his fingers could find no purchase, and he fell backwards into the mud.

The shift in position created just enough of a gap to allow water to flow between his foot and the sucking mud, and just like that, his left foot came free, not only of the mud but also the duct tape that had bound his ankles together. With renewed hope, he wrenched his right leg. The boot stayed fixed in place, but the laces relented and his right foot was free as well.

Yet he was still a prisoner of the bottom. The mud surrounded him; everywhere he put a hand or foot, it threatened to hold him fast. It would do no good to extricate himself from the mud if he could not swim to the surface, yet even with his feet free to kick, he just wasn't strong enough to swim to the surface with the added ballast of the weight belt. He tore at it, felt it slip around until the clasp was in the front. It came apart with astonishing ease and he kicked up, away from the mud.

He started to sink immediately. There was no air left in his lungs to buoy him up. He fought and thrashed, trying to climb through the water to the surface, but to no avail. Because he was immersed in darkness, he couldn't tell that his vision was tunneling as his brain started to shut down. There was nothing at all to mark his slide into unconsciousness or that moment when his need to breathe became absolute and he took a deep, involuntary breath.

○

Through the crystalline waters of the lake, Russell's bright dive light, illuminated every detail of Kismet' struggle for the passengers on the boat. When Kismet's grip on the ledge failed, Annie cried aloud, "Pull him up!"

She turned to Leeds, pleading. "He's no good to you dead."

The occult scholar watched without expression as Kismet disappeared in a cloud of silt upon touching down at the bottom. "It would seem I overestimated him."

"You can still save him," she cried. "Please!"

"She's right, Leeds." It was her father, unexpectedly rising to her defense. "He's more useful to us alive. Bring him up and let him try again."

Leeds looked away from the lake and fixed Higgins with an imperious stare. "Why?"

"You wanted him to find the cavern with the Fountain."

"And he has. The ledge where his hold failed is surely the cave entrance. Major Russell will run a line inside and explore the interior to see if there are dry spaces beyond. We are nearly there!" Leeds seemed positively exultant.

Horrified and helpless, Annie could only stare into the depths and the billowing sediment cloud that concealed Kismet's fate.

16

KISMET'S NEXT MEMORY WAS OF COUGHING violently, vomiting up water from his lungs, as he lay on a hard sloped surface. He was vaguely aware of a firm hand on his right arm, but his body continued to be racked with spasms and for a moment, that single imperative was the only thing that mattered. Finally, as the fit began to subside, he began looking around.

He didn't think about the fact that he could see until his eyes fell on a bright waterproof flashlight dangling above the gray-white stone surface beneath him. In its glow, he could make out the rest of his environment; he was in a low ceilinged tunnel—a mere crack in the limestone—that sloped up and away from the lake water, which still lapped gently at his feet. The light was tethered to the belt of the wet-suited figure leaning over him and still gripping his arm.

"I think you're going to make it," Russell announced.

"You saved me," Kismet said, between coughing fits. "What the hell did you do that for?"

The major eased back on his haunches. "I think we both know that this isn't going to end the way Leeds has planned. He's bitten off a lot more than he can chew."

"So, where does that leave you exactly? You save me, and then when the feds arrive and start arresting everyone, you can claim that you were one of the good guys?"

Russell shrugged. "Honestly, I don't know. You probably won't believe me when I say it, but I do have my orders. And right now, I'm doing my damnedest to follow those orders without letting that psychopath kill you."

The admission stunned Kismet, almost as much as Leeds' cryptic revelations about Prometheus. But before he could inquire further, Russell slid his diving mask down over his face.

"I need to get topside again. Pretty soon, everyone's going to be down here. Leeds still has your little girlfriend and he won't hesitate to hurt her to get you...or her father...to do what he wants. I suggest you just sit tight and wait. If you can refrain from rocking the boat, there's a chance we all might survive this."

With that, the man dropped back into the water, leaving Kismet in absolute darkness. He was still coughing intermittently, but in the quiet spaces in between, he tried to use his other senses to compensate for his total blindness. The musty air smelled disgusting, like something rotting, but it was breathable. The only sound he could hear was water sloshing at his feet, but the way it echoed gave the impression of being in a much larger space than what he had imagined based on his brief glimpse. Cautiously, he got to his hands and knees and then stood up.

With a hand stretched out in front of him, he started forward. The loss of a boot interfered with his gait, so he kicked the remaining one off and proceeded forward in just his socks, probing with both his toes and his outstretched hand before advancing.

He hadn't gone more than about fifty feet when a splashing noise echoed up the tunnel, accompanied by the glow from a pair of dive lights. He glanced back to find Russell, and another figure climbing out of the water. It was Elisabeth Neuell.

She wore no SCUBA gear—save for a face mask—and no wetsuit. Instead, she was clad only in matching lacy white bra and panties; dry, the undergarments wouldn't have left much to the imagination, and soaking wet, they were nearly transparent as well. She stripped off the mask, cursing when the rubber strap caught a strand of her golden hair, and then realized that she and Russell were not alone.

"Nick!"

For the briefest instant, her face clouded with something like worry, even fear, but then her expression transformed into a dazzlingly perfect, plastic Hollywood smile. She immediately began to shiver in the cool tunnel. Goose pimples appeared on the bare skin of her arms and she hugged herself for a moment, framing her breasts with her arms and accentuating her piercingly erect nipples. Her coquettish pose reminded him of their first meeting in Jin's fortress—the first time she had tried to arrange his death.

Another figure emerged from the water, one of Leeds' hirelings, likewise wearing just a face mask and underwear—Confederate battle flag boxer shorts. He was holding a dry bag, and upon seeing Kismet, quickly opened it and took out a pistol.

"Put that thing away," Elisabeth said. She tried to sound commanding but her shivering made her sound like a harried babysitter pleading with a wayward child.

"Screw you, lady. I'm fed up with jumping through hoops for you and that damn freak. So unless you' gonna do something with that ass ah yours 'sides wiggling it, I think I'll just have me a looksee at this here cave that y'all're so wound up about."

Kismet stepped aside as the man, still clutching the dry bag in one hand and the pistol in the other, charged up the sloping tunnel.

"I don't think that's a good idea," Russell cautioned belatedly.

The hand with the pistol came up, middle finger extended in the air. "Screw you, too. I ain't in your army."

Elisabeth was still sputtering with unfocused rage as the man reached the top of the rise and then stepped over, out of their line of sight.

A loud snap thrummed in the still air, followed immediately by a wet squishing noise. A grunted curse drifted back down the tunnel, and then something heavy crashed to the floor and everything was quiet again.

Kismet shared a confused look with Elisabeth and Russell, but before anyone could voice an inquiry, the pool behind them erupted in a plume like an underwater explosion, and Higgins, with a thrashing Annie locked under one arm, came into view.

FORTUNE FAVORS

Annie, who had only just a couple days earlier suffered a nearly paralyzing bout of claustrophobia, was in full panic mode. Kismet could only imagine her reaction to being ordered to dive into a dark, water-filled hole, and then told to swim into another dark hole with millions of tons of earth poised to bury her alive. He wondered why Leeds hadn't simply just left her topside and saved himself the trouble, but then realized the obvious answer; she was the leverage that would buy continued cooperation from himself and Kismet.

Annie had not stripped down for the swim, and so now was fully clothed but soaking wet. She remained on the verge of hysteria, but when she saw Kismet she brightened a little and wrestled free of her father's protective grasp to rush up the tunnel and embrace him.

"I thought you were dead."

He returned her embrace, holding her tight.

Her shaking relented a little, but she continued to cling to him, refusing to look anywhere but at his face. He eased her forward and continued up the passage to see what had befallen Leeds' hireling. Elisabeth and Russell were right behind them, while Higgins waited, alone and seemingly cast adrift, near the entrance pool.

The headstrong man stood frozen in mid-stride on the threshold of a much larger chamber. Kismet took another step forward and discovered why the man's explorations had ended there.

A pole of wood, bristling with sharp spikes now blocked the entrance to the cavern. Kismet recalled what he had read in Fontaneda's diary; he and the other explorers, besieged by angry natives, had turned the cavern into a fortress, with snares and booby traps as a passive defense against invasion. Evidently, he had left those measures in place, maintaining them over the years.

One of the stakes had impaled the man, who still wriggled soundlessly in his death throes like a worm on a fishhook. The man finally succeeded in pushing himself off of the deadly poniard and collapsed backwards, splashing onto the floor where the last of his lifeblood drained away. Elisabeth turned away in disgust.

Other faces now filled the entry tunnel below them; Dr. Leeds and two more of his hired thugs were advancing up the passageway.

Leeds' gaze went immediately to the motionless form on the ground. "What is going on here?"

"Your man tried to go on ahead without you," explained Russell. "I tried to stop him, but...something happened."

"A parting gift from our friend Fontaneda," supplied Kismet.

Dr. Leeds drew in a sharp breath. He whirled to face Russell, and savagely grabbed hold of the front of his wetsuit with his good hand, bringing the deadly hook on his other to the major's throat. "You saved him?"

Russell sputtered, trying to find an explanation for his actions that would satisfy the occultist, but Elisabeth spoke first. "John, there was a trap. He walked right into it."

Leeds paused, stifling his rage. "A trap?"

He thrust Russell away and turned to Kismet. "You knew about this, didn't you? The Spaniard did this?"

Kismet nodded and flashed a defiant grin. "Better watch your step."

One of Leeds' men knelt beside the body a let out a low wail. "Ah, shit. Lonnie!" Almost clumsily, he scooped up the dead man's pistol and brought it to bear on Kismet.

"Stop it," Leeds barked. "Put that away."

The man, almost blubbering, pointed at the corpse. "He's dead."

"You men knew there was risk in this endeavor. Great accomplishments require great risks, and sometimes, great sacrifices. Your friend took a stupid risk and has paid for his recklessness. But we may yet benefit from his sacrifice."

A wicked gleam flashed in Leeds' eyes as he turned to Kismet. "The Fates must have a reason to keep saving you. Who am I to argue with the forces of the universe? Since you seem so eager to discover the secrets of this place, why don't you take the lead?"

"Why should I do anything for you, Leeds?"

The occultist pointed his hook at Annie. It was answer enough.

Kismet sighed. "All right, Leeds. Let's finish this."

FORTUNE FAVORS

Leeds' party took a few minutes to unpack their gear and dress in dry clothes before pushing on. Russell remained in his wetsuit and carried his SCUBA gear with him, perhaps anticipating more submerged tunnels along their path. Annie had nothing to change into; her father had, against her protestations and without any preparatory measures, grabbed hold of her and jumped into the water. Still, she was better off than Kismet who had somehow lost his shoes, never mind that he looked like he'd been put through a wringer.

He stayed close to her, and that helped, but she was still in the grip of overwhelming emotions. She could not will her body to move; the nearness of the cavern walls smothered her, as did the knowledge that the only escape from this place was through stone and water. Yet, it was not just the irrational fear that stabbed at her heart.

Kismet was still alive, but how long would that last? Leeds was only keeping him around to accomplish his twisted purposes. And she was nothing more to the occultist than a lever to force Kismet—and her father as well, she supposed—to remain compliant. That realization sickened her.

With flashlights to show the way, the party advanced to the top of the rise. The spiked pole still barricaded the end of the passage like a deadly tollgate. Kismet was ordered to investigate the grisly trap while Dr. Leeds kept a firm grip on Annie's shoulder, ready to punish her at the first sign of resistance.

Kismet quickly discovered the trip wire that had triggered the trap and announced that it posed no further threat. One of Leeds' men produced Kismet's *kukri* and used the heavy blade to chop through the barrier, whereupon Leeds gestured for Kismet to proceed.

When Annie got her turn to pass from the tunnel, she discovered a wondrous underground room. Had she been slightly less intimidated by the location of the chamber, she might have been amazed by the discovery.

The walls of the chamber were a smooth, brilliantly white limestone, reflecting and amplifying the glow of the flashlights to fill up the entire area with illumination. There were a few mineral deposits—stalactites that looked like drips of milk frozen forever in time, and stalagmites that rose from the floor like anemic toadstools—which threw long, bizarre shadows against the bright walls. Flowing through the midst of the stone forest was a stream of water, seepage that had found its way down through the bedrock to ooze from the walls and ceiling.

Then Annie saw that not all of the lumps on the floor were stalagmites. There were also bones, picked clean of flesh, but still unquestionably the remains of human beings.

Kismet paused in the center of the cave and contemplated the path ahead. When Leeds approached to question him, he pointed to three separate holes in the limestone walls, passageways which each led in a different direction. "Fontaneda didn't mention anything about this."

"I defer to your judgment," replied the occultist casually.

A surge of quiet terror seized Annie. If they made a wrong turn now, pushing deeper into the bowels of the earth, they might wander forever, never reaching their goal, never escaping to see the light of day.

A closer inspection revealed that the right-hand passage was merely a niche in the wall, reducing their choices by one. Kismet chose to explore the center passage, which seemed to descend slightly. He had only taken a few steps into the shallows when he called an abrupt halt. "It's another trap."

The trip wire was hidden in debris that conspicuously littered the floor. The device, another spike trap like the first, was concealed in a depression in the wall. Only Kismet's cautious pace had prevented him from being skewered.

"Excellent," crooned Leeds. His dark clothes were a stark contrast with the brilliant white of the cavern, and when he spoke, it was if the words were emanating from a hole in the fabric of the universe. "We're on the right path. The Spaniard would not have bothered to defend a false passage."

"I'm going to trigger it," Kismet announced. "Stand back."

FORTUNE FAVORS

He pitched a head-sized rock onto the trip wire. There was a twang, followed by a snap and a blur of motion as the deadly spikes swung out of the wall across their path. An involuntary shriek tore from Annie's chest.

Kismet extended a palm, and to Annie's complete surprise, Leeds' man handed over the *kukri*, allowing Kismet to clear the passage. She was even more shocked when, after sliding the knife blade into his belt, Kismet reached out to her.

"Come on," he said, as if they were the only two people there. He handed her his flask. She accepted it and took a gulp, grimacing as the bourbon went down. Strangely, she did feel a little better.

He returned the container to his pocket and then gave her a hug. "Stick with me. We'll get through this."

Leeds made no move to interfere, but watched them with a bemused expression. "How touching. But be careful about making promises you can't keep Kismet."

"Oh, I keep my promises, Leeds."

"Keeping a promise requires power," retorted the occultist. "You are in my power, and you live or die at my command. Your life, and your ability to keep you word is dependent upon your cooperation."

Kismet just smiled, as if he knew something Leeds didn't, and put his arm around Annie. As they passed the splintered remains of Fontaneda's spike trap, Kismet whispered in her ear. "I swear to you, we'll get out of this, somehow."

A ways further on, Kismet spied another spiked barrier trap. After disarming it, they rounded a corner and came to an abrupt dead end; a massive wall of rough limestone blocked their way.

Leeds strode forward, his eyes now hungry and excited. "This is not possible. We are following the correct path, I am sure of it."

Russell also advanced and began examining the edges of the wall with his flashlight. "This isn't part of the cave. It's a loose rock...like a boulder. See here along the edges...it isn't connected to the walls." He shone his light overhead. "I think the tunnel continues. There might be room to crawl over at the top."

Kismet pulled himself partway up the boulder. "It's another of Fontaneda's traps. He must have rigged up a portion of the ceiling to collapse. This one was an accident waiting to happen. Who knows what triggered it? But if he set one rock to fall, we have to assume that he may have rigged the entire cave to collapse if his final sanctuary was violated."

"A chance we shall have to take," retorted Leeds. "Or rather, I think, that you will have to take."

Kismet's eyes narrowed but he made no retort. Instead, he continued up the rock wall. Annie watched as he picked out handholds and minute cracks in which to insinuate his fingers and toes. With each step, he left dark smudges on the white rock. The scattered chips of limestone debris, no doubt leftover from Fontaneda's engineering project, had cut right through his socks and blood was oozing from dozens of scrapes and cuts on his feet. The injuries however didn't seem to slow him down one bit. He pulled himself up high enough to inspect the top of the barrier then asked Russell to pass him up a flashlight.

"There must be an opening to the outside. I can feel the air moving. God, what a stench."

Major Russell, with a loop of climbing rope draped around his neck like a bandolier, scaled the rock to join Kismet, and quickly rigged up a belaying line.

Annie was an adept rock climber, but as she watched the rest of the group ascend, she was filled with an uncharacteristic panic. They were all squeezing into the narrow gap atop the rock, directly beneath a ceiling that had been rigged to collapse with the slightest disturbance.

"No." She shook her head when her turn came. "I can't."

"There's only one way I'm leaving you behind, Miss Crane," Leeds said, his soft tone making the threat all the more ominous. "And I don't think Kismet or your father would approve of that solution."

Higgins decisively took the fixed rope and secured it around her midsection. "Pull her up," he called to the men already atop the rock.

The ascent was brief, only a few seconds, but it stretched out like an eternity of torment, until at last, she found herself once more in Kismet's embrace. He freed her from the rope and then guided her through the narrow crawlspace and helped her down the other side.

An acrid odor, an animal smell, drifted in the light breeze that wafted through the tunnel, but Annie saw no evidence of anything living in the cave, nor any sign of an exit leading to the outside. Nevertheless, the gentle movement of air gave her hope. Maybe there was another way out, just around the corner...an end to this ungodly nightmare.

Kismet took the lead again, now watchful not only of the floor, which was deliberately littered with chips of limestone, but also the ceiling overhead. Thirty yards further along, he pointed up to an unnatural pattern of cracks outlining a ten foot long section of rock.

"It's Fontaneda's doing," he announced. "A trap, but I can't figure out what the trigger is. Probably a pressure plate on the floor."

Leeds was becoming impatient. "We'll have to trigger it and crawl over as before."

"That's insane. If we drop that rock, there's no telling what might happen. The crash could cave in the whole tunnel or open a crack to the lake and flood us out. We should go back."

Kismet's cautionary assessment set Annie's heart racing again, but seemed to have no effect at all on the occultist. "Find a way, Kismet. Or I'll send Miss Crane ahead in your place."

"No, damn it," rasped Higgins, pushing through to the front of the group. "I'll do it."

The unexpected declaration shook Annie out of her despair. "Dad, no!"

Her father was already striding purposefully toward the area beneath the snare. Kismet stepped in front of him. "Don't be stupid, Al. I don't know what's going on in your head any more, but I know you care about Annie. It won't do her any good if you get yourself killed."

Higgins stared back at Kismet, his expression pained and confused, as if he could no longer remember the reason for the choices he had made. He turned, looking meaningfully back at his daughter.

"Maybe it will," he whispered.

He sprang at Kismet, catching him in a low tackle and thrusting him against the tunnel wall. Kismet rebounded and sprawled face first into the impact zone as Higgins dashed past him, running all out as if pursued by a predator.

His first step crunched loudly on the littering of limestone chips.

Every movement and noise seemed to take place in slow motion as Annie watched; the crunch of her father's boots on the limestone chips, the sound of her own scream, distorted into a ghastly howl.

Higgins' left foot came down, six feet from where Kismet was struggling to rise, and suddenly, the floor beneath him buckled, collapsing away. He froze, his expression both terrified and purposeful.

It was the look of a martyr.

The entire section of floor beneath the cracked ceiling collapsed in chunks. Kismet too slipped forward, caught in a wave of rubble that was rushing into the newly exposed pit. A cloud of dust swirled up from the shower of rock.

Even louder than the rumble of the collapse however, was the twanging sound of a metal wire, concealed by a facade of limestone cement plastered to the cavern wall, being pulled away from the side of the tunnel.

Annie watched in horror as the singing wire exploded from the wall, working its way swiftly toward the ceiling where it would trigger the release of the enormous boulder onto her father and Kismet.

The wire went taut, like the string of a musical instrument stretched between the pit and the wall, just a few feet below the ceiling. It held there for a second, and then snapped with a final discordant twang. The loose end whipped around and disappeared into the rising cloud of dust above the pit.

Kismet felt a sting as the wire lashed across his back, but it was just one of a dozen sensory assaults that he barely noticed in his frantic scramble to get out of the shallow pit. He began clawing at the stone that was piling on top of him, trying to get free of its weight, and out of the pit before the ceiling crashed down upon him. Higgins lay nearby, half buried in the rubble. And in front of him, just a few steps away, was the far edge of pit.

Kismet grabbed the stunned Kiwi by the collar and heaved him forward. They reached the chest high wall of the pit, slipping uncertainly on the loose rubble, and desperately began clawing up the near vertical surface while overhead the rigged boulder groaned ominously.

And stayed exactly where it was.

When Fontaneda had first designed the trap, hewing the stone block out of the surrounding limestone, he had held it in place with just a few thin rock wedges, connected to the trip wire. When the wire pulled tight, the wedges would be dislodged and the block would drop, or so the Spaniard had intended. But centuries of moisture, seeping through the rock matrix and infused with mineral particles had effectively cemented the block in place. The stone remained poised overhead, seemingly ready to drop down and obliterate Kismet and Higgins, but it refused to move.

The trap was a dud.

Kismet lay on his back at the far edge of the pit, staring up in disbelief. Beside him, Higgins sat up, an expression of amazed disappointment replacing the frightened ecstasy of a moment before.

"You could have killed us all." He grabbed Higgins' shirtfront, but the other man just sagged in place, shaking his head miserably. He looked as if the universe, in refusing his sacrifice, had left him completely bereft and Kismet realized that maybe getting them all killed was exactly what Higgins had been trying to accomplish. The former Gurkha, the man he'd once fought beside and nearly died with, was caught in a trap of a very different sort, a web of his own desperate choices.

"Just whose side are you on, Al?" he whispered.

Higgins' wounded expression offered no insights.

"Well done, Mr. Higgins," said Leeds, standing on a narrow ledge that skirted the side of the pit. "Kismet's luck seems to have rubbed off on you. Fortune favors the bold. With men such as you leading the way, I cannot help but succeed."

Kismet turned on him. "You're insane, Leeds. These traps are getting more complex, and more dangerous. We're in over our heads, and we're all going to end up dead if we don't turn back."

"Nonsense. We are beating the Spaniard at his own game. Keep your eyes on the prize, Kismet. Onward!" To underscore the fact that his statement was a command, not an admonition, Leeds caught Annie's wrist in the crook of his prosthetic and pulled her along.

The tunnel turned just beyond the pit and grew increasingly cramped. The naturally formed walls seemed to close in around them, while the floor sloped up sharply. The rock underfoot was no longer the chalky white of limestone, but increasingly dark and oily, stained with a substance that reeked of ammonia and decay.

"Bat guano," Kismet whispered to Annie. "That's a good sign. It means there's an opening to the surface somewhere nearby."

He didn't add that, for a colony of bats to come and go as they pleased, the opening would need to be only a few inches wide.

The tunnel leveled out and then abruptly ended, but this time, instead of a solid rock wall, the passage was blocked by what looked like densely packed soil. Kismet probed it with the tip of his *kukri*, dislodging a large chunk and releasing an almost overwhelming stench of nitrates. Fontaneda's secret lay somewhere on the other side of an enormous heap of bat excrement.

Kismet could still feel the movement of air, and in the flashlight beams, he saw a narrow gap at the top of the mound. Reasoning that the accumulation was looser there, he started digging, using the *kukri* like an entrenching tool. In just a few seconds he broke through to the other side and through this hole he could see dust motes drifting in a shaft of sunlight that stabbed through the darkness of the cavern beyond.

The sight roused him. This was the chance he'd been waiting for. Though it would mean abandoning the search for the Fountain, probably allowing Leeds to seize his prize uncontested, he couldn't pass up this opportunity to escape.

FORTUNE FAVORS

He backed out of the narrow crawlspace he had dug. The rest of the group had backed away from the shower of guano dislodged by his excavation. "It's clear. No sign of any more surprises from our Spanish friend."

Leeds gazed up at him suspiciously. Kismet could almost see the wheels turning in the man's head. Was Kismet trying to trick him? He smiled and gestured forward. "Then by all means, lead on."

It was exactly what Kismet was hoping for. He looked directly at Higgins. "It's a pretty tight squeeze, Al. Keep Annie close so she doesn't freak out."

He couldn't tell if the other man had understood the subtle message, or the implicit offer of trust and forgiveness in his tone.

Are you reading me, Al? We fought on the same side once. I dragged you out of that hellhole in Iraq. Now do this for me.

Higgins just nodded and pulled his daughter close.

Kismet crawled back into the hole and pushed through to the other side, spilling forward down a forty-five degree slope into the cavern beyond. The floor was covered in a thick layer of moist guano, like a peat bog, and his feet sank several inches as he struggled to stand up. From the hole behind him, he could hear Annie whimpering, seemingly on the verge of hysteria, as Higgins prodded her forward.

Perfect!

Kismet scrambled up the crawlspace and reached in, seizing hold of Annie's arm, pulling her through. They tumbled down the slope together, but he quickly got her up and pointed to the shaft of sunlight streaming into the chamber, lighting the way to freedom.

That was when he realized that source of the light was at least twenty feet directly overhead. The almost perfectly round hole might have been big enough to crawl through, but it remained impossibly out of reach.

The ceiling around the hole began to ripple, like a still pond disturbed by a cast stone, and then large pieces of it came loose and started to fall—except they didn't fall. Instead, the shapes began to flit about, swooping back and forth through the air above them. In the brilliant beam of natural light, Kismet could just make out the winged shapes.

Bats.

Enormous bats.

Bats with bodies the size of housecats and leathery wings as long as his arms. There were thousands of them clinging to the ceiling overhead and they were waking up.

Kismet knew that most bats were insectivores, subsisting entirely on winged insects that they plucked out of mid-air with uncanny precision thanks to their natural sonar. Bats could often be found near large bodies of water, where mosquitos provided an endless food supply, which was an absolute necessity since their metabolism demanded that they consume a third of their body weight daily. Most bats weighed only a few ounces. Kismet didn't want to think about how much these monsters would have to eat to sustain themselves, but he doubted that they had gotten so large on a diet of insects alone. In fact, there wasn't any natural explanation for how these creatures had grown to grow to such an extraordinary size.

The Fountain. It's close!

The realization caused him to momentarily forget his disappointment at the aborted escape attempt.

Just ahead, on the wall opposite where they had come in, barely visible in the gloom and partially hidden behind the rising mass of guano, he spied another passage. He pulled Annie close and hastened toward it, even as shouted warnings from Leeds and his men, along with Elisabeth's strident curses, began to echo in the cavern. The noise multiplied, and suddenly the air was thick with giant bats, disturbed from their rest.

Kismet bulldozed through the accumulation of guano and tumbled through into the adjoining tunnel. It was cramped, the ceiling too low for them to stand, but the passage angled up and away from the escalating din in the cavern behind them and into the unknown darkness beyond.

Except it wasn't dark. Kismet could just barely distinguish the outline of the walls and as he drew Annie forward through the winding tunnel, the illumination reflected from the limestone surface grew increasingly brighter until he had no difficulty making out the details of their environment—striations in the color of the limestone, patches of lichen, even a distinctive trail of human footprints worn into the path of rock chips that covered the floor.

He froze in mid-step.

Although he could see, quite literally, the light at the end of the tunnel, a wave of dread crashed over him. In his haste, he'd forgotten to look for more of Fontaneda's traps, and now he felt as if he wandered into a minefield.

He stretched his foot out a few inches beyond what would have been his normal stride, stepping into the impression left, so he assumed, by the Spaniard. It was a gamble; did those tracks mark the safe route past another trap, or were they the bait designed to lure in the unwary?

Only one way to find out.

"Annie!" He gripped her by the shoulders and tried to hold her attention. "I need you to focus. If you want to get out of here, you have to do exactly as I say. Can you do that?"

A nod.

"There are footprints on the ground here. That's the only place it's safe to step...at least I think so. Got it? Step only in the footprints."

"Got it," she whispered.

The tunnel continued for only a few more steps, then opened into another chamber that was lit up like Times Square.

He suppressed the urge to rush forward. Between the place where he stood and the mouth of the cavern, a distance of about four feet, there were no footprints. Fontaneda always stepped or leaped that final interval.

He swung his arms back and then made the leap.

One foot touched down on the hard floor and then the other. Nothing else happened. As he turned, he saw a frame of wood, bristling with sharp stakes, poised just to the right of the tunnel mouth—Fontaneda's final trap.

"Big jump, Annie. You can do it."

She gave a furtive nod, and then took her own leap of faith. It wasn't her graceful best, but she made it with a few inches to spare, and fell into Kismet's embrace. He spun her away from the trap and turned to behold the wonder of Fontaneda's magnificent discovery.

Almost immediately, he felt a faint tickling on his skin, as if he had walked through a strand of spider web. He brushed at his face and felt the familiar sensation ripple across the backs of his hands.

Static electricity, he realized. The atmosphere was ionized like the air around a Tesla coil, and long streamers of plasma—hues of red and violet—danced in the air all around them. Kismet had the impression of standing at the edge of a bottomless pit filled with electrical energy, but then he realized that the lights below them were merely a reflection—a reflection from the mirror-like surface of a large pool that dominated the center of the cavern.

Kismet recalled the line from the letter Leeds showed him, and similar words written by a man calling himself Henry Fortune hundreds of years later.

A cavern where fire dances upon the surface of the water.

They had found it. Fortune's cavern. The Fountain of Youth.

17

ANNIE WATCHED BREATHLESSLY as Kismet advanced into the cavern, and for a moment, forgot completely that she was trapped underground.

The chamber was the largest of any of the caverns they had encountered thus far. It was roughly circular, at least a hundred feet across and nearly as high. The domed ceiling was spiked with stalactites that glistened with every hue of the spectrum and even a few shades that seemed completely unnatural. The pool dominated the floor of the chamber but a walkway—about ten feet wide—encircled it to form an unbroken ring, a near-perfect circle with only one minor deviation. At the rear of the chamber, the walkway became a staircase going up four of five steps to a platform that overlooked the water and another set of stairs that led back down to the walkway. There were carvings on the wall behind the dais and some kind of pedestal, an altar perhaps, but it was difficult to make out any details because the air between them was alive with brilliant discharges of energy.

The pool was the source of the light. Veils of color, red and violet, wove intricate patterns mere inches above the placid surface.

"How is this possible?" Annie asked.

"I think it's ionized plasma, kind of like the aurora borealis. What's making it happen here? I have no idea. But this is exactly what Fontaneda described, so whatever is causing it must be related to the...the power of the water." He shook his head as if trying to remember something. "Leeds talked about a source; a Seed of the Tree of Life, and how it could...I guess the word might be 'supercharge' ordinary water into something that can make a person immortal. Maybe there are other effects, like this plasma storm."

"Is it dangerous?"

"Fontaneda didn't say much more about it, but we should be careful nonetheless." He watched at the light show for a moment longer, and then glanced past her to the entrance. "Leeds' is the real danger. We have to find the source he talked about, the Seed."

"Then what?"

"Use it for leverage; threaten to destroy it if we have to." He took her hand and led her out onto the walkway.

As they neared the upraised platform, they passed a cairn of hewn limestone rocks, some as large as a man's head. At one end stood an ornately carved cross. There was a name carved on it and a pair of dates. Annie looked at Kismet for an explanation.

"Fontaneda wrote about this. In the end, his companions decided to die rather than drink..." His voice trailed off as he looked thoughtfully at the cross, and then looked down at his own hands—scraped raw and streaked with chalk dust and bat guano—and his feet which had been cut to bloody ribbons by the journey through the cave. "The Fountain didn't just give them youth. It healed their wounds. It made Fontaneda strong; supernaturally strong."

Then, seemingly apropos of nothing he took out his hip flask.

"You're drinking?" Annie gasped in disbelief. "At a time like this?"

"I can't think of a better time for a drink," he answered with a roguish smile. Then he upended the container and let its contents dribble out onto the floor. When it was empty, he moved cautiously toward the edge of the pool.

The effects of the plasma storm seemed to increase with his approach. A tendril of light reached out and caught the outstretched hand with the flask. The tongue of energy vanished instantly upon contact, but Kismet jerked his hand back and cradled it against his chest.

FORTUNE FAVORS

"Damn thing shocked me," he muttered, but nevertheless resumed his advance. For a moment, the cave grew dim, as if the jolt had somehow drained the static storm of its power, but after just a few seconds, it started growing brighter again. The brief respite permitted Kismet to reach his goal without being shocked again, and he knelt right next to the water's edge. Annie, braving the storm, moved to join him.

He cautiously probed the air above the water. Wispy tongues of static reached out to him, dancing at his fingertips, but evidently not with the same intensity as the earlier discharge. He drew back his hand and flexed his fingers, trying to shake the memory of the jolt from them. "Whatever is at work here, it's powerful."

Steeling his determination, he held the flask out over the water. The electricity arced into him again, conducting right through the metal of the container, but he resisted the instinctive urge to draw back and instead lowered the flask into the water.

A dull moan escaped his lips as energy began surging through him. A mist of crimson plasma began to swirl around his arm like a veil. Annie reached out instinctively, intending to pull him back, but through clenched teeth he hissed, "Don't touch me."

Through a sheer effort of will, he drew back his hand and with it a flask full of the potent water. The ferocity of the electricity began to diminish again as he moved away, his muscles still twitching uncontrollably from the shocks. A few tendrils of light clung tenaciously to him for a moment then vanished.

"Are you all right?" she asked. She wanted to reach out to him, but his earlier warning echoed in her mind. Was he now charged with electricity? Would a single touch from him knock her on her ass...or stop her heart?

He looked at her and opened his mouth tentatively, as if unsure that any sound would issue. "I will be," he croaked.

Then they both stared down at the prize he had retrieved. She extended a cautious and reverent hand toward it, placing her fingers against the metal.

"It tingles!"

He met Annie's stare, as if asking for her approval. She nodded reassuringly. "Do it."

Kismet raised the flask, as in salute, and then tipped it to his lips.

He felt energy crackle between the flask and his lips, and then the water was in his mouth. There was a faint lingering taste of bourbon, but as the liquid swirled and sizzled across his tongue his ability to perceive even that was overwhelmed. Then the electricity surged through his body, causing the muscles of his extremities to begin twitching uncontrollably. Yet, whereas the static on the surface of the Fountain had been painful, even injurious, the shocks he now felt seemed to revitalize and energize him. He felt the pins and needles of increased circulation in his arms and legs. The liquid, sliding down into his digestive system was like warm liquor in his throat and stomach, and he could feel it passing immediately into his bloodstream. He had taken only a small sip, but the effect was tremendous. His body was alive with energy, his nerves quivering with excitement.

He abruptly felt a profound, gnawing hunger in his belly. The spasms nearly caused him to double over in agony. He groaned a little, and Annie, sensing but not understanding his discomfort, took the flask from his hands and set it carefully on the floor.

She gripped his shoulders. "What's wrong?"

The hunger subsided to a dull throb, but a sense of fatigue quickly replaced it. Kismet felt as if vital energy was being sucked out every pore of his body, drawn down into his core; his muscles felt like jelly.

"Nick, is it the water? Is it poison?"

"No," he whispered.

No indeed.

Not poison. Not harmful in any way, at least not in the small amount he'd imbibed

FORTUNE FAVORS

He could almost see what was happening. His bone marrow was generating blood cells at an astounding rate. His arteries and veins of his body were swelling to accommodate the invigorated blood supply. He greedily sucked in breaths, charging the newly formed red blood cells with oxygen, and those new cells raced throughout his body, delivering their payload to his cells, which in turn began growing and dividing, healing the tissue that had been damaged by injuries too numerous to count.

The process wasn't altogether pleasant. Cells used oxygen as a catalyst, but the raw material needed for growth and regeneration was being drawn from his body's reserves. He didn't know what would happen once those were depleted.

Something else was happening, too. His nerves were being overloaded with sensation. At first it was a merely an annoying itch, but within seconds, the sensation racked him from head to toe—it was especially intense in his feet. The itch grew exponentially, not just on the surface of his skin, but internally, in his organs and musculature. He could not resist the impulse to begin scratching at the painful sensation. His fingernails were visibly longer than just a moment before, and he dug them into the exposed flesh of his feet.

Annie watched, horrified as the effects became starkly visible. In a matter of seconds, Kismet's hair and nails had grown longer. When he started tearing into the bare skin of his feet, she seized his wrists to prevent him, but then gasped in disbelief at what she saw next.

Under the ragged and bloodstained tatters of his socks, his feet had healed completely. Fresh, pink skin gleamed on the soles of his feet, marred only by red claw marks from his uncontrollable scratching, and even those vanished before her eyes.

The hands she held in her own were also healed. The outermost layer of skin, tattooed with scratches and scars, the physical record of the innumerable deadly encounters he had survived over the past few days, sloughed off like the shed skin of a molting reptile, and beneath it was virginal flesh, as pink as smooth as a baby's.

Kismet hugged his arm to his chest and clenched his teeth as he rode out the deluge of sensations. He understood now. This was indeed the Fountain of Youth, but it wasn't magic. When he'd drunk, a chemical message had gone out into his cells, stimulating them to do exactly what they did from the moment life began—create new cells and tissue to replace and repair the old. The only difference was that the water initiated an accelerated version of this process.

The sensory overload reached an almost transcendent peak then began to subside, but he could feel the potency of the Fountain's water tingling within him. It was still active, but for how much longer?

Annie still held him tight. He slowly unclasped his arms from around his chest, and reached out to return her embrace. "It's all right," he whispered. "I'm fine."

He was soaked in sweat, and a chill raised gooseflesh all over his flushed skin, but in every other way, he was perfectly healthy.

Something tickled his forehead, and he reached up to discover that his normally close-cropped hair had become a shaggy mass, a prodigious mane that fell down nearly to his eyes and tickled the back of his neck. A bushy beard had sprouted on his chin and cheeks as well.

He was still marveling at the transformation when he heard the sound of laughter.

Beyond the fantastic glow of the plasma storm, Dr. Leeds stood just inside the entrance to the cavern. The rest of the party had filed in behind him and were now spread out on the walkway to either side of him. They had all made it, though the journey had taken a toll. Elisabeth's legendary Hollywood beauty was concealed beneath layers of guano and dust. Russell was holding a hand protectively against his right side, just under the armpit—the final spike trap had caught him with a glancing blow. Higgins seemed shellshocked, gazing across the pool at his daughter and Kismet with a desultory stare. Leeds however, looked triumphant.

Kismet launched into motion. He thrust Annie aside, into the marginal cover of the limestone cairn, and began sprinting toward the ascending stairs and the dais, where he intuitively knew he would find the Seed from the Tree of Life.

He did not see Dr. Leeds nod sharply to one of his men. The only warning he received was Annie's screamed: "No!"

Something punched into his upper back, just below the right shoulder. The force of the blow spun him halfway around. Even as the report reached his ears, he knew that he'd been shot. A bullet—a .308 round from Higgins' Kimber rifle, though fired by one of Leeds' thugs—ripped through his torso, splattering the cave wall with a chaotic spray of crimson.

His momentum carried him several steps closer to his goal before the agony of the wound blossomed, paralyzing him with the pain. He stumbled headlong, clutching uselessly at the cascade of his precious lifeblood. The wave of pain crested, and then just as quickly subsided as traumatic shock plunged him into a surreal state of hyper-awareness.

He could feel his heart beating, fierce and rapid with adrenaline, but each contraction of the life-sustaining muscle pumped more blood out of the ragged holes in his torso. Blood was spilling inward too, filling his chest cavity, submerging his lungs, drowning him. The brightness of the plasma storm above the pool vanished into a hazy void, filled with white noise.

Annie was suddenly beside him, embracing him from out of the darkness, whispering tenderly in his ear. He opened his mouth to tell her...what? He couldn't seem to connect his thoughts.

Then suddenly he was no longer in the world, no longer in his body. The abyss opened up to receive him, and he had no choice but to plunge into it.

Annie reached Kismet with the report of the rifle still echoing in her ears. She lifted him in her arms, and was immediately drenched in his blood. His eyes were open, yet he seemed to unable to see her.

Tears bled from her eyes, tracing rivulets through the mask of dust on her cheeks, as she hugged him to her breast.

"Annie..."

"Nick. Oh, Nick. Hold on." The words poured from her without conscious thought. "Don't leave me. I love you."

"Seed..."

The effort of speaking that one word was too much. Whatever thought he had tried to communicate slipped from his lips in a trickle of blood.

In a flash of insight, she understood what he had been trying to tell her, and what she had to do next.

She eased his lifeless body to the ground and stood and faced the stairway, but before she could take even a single step, a steel grip clamped her upper left arm. She was hauled back, away from the dais—away from the thing Kismet had wanted her to take—and then spun around to face her captor.

Dr. Leeds glowered at her. "Oh, I don't think so. The Seed is mine."

She struggled, trying to break his grip, but his hook-hand looped around her wrist, turning it just enough to send a burst of pain stabbing through her. With a snort of derisive laughter he thrust her behind him, into the waiting arms of her father.

Higgins held her tight, but she struggled against his embrace. He had betrayed Kismet, betrayed them all. She struggled to the verge of exhaustion against his loathsome touch, but was unable to break free. Finally, she could do nothing but sag in his arms, weeping uncontrollably.

Dr. John Leeds gazed contemptuously down at Kismet's body, and then began ascending the steps.

The cavern might have been Mother Nature's handiwork, but the dais was unquestionably the product of human artifice. The steps were too perfectly cut to be the result of geological processes, but the real proof was the intricate carvings on the back wall; an elaborate scaled serpent, surrounded by wedge shaped marks that told a story in the language of ancient

Mesopotamia. He recognized some of it, and probably could have translated it given sufficient time, but he already knew the gist of what it said. It was a familiar tale; the story of the serpent that stole the source of immortality, a legend built on the bones of what had really happened thousands of years before. It was a story that would rewrite the history books.

The priests of the Serpent cult had stolen the source—the Seed of the Tree of Life—from the god-emperor of Chaldea, the man known to the Babylonians as Tammuz, but also as Gilgamesh and Nimrod. They had stolen the source of his power and immortality and fled east—just as Cain had been exiled into the land east of Eden—and their journey had eventually brought them here, where they had built this shrine.

The head of the carved serpent protruded from the carving, its mouth agape and hollow inside. Leeds realized that it had been crafted to disgorge a trickle of water directly onto the altar, which would in turn decant its contents into the pool, but the snake's mouth and the spout that extended over the pool were both bone dry; the water that had once fed the Fountain of Youth had been diverted.

No matter, he thought. *That's not what I came for anyway.*

Suddenly, the wall of cuneiform writing exploded in a spray of stone chips. Leeds recoiled, incredulous, and turned to see Major Russell, pistol in hand, adjusting his aim for another shot.

Several reports thundered in the cavern, but none of them from Russell's gun. The men he had recruited in Charleston had finally done something right for a change, and cut the treacherous army officer down with a concerted volley. Russell was blasted back into the wall, where he fell into a sitting position with his legs splayed out. He was still conscious, staring at his assailants in mute horror, and then his eyes turned pleadingly toward Elisabeth.

Elisabeth?

Had the ruthless bitch tried to organize a mutiny? Leeds had never completely trusted Russell, much less understood how the actress had been able to so easily win him over to their cause, but now he saw a glimmer of what was really going on.

She wanted the prize for herself. *Typical.* She had seduced the officer with a promise of some fairy tale life together. Perhaps she had intended to make a similar appeal to Kismet, or the brutish Higgins.

Well, let's just nip that little flower in the bud. He nodded to his loyal hirelings and then pointed at the actress, his meaning perfectly clear.

The two men brought their weapons around and took aim at the now surprisingly defiant Elisabeth...

Suddenly Leeds' men began twitching in place, their bodies exploding with gouts of blood.

At first, he thought it was some effect of the static storm above the pool. They had all felt its shocks upon entering, but no, this was something else.

The occultist watched in stunned disbelief as several men—all of them wearing dark military fatigues with matching tactical vests, faces concealed behind black balaclavas—swarmed into the cavern through the opening. Each man held a compact machine pistol equipped with a long sound suppressor, and they quickly moved into defensive positions, sweeping their gun barrels in all directions as if looking for targets.

Another man filed in behind the strike team, and strode purposefully toward Elisabeth. Through some trick of acoustics, Leeds could hear their voices as clearly as if they were right beside him.

"You took your sweet time getting here," Elisabeth complained.

"You didn't give us much time to prepare," the man said, his voice smooth and unperturbed. "And we had to sort out a few loose ends topside." He gestured at Russell, who still clung desperately to consciousness. "And it looks like you've started sorting them out down here as well."

"He was about to take it." She peered across the cavern and fixed her stare on Leeds. "I had to do something."

The statement snapped Leeds out of his paralysis. Though he still had no idea what was going on, he understood that success—no, survival—depended upon just one thing.

He spun back toward the dais and charged up the steps, reaching blindly toward the altar, intent on seizing—

"No! It can't be."

FORTUNE FAVORS

The words were barely out before he felt a series of tiny stings all over his body, like biting wasps burrowing through his clothes and into his skin. His hook hand caught on the edge of the altar for a moment, and he saw splashes of red—his own blood—decorating the serpent's head. Then he reeled sideways and pitched into the shimmering pool.

Annie felt her father's hold go slack. Higgins was transfixed by the events unfolding across the cavern, staring at the mysterious strike team as if they were ghosts. She looked past him, at Elisabeth conversing with the leader of the commando element—at Russell, gut shot and bleeding out—at the pool where the diabolical Dr. Leeds floated like a piece of discarded trash—and at Kismet, dead at her feet.

Then she saw the flask. She'd left it at the cairn when she'd seen Kismet shot. There was still some of the water in it—she could heal him, save him.

She pulled away from her father and retrieved the silvery container, then knelt beside Kismet.

He wasn't breathing. A bubble of blood sat on his lips, his last exhalation trapped within. She hugged his head to her breast, but his sightless eyes gazed right through her.

"Well that's a surprise," crooned a voice from just a few feet away.

Annie looked up and saw Elisabeth and her mysterious savior. Her eyes were blurred with tears and she couldn't bring herself to look at his face.

"I guess we can finally close the book on the great experiment," the man continued, chuckling sardonically. "Now, let's get what we came for."

She heard him speak again, a shout, but the words were unintelligible—an alien tongue she didn't recognize.

"Wait," Elisabeth said, hastily. "They're not part of this."

The man clucked disdainfully. "Loose ends, my dear."

"We can debrief them, bring them into the fold."

Annie started when she realized who Elisabeth was pleading for—Alex and herself.

"Please," Elisabeth begged. "Hasn't there been enough killing?"

"I'm sorry, my dear. To keep a secret such as ours, sacrifices are sometimes necessary."

Annie felt her blood go cold as the man shouted again. The language he used may have been completely foreign to her, but she knew exactly what he had said.

Kill them.

She cast her eyes down, at Kismet's unmoving face, and waited for the silenced bullet that would reunite them.

But the bullet didn't come. Instead, Annie heard a strange, guttural sound burbling across the surface of the pool. She looked up and saw someone standing waist deep in water, surrounded by a corona of violet electricity.

It was Dr. Leeds, and he was laughing.

18

"GUNS?" THE OCCULTIST, WREATHED IN TENDRILS of plasma, tipped his head back and chortled. "You'll have to do better than that."

The static field surrounded him like a diaphanous blanket. Energy swirled around him as if he had become the living nexus of the Fountain's strange power. He raised his hands and light coruscated between his fingertips.

Fingertips!

His hook was gone; his maimed hand had been completely restored.

The commandos opened fire without any prompting and, despite the supernatural power surrounding him, Leeds staggered back under the onslaught, falling once more into the water. But he recovered from the attack almost instantaneously, as if they had done nothing more than push him off balance. His black garments were perforated with dozens of holes, but underneath, his skin was unmarked and radiating brilliance.

He stood again and stretched his hands in the direction of the nearest gunman. A tongue of plasma arced across the water to engulf commando, who evaporated in a cloud of red mist that was sucked back along the tendril and into Leeds' body.

Like an angry god hurling fire at the unbelievers, Leeds reached out for another victim.

Annie felt her father's hands close around her and he began pulling her toward the cairn. She didn't have the strength to fight him, but she tightened her hold on Kismet's body and refused to let go. Higgins just dragged them both, and then covered his daughter with own body.

For several seconds, absolute pandemonium reigned.

She heard shouts and more laughter from Leeds, but there was another noise—a crackling sound like a hissing live wire—that soon drowned out everything else. The harsh smell of ozone filled her nostrils, scrubbing away the sulfurous odor of burnt gunpowder.

And the light—the cavern was lit up like daylight. At the center of the Fountain, Dr. Leeds was blazing like a supernova.

Annie struggled free of her father's protective embrace and gazed out at the chaos.

The remaining commandos continued to hurl rounds at the transformed occultist, but their resistance was merely a desperate effort to distract him so their leader and Elisabeth could escape. But instead of seizing that opportunity, the pair was trying to make their way to the dais.

Leeds seemed not to notice. He reached out from the heart of the plasma storm again, this time enveloping the still form of one of his fallen hirelings, instantly vaporizing him and consuming the resulting cloud of organic molecules. Annie felt a cold rush of horror as she realized what Leeds was doing.

He's feeding,

Behind the veil of pervasive energy, Leeds was undergoing a startling transformation. His hair spilled over his shoulders, a prodigious beard sprouted from what had been a clean-shaven face. Beneath it all, his skin had darkened to a feverish, ruddy hue, and before Annie's eyes, he started to swell.

Another finger of fire lanced out, striking Major Russell, whose scream was cut short as his wounded body disintegrated.

At the center of the raging tempest, Leeds' skin stretched like an overinflated balloon, and then burst, revealing new flesh underneath. Immersed as he was in the Fountain's waters, there was no end to the process; it just kept rebuilding him again and again, and would continue to do so as long as it had the raw materials to work with.

Tendrils of lightning began reaching out of his body, seemingly at random, without any conscious control. The plasma trails stroked the walls, disassembling stone as easily as flesh. Limestone, calcium carbonate, was nothing but than the remains of ancient life forms, compressed together by time and pressure—the perfect fuel for the fire of Leeds' astonishing and endless transformation.

The intensity of the lightning was both blinding and deafening. It soared up into the high reaches of the cavern, dancing between the dangling stalactites like sunbeams in a crystal chandelier. The cave resonated with thunderclaps, vibrations that shook the ground and sent cracks shooting across the smooth stone.

Leeds' clothes had been completely burned away, or perhaps vaporized and ingested like everything else, and he stood naked and exposed in the center of the pool. His skin was peeling away like bark from a tree, but as soon as it sloughed off, new flesh was revealed. Annie saw that something else had changed as well.

Dr. Leeds was growing.

When it had begun, he had been waist-deep in the pool, but now he stood like a titanic colossus with the water splashing around his knees.

Except something was wrong.

The growth wasn't proceeding uniformly. Some parts seemed to be growing faster than others, giving the impression of a hideously deformed creature. Under his beard, his face had become distorted beyond recognition. His torso had grown bloated, top-heavy, on legs that seemed to be atrophying before Annie's eyes. The ribbons of skin peeling away weren't dead layers of epidermis flaking off, but living tissue that also continued to grow haphazardly. In a space of time that might have been measured in heartbeats, Dr. Leeds ceased to be anything remotely human.

And still it did not end.

The misshapen giant form collapsed back into the pool; a grotesque island of flesh that grew like a tumor, drawing still more material into itself with cataclysmic discharges of energy.

Annie felt movement against her body and cried out as something squeezed her arm.

Was this what it felt like? Was it her turn to be ripped apart, reduced to a spray of molecules and consumed by the thing Leeds had become?

But it wasn't the jolt of an electrical discharge she felt.

It was a hand.

Kismet's hand.

○

Death, it seemed, had no secrets to reveal. Kismet's plunge into the abyss of darkness was unremarkable in its similarity to countless reports given of near death experiences. His world had collapsed into a tunnel of darkness, and at its end...heaven?

And he had died, hadn't he? His lungs had filled with blood, drowning him and causing asphyxia. His brain deprived of oxygen, shut down. The electrical impulses from his central nervous system that regulated the rhythm of his heart were cut off. Neurological flat-line; the clinical definition of 'dead.'

And yet, every few seconds, his heart contracted within his chest.

Another source of electrical stimulation was at work within him. The mysterious element that had empowered the water of the pool to rejuvenate his cells—the very substance that reacted with that water to create the stunning plasma storm in the air above the Fountain—was generating random and discordant electrical shocks throughout his muscles.

His blood pressure had dropped to virtually nothing, no oxygen was being carried by the red blood cells that remained in his circulatory system, but something more important was going on. There were still traces of the

FORTUNE FAVORS

Fountain's water in his body, generating those tiny sparks as they went to work stimulating his cells to keep regenerating and reproducing.

What had happened to Leeds on a grand scale was happening to Kismet at the microscopic level. Damaged and ruined cells were consumed, broken down into raw material, transformed into healthy tissue.

After a time, perhaps only a minute or two, his blood vessels were whole again, his chest cavity repaired, the deluge of blood absorbed back into his body. His diaphragm twitched and the tiniest gasp of air was drawn in. His heart gave a spasm, and the blood in his arteries and capillaries and veins...moved.

Kismet sat up, like a sleeper awakening from a bad dream, only to discover that he was in the middle of a much more terrifying nightmare.

"What the...?"

He looked up into Annie's eyes, then past her to Higgins...

Higgins! He felt a surge of anger as he recalled how his old comrade in arms had betrayed him, held him at gunpoint turned him over to Leeds...why exactly, he couldn't remember.

Then what?

It came back to him in chunks. The ordeal on the lake bottom...traps...giant bats...*The Fountain. I drank from the Fountain of Youth!*

And that was it. The last thing he remembered.

He stared into the heart of the raging tempest at the center of the pool; there was something alive there, something that had once been human.

"Leeds?"

Annie nodded.

The sight held him rooted in place. He could vaguely recall what he had felt after tasting the water, and thought he had at least a rudimentary grasp of the principles at work. It was probably beyond the grasp of science to explain, but there was certainly no magic to it. But what was happening in the center of the Fountain was like nothing he could have imagined.

Then he recalled something else, the thing Leeds had truly sought—the Seed.

He turned toward the elevated dais, and that was when he saw the man standing next to Elisabeth.

It had been twenty years since their last encounter, but he recognized the man as easily as if it had only been yesterday.

"Hauser!"

It was a barely a whisper, but somehow the man standing on the platform and likewise captivated, heard him.

Kismet felt a cold chill wash over him that had nothing to do with the cataclysm building in the pool.

Ulrich Hauser.

That was what the man had called himself—the man from Prometheus—the man who had somehow known all about him.

You are their grand experiment.

Ulrich Hauser had left him to die in Iraq—

Or had he?

Kismet, if I killed you, your mother would have my head.

Hauser had said that, all those years ago, just before leaving him on his own—he and Higgins had been captured, tortured—and then, for no apparent reason, they'd been allowed to escape. Had Hauser, or someone else acting on his orders, orchestrated that?

Higgins was right, he realized. *I've never been anything but their bloodhound, their puppet. I found the goddamned Fountain of Youth, and here they are—here he is—to take it away.*

Kismet had wondered if Leeds might be an agent of Prometheus; how else to explain his knowledge of a society so secret that twenty years of searching had not revealed to Kismet even a single clue regarding its existence. Leeds had used his knowledge of Prometheus to coax Higgins into joining his cause, and neither man had suspected even for a moment that their agent was already in place; the beautiful blonde—the disillusioned Sultana, the actress, the professional liar.

In hindsight, it all made perfect sense now. Elisabeth's sham marriage to the Sultan, at the height of her career—the pirate raid on the cruise ship—there was a commonality there: the relics of the ancient world, illicitly acquired by the Sultan's father. And then Nick Kismet—the great experiment—had wandered onstage.

She had tried to kill him, or had she really? She had seduced him—why? And then she had joined forces with Leeds, subtly goading both men into a rivalry that would not only add yet another fantastic treasure—a Seed of the Tree of Life—to Prometheus' secret storehouse of mysteries, but would also give them a chance to put their grand experiment to the ultimate test.

God, she's good.

"Hauser!" he shouted, getting to his feet. He felt strong, surprisingly so, given what he felt sure he had just gone through. "Not this time, Hauser. You're not taking this one away."

The blond man stared back at, turning his head a little as if to bring something distant into focus, and for good reason—his left eye was covered by a square of black cloth.

Well that's new.

He started running, only peripherally aware of the tongues of fire scorching the air above him, licking the cave walls, shattering the limestone with their kiss. Hauser lurched into motion, turning back to his goal.

Kismet knew he wasn't going to make it time, but he tried anyway.

Elisabeth stepped into his path, aiming a compact semi-automatic at his forehead. "Don't," she warned. "I don't know if a bullet will even kill you now, but I'll pull the trigger if I have to."

There was just enough hesitancy in her voice that he believed her. "What about your experiment? What would my mother say?"

She cocked her head sideways. "You really have no idea what's going on, do you?"

A retort was on his lips when Hauser erupted in a string of curses. His rage was so palpable that even Elisabeth winced, dropping her guard for just a moment. Kismet took the chance and brushed past her, vaulting up the steps. He ascended the dais just as Hauser wrapped his arms around the base of the altar, picked it up, and hurled it into the pool.

It took Kismet a moment to understand the reason for the other man's rage.

It's not there. The Seed is gone. Did Leeds...? No, someone else.

His mind turned the possibilities like the pages of a flipbook.

"Where is it?" Hauser raged. "Where in the hell is it?"

"Looks like you were late to this party," Kismet remarked. "No Seed. The Fountain of Youth..." He glanced back at the pool and the storm; the cavern was about to implode, and when it went, that would be the end of the Fountain of Youth. "You lose. I imagine that's a new experience for you."

Hauser wheeled on him. "Where is it, Kismet?"

"Why should I tell you?"

For a moment, the other man just glowered at him. Then his lips pulled back in that Big Bad Wolf smile that Kismet remembered so well. "You know where it is, don't you? What say we make a deal? You tell me where it is, and I let the girl keep on breathing."

Kismet glanced over a shoulder and saw Elisabeth moving toward Annie, the pistol already trained on her. Higgins just stood there, rooted in place.

Kismet wanted to scream at the man. *Damn it, Al. Stand up to them; she's your daughter for God's sake!*

He turned away. "You were probably going to kill us all anyway, right? Oh, maybe you'd let me live for the sake of your great experiment, but as I recall, you have no qualms about leaving me in a room full of dead people. So why should I tell you anything?"

Hauser leaned close, nostrils flaring. "Because there are worse fates in the world than death."

Kismet matched his stare for a moment. "Promise me that you'll leave her alone, and I'll tell you."

The lupine lips curled ever so slightly. "I swear on my mother's life."

"Is that some kind of joke?"

FORTUNE FAVORS

Lightning crackled between the stalactites and a chunk of stone the size of Smart Car crashed down and obliterated a section of the walkway on the far side of the pool. The impact sent a tremor through the entire cavern, opening gaping fissures in the walls, from which water began to pour.

He didn't trust Hauser, but in a few minutes, it wouldn't matter. "Fontaneda took it back to Spain with him."

"How do you know?" Hauser pressed.

"He wrote that he planned to hide it in the Alhambra Palace in Granada."

Hauser fixed him with a single-eyed stare, looking for any hint of duplicity. Then, without another word he turned and fled down the stairs.

Kismet started after him, but Elisabeth warned him off. "Not another step."

"You promised, Hauser. No harm."

"A promise I intend to keep," the one-eyed man assured him. "As long as you stay the hell away from me."

He bent down and seized Annie's arm, pulling her erect.

Kismet took another step forward, but Elisabeth waggled the gun meaningfully.

Another thunderous discharge shuddered through the cavern. The pool was boiling now, and at its center, a hideous mass of wriggling flesh continued to grow.

"Then go!" Kismet shouted. "Get the hell out of here before we all die."

Hauser pulled Annie after him and headed for the exit where the last remnants of his commando force waited. Elisabeth however lingered. "Alex? Are you with us?"

The question seemed to perplex the former Gurkha. He stared back at her, and then turned his desolate gaze on Kismet. His lips formed words: *I'm sorry.*

There was only one thing left to say. "Take care of her, Al. Keep her safe."

Higgins nodded and moved to follow Elisabeth.

"Hey, Al."

303

Higgins paused but didn't look back.

"See you in the next life."

19

AS SOON AS HIGGINS AND ELISABETH passed through the exit, Kismet started a mental ten count. He only got as far as three, when Hauser reappeared in the doorway, holding what looked like a woman's shoulder bag, sewn of olive drab fabric.

"You probably won't die right away," Hauser shouted. "In fact, you might not die for several years. Enjoy your stay!"

With that, he dropped the bag and took off running.

Kismet ran too, back toward the relative safety of the cairn. He threw himself flat behind the piled rocks an instant before the satchel charge detonated.

The explosion was tremendous. Kismet felt the concussion ripple through his body. He'd kept his mouth open slightly the whole time so that the overpressure wouldn't rupture the membranes of his inner ear, but the blast left him stunned.

Because the bomb had gone off almost exactly in the entrance, fully half of the explosive energy had been directed away from the cavern. Nevertheless, the half that had blasted inward was more than enough to finish what had already begun. The already gaping cracks widened, and between them, huge sections of the wall began moving independently, undulating—collapsing.

Suddenly, Kismet's wildly long hair bristled up on end, surrounding his head like a halo, alive with a crackle of building static. Something big was about to happen.

He threw himself flat on the shattered floor.

A bolt of pure blue-white lightning arced between the ceiling and the center of the Fountain. Overhead, the few remaining stalactites began to vibrate violently and explode in a spray of deadly fragments.

In the pool, the thing that had once been Dr. John Leeds exploded in a geyser of blood and tissue.

Annie followed unwillingly but without resistance as the one-eyed man—the man Kismet had called Hauser—led her through the cave with the bats.

Most of the winged creatures were gone, frightened from their dwelling by the release of energies from the nearby cavern, though a few still flitted about overhead. The fleeing group barely took notice.

As they passed beneath it, Annie saw that the opening overhead was larger now, giving her a much-needed view of the sky above the surface world, where she desperately longed to be.

Like the other chamber, the bat den was being reshaped by the cataclysm. The walls, riddled with fissures, were groaning, shifting back and forth like earthquake fault lines. But even more ominous was the sound of rushing waters."

"Hurry!" Hauser urged. "The entire cavern is flooding."

Water began to pour in; just a trickle at first, like a leak in an old roof. The tremors had uncovered ancient reservoirs—pockets of groundwater that would have naturally seeped through the rock and into the nearby lake—and was diverting them into the hollow channels of the cave network. The limestone walls were but a thin membrane, holding back a tremendous underground deluge, and as those walls fractured, an irreversible chain of geological events would transform the labyrinth into a sinkhole, ultimately expanding the boundaries of Lake George.

Though it would be no more significant than any other fishing hole on the lake, the Fountain of Youth was about to be revealed to the outside world.

None of Fontaneda's traps remained to slow their flight, but when they reached the corridor where the boulder-sized stone block traps had earlier daunted Leeds' group, they discovered that the fragile cement holding the remaining block in place had crumbled, triggering the last of the Spaniard's defense mechanisms. They had to crawl over both of the stone blocks to escape. This time, Annie felt not even a twinge of claustrophobia; they were heading for the surface and that was good. If she hesitated, she would die, crushed by stone and water, so the only option was to keep moving.

Suddenly, a massive detonation from deep within the cavern split the length of the tunnel wide open. Annie was knocked flat by the violence of the tremor, which was an order of magnitude more powerful than the satchel charge Hauser had left behind to kill Kismet.

Nick?

She tried to thrust that thought from her mind. She couldn't do anything about it now; she had to get out of this place. But before she could raise her head, water began pouring from the walls, and a freezing wave engulfed her.

○

The climactic blast lifted Kismet off the floor and flung him against the cavern wall, fifteen feet from where he had been standing. He felt as though his body had become a single massive bruise, though as he struggled to rise, the pain receded quickly, replaced by a tingling in his nerves.

He recalled Hauser's parting shot, and wondered how long the potency of the Fountain's water would remain active within him? What if he survived everything—the crushing collapse of the cave, the rising flood of water—and wound up trapped forever, unable to find even the release of death.

Screw that.

A gleaming piece of metal lay nearby; it was his flask. The container was nearly full of water from the Fountain and the metal tingled beneath his fingertips. He stashed it in his pocket, then turned to survey the damage caused by the explosion.

Where the Fountain of Youth had once existed, ablaze with seemingly supernatural energy and a promise of rejuvenation, there was now only a void. A smoking crater, deeper than Kismet's eyes could penetrate, marked the place where it had flourished.

The mass of flesh and organic matter—otherwise known as Dr. John Leeds—had been completely immolated in the eruption. The walkway around the crater was almost completely gone, shattered beyond recognition, impassible, and littered with enormous chunks of rock falling out of the walls and down from the ceiling overhead. The pieces were falling all around Kismet; the next one might, without even a hint of warning, smash him to a bloody pulp.

He had to get out of here.

As he searched for an exit, he realized that, despite the fact that the plasma storm was no more, he could still see. Daylight was streaming in through a rent in the fabric of the cavern's dome. The explosive force of that final discharge had blown a hole in the roof directly over where the Fountain had been. It was ten feet across and getting wider as the edges continued to crumble away. As he watched, a huge block of stone, larger than the original hole, pulled away with a splitting noise. It seemed to hang indecisively for a moment before succumbing to gravity, plunging into the depths of the crater below. The floor trembled with its impact.

A surge of water abruptly exploded into the cavern. Kismet had time only to look up before the wave caught him. The rushing waters lifted him effortlessly, pitching his battered carcass against the fractured wall. It took a moment for him to regain the wherewithal to begin treading the turbulent water, and he bobbed up to the roiling surface as the water rose beneath him.

The suddenness of the collapse made him fear for Annie's safety. How long had it taken Leeds' group to reach the Fountain? An hour? Maybe the return trip wouldn't take as long, but he feared the worst. Nevertheless, one way or another, Annie's fate had already been decided. It was his own fate that remained uncertain.

He tried to swim for the center of the cavern where there was the least chance of being crushed, but the swirling eddies caused by the inflow kept him all but pinned against the back wall, above where the last fragments of cuneiform remained as the only proof that anything he had witnessed here. He fought the currents with all his strength, but was already feeling a profound fatigue. His body had used up the last of its reserves; he had nothing left to give.

Someone pulled Annie out of the water and started dragging her along. She struggled to get her feet under her. Everything was happening too fast. The water was rising rapidly, swirling around her knees, but she found the strength to keep running.

The rushing waters threatened to knock her down again, but the flow of the current was pushing the fleeing group toward their goal. Although the passage was now entirely filled with water, they all knew it was the final hurdle in the path of their escape, and plunged blindly into it.

Annie felt her paralyzing claustrophobia rise again, but that was not the only source of despair. Kismet was gone; he'd been returned to the land of the living only to perish again. There could have been no escape from the collapse of the cavern where they had found the Fountain of Youth. In her heart, she was certain that she would be joining him soon, entombed forever in the constant night of the underworld. Nevertheless, she did not resist as someone took hold of her and pulled her into the water.

Unprepared for the dive, she immediately sucked in a mouthful of brackish water. The liquid ran up her nose and down into her windpipe, causing an uncontrollable spasm. Someone was holding her tight however, and she succeeded in pressing her hands to her face to avoid inhaling any more. She existed for what seemed an eternity in the dark chute, aware that he was pulling her downward, deeper, away from the surface and salvation. Then, just as abruptly, she was rising through the twilight shadows in the depths of the lake. Daylight loomed above her, closer with each passing second, yet impossibly far away.

She broke through the surface, hungrily sucking in breaths. There were dark shapes moving around her in the water. She felt a rush of panic as she recalled the alligators that had attacked Kismet earlier—but no, these were humans—the last remnants of Hauser's assault force. The one-eyed man was there, as was Elisabeth. Then she got a look at the man who had refused to leave her behind.

It was her father. Alex Higgins had rescued her from the horror of the cave, and snatched her from the lake.

The pontoon boat Leeds had used to mount his ill-fated expedition into the depths bobbed nearby, and the survivors were clambering aboard. Higgins propelled her up onto its deck, and then hauled himself up as well.

"Get us out of here." Hauser's breathless command warned her that the danger was not yet past.

An outboard engine roared to life and the boat began steering away from the shore, heading out toward open water. Annie glanced back and saw the lake's perimeter transformed in an instant.

The shoreline crumbled away, vanishing into the water, sending out waves that rocked the retreating boat. Cypress trees groaned and toppled into the newly created voids. The serpent mound, which had once pointed the way to the Fountain, seemed to come alive, crawling and undulating into the depths.

Kismet was down there somewhere—lost forever.

Despair and exhaustion overcame her, and when she closed her eyes to hold back the tears, unconsciousness quickly claimed her.

FORTUNE FAVORS

Something splashed in the water next to Kismet, not a dislodged piece of stone, but something else. For a second, it looked like a snake and he instinctively tried to draw back from it, but then he realized that it was a rope, hanging down from the darkness overhead.

What the hell...?

It was like some kind of insane practical joke; a rope appearing out of nowhere, leading—where?

He reached for the line, snaring it on his second try, and clutched it greedily to his chest, but try as he might, he could not make the ascent. His arms were just too tired; his bare feet slipped uncertainly on the wet threads. With the last of his fading strength, he wrapped the line around his waist twice, tying it off with a crude knot, and then sagged in the noose, awaiting whatever would follow.

The rope went taut and Kismet was yanked straight up, out of the water. The line was pulled in steadily, as if attached to a reel, and after just a couple seconds, the ceiling of the cavern loomed close...and then swallowed him whole.

He spent just a moment in the total darkness of a vertical shaft, before hands reached out to draw him over a stone lip and onto a ledge. There was light here; a flashlight beam shone directly onto his face.

"Come on! Run!"

The voice was familiar, but he couldn't place it, and there was not a single reason in the world to ignore the exhortation. He took off blindly, finding his way along the tunnel by following the cone of illumination cast by his guide's flashlight.

The escape route chosen by Kismet's barely glimpsed benefactor was more of an obstacle course than a tunnel. The passage had been carved out by nature, streams of water seeking the path of least resistance over the course of thousands, or more probably, millions of years, burrowing through softer portions of the rock matrix, driven by gravity and pressure. There were cramped spaces only a foot or two high where Kismet had to crawl, squirming around sharp corners and through choke points. There were places where he had to climb, groping blindly in the almost total darkness to find his way up to the next passage, visible only because of the indirect light from his savior's lamp. The only constant was that they were going up.

The entire journey lasted only a few minutes and covered a distance of only a few hundred yards, but the tremors shuddering through the rock beneath him were a constant reminder that, at any moment, the whole place might collapse on top of him, smashing him to oblivion. And then, without any hint that the end—one way or another—was close, he spilled out into daylight.

He lay in a foot of water at the bottom of a limestone depression, a naturally occurring well perhaps twenty feet across. Above him, a vertical distance of about twelve feet, he saw the tree limbs waving gently, backlit by the azure Florida sky. Dangling down one side of the pit was a rope ladder. The man that had saved him was already halfway up, and at its top, a young African-American woman was shouting down at Kismet, urging him to climb.

He struggled to his feet, slipping uncertainly on the slimy stone at the bottom of the hole. The ground continued to shudder violently, but he managed to reach the smooth rock wall and used it to steady himself as he circled to the ladder. When his fingers curled around the rope rungs, he felt a surge of energy in his tired limbs.

The ascent was like a final insult, a parting shot from the hellish underworld he had just escaped. His bare feet couldn't seem to find a purchase on the woven fibers, and when they did, the rope pressed painfully into the soles of his feet. Every time he tried to pull himself up, his arms felt he was lifting the weight of the world. But then, as he neared the top, he saw hands reaching down to him, and at last glimpsed the familiar face of his savior.

"Joe?"

The shoreline of Lake George expanded, claiming the new depths for itself. Standing at its edge, watching as the lake poured into the newly created sinkhole, Kismet saw that the cavern which had concealed the Fountain of Youth for untold millennia had not been far at all from the boundaries of the lake. In time, perhaps a few more centuries of pounding by tropical storms, the cavern would have flooded naturally, achieving the same result.

That he decided, would probably have been a better outcome.

Farther out, he could see the pontoon boat, scurrying away from the scene of destruction, heading north toward some unknown rendezvous with more of Hauser's Prometheus allies. The passengers were mostly just dark shapes; he couldn't tell if Annie was among them. He decided to believe that she was, and he knew exactly what he was going to have to do to save her.

He turned to face the pair that had rescued him: Joe—the young man from Charleston who had claimed to be Joseph King's grandson—and his companion, an equally youthful woman. It had taken a few minutes of scrutiny for him to recognize her, but when at last he had, all the pieces of the puzzle fell into place.

It was almost too much to process. He didn't know whether to be grateful for their last minute intervention, or angry for the deception that had thrown him into the nightmare in the first place. "Are you ready to tell me the truth now?"

Joe's expression was contrite. "I'm not really sure where to begin."

Kismet turned to the woman. "Let's go with an easy one then: Are you really Joseph King's daughter?"

The young woman, who had, the last time he'd seen her appeared to be at least in her seventies, just nodded.

Kismet turned to Joe. "Father and daughter. Joseph and Candace—those are your real names?"

Joe's mouth twitched into a nostalgic smile. "Candace was the name given to the queens of the ancient African people, the Nubians and the Ethiopians. It seemed like a good Christian name for her. I've been Joseph King—Joe—for so long that I don't think of myself by any other name. When I was with Hernando, I was Jose Esclavo del Cristo Rey, but that wasn't my real name either."

"Joseph, slave of Christ the King."

"I don't know what my parents named me..." Joe trailed off as if trying to access that memory was particularly painful, then shrugged.

"You were with him from the beginning then. One of his explorers."

Joe nodded. "I remember that I was the slave of a Moorish nobleman. After the *Reconquista*, I earned my freedom, but that didn't exactly count for much back then. When the Inquisition started persecuting the Moriscos, anyone with black skin was a suspect. So I joined with Fontaneda and sailed to New Spain, hoping to find my fortune. I did, and as it turns out, a whole lot more."

Kismet recalled Fontaneda's account of the discovery of the Fountain and the long ordeal that followed. "He wrote about two survivors that returned with him to the Fountain, and how they chose to die rather than drink again from the Fountain. But there was only one grave down there."

"I almost died, too." The wistful look came back. "Can't remember exactly why I thought that was a good idea. When I was too weak to resist, he saved me. After that...Well, as you can imagine, it's a long story."

"You killed Fontaneda, didn't you?"

Joe sucked in a breath at the abruptness of the accusation, but Kismet didn't wait for a response. "I'm sure you had your reasons, and I don't care about any of that. Right now, I need something from you."

Joe's expression was no longer wistful or contrite. "Something more than saving your hide?"

"They have Annie. They want the thing that gave the Fountain its power—a Seed from the Tree of Life, and if I'm going to save her, I need to give it to them." He fixed Joe with an unflinching stare. "So I need you to give it to me."

FORTUNE FAVORS

20

Granada, Spain

AS SHE TRAVERSED THE WOODED PATH leading up the hill to La Alhambra, Annie wondered how many more times she would have to make this journey.

The magnificent palace, built by Berber conquerors in the 10th century, the very place from which Isabella and Ferdinand had, at the end of the 15th century, set in motion the discovery, exploration and exploitation of the Americas, was like something from a fairy tale. The architecture was stunning, with arches and arabesques that looked like they belonged in a tale from the Arabian Nights. The complex, situated on a hilltop overlooking the city of Granada, had endured the tides of history, sometimes falling into disrepair only to be restored again like the treasure it was. Though it was no longer a nexus of historic events, it remained fixed in the human consciousness as a place of great beauty. It wasn't at all surprising that the Spaniard, Fontaneda, had brought the Seed here.

That was what Hauser had told her—told them all. A child of the southern hemisphere, Annie didn't really know much about European history.

It was the start of their third full day in Granada. Hauser had somehow arranged to have the entire complex closed for "urgent renovations," and brought in a team of experts—art historians, architectural consultants, sonar imaging technicians—and truckloads of equipment to survey every square inch of the historic palace. Thus far, the search had yielded no results, and today promised to be more of the same.

Not that she was involved in the actual searching. Hauser brought her along for one simple reason; he wanted to keep her where he could see her. It was a constant reminder that she was his prisoner, not his guest.

Although surrounded by people, she felt completely alone. She had her own room at the nearby Alhambra Palace hotel, a luxurious suite with a gorgeous view of the city from the balcony, but someone was always with her—either one of Hauser's men who worked rotating shifts as her minders, or the man himself. Her father was involved in the search effort, but while she saw him daily, she wasn't permitted to talk to him.

Not that she had any particular inclination to do so.

She had figured out a few things. Hauser, and evidently Elisabeth as well, were part of the group that Dr. Leeds had told them about in Central Park: Prometheus, a cabal of intellectuals bent on hiding away the mysteries of the world; mysteries like the Fountain of Youth and the Tree of Life.

Why?

That was still a bit unclear. Maybe they didn't trust what humanity might do with such knowledge and power—*who can blame them?*—or maybe they just wanted it all for themselves.

What really troubled her was the fact that her father was now working with them. She had worked out that Alex Higgins blamed Prometheus for the deaths of his teammates in Iraq during the mission in which he first met Kismet; how else to explain his willingness to throw in his lot with the psychopathic Dr. Leeds? But then he had switched again, and joined forces with the very people who dealt that blow in the first place.

She knew why of course. He was with Elisabeth now, Annie was almost certain of it. She had seen them together once or twice, walking across a courtyard or examining the magnificent arabesque and arches that seemed to be everywhere, and it hadn't been too hard to draw that conclusion. Elisabeth might have been faking it; she was a professional actor after all, but Annie could read her dad like a book.

FORTUNE FAVORS

She wanted to scream at him—*Finally got what you wanted, did you? Hope it's worth the price you paid*—but she didn't. It hurt too much to think about his betrayal and just how costly the journey had been.

Her minder this morning was Karl, but that was the extent of her knowledge about the burly man who walked a few steps behind her. They passed through the *Puerta de las Granadas* and made the climb up to the *Puerta de la Justicia*, the original 14th century entrance to the palace.

Hauser was there already, addressing a group of searchers that included her father and Elisabeth Neuell. "Today we're going to have to expand the search into the Alcazaba. We'll start with radar and acoustic imaging. We've got to think like this Spaniard, put ourselves in his shoes. When was he here? What places would he have had access to? Was he the kind of person who would hide it in a place of importance, or in the most inconspicuous location he could find?"

Annie tuned him out. She didn't know whether to hope for their success or continued failure. How long would they keep looking? How long would they keep her hostage? She wondered what Alex's defection would mean for her when the search ended, successfully or otherwise? What had Hauser said back in the Fountain cavern? Something about loose ends; was that all she was?

A sudden murmur from the group brought her attention back to Hauser, who now stood in silent consternation as one of his men whispered in his ear. His blond head came up suddenly, and his one good eye focused directly on her. Then, without another word, he strode over to her, grabbed her arm possessively, and began dragging her along as he strode into the heart of the complex.

Something was happening, something big. Annie didn't get the sense that Hauser was angry, but he was definitely anxious about something. She offered no resistance, quickening her steps to keep up with him as they entered the Charles V palace, which housed the museum, but as they moved briskly through a maze of interior halls and corridors, some of which were an unpleasant reminder of the caverns in Florida, she felt her own anxiety mounting. Then, she saw daylight again, streaming through the arched colonnade leading to the *Patio de los Leones*—the Court of the Lions.

Another of Hauser's men—not a technician, but one of the security team that had been with them since Florida—approached and quickly briefed him, using the same strange language that she had first heard in the Fountain cavern, and many times since, whenever they wanted to keep a secret from her.

Hauser nodded, and then pulled Annie around in front of himself, positioning her like a human shield. "Move. But don't do anything stupid."

She complied, letting him guide her through the colonnade and out into the open courtyard, with its majestic centerpiece, an alabaster fountain resting on the back of twelve white marble lions. The fountain had been the very first place Hauser had looked for the Seed.

Several members of the security team were deployed throughout the plaza. Their guns were drawn, but pointed at the ground in anticipation of further orders.

Then Annie's heart lurched in her chest and she almost stumbled. In the center of the courtyard, standing patiently right in front of lions was Nick Kismet.

He looked consider better than he had when she'd last seen him. His wild hair was shorter now, though very full and falling over his ears, and he still wore a beard that looked just a little on the scraggly side, but he was otherwise the very picture of health. Annie actually thought he looked about ten years younger.

Of course he does.

Kismet smiled at her then turned his stare to Hauser. "Hiding behind a woman, Ulrich?" He made a clucking noise of disapproval. "But I suppose that's always been your style. Let others do the work, take the risks—I think that's called 'cowardice.'"

Hauser tightened his grip on Annie's arm, evoking a low whimper, but he ignored the taunt. "It's not here, is it? It was never here. You lied to me."

Kismet grinned. "Everything was so crazy—lights were flashing, the world was ending—I just said the first thing that popped into my head."

His expression became more serious. "I needed to keep you busy for a while, somewhere I could find you when I was ready, when I finally had something to bargain with."

"And you have it now?"

Kismet didn't answer immediately, but looked past him as Higgins and Elisabeth stepped past the pillars at the edge of the courtyard, the latter holding her semi-automatic pistol aimed at Kismet. "Well, well, the gang's all here."

"Where is it?" Hauser pressed, jerking Annie's arm again.

Kismet gave a deep sigh. "You know, I've been looking for you for a really long time. At the risk of sounding melodramatic, you really messed up my life."

To Annie's surprise, Hauser laughed. "You were never meant for normal things, Kismet."

"See, that's what I'm talking about. You seem to know all about me, and I know...well, nothing about me."

The one-eyed man shook his head ruefully. "And you never will."

"Not even if I give you what you want? The Seed of the Tree of Life?"

"Not even for that. It is important to us, but not that important. And in the end, we will have it anyway. The question you should be asking is: how much is it worth to you?" He shook Annie meaningfully.

Kismet's eyes flitted to hers, and then to Higgins, before coming back to Hauser. "I figured you'd say something like that. Fine. Let her go and I'll give it to you."

"You first. Where is it?"

Kismet shrugged then took something from his back pocket and held it out on his open palm. It was a small heart-shaped silver box. He flipped it open and tilted it down to show the contents. Annie saw what looked like a large unshelled almond or maybe the stone from a peach. A faint blue light seemed to be oozing from the tiny pores that perforated its outer surface. Then Kismet snapped the lid shut on it.

"That's a fake. You aren't stupid enough to bring it here."

Kismet ducked his head in feigned embarrassment. "That's mean."

319

"Where was it?" Despite the intensity of her captors hold, Annie turned in surprise, not because of the question, but rather the person who had asked it: her father.

"It's quite a story really. You see, four hundred and fifty years ago, when Hernando Fontaneda found the Fountain of Youth, he wasn't alone. He had with him several companions, including freed slaves who signed on as mercenaries. Fontaneda wrote that most of them died during the search. Only a few survived long enough to reach the Fountain, and only he survived to return to civilization. Turns out, that wasn't exactly true. There was one other. You've already met him, Al. In fact, you saved his life back in Charleston."

"Joe?"

Kismet nodded. "King and Fontaneda didn't dare share their secret within anyone else. There was no telling what might happen if they did. They tried to integrate themselves into the colonies in the New World; Fontaneda established himself as a wealthy gentleman, and King was his slave. There were some hiccups at first; they nearly got caught in Saint Augustine, and had to completely start over. Over the next three hundred years they managed to work out a system that allowed them to live among the rest of us poor fragile mortals for a while without attracting too much attention. The Fountain regenerates—regenerated rather, but then after a while, the natural aging process resumes. They would stay in one place for twenty or thirty years, and then pop back down to Florida, take a sip, and start all over again somewhere else with a new name. Fortunato, Fortune, Fontaine, and always accompanied by his faithful manservant Joseph."

"The Spaniard hated slavery," Higgins countered. "He was an Abolitionist."

Kismet nodded. "It was a different world. They had to stay close to the Fountain, so it was necessary to live a lie. Fontaneda never mistreated King, or if he did, it was just for appearance's sake. I think his decision to help fugitive slaves was, in part, to soothe his sense of guilt about the situation. They were equal sharers in the secret of the Fountain's existence, but Fontaneda lived the good life, while King was relegated to the slave house.

"Then the world changed. The Civil War ended slavery and they could no longer maintain the old lie. And King wasn't under Fontaneda's thumb anymore. Not that things were much better for King, but he was finally able to stop pretending to be a slave.

"He married and started a family. Not his first of course. Both men had married, fathered children, and then watched them grow old and die, never daring to reveal their secret or use it to save their loved ones. But that had always been Fontaneda's decision. Now that King was a free man, he could do as he pleased. His wife died in childbirth—no chance to save her—but King vowed that he would not lose his daughter, Candace, I believe you met her, Elisabeth, though I doubt you'd recognize her now."

The actress glowered but said nothing.

"Fontaneda tried to prevent King, and when that failed, he decided to take the Seed for himself—he'd figured out its importance long before that—and reveal the existence of the cavern to the world through the United Nations. I'm not sure if he meant it to be an act of altruism, or just a way to put King in his place one final time. In the end, King got the last laugh. They fought and King killed Fontaneda in self-defense—well, he says it was self-defense. Remember that strange mark on the map? Like a scar? King cut out Fontaneda's heart, just to make sure he wouldn't get back up again."

Annie shuddered a little at the mental image. It was hard to reconcile Kismet's description of King with the youthful man they had met in the Charleston cemetery, and even harder to picture Joe cold-bloodedly murdering a man and desecrating his corpse.

"How do you know all this?" asked Hauser, evidently curious in spite of himself.

"King told me the whole story, right after he and Candace pulled me out of that cave. I had figured out a lot of the 'what' already; King just supplied the 'why.'" Kismet now focused his stare like a laser on the one-eyed man. "And of course, he gave me the Seed."

"Because you asked so nicely?" Hauser scoffed.

"Because I threatened to expose their secret. When we showed up, asking about the Fountain, they knew the jig was finally up. They just wanted a

321

chance to start over one last time, so after we left, they headed down to Florida ahead of us, used a back door—which would have been really nice to know about ahead of time—and took the Seed. Lucky for me, they decided to hang around a while longer to see how it all played out, and were there to rescue me."

Hauser shook his head. "How nice for you. What an entertaining story. And you expect me to believe that's really the Seed? That you just brought it here, knowing that I could just take it from you."

"You could try. But really, why make it so difficult?" He waggled the heart-shaped box. "You want it, I want her."

"No!" protested Annie. "Nick, you can't give it to him. You've no idea what he'll do with it."

"I know exactly what he has planned." He glanced at Hauser then at Higgins. "What he always does. He'll hide it away forever. I can live with that. But I promise you this, you won't get a thing if you don't let her go. It's that simple."

"I'll make it even simpler," Hauser threatened. He held up his semi-automatic. "I'll just kill you and take it."

"Not a good idea. For starters, while I'm holding this, I'm not sure it's possible to kill me. I can feel it working on me right now. Hell, my fingernails have grown while I've been standing here."

Annie thought his hair and beard looked like they'd grown as well.

"You could probably knock me down with a bullet," he continued. "Put me out for the count long enough to take this. But before you do, there's something you should know.

"In addition to the Seed, this little box also contains twenty grams of C4. Not a lot, I grant you, but then that's the idea. When I closed it just now, I armed the trigger. Open it again, and it will blow up. If you shoot me and I drop it..." he shrugged. "It might not blow up. And I'm sure you could probably bring in someone to try to defuse it—he might even succeed. But it's just as likely that, if you try to take it by force, I'll open it and blow it to hell.

"So, were back to the easy way. Let Annie go, and I'll give it to you, simple as that."

Hauser cocked his head sideways and squinted with his good eye. "You're bluffing. You wouldn't destroy it. And I don't think you'd part with it either."

"That's where you're wrong," Kismet said, without a trace of his earlier flippancy. "I never cared about any of this. Legendary relics, mythical powers—I only ever started looking for these things because I hoped it would lead me to you."

He spread his hands. "And here we are. I want to be done with you, Hauser. If you aren't going to tell me what you know, then leave me the hell alone."

Hauser regarded him a moment longer, and then broke into a wolfish grin. "Mother will be so disappointed to hear that."

Kismet's confident expression slipped a little. Annie thought he looked like he'd been sucker-punched. In a low voice he said: "Whose mother?"

Hauser threw back his head and laughed. "Very well, I accept your terms."

Throughout the conversation, Annie had kept waiting for Kismet to do something, pull a rabbit out of the hat, rescue her and keep the Seed out of Hauser's hands. Now, she saw that he was serious; he was going to give Hauser and Prometheus exactly what they wanted, and he was going to do it in order to save her.

That was unacceptable.

"Nick, don't." She wasn't sure anymore what she could say or do to stop him, but she had to try. "You can't let them have this. They might hide it away, or they might do something much worse. Power like that...I don't know what they'll do with it, but you can't give it to them, no matter what they do to me."

Kismet offered a rueful smile, but Annie saw his gaze move slowly toward...her father? "It doesn't matter, Annie. If it's not the Seed, it will be something else. If it's not Prometheus, then some*one* else. But I can do something good, right now. I can get you out of here, and that's all that matters to me."

He turned to Hauser. "Just let her go. I'll put the Seed on the ground and walk away."

"And your explosive device?"

"Like I said, you should be able to figure out how to bypass the trigger. I'd promise to send you the code to disarm it once Annie and I are safely out of here, but you probably wouldn't believe me anyway."

Hauser considered this a moment longer, then shook his head. "No. It's a fake. Has to be."

Kismet held the box up. "Elisabeth, do you think I'm lying?"

The actress gazed back at him, almost defiantly at first, but then softened. "No. Subtlety isn't your style."

He nodded. "Here's how this can work. Elisabeth comes and gets the Seed from me. One touch, and she'll know it's the real deal. At the same time, Al walks Annie over to me."

Hauser nodded his assent, and Elisabeth immediately strode across the courtyard, tucking her gun in her waistband as she moved. She reached Kismet a few seconds later and placed a tentative finger on the box.

"Oh." Her eyes rolled back in undisguised ecstasy. She stood up a little straighter, as if playing to a hidden camera. "Yes, it's real. I can feel the energy flowing into me."

Higgins reached Annie's side, but she resisted him. "Damn it, Nick. You can't do this."

"Come on, Annie girl," Higgins urged. His voice was strained, like a piano string tuned so tight it was about to snap. "It's going to be over soon."

"Is that good enough for you, Hauser?" Kismet called, his fingers tight on the box, resisting Elisabeth's stolid efforts to take it away. "Now, let her go."

In the same way that Annie had believed, right up to that moment, that Kismet would play some unexpected wild card to save the day and keep the prize away from Prometheus, she expected Hauser to somehow play false at the end. She was wrong on both counts.

FORTUNE FAVORS

The one-eyed man relaxed his grip on her, and her father reached out to draw her into his embrace. She was too dumbfounded to even resist.

Kismet uncurled his fingers, and surrendered the Seed of the Tree of Life to Elisabeth Neuell.

She almost ran back toward Hauser, holding the box before her with equal parts fear and awe. Higgins, half-dragging Annie, had barely gotten a few steps away when Elisabeth raced past, holding the Seed out to Hauser.

That was when everything started to happen.

Higgins, with preternatural calm, reached out and snatched the pistol from Elisabeth's waistband. She felt it, and started to turn, but her momentum had already brought her within reach of Hauser, who was unaware of what Higgins had done and too caught up in his imminent victory.

Hauser greedily snatched the box from Elisabeth and hugged it to his chest.

Higgins spun Annie toward Kismet and gave her a shove, propelling her across the courtyard, into his arms. Then, the old Gurkha raised the pistol and aimed it at Kismet.

The rest of the Prometheus security team had instantly come alert and brought their weapons up, but none of them could seem to decide where to aim.

Hauser suddenly gave a low cry and doubled over. Then, as he straightened, he reached up with his free hand and tore the eye patch away. He winced as light flooded into the restored orb, and covered it again with his hand. That was when he caught a glimpse of Higgins, aiming a gun at Kismet.

"Dad, no." Annie's pleas seemed to fall on deaf ears, but she did not give up. "Just let us walk away."

"Do what you have to do," whispered Kismet, nodding to Higgins.

Hauser fixed both eyes on Kismet. He raised the box with the Seed and waved it triumphantly. "Game, set and match, Kismet."

"What about the experiment?"

Hauser laughed. "There was only ever one rule to the experiment; do not interfere. Oh, I've wanted you dead so bad I can taste it, believe me. I had hoped you would die in that Iraqi hellhole, but someone—" He rolled his eyes—his perfect, unblemished blue eyes—and mouthed a single word: *Mom*. "Decided that I had interfered by blowing up your ride and leaving you stranded, so she pulled strings like you can't imagine, to 'balance the scales.'

"Her interference made it so much easier for me to take over." He had lowered his voice to a barely audible mutter for the aside, but then spoke clearly again. "But rules are rules. I'm not going to tell Higgins to kill you. But I am certainly not going to stop him."

Kismet nodded to his nemesis—*brother?* "Then I guess I'll see you in Hell."

As if Kismet's words were the signal he'd been waiting for, Higgins' thumb extended up to pull back the hammer, cocking the pistol and readying it to fire.

Time seemed to freeze. Elisabeth, standing beside Hauser, clutched his arm as if he were a prize she'd finally won. The security team around the perimeter of the courtyard had lowered their weapons again, and were watching as if hypnotized. Hauser continued to stare across the plaza at Kismet, holding the box above his head, as if daring the heavens to take it away...

And in a heartbeat, they did.

Higgins turned, swinging around slowly, almost ethereally, away from Kismet. His movements seemed almost without volition, as if he had been programmed like an automaton. His hand kept moving, smoothly adjusting, elevating slightly, and then he pulled the trigger.

The firing pin was released with a sharp 'click' and pivoted forward, striking the primer on the brass cartridge dead-center. The gunpowder charge ignited into a ball of expanding gas, driving the lead projectile out of the barrel at nearly the speed of sound. The bullet screamed through the air, but traveled only about thirty feet before striking its target with unfailing accuracy.

The metal box containing the last Seed of the Tree of Life rang for a split second with the impact of the 9-millimeter round.

FORTUNE FAVORS

An instant later, it erupted with a thunderclap that dwarfed the barely heard report of the pistol.

○

The detonation threw everyone aside like so much chaff. Kismet lay stunned in the aftermath, momentarily forgetting who and where he was. His senses returned after a blurred moment and he groped for Annie. She lay, dazed but apparently unhurt, a few feet away. Higgins lay supine, the pistol flung away.

Hauser and Elisabeth were standing, dazed and peppered with shrapnel wounds, locked together at the heart of a blazing inferno of violet light. Hauser's arm was still outstretched, but it ended at his wrist, which was now just a ragged, oozing stump.

The flames grew around the pair like a blanket, dancing lovingly on the ravaged flesh of Hauser's wounds. Tendrils of energy, the same hue as that which had burned in the cavern of the Fountain of Youth, caressed his skin, crackling on the stump of his maimed arm, probing into the deep shrapnel wounds, and wherever the flames lit, the injuries seemed to evaporate like smoke.

Kismet pulled Annie to him, and then together they crawled toward her father. Higgins was stirring, apparently unhurt. "Nick?" His voice was a distillation of misery. "I had to do it. Couldn't let them have it—had to save Annie—it was the only way."

The words struck Kismet. The betrayal in Florida seemed a distant memory, something he'd managed to push to the back of his mind in order to focus on his sole objective—getting Annie back from Prometheus at any cost. He didn't want to think about what had motivated Higgins, and didn't have the mental energy to second guess the man's desperate decisions.

"It's okay, Al."

"I can't see."

There was a shriek from behind them and Kismet looked up in time to see Hauser, his clothes in burning tatters but his flesh perfectly restored, thrust Elisabeth aside. She stumbled back, screaming as fingers of plasma reached out from Hauser to caress her, and then tightened around her like a cocoon.

There was a flash, and Elisabeth evaporated.

The flames arced back into an exultant Hauser. He stood there, contemplating the power coruscating down his arms and at his fingertips. Energy flowed like liquid into his nostrils and mouth, and for a moment, the fire seemed to be burning from beneath his skin, growing in intensity until the brilliance forced Kismet to cover his eyes.

He recalled something Leeds had told him during their first encounter, an idling speculation about how the miracles of Jesus Christ might be attributable to his possession of a similar Seed. Leeds had hypothesized that Jesus had somehow integrated a Seed into his own body, and that when a Roman centurion had pierced him during the crucifixion, the energies released had transformed the dying Christ into a divine being—an entity of pure energy.

That had been Leeds' ambition all along. To find the Seed and turn himself into a god. And now it seemed that Hauser was undergoing such an apotheosis.

The Prometheus leader inhaled the potent forces, as if consciously willing them to pervade every molecule of his body, to infuse every atom of his being. As the unleashed power of the Seed grew from a violet flame to a burning white-hot fever pitch, his flesh was transmuted into living energy. Tissue boiled away, replaced by a vague outline of energy that flared brighter and brighter—

And then winked out completely.

EPILOGUE

FOR A FEW MINUTES, KISMET wasn't even sure that he was still alive. The light and fury of Hauser's transformation had reached a crescendo and then...nothing.

He couldn't see or hear anything.

But gradually, his other senses began filling in the gaps. The air was alive with ozone. His hands were touching something that was both soft and firm, and he recalled that he had been huddled together with Annie and Higgins...yes, he could feel human warmth in his fingertips, and a faint pulse of life.

The darkness was receding a bit. Familiar shapes were emerging out of a brown haze as his eyes began to recover sensitivity, one wavelength of the spectrum at a time. He saw the pillars of the colonnade surrounding the Court of Lions, but for a moment couldn't penetrate the shadows beyond.

"What just happened?" Annie whispered.

Kismet shook his head; he didn't have an answer.

Hauser and Elisabeth were gone, but so also was the Prometheus security team, vanished just as surely as if they'd been caught up in the conflagration.

He discounted that idea. It was more likely that, upon witnessing the destruction of the Seed and Hauser's—death?—they had decided to evacuate the site. With the Seed gone, there wasn't any reason to stay anymore.

And as Hauser had said, there was just one rule where Nick Kismet was concerned: Don't interfere.

"Is it over?" Higgins' asked.

Kismet could tell by the way Higgins' eyes darted back and forth that his vision hadn't recovered yet. He had been looking right at the Seed when it exploded, struck blind gazing upon the glory of God...

Something like that anyway.

Annie was tearfully hugging her father. Kismet wasn't sure what to think or feel about the other man now. He understood Higgins' motivations; they weren't all that different from his own. His decision—his betrayal—had probably saved them all in Florida.

But it still stung like a son of a bitch.

He sighed. Some wounds took longer to heal, even with magic potions.

"It's over. Come on. Let's get out of here." He gripped Higgins' biceps and started guiding him toward the nearest gate.

"What happened?" Annie asked again, staring in disbelief at the spot where Hauser and Elisabeth stood a few minutes before. There was a faint starburst pattern on the paving stones, as if that place alone had been bleached by the sun, but that was the extent of the damage to the courtyard. "The Seed...what was it? Was it really from the Tree of Life?"

"I don't know," Kismet answered honestly. He had examined it briefly after Joseph King had handed it over; it did look like something from a fruit. But it could just as easily have been an artifact, something crafted as a receptacle for the unique energy that had sustained a select few legendary men throughout history and infused the water in a Florida cave with the power to restore life. He had once remarked that it was science, not magic, but now he wasn't so sure. If it was some application of science, then it utilized principles that were beyond the grasp of anything he'd ever heard about—and wasn't that the very definition of magic?

"I don't know if there ever really was a special Tree," he continued, "Or a Garden of Eden. Maybe everyone got it backwards. Maybe the whole idea of the Tree came from the fact that it kind of looked like a seed."

"But...how did it do all that? Heal and destroy at the same time? And what happened to Hauser? Is he dead?"

Kismet just shook his head. "He's gone. Maybe he transcended the flesh, became one with the universe...Maybe he just went 'poof.' The important thing is that it's finally over."

"You came back for me," Annie realized aloud.

Kismet suddenly found himself locked in her embrace, her lips pressing against his. He did not resist. A moment later, she leaned back and tousled his hair. "So...you're not exactly the older man anymore."

"I'm sure the effects are just temporary. I hope they are. I have to shave twice a day just to keep this beard under control."

"I kind of like it." She kissed him again. "And I'm flattered that you were willing to sacrifice the secret of immortality to save me. I just hope it was worth it."

Kismet gazed back at her, and then glanced at Higgins, who shuffled sightlessly along. The ordeal had cost a lot more than just the Seed.

But maybe the old saying was true, maybe time really did heal all wounds. It had taken more than twenty years, but it finally felt like the ordeal that had begun that night in Iraq was over. The chains that had bound Higgins to him were finally broken. He didn't know if their relationship—friendship, camaraderie, brotherhood, whatever it was—would endure, but at least the shadow that had corrupted it was gone.

"Definitely," he answered finally. "Because I got my friends back. Both of you."

Higgins gave a wan smile and nodded, though Kismet could tell that his eyesight hadn't yet returned. Maybe because he'd been staring right at the blast, it wouldn't...

He took out his hip flask. "Al, you look like you could use a drink."

ABOUT THE AUTHOR

SEAN ELLIS is the author of several novels. He is a veteran of Operation Enduring Freedom, and has a Bachelor of Science degree in Natural Resources Policy from Oregon State University. He lives in Arizona, where he divides his time between writing, adventure sports, and trying to figure out how to save the world. You can find out more about Sean at his website: www.seanellisthrillers.webs.com.

Made in the USA
Middletown, DE
17 November 2018